SLAB OF PEACOCK

SLAB OF PEACOCK

Narasimha Rao Mamunooru

PARTRIDGE
A Penguin Random House Company

To order additional copies of this book, contact
Partridge India
000 800 10062 62
orders.india@partridgepublishing.com

www.partridgepublishing.com/india

To the Loving Memory of
My Father: Krishna Rao
Mother: Durgamba
And
In fond remembrance of MAMUNOORU, my birthplace
And
The Villagers of Mamunooru.

Acknowledgements

In the first instance, I owe the activation of my career of creative writing to my wife, Smt. Rukmini Devi, who bore the entire burden of running the house and gave me the required time and peace to preoccupy myself with reading and writing. I thank her profusely.

I thank my children Krishna, Kalyani—Sunil, Mahesh and Thiru who took care of their education and career without my intervention at any point. In particular, I thank my daughter (in law) Chi. Sow. Mamunooru Bhargavi, who should get half of the credit for the completion of this work and the publication of it.

I thank the Partridge Publishing House for accepting and bringing out the book. Also I owe my gratitude to Ms. Melissa Tan, the Publishing Consultant of Partridge Publishing House for putting me in the right course in the matter of publication of this work.

I thank Mr. Joe Anderson, my Publishing Service Associate (PSA) of Partridge Publishing House for guiding me through the different stages of publication.

I thank Mr. Gopi, the Artist, who has given the imaginative cover page and the contextual illustrations.

Finally I owe my thanks to one and all who may have helped me in different ways in the completion of this work.

Nobody in that village knew the age of their village or how it had got its name. They, in fact, never bothered about these things. When their forebears had started to build the village, they perhaps laid the foundation by building a small shrine for the village deity, Muthyalamma, and went on building their mud-walled houses around the shrine in a plan born of their native wisdom and the streets or rather the lanes took shape between the rows of houses. At the axial point, in their plan, they raised the ground level a little and laid on it, an unusually long stone slab, about ten feet long and seven-to-eight feet wide and they made it the seat of their village assembly, the village arbitration court and the village club—a three-in-one—and they called it 'the slab'. However, with the passage of time, the slab had shed most of its functions and though still organically part of the village, it now remained largely vestigial. Nonetheless, the commoners of the village did not lose their awe and fondness for it, and occasionally they even acted as though it were still the whole and soul of their village.

The slab had lately undergone a renovation; the landed gentry pooled money with which they built a rectangular brick structure in place of the slab and a long cemented strip, abutting on the compound wall of the merchant Venkatnarayana's house—the wall serving like the back of a bench, to lean against. They called it the 'chimti bench'. It became their bench and their bed also, for, quite a few young men and some unmarried men too reclined on it and snored away their nights, the coiled-up 'shoulder cloth' placed under their heads for cushion comfort.

On the slab, the villagers, some of whom were peasants and some daily wage earners, assembled. The gathering was a mix of adults and young men; occasionally some old men, who suffered from insomnia, joined them. They all assembled there after supper, passed time in chitchat on public and private issues and when one-to-one 'exchanged notes' on sleazy scandals.

Following the construction of the cement slab, they pushed the original stone to a side and there it remained like an ignored patriarch sulking silently; but as a point of solace, it had its customers in old men, who obsequiously chose their perches on the old stone slab.

At the back of the slab stood a big Bo tree, on whose huge trunk stood a canopy of branches with their rich foliage, spread like the hood of a gigantic cobra.

On a full-moon night the glorious moonlight sieving through the thickset foliage, cast soft prints of light and shade on the slab. Here and there a few leaves, whose angle of repose caught the moonlight straight shone like silver medallions.

The sounds produced by the rustling leaves soothed the ears of the tired men resting on the slab and its wings.

Indistinct reports of voices of men, women, a crying child and now and then the howl of a street dog, chimed in and at times, the warbling notes of folk music, played by an aficionado on the long flute, floated on a slow-moving wind.

The big bungalow of the Banzardar stood right in front of the slab. The bungalow and the slab were so near to each other that the pleasantries, the Banzardar's daughters and their spouses traded among themselves on the terrace, reached the slab, intermixed with the jingling sounds of the bangles.

This had become a routine since the cementation of the slab; men converged at the slab, some fifteen to twenty of them, during the nights in summer, in winter and even in rainy season, to listen to the tales narrated by Pagadaiah.

On one such evening,

Kannam came to the slab took a close look at the faces of the men resting on the 'chimti' bench and settled himself by the side of his friend Gopaiah.

"So, he hasn't come yet-eh?" enquired Kannam, as he dug out a beedi from the deep pocket of his undershirt.

Gopaiah smiled in appreciation of the jesting enquiry.

Bademaya heard them and said, "So, here you are, to mess up the things!"

"You heard him say that, Gopa? Now, whatever have I done, man?" said Kannam, with a mischievous smile on his lips.

Gopaiah too smiled, once again.

Pagadaiah recited tales to the men that gathered at the slab in the evenings. The tale held out for a long time; sometimes it went past the midnight, stretching out into the last quarter of the night and once in a while it ran up to the first crow of the cock too. At times, it took the form of a serial saga—an episode a night, the villagers' version of soap.

However, on occasions the story ended well before midnight, but that was a rare eventuality. If ever his story ended abruptly, it meant that Pagadaiah was pretty certain that the usually elusive sleep was ready to take him into 'her lap'; otherwise, they were at his mercy-the tale and the listeners; neither the story could be wound-up nor the audience could abort it.

"Arre Gopa-What was the story he told the other night? Ah, this was it—the queen transformed herself into a demon, went stealthily into the royal stables to devour the horses and elephants! Hha ha," Kannam burst into loud laughter as he recollected, "Why go so stealthily if it is a demon? It can vanish in the palace and appear there in the stables, can't it? A demon has such powers, they say. What do you say, what do you say, Gopa? Why don't you say something?"

Gopaiah sat up as he warmed up to the chat, "Ok, let it be so, whatever it is; but the fact of the matter is—demon's feet are turned-back, they are not in the normal way, are they? Could not that son-of-a-whore, the minister, detect it? And Pagadaiah says the fellow was a paragon of wisdom!"

Pagadaiah was not there to defend himself; but he had his allies in the assemblage; Bademaya was one of them; he rose to the occasion, "How could the poor minister know, Gopaiah? He himself got hitched to the second demon, and moreover, would a devil, clever that it is, ever reveal its turned-back feet?"

Kannam continued to laugh, "Tell me a hundred things," waving his palm across in dismissal, he said, "I won't buy these tales. Then, Gopa, what was that tale he told us the other night? Ah, here it is, there was a queen who flirted with the stableman and the king lusted for that hunchback wife of the potter, ha-ha! Uff these tales that he tells . . . !"

Bademaya had no arrows to counter this salvo. After a thoughtful while, he sought to conclude the war of words, "Why all this flak, Kannam? If you don't like them just don't listen to him; after all, Pagadaiah has not solicited your attention. Why do you spoil a story session, for which all these men have come . . ."

At this juncture, they heard the cough, the cough which always heralded the arrival of the raconteur as he turned the corner of the lane; at that, some men who had lain there evincing no interest in the debate running, sat bolt upright and looked in the direction of the lane.

Pagadaiah was his usual dignified self; he called out the names, much in the fashion of a schoolmaster. Then he fixed that green leaf-roll of tobacco between his lips, smiled contentedly and queried, "Have they all come? If someone comes late and asks me to start it all again, I won't do that, I tell you, know you that." Then he stretched his hand for the matches; as usual, he was very composed.

"Of course, of course, all are here and the fellow Kannam is also there," said Naginboina in a shrill voice that he employed whenever he mixed a fact with fun.

"What do I care who comes!" Pagadaiah remarked, summoning up his self-assurance, "The one who is interested would listen and the one, who is not, won't."

Kannam took no notice of the remark and changed into a reclining posture. 'Uff, these tales Pagadaiah tells!' he reflected, 'Martha Lakshmanna's anecdotes from his life are far more interesting than these tales. One must 'first utter the name of Martha Lakshmanna and only then utter the words courage and bravery'! With one leg gone, Martha Lakshmanna was still the first choice for any big farmer for the job of watchman over the crop field. Why do they all treat his services as a favour, why? Is it because they love or like him? No, it is because Martha Lakshmanna does not care whether he loses a limb or life; his priority is always the protection of the crop. It is for that reason they seek his services.'

Pagadaiah began the narration.

Kannam could hear from his perch.

Kings, queens, princes, princesses, ministers, courtiers, courtesans, 'horses with the five favorable signs', caparisoned elephants and so on and so forth—Pagadaiah paraded them all at the slab, for his listeners, as the tale progressed

They all listened to him, mesmerized; but not Kannam, whom even the sizzling 'beauties, matchless in the three worlds', could not enthuse into the tale.

At a point, the tale gained tempo.

Cigar-ends burned bright; smokers sent bales and bales of smoke into the air and acclamations and applauses punctuated the progress of the tale.

Pagadaiah's aplomb was steamed up by the listeners' intentness. He felt happy; he liked it that way; but occasionally, tickled by a sudden desire to test the extent of their interest and attentiveness he applied a sudden brake.

The story screeched to a halt, throwing the shocked listeners into desperate guesses—'what next?' 'How then come . . .' 'Where do we go from here?' 'Would the story go on or would he defer it to tomorrow . . .'

Such halts and jolts were the common lot of Pagadaiah's audience or rather they were Pagadaiah's tricks of the trade and after employing them he would dodge even further. He would throw away the beedi, even when it burned right and straight and seek a fresh one from his clientele or if he had been smoking a cigar, he would smother the burning tip, rub it on the 'chimti' bench and light it afresh or he would go to relieve himself, take a long time and return unrelieved or he would announce 'vontale bell' ('interval') . . . Plenty of those tricks were there in his bag!

Notwithstanding all that, Pagadaiah always gave a start at the mention of Kannam's name and felt discomfited to have him among his listeners.

As a child, Kannam had gone to school and studied up to fourth standard, a feat Pagadaiah could not boast of and was conscious of. The sudden death of Kannam's father put an end to the son's studies and Kannam settled as a cowherd in the Banjardar's house. His maternal uncles proposed to take him to their village; but Kannam's mother dissented and Kannam remained in the village to become, in later years, a thorn in the flesh to Pagadaiah, the raconteur.

"Once upon a time, there was a hermit in a village," Pagadaiah would begin a tale.

"What, a hermit in a village . . . ? His hut and haunt are in the forest. What is he doing in a village?" Kannam would controvert.

Touched to the quick, Pagadaiah would shout, "He would live wherever he liked; of what concern is that to you?" and he would continue the tale, "So, that hermit, who lived in a village, had a sword and a tumbler-"

"Stop", Kannam would raise his palm and say, "A tumbler—ok, we would grant that, but what business does a hermit have with a sword, warrior is the rightful owner of that—?"

"Tut, you fellow," an exasperated Pagadaiah would now appeal to his audience, "Do you want this tale to go on or not? Tell me."

Some would admonish Kannam; some would appeal to his good sense and some would enjoy all this as a theatrical farce.

Kannam would then wave his hand to them to get along, "'Die the way you want to', you ignoramuses!" With that, he would quit the arena.

Pagadaiah would then loudly clear his throat, in celebration of his triumph over his bugbear and would ask someone to roll a green cigar for him.

In summer, during moonlit nights, kings with their retinue, princes and princesses and their paramours, their counterparts from the neighboring lands-all of them, kept lingering around the slab, awaiting a propitious mood of the raconteur.

By the time it was past the second quarter of the night, Pagadaiah brought the narration to a halt and adjourned the session to the next night.

Eyelids drooping with sleep, Pagadaiah headed for home; at the slab some farsighted men in the assembly had already slipped into slumber and were snoring robustly.

Most of the dwellings in the village were thatched houses; they had for compound walls mud structures of three feet height. Whether they had built them all to the same height by design, or, exposed to the ravages of time, they came to stand as remnants of what had once been taller structures, no one could vouch for. For all that, their height served to bring about a weird uniformity, so weird a uniformity that it all seemed to be the work of time and weather at one time and at other times appeared to be the result of a strange and naive regard for tradition and historicity of the things.

Tonight, the architectural singularity was to discomfit Pagadaiah in a strange way.

To the right of Pagadaiah, who was walking along the north street, was the house of Rosaiah, the younger brother of the merchant Venkatnarayana. The backyard of the house, bordering on the north street, was clearly visible to the passersby.

At that late hour, Rosaiah's lately married son was engaged in amatory acts with his bride and Pagadaiah inadvertently eyed it. For a time he found himself stayed put, noticing which, the couple disengaged themselves from their activity.

Embarrassed at being detected peeping, Pagadaiah hurried on his way, but in a deeply shaken mood.

Opening the door of his hut, he dragged out the hemp-cord cot and putting the hay-filled sac under his head, tried to get some sleep; but finding the headrest uncomfortable, threw it away and placed his rolled-up shoulder-cloth under his head; it too was of no avail.

He tossed about desperately trying to get some sleep; but sleep, which had come and rested on his shoulder, like a dove when he was at the slab, flew away like a fickle-minded bird.

His mind refused to be reined in and began to recall the past. The reminiscences as usual centred round his wife, Rattamma.

Rattamma had lived with him for a brief period before she went away to her mother's house. That was years ago. Since her departure, recitation of tales had become the mainstay of activity for him, during the nights.

His body ached for sensual pleasures and comforts; but his situation in life denied them to him. He knew that others in similar predicament found ways to gratify their desires by haunting fleshpots in the nearby town-and why go so far— even in his village, their local versions existed and he knew that. Somehow, he could not get into that line of thinking; women of easy virtue gave him bad vibes.

Therefore, he took to this pastime, the narration of tales, as a palliative, a night without which upset his equanimity. On the other hand, when he narrated a tale, he felt refreshed; it recharged his sagging spirit and revived his zest for life.

When he was thus engrossed in the narration of a story, the tale and the time stretched themselves. He had a pliant audience, barring that bugbear, Kannam. They would all collect at the slab or if it was rainy season, on those cement benches under the thatch-roof fronting the house of Mme Durgamba. Young fellows and adults, serving as farm hands, assembled and waited for him. If, for some reason, there was a change of venue, someone came and informed. How those poor young creatures hungered for the fiction! How they lusted for an account of the beautiful damsels in distress that teemed in his tales! Maybe, they dreamt of them when they slept, and fantasized on them when awake.

During the winter nights, the young and unmarried men assembled in good number; they brought touchwood, twigs and one or two logs, lit up a bonfire and huddled round it, casting looks of admiration and wonderment at him, the narrator.

He, the raconteur sat in the middle, reeled off episode after episode, rolling that green cigar from one corner to the other between his lips, biting off bits of the green leaf and playfully indulging in a host of complementary acts, which, he knew, added a tang to the tale.

However, at times his enterprise ran into rough weather, especially after the harvesting and hay stacking of millet crop were over. That was the time when the dry land farmers found time to recline and rest. Someone would invariably go to a neighboring village and book puppet players or a repertory performing there. Finish! That was all—the slab would wear a deserted look!

Pagadaiah moved restlessly in the cot; two or three cords snapped.

No respite appeared likely; he went into the backyard 'to fold legs'.

Coming back, he resettled himself on the cot and lit a leaf cigar. He looked at the starry sky; it was fourth quarter of the night.

He bit and nibbled on the green leaf of the cigar with relish as he continued to brood on his marital life. 'Is she not a normal woman? Is she the odd one among them?' he wondered aloud.

Hearing his master's voice, his pet came out from under the cot and waving its tail looked hither and thither and finding nothing noteworthy, came back to whine about that 'much ado about nothing' and resettle itself at its master's feet.

Pagadaiah patted on its back and continued to reminisce. Rattamma his wife, who had stubbornly shunned him as bedmate, continued to dangle in his mind. 'Away from her rightful husband for years and continuing to live at her mother's!' he mused.

'Four years after the wedding, his in-laws were still reluctant to send their daughter to the husband's house for marital life!' Somehow he managed to bring her to his house, thankfully due to his sister's negotiating skills, but what good came of it! Rattamma continued to be her adamant self, declining to oblige her husband to bed. When he tried to take her, she brought down the house with her ear-piercing screams, waking up all the sleeping souls in the vicinity. The follow-up put him to shame for something that was not of his making!

God appeared to have His own design for the men He made; however, sometimes He chose some men for the bestowal of an odd gift!

The irony of it all was that his wife herself became the instrument of the rake-up, which, in his scheme of things, was completely uncalled for. Nevertheless, there it was—Rattamma was baffled and bewildered by what lay in prospect for her. Frightened, she confided it to her mother and the mother, that senseless creature, made a mess of things by making a public declamation of it to a gathering of men and women, who appeared pleased with the treat they had received in recompense for their disturbed sleep.

'Are the things like birth, nature, the complexion of the body and the length and breadth of the limbs and organs, matters of human choice? Maybe, in God's plan an oddity has a purpose! Who can fathom these things'? He had heard the epic-singer mention the fact that Arjuna, (a main character in the epic Mahabharata) did not have a moustache and beard, when he was in the court of King Virata. One might say that was so because he was in disguise and also because he was serving the term of a curse by the celestial danseuse Urvasi, whose amorous advances he had declined. There was also the case of Krishna, the lord incarnate of God Vishnu. He saw many mythological plays but never saw Krishna sporting a moustache. 'Why, Pray why? There definitely is a reason for it; yes, there is a divine plan in it though it remains unknown'; But Rattamma, that ignorant woman, how could she understand these complex matters?

He heard a commotion in the cattle-shed, the sound of stamping hooves—'the quadrupeds' way of communicating-It was the God's way for them.'

Pagadaiah went to the shed put some hay in the trough and returned to delve back into recollections.

Despite that shaming incident, Rattamma remained in his house for a few more days, and by God's grace, he managed to consummate the matrimony! How unforgettable the experience was! But, before it sank in, his mother-in-law had returned to take her daughter away, on the plea that Rattamma's father was pining to see his lone child.

Ten months later the news came; Rattamma had given birth to a boy. That was the fulfillment of a cherished desire for him.

Duly he went to his in-law's village; his sister also accompanied him. They partook in the naming ritual. He gave the child the name he had chosen long back—Balaraju (the boy king), the eponymous character of the movie, played by that great thespian, Nageshwar Rao. He admired that actor to the point of obsession. In fact, when, at the age of ten, he had seen the movie he took a spontaneous decision to name his son after one of the characters played by Nageshwar Rao.

When his sister proposed to take Rattamma and the child to their village, the parents of Rattamma did not show the temerity to say 'no'.

Thus, Pagadaiah brought home his wife and child. He had his sister to thank for all that; her personality exuded the strength of her character, so domineering that they just had to fall in line with whatever decision she took.

To Pagadaiah it always seemed that the fullness and dignity of the personality came to his sister, Aademma, when she wore that chain laced with gold coins, round her neck and those gold bangles on her wrists!

Rattamma's mother had accompanied her daughter, leaving her old man to burn his fingers in kitchen.

Balaraju's physique made Pagadaiah feel proud; but a gnawing doubt persisted; would his son, when he grew up, have his moustache and beard or at least, a moustache?

He examined the boy very closely, limb by limb and cheek by cheek. His careful survey revealed nothing, which might, later in life turn out to be a source of embarrassment to the boy.

In a way, he should thank Rattamma, he thought, for bearing a son to him; but on second thoughts, he chose to thank the God, for the merciful act. He was indebted to Rattamma in no way. If not she, some other woman would have done that. However, definitely he would have thanked Rattamma, had she continued to live with him in his house, like all the housewives.

Rattamma continued to be her evasive and troublesome self when she was with him. She always clung to the sari-frills of her mother; for she hoped that her mother would rescue her in case there was another 'calamitous encounter'.

The second coming of Rattamma had been no better than the first one. It didn't contribute to any marital happiness. Theirs was just commensalism of a kind.

All of it turned out to be very poignant to him, since he noticed how shapely and supple Rattamma had become. Her bosom swelled and her complexion improved. She looked more poised than ever before. Her postures and gestures revealed a maturity that was not there hitherto. He coveted her, not just for bodily pleasure; he wanted to open up a new chapter of courtship with her. There was no way for him to convey all those sentiments to her; she never gave him a chance to convince her that he sincerely wanted both of them to lead a family life acceptable to themselves and to the community.

While he thus felt freshly drawn towards her, there was no trace of any such inclination in her bearing. Still, he wanted to go close to her and take her into confidence; but there was that devil of a woman, the mother-in-law, who moved menacingly close by.

One day he said to his mother-in-law suggestively, "Uncle must be having a horrid time alone there; it is time . . ."

Cutting him short, the mother-in-law quipped, "I know what I should do; I haven't come to live here, you must know that. I am worried because my child is in a frightened state of mind. I just don't know how to help my child out of this terrible plight."

He felt nettled by that remark and impulsively rebuffed, "What fright and what plight? Why fright? Frightened of marital life . . . ? Then, why did you perform your daughter's marriage? Whom are you trying to fool?"

She fumed at him and made grotesque gesticulations. Her left hand held her right elbow and she moved her right forearm up and down showing it to a lewd purport, "Why? You ask that question, 'why' . . . ? I will tell you. Yes, the time has come for that. I had never suspected this calamity, the one that my child has come up against. I had never imagined that my brainless old man, that wretched son of a widow, would fix this over-aged, over-sized, no moustache no beard man for my golden doll . . . such a sweet and agreeable girl of tender age! Are we cursed to spend the rest of our lives crying our hearts out! Oh God, this was not the thing I had expected from you! Oh my God what have you done to us?"

His sister being away, he was left to fend for himself, "You say your daughter is a child, so tender—an infant? One who had attained puberty four long years before the wedding, and you call her a babe? Don't think that you can get away with that bluff."

The mother-in-law's face went into contortions as she howled and waved her index finger convulsively, in warning, "Rre . . . You are talking indecently. Beware-my child was just twelve years old at the time of marriage and you-? You, son of a donkey, you were already past twenty-five! Who does not know that! Let somebody come and contradict that, you 'son of a stealthy widow'!"

A mixed feeling of indignation, humiliation and dejection overtook him as he recalled the incident in all its vividness.

That was the end of the things. The next morning, mother and daughter set out for their village. The mother-in-law was dressing up Balaraju; obviously, she was intending to take him with them.

That was the last straw for him; he sprang to his feet and in a flash took out the sickle from the twig screen. He brandished it at the wretched woman, "If you are itching for it, both of you go and 'jump into a well of your choice'; but if you touch that son of mine, you would be dead the next moment, you dirty bitches; mind that!"

They shrieked in horror.

Balaraju was scared and started to cry. He took him brusquely into his hands and that frightened the boy into silence.

That bitch, the mother-in-law trembled and Rattamma looked with apprehension.

They went away like that. Years passed. They did not show their faces again; even Rattamma, the mother of the child, didn't. 'What kind of woman one could call her!'

One day, 'the brainless old man' came and beseeched him to send the child with him once, promising to send back the boy after a week.

"You have discarded me. How can I send my son with you? I would not send my boy. You may 'go back the way you have come' and mind it, do not come to my place again. If you want to reestablish the connection, send my wife back. That is the only way out for you," His answer was firm.

The fellow almost fell on his feet! Funny, a father-in-law falling on the feet of the son-in-law! Poor fellow, what could he do! Rattamma was their only child, hence this craving for the grandson, whom they wanted to adopt, perhaps as the heir to their property.

He recalled how he had walked a distance of ten miles to see the movie 'Balaraju'. 'How dazzling was Nageshwar Rao in the movie!' He wanted his son also to grow into a handsome young man like that hero, Nageshwar Rao. 'Would he? Only time would reveal.'

'So, the marriage, the nuptials, the childbirth and the separation-all have passed off quickly! Passed off like a dream! Oh, what a woman that bitch Rattamma is! Has neither the desire to live with her mate nor does she have that tender love for her son! And that mother-in-law, the one and only abnormal kind of woman in the 'whole-entire globe-earth-world', so to say, fit neither to be a wife nor to be a mother nor to be a mother-in-law nor to be anything else to anybody else—Why does God create such creatures, wasting His time!'

Pagadaiah heard the cock's crow, and before he had time to wonder about the time of the night or dawn, he began to hear the hustle and bustle of men and women going about their chores.

He went into the hut, dragging the cot with him and closing the door, fell on the cot, sleeping at last!

Another night, Pagadaiah went to the slab a bit late. There were not many men on the slab; the few that were there did not appear to have noticed his arrival.

'There is something the matter', he thought.

Normally they all waited for him and waited on him; the moment they heard his cough with which he usually announced his arrival, some of them even came a few paces to receive him.

Some of them called him 'uncle' (maternal or paternal) and escorted him to the slab, on which they seated him at a vantage point, after dusting it for him with their shoulder-cloths. Such were the instances that silver lined his career as a narrator of stories.

'Somehow, today the situation looks a bit different!' thought Pagadaiah.

The slab resembled a boa-constrictor, its central part bulging, as though the reptile had just swallowed a lamb and on either side the cemented strips of the bench ran straight like the frontal and rear parts of the reptile.

Here and there, on the slab, some young men rested, half-seated, half-lying, in postures indefinable; some were communicating in hushed voices. For once, every one of them appeared intent on hearing what the other was saying.

Pagadaiah surveyed the scene and gave another cough to hint his presence. It was of no avail; one or two among them turned to him and responded in a consoling way. After that cursory greeting, they once again turned back to the activity they had been engaged in.

Pagadaiah felt annoyed. He had left the prince on a bare stone in the thick of a thick forest, infested with dangerous beasts and here, these fellows appeared least bothered about the plight of that poor prince! God, had he known this attitude of theirs he wouldn't have taken that royal lad to the forest at all! No raconteur in his right senses would've done that, in fact.

He moved nearer to them in an effort to listen to what they were talking about.

"Even last year it didn't rain much. You couldn't call it a rainy season actually," Mme Pullamma's husband was saying.

"Just a few 'dress-wetting drizzles', that's all; but those two cyclones saved the year for us; otherwise, people would've died of thirst!"

'So that's it,' thought Pagadaiah, 'Paddy plants in the nursery beds were ready for transplantation; but, with the rains playing truant, how was one to plough the field and roll-plough it into readiness for transplantation? By this time three to four big rains should have occurred; but that had not been the case,' He reasoned it out; but it hurt him to think that they did not take him into confidence and his advice was not sought in this important matter.

Pagadaiah thought that he should take things into his hands to restore the parity at the slab and took the initiative.

First thing he did was to push aside Bademaya, who had not only been his prop, but was the one that had always pestered him for tales and tales; he moved into a pivotal position; then, he ran his palms on his thighs, shifted that leaf-cigar to a corner between his lips and forged ahead in that battle of wits, "What is bothering you, failure of rains? Why, there would be rains, what else the clouds can do? There would be rains; but it is the prerogative of the rain-god, Varun; he knows when to rain, where to rain and how much to rain; that's it?"

"What is the use if it rains after the season is over? That would only spoil the dry crops!"

Pagadaiah was nonplussed; but he knew how to deal with them in such situations. He took out the leaf-cigar and went to that row of Mangalgiri fence plants, expectorated thrice, wiped his lips with the edge of his 'panche' (a cloth of five yards length worn round the waist-'panche') and walked back slowly; he knew that they would be restlessly waiting for him to come and show them a way out of the quandary.

Reoccupying his seat, he said to them with the air of one who knew the things inside out, "It could be that there is an extra month this year (the traditional Indian calendar, 'panchang' allows an extra month or a void month in a year, in its periodicity.)"

"What, an extra month? But the priest-sir hasn't told us of that!"

Immediately Pagadaiah gave the other alternative, "Or there is a deficit of a month. One can confirm only after studying the calendar. Anyway, there is always a reason for these things. This idle talk of yours is useless, know you that." Thus, he drove home the point that things happening in this mortal world had their own reasons and the reasons were known only to the priest-sir or to a few cognoscenti like him.

However, the gathering there did not appear ready to accept it without a discussion. Therefore, everyone came up with an explanation, on the factors that were responsible for the prevailing drought conditions.

When Pagadaiah gave his reasons, they all fell in line, as expected. "Sinfulness is on the rise in this entire 'globe-earth-world'. Morality and ethics have completely disappeared. That is the main reason for the dysfunction of the seasons . . ."

In support of Pagadaiah's theory, they began to cite examples, "Definitely sinful people are responsible for this wrath of the Rain-God," they averred.

Meanwhile Kannam arrived on the scene, crooning a tune.

Pagadaiah flinched for a moment when he heard that; but steadied himself, bracing up for a possible tiff. He abruptly turned to the old man Hulakki who sat by him innocently, chewing on his gums and said loudly so as to be audible to Kannam, "Uncle Hulakki, you tell me the reason for this bad state of affairs in the world—is it not due to the moral depravity of the man? Has it not become a fashion for the people to deny the existence of the Deity and Devil? How the youth of today are showing disrespect to the elderly and enlightened people? Is it not this trait that is destroying the community, Uncle Hulakki?"

Hulakki was happy that, for once, an issue had been referred to him.

Kannam understood that the innuendo was aimed at him and he cleared his throat stridently to indicate his readiness for a showdown.

Men, who had been lackadaisical to the ongoing exchange of words, suddenly sensed that a peppy drama was opening for them.

Showing a stop signal, with his palm, to Kannam and addressing Hulakki, Pagadaiah initiated the debate, "Tell me, Uncle Hulakki, on the day of Dasara (a festival day for the worship of the deity Durga), we all see Satti possessed. The incense brought from the temple sends her into a state divine frenzy. In that state, she comes up with many revelations. How is she able to do that, if it is not due to the divine power given by the Goddess? How does she do it, Uncle Hulakki, Pray how? And then, Uncle Hulakki, on the day of Mohurram festival Gali Saheb and Pentu Saheb walk on red-hot embers; and why doesn't it burn the soles of their feet? Tell me, Uncle Hulakki, what is the reason? And then, when a cow or a bull comes home, bitten by a snake, is not the spell of hymns cast by the priest-sir, reviving it? Have not we all seen it? How do these things happen, if not by a divine power? Tell me, tell me Uncle Hulakki?" Pagadaiah thundered.

Uncle Hulakki looked grim; he was perplexed, 'Why is he asking me, of all? Why is he pitching me into trouble?' he thought and with eyebrows knit, he began to look a worried man.

"Why, Cousin Pagadaiah, who can deny the truth of what you have said! Definitely deity and devil have a right of their own to exist; otherwise, where would they go, poor creatures!" Borrababu intervened to assuage the feelings of Pagadaiah.

Pagadaiah gaped at Borrababu.

That reassured and comforted Uncle Hulakki; he heaved a sigh of relief and guardedly moved to a safe distance.

"All that is empty talk; tell me, have you ever seen any dead man coming back to life, in response to a spell, I mean, by the incantations? Show me a single instance, just one instance!" challenged Kannam.

Mme Pullamma's man rushed forth from a distant corner; he even pushed aside a man and occupied his strategic seat. For quite a long time he had been planning to participate in a polemic, taking place at the slab. He said, showing some verve, "What are you talking, Kannam! Only the other day, didn't Uncle Pagadaiah tell us? When the old magician was killed, did not his junior restore him to life with an incantation?"

Pagadaiah was amazed at this rush of support from an unexpected quarter.

"Trash, don't tell me these cock-and-bull stories," Kannam dismissed the attempt of the debutant.

Another ally of Pagadaiah tried to be of help, "What about Satti then? How is she able to divulge so many things? And nobody ever denied the truth of what she had revealed!"

Men nodded appreciatively at that man.

"Ah, that Satti, that demented creature and her revelations!" Kannam pooh-poohed, "Who doesn't know the things, you say, she reveals? Most of them are scandals known to everyone. The thing is, nobody likes to divulge them in public. She blurts them out fearlessly because they all accept that she is in a state of divine frenzy and that gives her a sort of immunity. Well, if we empty on your head a few pots of cold water and put those pungent fumes of incense into your nostrils, you would also come into that divine frenzy. Are you ready to try it once, and see it for yourself?"

Now, to an old man sitting by, listening, things appeared to be going out of the bounds! "No, Kannam, you cannot talk like that," he ruled; all the time he had been chewing on his gums; now he got his chance and he grabbed it with both hands and straightaway went into profundities, "A revelation is a revelation whether known to all or unknown to anybody," he ruled, "Here the point is that Satti is able to pronounce them! That is the most important point. No one, not divinely possessed, can reveal like that. This is an age-old piece of wisdom. Don't ever pooh-pooh that if you want to live a long life. Yes, that's it."

The censure from the old man was followed by grave silence; later, accolades came the old man's way—"Yes, indeed," "Truly," "You have put that well."

Changing the strategy, Kannam shifted into a conciliatory tone, "I admit the truth of the grand old man's remarks; but gentlemen, I would like to ask you one thing. I will bring a stranger from an adjoining village. If Satti, in her divine frenzy, can reveal the identity of that person and the facts of his life, I would accept your views on that 'frenzy and revelations stuff'."

Pagadaiah had already washed his hands off the issue and was now seated leaning against the wall in a relaxed manner; but he had to react and so, he said, "Aye, she would—she would reveal; what other business is left for her, than doing your bidding!",

'So, he has retreated' thought Kannam; he mumbled something and Pagadaiah muttered in return; both were largely inaudible, each to the other as also to many avid listeners.

Hulakki was sincere in his efforts; he craned his neck and tried to listen; but it was of no avail. He disapproved of their method of communication, 'Wherever have they learnt this technique of talking so inaudibly!' he wondered.

To members who had expected a grand treat, it turned out to be a disappointment. 'That was a tame finish to something that had started on a great note!' they lamented—most of them.

"Leave all this futile talk. How are we to tackle this drought situation? Think about that first," another toothless old man, Pitchaiah said. That diverted the attention of the gathering from the great treat they were having.

It was precisely this break Pagadaiah had been looking for, to upstage himself. "There is a way out," he said quickly, "We have to arrange the recital of the cow-filching episode from the Mahabharata."

"What, what . . ?"

"Cow-filching episode of Mahabharata," Pagadaiah said with poise.

"Will that do?" enquired Naginaboina, "Will that bring rains?"

"Can you recite that story, Uncle Pagadaiah?" asked Bushaiah.

Pagadaiah did not need to respond to that query; one of his allies did that for him, "Why not! You idiot, is there a tale not known to him, in the entire globe-earth-world?"

At that Pagadaiah smiled modestly, "Of course, I can; but it has to be a singing recitation by a Haridas (an epic-singer), that is, a Harikatha (the story of God), yes, Harikatha."

"Oh my God, Harikatha . . . ? Of all the things, Harikatha?" lamented Hulakki, beating his breast, "That is something, even all of us put-together cannot do."

Then they put their heads together, wondering whether there was an epic-singer in any of the villages around.

Somebody informed the gathering that there was a deaf music teacher in a neighboring village—the one, who taught the nubile girls music on harmonium so as to qualify them for marriage. He was an itinerant music master; periodically visiting his girl-students located in different villages within a radius twenty miles—his name—Sita Ramaiah.

It was decided to arrange a Harikatha; they would report it to the Banzardar, the Patwari, and the village gentry because they were the ones who would be defraying the expenditure.

The gathering at the slab unanimously elected Pagadaiah to be the man to go on a scouting trip, find that deaf music master and an epic-singer and finalize the programme. They thought he was eminently suitable for the task; he would do it successfully, just as the prince of his tales went in search of his dream-girl and succeeded in finding her. Pagadaiah would definitely accomplish the task, yes, he would.

So, a remedial measure was found.

Hulakki kept showering looks of admiration on Pagadaiah.

Once the initial things were finalized, Pagadaiah went on with his avocation, methodically. First things first—the prince, whose hands and legs were bound together tight in iron chains, was freed; this, the prince's companion did with the help of a bear, which was actually a Gandharva (a celestial being) who was serving the term of a curse. When redeemed from the curse by the prince's companion, the Gandharva gave a floral plane, Pushpak, as a token of his gratitude. Pagadaiah sent the prince to the royal palace and then mercilessly dispatched the princess, a beauty of the three worlds, to the nsorcerer's subterranean den-complex, situated yojanas and yojanas away, way beyond the seven seas and hundreds of islands!

Then Pagadaiah walked home, his mind at rest.

All of them—the Banzardar, the Patwari the gentry and the commoners agreed that an epic singer should be found to recite a story from the Mahabharata to propitiate the Rain-God and get rains; they welcomed the move.

Four years ago, when similar conditions prevailed, the villagers bathed the village deity, Muthyalamma, pouring a thousand pans of water on her head, the waters that streamed from the exercise flowing into that deep, cavernous, dried-up well at the end of the north alley.

The next day it rained torrentially. What else could the Rain-God do! There just was no option to him, the Rain-God!

However, that was the ultimate choice; they would take it up, in case the Harikatha failed.

Pagadaiah went on the mission assigned to him; the members of the slab gave him a touching farewell as he set out.

"It is for the good of the village that he has taken upon himself this stupendous task," Naginaboina said in praise of Pagadaiah.

They were all sitting at the slab.

"Anybody in his place would go. What else has he to do at home? He has no wife at home; his sister is taking care of his son. Even the two—acre piece of his land is being cultivated for him by his sister."

Naginaboina showed his disgust at the crabby mindset of Kannam, "Kannam you must change your attitude; you see no virtue even in the best of the men. Pagadaiah is such a noble man! You pounce on him at every chance to insult him and yet he doesn't bear a grudge against you!"

Kannam was mulling over ways to counter this accusation of Naginaboina; but before he could come into action, Naginaboina left the place.

Three days passed; on all the three days the men at the slab talked about the Harikatha and Pagadaiah. They even discussed the available alternatives in the event of a prolonged drought.

Kannam silently sat listening to all that, pitying his village men and dismayed by their dogged faith in the deities and their powers.

"Even God cannot save stupid people," said Kannam to his chum, Gopaya.

Gopaya was looking in the direction of the lane in front and said, "There he is, Pagadaiah, he is coming back. The way he is walking doesn't suggest success in the mission."

All of them looked and saw Pagadaiah coming.

He wore that slightly water-reddened white dress (clothes acquired the colour, called 'neerkavi', when regularly washed without using any detergent), which added a touch of grandeur to a villager's dress. So dressed, he wore on his head a pink turban and looked majestic. When one viewed him from the rear, the slipknot showed his class! ('The slipknot is not the same as a ponytail; in a ponytail hair flows down from the knot, whereas in a slip-knot the knot binds the hair at the bottom, symbolically conveying the idea that the man who sports the slip-knot can control his mind!' explained Pagadaiah once.)

He was coming, after running an errand for them all. Most of them sitting on the slab got off and walked a few steps to receive him in a ceremonious way.

Pagadaiah humbly accepted the reception and walked slowly, seemingly exhausted, wiping the sweat on his forehead and looking at them with a weak smile on his lips.

Escorted to the slab, he sat at a place one of them had cleaned for him.

"He looks fatigued; must have walked quite a distance. Even the nearest village is three miles away and how many villages he must have visited!" Hulakki wondered aloud.

"He must have walked a lot of distance. I just don't know how many villages, each far from the other, he had had to survey!" said Borrababu, in an aside to Hulakki.

Lowering his voice Hulakki responded, "I too don't know; in fact it is difficult to know such things."

Borrababu gawped at him and quickly moved away from him.

Hulakki was baffled at this move of Borrababu; but felt comforted when Pullamma's husband came and sat by him.

Now, a little away from Hulakki, Pagadaiah was making a statement on his tour, to those who were making enquiries about the epic-singer, the date of the programme, deaf Sitaramaiah's role in all this and so on and so forth.

"I met deaf Sitaramaiah at Devarampalli; but actually he belongs to Ramannapet. He is indeed a gentleman. Some of the gentry of Devarampalli said they were also contemplating a Harikatha in their village. In fact Sitaramaiah was at Devarampalli to advise the villagers on that."

"Have you talked to him about our programme?" asked Borrababu.

"Yes, that is the purpose of my trip; otherwise why would I undertake such a grueling journey in this mid-summer!"

"What had he to say?"

Pagadaiah raised his palm and said, "I will tell you everything if you give me a little breathing time," Obviously, he was displeased with the curt attitude of the slab members.

Immediately there was a hush.

To Pullamma's man, something important appeared to be happening at that part of the slab. Therefore, he hurriedly parted company with Hulakki and walked briskly to the prominent part of the slab.

Hulakki was aghast; 'in just three minutes the fellow borrowed two beedis and puffed them away, and now, he is gone!' He felt cheated; but he too felt the pull of that spot and slowly walked there.

"Deaf Sita Ramaiah-sir was very obliging. He is prepared to do this programme for us, at our place. Finding an epic-singer is no big problem for him. Actually he has a cousin, who can do the job; but . . ."

"What does 'but' mean?"

"Yes, there is a problem; the problem is with Sita Ramaiah himself."

"Problem with SitaRamaiah . . . ? That sounds bewildering!"

Their faces wore a look of worry.

"Yes, it is my perception, though. As you know, Sita Ramaiah is going to provide the harmonium accompaniment to the epic-singer; but the fact is that Sita Ramaiah-sir is deaf; how is he going to provide that support?" Pagadaiah wondered openly, for them.

"Oh my God, deaf Sita Ramaiah is deaf?" Uncle Hulakki was dismayed.

"But that is his problem; what do we have to do with that?" Mme Pullamma's man thought it was none of their problem.

"No, no," Pagadaiah laughed at the naiveté of his clientele, "Actually it is our problem, more than being his."

"But, how . . . ?"

"I will tell you how," Pagadaiah smiled. Then he joined the tips of his right hand thumb and index finger and kept the other fingers straight, conjuring up the age-old preaching gesture of the saints. Then, with eyes half-closed, he explained in style, "You see when an epic-singer is performing, and a harmonium accompaniment is giving him support, the pitches of the singer's voice and that of the instrument should agree. Otherwise . . ."

"What is he saying?" Hulakki shook the arm of Borrababu vigorously.

Borrababu turned his palms clockwise, anti clockwise and grinned sheepishly.

'The fellow is hiding something' thought Hulakki and fell back on the wisdom of Pullamma's man, "Pullamma's man, what is this Pagadaiah is saying about the epic-singer and the deaf man?"

Pullamma's husband was desperately looking for a charitable man to borrow a beedi from. Therefore, he readily stretched his hand in a 'this-for-that' proposal.

Hulakki looked at Mme Pullamma's man with abhorrence, 'what a detestable creature the fellow is! How is Mme Pullamma able to stand the fellow!' he wondered to himself. The next moment he found the fellow smoking a beedi by the side of another member, his right leg placed on the left knee in a lordly style! 'That's why the proverb—the one that cooks has only two dishes, whereas the one that begs has twenty dishes!' he thought.

As he was so lost in thought, the explanation of Pagadaiah was over and the members of the slab sitting nearby were nodding their heads in appreciation of the point. 'As usual, I have missed a vital point!' Hulakki grieved.

So it was fixed—the Harikatha was only three days away. It was decided to transform the slab into a makeshift stage with an improvised roof.

Pagadaiah appealed to the members to come forward voluntarily to work at the slab.

On the day of Harikatha, the slab witnessed some brisk activity by the members. There were more volunteers than were required; but Pagadaiah allowed all of them to participate in the preparatory work—setting-up of the stage; after all, it was the work of the community.

They dug the holes, pitched the poles, and arranged a makeshift roof; only a little sprucing up was needed.

Meanwhile the Banzardar and the Patwari (the village officer) arrived and made a cursory survey of the preparations. They expressed their satisfaction at the state of things and asking Pagadaiah to approach them if anything was needed, they went away.

Pagadaiah was at the center of the activity; wielding a crowbar—a pickaxe—a scythe or any other tool, it was he all the way!

Mme Pullamma's man was another member who caught people's attention. For once, now there was no dearth of beedis for him and he was there for all to see, with smoke perpetually issuing from his mouth and nostrils, making him look like a 'smoldering' man.

The men smiled relishing his gusto.

The only odd one in this entire hullabaloo was Kannam; he was there at the slab, but kept away from the buzz of the activity; as he watched everything, his lips curved into a sarcastic smile.

Hulakki kept a wary eye on Kannam. 'Wouldn't the fellow involve himself in this important community work?' He could not answer the question. 'There is only one person who can answer the question and that is Pagadaiah,' he thought, but, he did not have the courage to pose the question to Pagadaiah, at least at that juncture.

The artists—deaf Sita Ramaiah, his cousin and another person, arrived well in advance of the time.

The slab, decked out for the occasion, looked spick and span. At the centre, a stage was set up for the performers-the epic singer and the accompanists. The slab and it's 'chimti' wings had been swept clean and washed; the foreground was sprinkled with cow-dung water. Three gaslights were lit.

The epic-singer and the accompanists—deaf Sita Ramaiah being the kingpin of them—had been a good team of performers in this art of epic singing. They had been giving these programmes for quite some time.

It was only a few years ago that deafness had afflicted Sita Ramaiah and the affliction was so telling that a few programs they gave after the affliction were enough to earn him the epithet 'Deaf'. He tried his best to listen and track the melodic scales selected for the verses by the epic singer; but despite his frantic efforts he consistently missed some notes. After two such low-key performances, the epic singer took him to Bezwada and Sita Ramaiah came back equipped with a hearing aid; so the tag stayed stuck.

People began to trickle in, quite early. The earliest ones were the protégés of Pagadaiah-led by Bademaya; later came the bugbear Kannam with his friends. The last to come were the Banzardar, the Patwari and the Mali Patel and they sat in the chairs close to the dais.

A sizeable number of brats sat ganged up in a place where they were starkly face-to-face with the singer and the accompanists. Pagadaiah noted it. As a precautionary measure, he went and sat at the head of the gang heeding to the suggestion of the artists, who had sensed trouble.

The story was from the Mahabharata.

'The Pandavas are living incognito as per the terms of settlement entered into with the Kauravas. King Virata gives them shelter. The Kauravas steal the cattle of King Virata and Prince Uttarakumara brags that he can easily defeat the enemies and bring back the cattle if only an able charioteer was there. Arjuna, living there disguised as a dance teacher, offers to drive the chariot for the bragging prince. When they reach the battlefield, the Prince develops cold feet and jumps off the chariot to run away; but Arjuna comes out of disguise and saves the day for the army of Virata . . .'

The epic singer found it difficult to read the response of the gathering. Most of them appeared mystified by this strange thing, called epic singing. Some were snoozing; some were searching for a place to get into a comfortable posture.

The most active of all were the urchins, who kept their eyes riveted on the epic singer and deaf Sita Ramaiah alternately; but the glint in their eyes looked foreboding to the epic singer!

As for Pagadaiah, he looked absorbed, too absorbed to monitor the movements of the mischievous gang of urchins.

The young lot liked the character of the chicken-hearted prince and the singer concentrated on it, creating a humour of sorts at which the front-row elite knitted their brows. The singer saw the elite's expression; but opted to keep the urchins in good humour.

Now, after a time, the brats lost interest in the epic and singing and were on the lookout for a fresh excitement; just at that fateful moment, the eyes of an urchin fell on Pagadaiah's slipknot; that opened up for them a new channel of entertainment.

Meanwhile, the weather became stuffy and all of them in the gathering began to feel a sudden discomfort; the wind had stopped blowing. Everyone took their headwear off to fan themselves with and when Pagadaiah also did the same thing the young rogues gasped exultantly at the fortuitous way things unfolded for them.

The stillness of the wind also affected the Banzardar's daughters and sons-in-laws, resting on the terrace of the bungalow; they had come for the summer vacation. They could view the programme from the terrace. Their comments, interspersed with the other accompanying sounds were reaching the slab.

Every time a comment was heard, the heads of the audience turned towards the roof of the bungalow; some looked pleased at the prospect of watching two programmes.

Once or twice, the epic singer stopped singing in an effort to get the undivided attention of the audience; but it did not have any salutary effect on the gathering.

"For days the fellows had been chanting 'Arikatha-Arikatha'; but they haven't bothered to arrange 'mykam' (mike set), so characteristic of the nature of our villagers!" wailed an old man, hard of hearing.

"Don't you wail, old man, it doesn't matter to Rain-God whether you have heard the epic song or not, it's enough if Rain-God hears."

"'Mykam' means forty rupees; who would give it, Sir?" another member of the gathering asked the old man.

"Who has paid for all this?" Waving his hand all around, the old man retorted, "Same fellow could have paid for 'mykam' also!"

"Why do you always expect that fellow and this fellow to pay? Why don't you yourself pay? At least, once in a lifetime . . ." A young man shouted at the old man.

The performers now stopped the program and waited for the verbal exchanges to stop.

"Shh, would you please stop this nonsense and allow us to listen to the epic song? We have come here to listen to the epic song, not to listen to your squabble, understand? If you don't want to listen to the epic song, you can go home and do some domestic work, at least; the womenfolk will appreciate that."

A section of the audience laughed loudly, at which the singer stopped the performance

The heads of the Banzardar, Malipatel and Patwari turned to that side and that did the needful.

Then ensued silence; the epic singer took it as 'go-ahead' signal and cleared his throat.

Pagadaiah was looking for this excellent opportunity. With a jerk, he stood up and shouted, "Go home, you bloody brats. What can you understand of this? This is not for you, you, loutish young rogues! Get lost!"

Some of the kids were unnerved and were dusting their knickers; but the one, who was the architect and executive engineer of the 'grab the slip-knot' plan was undaunted.

Pagadaiah knew that it was this boy, who was playing cat-and-mouse with his slipknot. He caught the boy by the hand and shouted, "What were you doing? Tell me, you rogue! What were you doing, along with that bunch of monkeys in your gang? Answer my question, or else I will box your ears. Whose son are you, you good-for-nothing fellow?"

The boy insolently looked Pagadaiah in the eye, pulled back his hand and said unfazed, "I have come to listen to the Arikatha. My mom has asked me to go and listen."

Pagadaiah scratched his pate in an effort to think of the next move.

"Pagadaiah, what is going on there? Shall we listen to the Harikatha or listen to your katha?" asked the Banzardar peremptorily.

With that, Pagadaiah had to stop his efforts at bringing the urchin around and the boy stuck to the place he had been sitting at. One after another, the other members of his gang regrouped with him, with a look of triumph on their faces.

Pagadaiah looked crestfallen and he moved away from the spot.

Hulakki sympathetically looked at Pagadaiah and sighed philosophically. Then becoming a little thoughtful, he safe-deposited his own slipknot inside a tightly tied-up turban.

The epic singer had just gulped down a glass of hot milk with pepper and dry ginger powder and looked fresh as he resumed the Harikatha.

Then the program encountered another hurdle. Big raindrops began to splatter the slab and its environs and after a few moments they gained momentum.

There was a tumult in the crowd as people rose and began to dust up their dresses.

The epic singer folded his hands and appealed to them "My dear friends and worshippers of Varuna, the Rain-God, please have patience and don't leave. We have all seen that the Rain-God is pleased with your devotion and these rain-drops are an indication of God's favour."

Pagadaiah also appealed to the gathering with his palms joined, "You must all sit and show the strength of your will and devotion. It is a testing time. The God is testing us. Let us not fail in this test of God."

The young brats were, of course, in no mood to leave.

Then the raindrops stopped falling and the epic singer resumed the Song of God.

For the children, it was like the second act of the play and they were looking for another chance to upstage Pagadaiah.

The epic singer now wanted to draw the crowd into his fold by taking up a risky digression and he began to dance to the fast beat played by the percussionist. There was no singing, no narration of the story. Just dancing—eyes half closed, hands and feet moving in perfect coordination, dexterously translating the nuances of the beat into fleeting pictures of graceful gestures and pleasing postures.

The essay on the part of the epic singer drew forth a spontaneous applause from the crowd, which came as a pleasant surprise to the singer and the percussionist.

The epic singer humbly thanked the crowd with folded hands and proceeded with the story.

However, with the intermittent breaks, the epic singer appeared to have lost his rhythm; but he continued in a determined manner.

The programme went on for some more time. Then the raindrops began to fall again, this time they were much bigger, of the size of peanuts and they began to fall with greater force.

"There, there, it has started to rain! Even before the completion of the Harikatha! That is the power of 'the Arikatha'! Rain-God is great. Hail Rain-God!"

"Oh, this wretched rain, looks like it wouldn't stop until we run downstairs," From the terrace of the Banzardar's bungalow, one of the Banzardar's daughters cursed the rain.

"I will break a coconut to the Rain-God tomorrow at the temple, if it rains heavily tonight," Bushaiah, a farmer, declared at the slab.

"I will keep a watch on you and see whether you would really do that. As far as I know you have never broken a coconut anywhere, leave alone at the temple."

The raindrops fell faster and faster.

The villagers began to run to their dwellings, muttering, talking, shouting, and thanking and cursing the Rain-God and their fate, in a mixed-up reaction.

The epic singer and the accompanists were taken to the house of the Patwari.

Soon the slab and its two wings became vacant.

Then abruptly, the rain or the raindrops or the drizzle, or whatever it was, stopped; but nobody thought of a restart of the programme, not even Pagadaiah and nobody spoke of the Rain-God.

Next day onwards, the Sun God went berserk. He scorched the earth, seared the vegetation and made them bear the marks of his wrath.

The soil with the cracks, clefts and fissures became an eyesore to the farmers. The pulverized topsoil rose and floated in the wind, like a cloud. Ponds in the agricultural farms had gone dry long back; now the pond beds showed not even a trace of the green grass.

When one looked at the horizon one could see the phantom forms of horses galloping in the hot air. The west wind blew straight over the blacksmith's forge, as it were.

All through the day clouds moved in the sky, taking fanciful shapes of black humped bulls, elephants and playfully ambling calves; but in the evenings the sky presented a picture of cleansed slate.

'If it continues like this, how would we live? What would we feed the cattle with? What would be there for us to eat, my brother . . . ?

'What would we eat? Why, God would show us some way to survive. He would not see us die! I tell you from experience—listen; in the Dhatha year, there was a terrible famine, but famine of a different type. What we are seeing now is nothing when compared to that. Ask any old man; he would tell you. I am not lying, you should know. I tell you I never speak lies. You can ask anybody, understand?'

'Yes, I know that, uncle; but tell me about that famine of the Dhatha year.'

'Tell what?'

'About the famine of the Dhatha year: how did the people survive that severe drought? What did they eat to live?'

'I don't know about the others; but my grandpa mixed curd with the slushy clay and slurped it.'

'Curd, where did they get it from?'

'Boy, that was a wet famine; I told you that. It means excess and excess of rains. No agriculture was possible; so, no food grains. Grass was plenty; no famine for cattle, famine only for mankind . . .'

'Too bad they had to do that; but there was lot of water, you say; there must have been lots and lots of grass; they could've eaten the seeds of grass.'

'No, they couldn't have done that; after all, grass is the food of animals!'

'Now, boy, there is not going to be any curd or slushy clay. Now, man has to eat just dust . . .'

'Why dust? There are trees and there are leaves on them. I tell you, humankind has fallen on evil times, because of their sinfulness. When men fail to do what God has ordained for them, the seasons go awry; it's all an interconnected system . . .'

'But, why punish the entire humankind for the lapses and failings of a few men? Has the whole humankind become so wicked just this year? Were they virtuous last year and the year before? I do not see any logic in the argument . . .

'Today I got up early in the morning, removed the clods of cattle dung, put them in the manure pit, and went to the well to draw water and fill the tubs. Lo, there I saw the bottom of the well! There was no trace of the tortoise! Where has the tortoise gone, the big tortoise? Why don't I see the tortoise in the well . . . ?

'Hey, where are you, Lady of the House?'

'Who are you talking to and what is it you are you saying? Tortoise . . . ? Worrying about the tortoise now . . . ? It must have left the well three years ago, when the heavy rains brought the well water to the ground level. You remember those torrential rains, don't you? The entire village appeared to be floating in water! The tortoise must have left the well then; you know, tortoises can foresee the future; you need not worry about the tortoise now; I am sure it is safe somewhere . . .

'Come, you have to take the cow to the forest. See how emaciated the creature has become! I thought it would give us a calf this year; but her feet cannot bear the weight of her body; how can she bear the weight of a bull . . .'

At the slab,

Muneyya was pacing up and down restlessly. He looked a worried man. He had taken a two-acre land patch on lease, three years ago. He grew vegetables on that land and supplied them to a nearby town. Last two years, his efforts earned him a tiny profit; but this year, the outlook appeared bleak. If the drought conditions persisted, what were to be his options?

After the night of Harikatha, things changed a little at the slab. Pagadaiah was his usual self, ready to narrate a tale; but he was a crafty customer; he waited until the request came. He weighed the earnestness of the listeners and then chose his response. However if he did not narrate a story he always felt uneasy; but there was no request!

As for the villagers, the men that regularly attended the assembly at the slab were in a state of indecision. After their supper, their feet dragged them to the slab; there was no stopping that, but once they were at the slab what were they to do? Should they flock around Pagadaiah along with others and pass the time listening to whatever he told, or, bond with another group and indulge in chitchat; but they seemed to have lost interest in both. Still, they did not feel like going home. What would they do at home at this time? It was slab-time for all men, rains or no rains.

"Sssss . . ." Muneyya heaved a sigh of anguish and said in an aside, "It's very stuffy. Looks like it would rain tonight heavily"

"Aye, it would, it would indeed! Keep waiting," Said Kannam sarcastically.

"Indeed, it would, it would . . ." Retorted Pagadaiah, "Especially, when there are blessed and righteous men, in the village!" the pointblank innuendo was, evidently, aimed at Kannam.

The comment of Pagadaiah drew ripples of laughter.

"If it were in your hands, you would have arranged a rain a night!" Kannam hit back, "You have even arranged the singing of the epic tale! We should now get very good rains."

"Yes, why not . . . ? As per my count, your farmland should get the best amount of rainfall."

"Oh, so you know these calculations and quotas too! Then, by your count, was that rain we had on the night of the epic singing enough recompense for that story, since you are a master of stories?"

"Again you say 'story'! You are saying that by and by. What do you think you know about the power of a story? Do you know the power of a story?" Pagadaiah climbed down from the slab and mustered up whatever theatrical talents he had, as he said, "A story can light up an earthen lamp with water in it! A story can revive a dried up trunk into a lush green flowering tree! Do you know that? A story can bring cool showers in scorching summer! You must know that?

A man of your standing deriding the story and its power, Hm . . . !"

'Damn you, brainy fellow!' Hulakki cast a look of admiration and amazement at Pagadaiah.

"Is that so, Sir? How do we, the naïve, know these complex things? Pagadaiah Sir, why don't you light up a lamp once, or revive a piece of dead wood once, or bring on a welcome shower once, with the power of your stories? I will fall at your feet and will serve you like a slave for the rest of my life. Pray, do any one of them things, here and now and dispel our ignorance," Kannam concluded his part of the argument, with a display of his theatrical skills.

Hulakki was equally impressed by the knack with which Kannam presented his case. Pursing his lips into a tight smile, he kept nodding his head rhythmically, in admiration, as Kannam spoke.

Now, silence descended on the slab. For a few minutes none spoke. Intrigued by the silence a few passersby got stuck up at the slab.

Hulakki was miffed by the situation.

"What next?" said Gopaiah in an apparent effort to end the impasse and pin down Pagadaiah?

"If you say what next, well, I am waiting to prostrate before Pagadaiah Sir."

"Do that, then." Pagadaiah stretched his feet, inviting Kannam to touch them and ask for pardon.

"I will do that, but, first demonstrate the power of your stories," Kannam replied as his blood rushed; he repeated, "I would definitely do that, Sir; but first I beg you to demonstrate the power of your story by doing one of those things you have spoken of."

Led by Hulakki, every head kept turning towards Pagadaiah and Kannam, in line with their turns of speaking.

Pagadaiah felt cornered; for once, he ran out of ideas and wished he were able to vanish like one of those magicians in his tales.

Hulakki felt restlessly happy; for him this was the best of the evenings at the slab. To him, Pagadaiah and Kannam looked like two champion wrestlers in the fray, each displaying his strength and skills.

A late onlooker, who was intrigued by the tense silence at the slab, queried innocently, "What has happened, you are all so silent?"

That was the half-chance Pagadaiah was waiting to come his way as Godsend and he lapped it up, with a twinkle in his eye, "Nothing happened as yet, Cousin Singaiah; but there are people, who want something or other to happen in this village. You know these things well enough; you have seen the world and it is not for nothing that people talk about your wisdom and sagacity . . ."

Singaiah bowed his head showing modesty and queried further, "That's right, my elder brother Pagadaiah, but what has gone wrong on the slab, and with you there?"

"Don't shame me further Cousin Singaiah. You and I are from the old world. I don't want to spoil your day with these silly and disgraceful things,"

Suddenly it dawned on Hulakki that as a responsible member of the slab he should explain the things to the latecomer, and relishing his luck, he went about it, "Actually, it all started as a talk on what should be done to bring rains. You know, we arranged a Harikatha on the cattle-filching episode from the Mahabharata; but the program didn't bring rain as expected . . ."

Then Pagadaiah interrupted Hulakki with a reentry into the debate; he thundered, startling the assembly of men, "It would've rained, I say it would've rained; but the story was not completed; that is the unfortunate thing. Was it completed—the Hari Katha, was it?" he turned to the gathering as a whole.

Hulakki picked up the thread, "Actually it would've been completed; but there was rain."

"So, it was the rain that interrupted the program of HariKatha?"

"Yes, but it was the katha that brought about the rain."

"So, there was rain, then?"

"Yes, but not much of it."

"Why not, pray?"

"Because the story wasn't completed; had it been completed there would've been plenty of rain."

Kannam broke into a loud laughter, "Things are interlocked, hhahhaha."

Pagadaiah looked at Kannam, half-in anger and half in dismay, "Crazy fellow!"

"I'm not the one who is crazy. Everyone knows who is crazy."

"I am also saying the same thing; everyone knows who is crazy. Come on, men; give your verdict. Who is crazy?"

All this didn't look nice to Cousin Singaiah; so he tried to pacify them and adjudicate on the issue. "It is not correct to precipitate things like this. What you want is rains. You should go for the next available option. That is what you should do; isn't it so?"

"What should we do, then?"

"Give the Goddess Muthyalamma a thousand-pan bath!"

"Yes, yes, that's the right thing. We should have done that in the first instance itself."

"Would that do? Would that bring us rain, Uncle Singaiah?"

"That would bring you rains. Yes, that should . . ."

"Suppose, it doesn't . . ."

"What 'suppose, it doesn't'? What do you mean by 'suppose it doesn't'?"

"I mean, if the effort fails to get us rains . . . then?"

"Then . . . ? Then, we will pull that icon of Muthyalamma out of ground and throw it into that abandoned well," Hussainaiah said, "That's where she deserves to be put, if she can't get us rains."

"Now, enough of that; don't bring disaster on the village by uttering such blasphemies!"

Hulakki looked aghast and turned towards Pagadaiah awaiting a censure. Of all the people, he was the person most qualified to reprimand; but Pagadaiah had learnt enough from his experience.

Furthermore, Pagadaiah knew how Hussainaiah had done a hundred circumambulations round the shrine of Muththalamma, praying for a son. For two years after marriage he had devoutly worshipped the deity; everyone in the village knew that; but Muthyalamma had not been kind to Hussainaiah; such things hurt, he knew.

Hulakki found Pagadaiah nodding his head in sympathy and immediately commissioned his head to do the same; he was intelligent, Hulakki; he could read people's minds from gestures!

"Yes, we will pull her out and throw her away."

"Shh, Hussainaiah, have you gone mad! Do you want the village to become a graveyard? One more such impiety from any, I will pull out that fellow's tongue and throw it in that abandoned well! Do you all understand?" Singaiah roared like an old lion that had lost its teeth; he lost a few phonemes in his words, but managed to get the tune right.

Members of the slab were stunned! 'Now, what next . . . ?'

"It has become a fashion to talk like that, Uncle Singaiah. Some rascal starts it and it catches on. In a way, it is good that you have come to the slab today, Uncle Singaiah. I cried my voice hoarse over this trend, several times. Some day somebody should be given a treat with a whip. Until then, this thing would persist," Pagadaiah supported the old man.

Kannam sat silently; he saw, in every word uttered by Pagadaiah, an attempt to blame him. He wondered whether the man was harboring a plan to get him whipped at the slab. He began to feel uneasy and after a while left the spot.

"People are becoming completely unruly. They do not respect the age or tradition nor do they revere the deity; this way, where would we end up?" Singaiah still hissed; 'after all, at the slab, it is not every day that you get listened to,' he told himself.

"Calm down, Uncle Singaiah," Said Pagadaiah in a low voice, "He has gone away."

Singaiah had no knowledge of the equations at the slab; so, he continued with his disapproval of the things he heard, "That is alright, one who has gone away is gone; the one who stays there, stays; the world goes on as usual. We are all puppets in the hands of . . ." he left it incomplete for Pagadaiah to complete.

"In the hands of Muthyalamma," Hulakki completed.

For once Pagadaiah was left staring, 'What temerity, what temerity!'

Then they decided to report the proceedings of the slab meetings to the Banzardar and Patwari. A delegation consisting of Pagadaiah, Lingaiah and the guest member Singaiah was chosen for the mission. Hulakki chose himself to be the surprise member of the team.

At the Banzardar's house, Pagadaiah recounted the discussions that had taken place at the slab and the decision taken by them.

Appaiah-lord-sir heard patiently and agreed that they should give Muthyalamma a chance. "Fair enough, who knows, she might succeed in getting us rains ... I would send the two juniors from my farmhands to share in the ritual work. Regarding access to the well, you know I have two wells. You may draw water from the one in the foreyard; but do not come to the well in the backyard; my children have come for the vacation. We need that well for ourselves. I am making it clear, well in advance, do you people understand ... ?"

Pagadaiah and company nodded in agreement. Then they went to the temple and requested the Priest-sir to fix up an auspicious day for the ceremonial bath they were planning to offer to the Deity, Muthyalamma.

The ritual of bathing Muthyalamma with one thousand pans of water was fixed for the full-moon day, which was ten days away. Pagadaiah would be in charge of the programme, as he had been and would be, on all such occasions.

By this time, Kannam, Gopaiah and a few others regrouped at the slab. The conversation that took place at the Banzardar's house was quite audible to them and what they had heard triggered a minor debate.

"I knew it would come to this. Pagadaiah can never solve a problem; he would only create a fresh problem; by nature he is like that."

"And by nature, we are naïve."

"Even if you are shrewd, who would listen to your voice?"

The few members that were there nodded.

"So, next full-moon day, the wells are set to go dry!"

"What would you drink and what would the poor cattle drink? Definitely, this is a very hasty decision."

"Bathing Muthyalamma with one thousand pans of water . . . ! It is not as easy as saying; the water has to flow all the way to that abandoned well and with the earth so scorched up, how long would it take for the water to flow to the well!"

"That's not all; the water thus flown into that dry well must amount to an ankle-deep pool! It is like, as they say, 'applying a medicine for the pharyngitis only to lose the tongue in the processes!"

"That was aptly said, aptly said! Moreover, the way to that abandoned well is so long and meandering . . . ! Oh, upon my mother . . . ! I, for one, am losing my head, at the very thought of it!"

"Let it be lost. What good is it to have a head in the present situation, anyway?"

Presently, the delegation was seen coming out of the Banzardar's house and silence descended at the slab once again.

Pagadaiah was his usual ebullient self on the full-moon day and no one was surprised at that—'if not Pagadaiah who else would be excited! On the day of Sri Rama Navami, the birthday of Rama, Pagadaiah erects the pavilion. On the day of Sri Krishnaashtami, the birthday of Krishna, it is Pagadaiah who would arrange that rope-with-butter pot, and then pull it up and down tantalizingly, teasing and taunting the youth aspiring to touch and grab the butter pot. Again, on the day of Vijaydasami, it would be Pagadaiah to take the deity to the Sami (acacia) tree and back to the temple, safe and secure. It is Pagadaiah all the way. Yes, it has been and it would be he all the way! If Pagadaiah were not there, the Priest-sir would be working with just one and only one hand, so to say.'

That day, Pagadaiah woke up very early, pounded the millet, drank 'kyapi' water (coffee) and kept some for his son Balaraju. When the little fellow came from his maternal aunt's house, he gave him some kyapi, bathed and dressed him up and then drove the two cows into the herd of Bandi Ramaiah's cattle going to the grazing land at the foot of the hills. Then he took head-bath and put on that long-sleeved shirt and the fine sixty-count panche, he had bought at Bezwada. Finally, when he put that vermillion mark on his forehead he looked respectable and presentable.

By the time the sun ascended the Pandava hill he reached the slab. He found the spot almost empty; only Bademaya and one or two others were there.

'Woe these prankish youngsters, how unbridled they have become!' Pagadaiah felt disgusted and sent Bademaya to summon a few men, he named.

It took the lads from the Banzardar's house some time to come for the community work.

They waited.

Then gradually people started coming and their number began to swell, some of them curious onlookers though.

Potter Sonaddiri and his wife were among the first few who showed an awareness of the seriousness of the occasion; the spouse, in particular, looked grand with her washed-up hair hanging long and loose and with that rupee-size vermillion mark on her forehead looking resplendent. As she walked majestically, Sonaddiri trudged behind, carrying a pair of new earthenware in one hand and a fowl for sacrifice, in the other.

Pagadaiah watched the duo with pride; they were the salt of the community! God cared for this world only because a few such people were there in the world, he thought.

Soon, others also followed with pans, pitchers, pails, and rounds of ropes to draw water from the wells.

The Priest-sir came, chanted some hymns, and gave them the signal to start the proceedings.

Sonaddiri walked forward and with one stroke severed the body of the bird from its head, and without any further ado, gave way to his wife and stood behind her, hands folded.

"So quick and well . . ." An old man said.

Pagadaiah was highly impressed with the workman-like act of Sonaddiri.

Then came the turn of Hussainaiah who did it all clumsily and the place resounded with the cackle and curse of the bird. He looked glum; that was the last chance he was giving to Muthyalamma, he told himself.

Then came the Banzardar Appaiah Esq., the Patwari and the Mali Patel and a few of the landed gentry; they poured, each a pan of water ceremonially and made way for the plebeians.

Then followed the central act; they started from the nearest well and soon their work gained a lyrical abandon.

They were on run, on run, on run . . .

'What excitement, what elation . . . ! Ah, Narasimha, Lord of the Lion-hill, Appanna, of the Lion hill, all this is your glory, your greatness . . . ! How light-footed and free of fatigue your divine highness has made them, your votaries, Lord Narasimha! They are sweating; the sweat is streaming; they are hot like engines; does not matter, doesn't matter . . .

'Let Muthyalamma, shiver with the chill, caused by the long, long bath! Let her teeth clatter—tuk-tuk-tuk-tuk . . . May the scorching month of Jyeshta metamorphose into the rainy month of Bhadrapada! May the Mother Earth feel goose skins at the sight of her devotees' fervor . . . !

'May this water, poured on the deity, vaporize, rise high into the skies into the cloud-zone and become a dark rain-bearing cloud. How sweet the rumble and roar of the clouds is to the ears and heart! The black cloud-formations look like awe-inspiring bulls reveling in the grazing field at the foot of the Pandava hills, digging up and throwing back the red soil with their horns and hooves of their forelegs! How closely the clash of the clouds recalls a bullfight, a sublime heartwarming sight . . .'

'The rumble of the clouds frightens the tender hearts and evokes the incantation of the names of the Pandava hero (Arjuna, Phalguna, Partha, Kiriti . . .). Those with strong hearts smile fondly at the fear and faith of the folks. Then, the cloudburst comes; the celestial elephants pour water with their trunks. There appear on the plough fields ruts and gorges rippling with water. Rivulets run hurriedly to enrich the rivers. In a matter of a few days, the earth would be green carpeted. How nice the sequence of events had been until two years back! Why has the nature suddenly become devious? What and where have things gone wrong? Why did it rain thrice in a month when Rama ruled as king? Why does not it rain so, now? Pray, why, Lord Narasimha! Why doesn't it rain like in old times?'

The eternal debate goes on, at the temple, at the slab or at any place where more than two men gather. Nothing is left unexplained and no explanation is contradicted; still things remain the same, as they were, mystifying and ominous. Why . . . Pray why?

Near the slab, things were not looking as bright as they had looked at the beginning. For quite some time the soil had been sucking the water the minute it was poured and so, it took some time for the water to flow as a small stream.

The men at work discovered that the water had not flown much of the distance to be covered; most of it had been sucked in by the thirsty soil and by that time, the pans and buckets had begun to draw blank. The empty bottoms of the nearby wells gaped at the men.

'Now, what should we do?' the men asked themselves. There were only two wells, untapped nearby—one, of the Banzardar's, another, of Kannam's.

No question of going to Kannam's well, Pagadaiah ruled. Now the option was to go to the Banzardar's well; but he had already asked them not to access his second well.

Bademaya had other ideas. "Come on; let's go to the well. By afternoon, the water should fall into the well."

"To which well and into which well, Bademaya Sir?" said Gopaya in a jeering tone.

"Let us go to Kannam's house, to the well in his backyard."

Pagadaiah cautiously kept silent; anything involving Kannam was making him queasy. Further, Kannam had not joined in the ritual.

"The fellow is a pervert. We just don't know how that 'son of a widow' would react."

Bademaya was unfazed and walked, all alone, like a soldier, into the foreyard of Kannam's hut, holding the pot in his hand, like a shield.

Kannam greeted them with folded hands, "There is only a little water in my well. If that is tapped, we and our cattle would have no water to drink."

Bademaya gaped, "How, then . . . ?"

"How do I know? Go and tap that well in the backyard of the Lord— Sir's house; it never goes dry. Further, it is near to the shrine of Muthyalamma," suggested Kannam.

"But, Lord-Sir has asked us not to touch that well . . ."

Then Pagadaiah intervened, "So you wouldn't give water to bathe Muthyalamma; is that your final answer? I tell you, you will have to pay heavily for this . . ."

At that, Kannam flinched a little, "Uncle Pagadaiah, this well in my yard is a source of water for four families. Just imagine our plight if it goes empty. I am unable to understand the logic of all this frenzy and wastage of water, when we are already short of water."

"Ok, go your way then. We will see . . ."

"Where do you want me to go?" Kannam said, needling Pagadaiah.

"Wherever you want to, to hell or heaven . . ." Saying that Pagadaiah turned to his men, "Come on, I told you it would come to this. Now let us get away from here as fast as we can. Let us go to the house of Lord—Sir; he wouldn't say no."

"When is this thing going to be settled and when are we going to resume! By that time, it would all dry up and maybe we have to start it all again. Oh Mother Muthyalamma, Oh Mother, help us!"

Banzardar Lord Appaiah scratched his head, seeing them. "What is this Pagadaiah? I have already told you that we require that well for ourselves. Two times a day my children have to bathe and then, unless at least fifteen to twenty pans of water are sprinkled on the terrace, my children cannot sleep on that terrace. I have already told you and here you have come back!" Then he pondered over the matter for a while and said, "Anyway let us see what can be done.

Meanwhile, go and ask the Priest Sir to come here. Maybe, he would offer a solution."

Bademaya went and came back with the Priest-sir, Suraiah.

The Priest Suraiah heard it all, scratched his pate and came up with a solution, "Actually, we should not take it literally; it is only a symbolic ritual. Muthyalamma is none other than one of the many aspects of Parvathi, the consort of Lord Siva; that way, it is nothing but performing the 'abhishekam' to Lord Siva. Since we have no temple of Siva in our village, we are giving this bath to Mother Muthyalamma . . ."

"Suraiah Sir, You haven't grasped the problem. The problem is: these people have been laboring since early morning and the flow of water hasn't gone even half the way. Most of the wells have showed the bottom. What is the way out?"

"Way-out means . . . Yes, of course there is a way-out . . ."

"Do reveal that at once, Sir. There isn't much time left," Said Pagadaiah impatiently.

"Actually, abhishekam means, as per the lore, bathing the deity with a thousand pans. Judging by what you say, you must have already poured a thousand pans of water . . ."

"Oh yes, why, it must have been much more than that . . ."

"Then there is no problem . . ."

"But the water has to fall into that abandoned well," Said Pagadaiah.

"As I said, there is a way. All that you have to do is, just go on adding flow to flow from successive pans. Do it in such a way that the flow is continuous; there should not be any break. Is that clear? I will explain again . . ."

"We have understood; in fact, we were thinking on the same lines," They said in unison and the next moment they were running back. In doing so, they never bothered to consult the master of the ceremonies, Pagadaiah.

Pagadaiah walked behind them. He did not want it to become so simple; but there was nothing he could do about it. He would have been happy, if someone had dragged the name of Kannam into the issue. He was also annoyed with the priest; he could not find a single point from the lore to nail down Kannam. It was rather strange, he thought.

The problem was solved and they managed to take that slender flow of water into that abandoned well, at the end of the alley.

By the evening, the sky became pitch black with clouds. All of them began to wonder at the strange and spectacular way the sky had started with a pan-sized black spot and in a matter of few hours came to be totally cloud-cast. After initial delight, people began to feel nervous at the alarming size of the cloud blanket; to them, the quick and sudden development looked rather ominous than felicitous.

"What is this that we see? Oh my, such a thick, ponderous cover of clouds . . . ! Are we in for a rainfall or a calamity of deluge! I haven't seen anything like this in my life; I for one do not think it augers well. What do you say?" Said Hussainaiah without actually seeing who was sitting nearby.

It was the ubiquitous man, Mme Pullamma's husband, as usual.

"I knew it would come to this. I thought of telling you; but you were so busy with that sacrifice thing; one fat cock lost so thoughtlessly!"

This aside between Hussainaiah and Mme.Pullamma's husband was not heard or if heard was not paid attention to. The men who gathered were restively waiting for the rain;

but more and more of them began to become apprehensive of the nature of the likely outcome.

An oppressive atmosphere hung heavily on the gathering at the slab. The overhanging branches of the Bo tree eavesdropped on them grimly, as though at the bidding of some supernatural force.

The slab was packed with men like the sky was packed with clouds, each engrossed in their own thoughts, but the collective mood was that of a gathering of men waiting for the feast or a gathering of workers awaiting the payment of wages for their toil.

"Cousin Bademaya, give me a beedi."

"Here, take it," Three or four of them offered; charity, for once, was overflowing.

All the members recalled it; how a little after the sun had gone past the meridian, a small cloud had appeared in a corner of the sky, how, by some celestial magic, it went on growing in size and thickness of black colour to larger and larger proportions till it spread menacingly over the entire sky. Nobody had seen anything like that in their lifetime.

To those sitting on the slab, what was happening in the sky was a display of the God's sleight of hand, quite a breath-taking fare all right; but what would it all come to?

Hussainaiah, in particular, was in a disturbed state of mind. Was this all the work of Muthyalamma? Was she just reprimanding him or was she set on punishing him?

A few feet away, Muneyya, a small time tenant from the neighboring village was restlessly pacing about. The small three-acre patch of land he had taken on lease stood him in good stead, in the first year; but last year the rains failed and this year was threatening to be worse. What would his family eat this year?

An assortment of the usual dusk-time sounds was afloat in the air, of someone pounding the millet in mortar, of cows and calves calling each other with affection, of bulls and cows jerking their body and lashing their tail to drive away the flies, the cries of infants, coughs of old men . . .

"Uncle Pagadaiah, tell us a nice story now," Someone suggested.

Pagadaiah laughed at that; he knew the impropriety of it; he said, "This is not the time for tales."

"Indeed, who would listen to stories now? The sky should recite the story; that would be the story of stories for us," Bademaya was in an effusive mood.

"That was well said, Bademaya. Once in a while you too talk some sense, really," Gopaya said.

There was a roar of approval from the gathering.

Bademaya felt stung by the comment and retorted, "Is that so Gopaya? So, you always talk sense, you and your talk of sense, eh. Now, where is your big brother? I see you on your own, for once."

From a corner of the chimti bench, Kannam was heard clearing his throat, to notify his presence.

"My goodness, so, you are there, big brother!"

The badinage went on and the crowd relished it. It was this entertainment that drew men to the slab night after night.

Now, a cool wave of wind blew across the alley to the slab and the stench it carried made them wince; but nobody made any remark; it was nothing new, after all.

Another wave dutifully sailed on to the terrace of the Banzardar's building where the daughters and sons-in-law were engrossed in chitchat.

The town-dwelling young women, on the terrace broke into disparaging shouts, "Thoo, thoo, chichee, how horrible this dirty stench is!"

Muneyya gave a start at that denunciation and covered his thighs with the garment, giving his fingernails some well-earned rest; then he looked sheepishly towards the terrace.

Pagadaiah's green leaf cigar was giving him trouble; it stopped burning. "Oh, this cigar is dead again," He scoffed at the cigar and made an appeal to the men around, "Oye, you fellows, would somebody give me a beedi and matches."

The next moment a bundle of beedis from one direction and from another quarter a box of matches fell into his lap. 'Have as many beedis as you wish. Don't disturb us. We are all busy looking for the rain,' was what the offers meant to Pagadaiah.

Pagadaiah resettled himself, leaning against the wall. He felt a little slighted by the brusque way the beedis were offered, and sulkily thought, 'No one is sitting here for anything else. Was it not for the rains that he had been taking all the pains! Woe betides these fellows, these 'sons of widows'! They have no sense of sense, these sons of donkeys!' He muttered comforting himself.

Pagadaiah knew that he would be right whatever the result was. If it rained, it would vindicate the validity of his prescription—the epic singing and the bathing of Muthyalamma. If it did not rain, he would still be right; for, had he not consistently theorized on the evil effect of the growing sin, on the nature of the seasons and times?

However, he wanted it to rain. He owned a patch of land. He could not say, with certainty whether it was wetland or dry land. For three years until last year, it sure was wetland. Last year it did not produce anything. This year, once again, it was a big question.

Muneyya was busy, sitting in a corner, using the fingernails of both hands dexterously, moving the beedi between the lips, corner to corner. His mind was restlessly analyzing his predicament. The land he had taken on lease was like a 'condemned widow'; he realized it rather late. What could he do now? All that he had to do now was to raise a good cash crop on it and with that, clear off the debts he had incurred on his son's marriage.

On the slab, some were lost in thought; some were locked up in a head to head chat and some were just staring into the big black sky above; the wait continued.

A distant rumble now, a faint lightning then—in a remote corner of the cloudscape kept spurring them on to look at the sky.

The birds in the branches of the Bo tree flapped their wings and cackled now and then; 'if it rained, where would we go?'

At that juncture, they heard a familiar sound—the sound of a low-key trumpet.

"Rosaiah Sir is coming," Somebody announced with a smile.

"Yes, yes, we all know that; 'doesn't' your maternal uncle know your mother's birthplace'?"

"He is a gentleman; always announces himself."

When Rosaiah reached the slab the comments stopped and he, as usual expressed his wonder, "Oh, there are so many here! The slab is full. Is he reciting a story, Cousin Pagadaiah?"

"Oh no, Rosaiah Sir, There is no question of any story tonight; this is the night of the rain."

"Ah," Rosaiah clucked his tongue striking off the possibility "There will be no rain or vain; times are bad this year," He said as if he knew those things quite well.

"Tut, Rosaiah Sir, what a foul tongue you have! Have you ever made a good forecast?

"Ah, don't expect good things from that tongue. That alley is better and cleaner than that tongue."

Rosaiah boisterously laughed and said, "Arre, you fellows, how you are all rushing into an attack on me! Do things happen the way I say? Am I an astrologer?"

"On my mother, I tell you Rosaiah Sir; if it would not rain tonight, we would lift and carry you to roll you round and round in that alley," Said Balakoti, carefully pitching his voice low.

"Arre, Balakoti, stop it, you fellow. Have you no sense of respect for the elders?" Hussainaiah chided.

Rosaiah's face showed hurt; but in that darkness, nobody noticed it. "What a 'good' refrain you have all got into! 'Thunder roared and roared only to fall onto the frying pan', they say. Your attitude is like that," Rosaiah remarked, turned back and lumbered off.

As he turned into eastern lane, they heard the trumpet sound again.

While the slab members broke afresh into laughter, the young first time visitors rolled about in mirth unable to contain themselves.

"Yakhyakh, thoothoo, Chichee!" The occupants of the bungalow terrace sounded their abhorrence.

The wind became cooler and stronger now.

A raindrop fell on someone's little finger, the burning end of someone's beedi was extinguished by a raindrop; somebody felt the fall of a raindrop on his bald pate.

It was the waning phase of the moon; so it was quite dark. 'Are there those rain bearing clouds in the sky?' They enquired among themselves. The faint lightning and the weak rumble of the clouds hinted in the affirmative and when the wind carried a sweet fragrance released by the earth at the caressing touch of the first drizzle, the message was clear; it was raining somewhere, maybe, nearby; but it was raining somewhere.

Badinage and repartees ceased. A veil of silence made a sudden descent on the slab. They all sat mute—'wild animals in a silent conference',—their tongues humbled by a thoughtful silence.

The slab, then, heard the sounds—sounds of brisk-walking steps, which soon became the sounds of running steps—the sounds of raindrops falling on the parched up earth, puffing up the dust.

"Yes, yes, it's raining, it's raining. Oh my God, how big these raindrops are! I have never seen the likes of them."

"Shh, don't make noise. Sit down in silence; let them fall, let them fall."

The confirmation of the start of the rain came from the Banzardar's roof-terrace, "Oh, this cursed rain! Looks like it would not allow us to sleep tonight. Naganna, come here quickly, bundle up and carry these beds down. Quick Naganna, wherever are you? Oh, this nasty rain . . ."

Downstairs, the Banzardar was also restlessly pacing up and down in his verandah, watching the activity in the sky. When he heard the ill humored remarks from the terrace he could not help chiding his dear daughters, "Oh, my children please don't talk like that, dearies. This rain, we are all awaiting, is lifeline for us, for our fields and our livestock. If it would not rain, we will be in for bad days, dearies; don't forget that, my children"

"As you wish Daddy Sir . . . Naganna keep those beds as they are. Daddy Sir wants them to bring rain. Now, take these children downstairs carefully, lest they should catch cold . . ."

At that, the Banzardar muttered, "Hm, catch cold! When would you grow up my children?"

Now the raindrops became more strident, large raindrops, the size of soap nuts, drumming a beat on the dry earth.

Hulakki got down from the slab and began to fasten the slip of his lower garment.

Pagadaiah noticed him preparing to go and stretched his arm across as a signal, "No one shall leave the slab. We have all bathed the deity, with one thousand pans. Now, let us all stay here to bathe in the bounty of rain."

In reply to that, Hulakki stretched his palm vertically and tried to comfort Pagadaiah, "Don't worry Pagadaiah, it can't fail now. It has got to rain; what else can it do? It will rain. I am with you all in this. Where would I go, let me just go and 'fold my legs'; I will be right back . . ."

From the roof-terrace of the Banzardar's house, the beds and children were brought downstairs safe and asleep.

As the raindrops turned into a drizzle, Pagadaiah became ecstatic.

For once, Muneyya lost himself in an eerie delight and in a new urge to dance; but he controlled his urge and limited his response to toe tapping.

However, the rest of the men in the gathering were walking homeward at a brisk pace, Pagadaiah's appeal notwithstanding.

Pagadaiah stood his ground like a valiant general trying to prevent his troops from fleeing the battlefield. When his efforts failed, he went and stood in front of the slab, akimbo and chin up—cutting the picture of the Lord Siva in a posture of readiness to receive the celestial river Ganga in his matted hair and Muneyya stood by him like that devout votary, Bhagiratha, who had, with the rigor of his penance, labored to bring the celestial Ganga down to the earth.

However, the river Ganga was in no mood to descend from the heights of the heavens and after a while, barring a remote lightning here and a weak thunder there, all trace of rain disappeared and from the sky stars twinkled or rather heckled at them as it appeared to them.

"Pagadaiah, oh this rain, how it has duped us all!"

"Indeed, Uncle Hulakki, what can we do?"

"They say it rained heavily in Kasaram, Molgumadu and a few more villages. How strange this vagary of the Rain-God is! We have arranged the epic singing and we have given the deity Muthyalamma a grand bath too. Still, 'its mother', the rain has not favored us," Said Muneyya. He was contemplating shifting to Kasaram or Molgumadu next year.

"Uncle Pagadaiah,"

"Yes, Hussainaiah . . . ?"

"Uff, its mother, you have emptied our well, Uncle," Hussainaiah gave a pale smile, "We need at least twenty pans of water for us and our livestock. Now, we hardly get ten pans of water from the well . . ."

"Why, I say, why do you need twenty pans? For just the two of you—man and wife, you say you require twenty pans. Take my case. I need thirty pans for the cattle and the sprinkling in the yard. After every two hours, I have to wait for three hours for two pans of water to collect in our well! Now what do you say? I say, definitely you are better off," Said Bushaiah, "Now what do you say?"

Pagadaiah lighted his beedi and said, after a couple of puffs, "What is there to say, get the wells de-silted."

"How to pay for that?" questioned Bushaiah, "I have been thinking of asking you, Uncle Pagadaiah, could you lend me two bags of grain on interest-just two bags?"

"What!" Pagadaiah almost shouted, "Are you joking?"

Bushaiah could only whimper in return and that was reproach enough; it was a tacit declaration that he had expected that kind of reply.

Pagadaiah sensed it, "Really my boy Bushaiah, I swear on my mother. If I have, so much that I can lend, would I deny it to you? If you are not convinced still, you can come into my hut and check for yourself . . . why don't you try with Hussainaiah? That is a possible source."

"Oh, Hussainaiah is planning to join the laborers' team."

Pagadaiah could not digest the fact that King Virata and deity Muthyalamma had given them the slip.

Everyday clouds formed in the sky, changed their color from light black to thick black, rumbled a little and doled a drizzle of diminutive duration, at the end of which the wind-god wafted them, way away and way away. Or else it rained a pittance on the Pandava hill.

Most of them in the village were petty peasants holding two or three-acre pieces of land. The big ones were there too; but, there were only three of them, the Banzardar, the Patwari and the absentee proprietor who lived in the town and did some business; a bad season or even two would not affect them in any significant way.

For the peasants, their occupation had become a game of dice with the rain-god; year after year invariably they lost to him; so, the cellar corn-pit, the high basket of grain became only ideas or expressions for them, buffer stock-merely a concept; they never had them. With a nonexistent buffer, if the monsoon played derelict for the second and third year in succession, where would the situation take them!

Most of the men in the village cultivated millet, a monsoon-dependent dry crop; they pounded the grain, washed and ate it cooked; the raw millet, they cooked and used as feed for the farm animals.

Some villagers had dug small lakes to store water in their farm lands; they called them 'kuntas'; they grew Kharif paddy with that water; but it was a very strenuous exercise, successful only when the rainfall was good and taken up only by them who longed to eat rice.

The big landowners, of course, had dug big wells and got the sides of the wells lined with stone; they irrigated their paddy plots with that well-water using the devices of mhote and Persian-wheel. The petty peasants too dug wells but of humble size, wells which were halfway between a well and a pool, but, were enough in size to give water for a Kharif crop of rice and if the monsoon was long and strong a Rabi crop too, which was rare though. To the husbandmen and the members of their family, it was a pleasure using, manually, those age-old devices like the swinging buckets and the wooden scoops; even passersby stood and stared, enjoying the spectacle; but nature granted those pleasures once in a decade at the most. However, if the rains played truant, in just one season invariably the bottoms of the wells gaped; 'nobody enjoyed an indemnity from that law of the tropical lands'— big farmer or the small farmer.

They all knew, in the village, that the only panacea for their misery was a water reservoir; they called it 'the tank'; only a big tank would solve their multiple problems and a long defunct big tank that was there in the upland region always beckoned them to dream of making it a live reservoir to be in their service. They dreamed of rebuilding that tank occasionally but were content with dreaming. Converting the dream into a reality was beyond their ability, they knew; they just had to live with the reality and that reality compelled them to suffer silently something that cannot be evaded or avoided.

Necessity had been the mother of invention for them peasants too. They came up with many smart ideas, like cutting down the number of daily meals from three to two, from two to one and shifting from one daily meal to a meal once in two days or thrice in a week, depending upon the size of the family and the circumstances.

A concomitant of the problem was the worry of finding fodder for the cattle. Fortunately, the districts that produced three crops a year were there for them, nearby; or rather, God had placed them nearby, and the government chipped in with a subsidy with which each group of peasants purchased a truckload of fodder and shared it among themselves.

Of course, there were a few other alternatives as well to earn a living. One was, to enlist in a gang of daily workers; there were two such groups—one led by Seelam Punnaiah and the other under Martha Ranga's leadership. There was not much to choose between them; each was as good or as bad as the other was. However, joining a group was not a smooth affair; they had to worm their way into the group leader's favor; but once it was done, the rest was a smooth affair, the already enlisted said.

Another alternative was to fetch the miscellaneous commodities for the retail trader Rosaiah from the wholesaler in the town; but the option was available only thrice or twice in a week and then the wages would be in the form of grocery items, and that at the seller's price.

There was yet another option, yes, there was another option, a risky one rather—that of going to the forest on the Pandava hill with an axe, getting some bamboo wood or some other valuable wood like teak or rosewood and selling them to someone in the village. If no one offered a good price, one could go to the neighboring town and sell the load at the timber depot; but one had to avoid the snare of the forest guard. The most important point one had to keep in mind was that it was a stealthy operation, requiring utmost precaution.

It was early hours of the morning, one day.

Kannam and his confidant Gopaya were headed in the direction of the Pandava hill forest; they were surprised to hear the voice of Hussainaiah, from behind.

A man of frail constitution, Hussainaiah measured up to Kannam's shoulders. Panting, he said, "My God, what a pace of walk yours is! And you don't heed to someone shouting for you!"

Gopaya looked at him up and down, "How did you get the scent of our trip?"

"And, see that axe in his hand! Would the forest survive your attack, Hussainaiah?

Hussainaiah smiled, "That is all right; but, what about the rain, Kannam? So, the deities also cheat, don't they?"

Kannam and Gopaya stopped walking and looked intently at Hussainaiah.

Hussainaiah prolonged the debate, "And they all agreed that they would uproot and throw away that deity if it didn't rain. Haven't they said so much?" Raising his eyebrows at their silence, he stridently said, "Why don't you open your mouths?"

"We will come to all that, later. First tell us, who told you about our going to the forest?"

"Nobody told me. I set out for the forest on my own. It is just by chance that we have met," Said Hussainaiah, "But, why are you shying away from the point?"

Hussainaiah had been married for a few years now; the couple remained issueless. He had vowed to Muthyalamma that if they were blessed with a boy or a girl he would name the child after the deity. He had waited for three years, a long enough period. In between, he sent the deity a few reminders; but she just was not paying any heed. How long would she expect him to wait? Hadn't she given three boys in a row to the younger brother of merchant Rosaiah's deceased wife? Strangely, the fellow never appeared to have gone to the shrine of Muthyalamma. 'Strange creatures these Deities are indeed!'—He thought.

They walked at a steady pace. There was a wholesome freshness in the wind and unknowingly they were enjoying the experience.

Presently they climbed up the steep bund of the Vindhyadramma tank. When they looked at the deep fall from that height, they felt dizzy. It was the work of the kings, or their assistants who had ruled in these parts hundreds of years ago. What a giant of a construction the bund was indeed!

Interestingly, how did they get the idea of building this tank here, in this hilly area?

Pagadaiah had narrated that story once, at the slab.

'In those times, that is hundreds of years ago, rains failed so frequently that every alternate year was one of drought. Dharmapala was the king then; true to the name he was a righteous ruler; clueless on what he should do to save his people from the recurring misery of drought, he called on his family priest at the family deity's shrine and said to him, 'Priest-Sir, people are suffering due to this continual failure of rains; they are unable to raise crops; the wells and lakes have gone dry; pasture lands have become parched up and the dumb creatures are perishing in this drought. Pray tell me, Sir, what I should do to save my people from this distress . . .'

'The priest stood silent in thoughtfulness for a long time and said, 'Oh king, the Terrestrial God, I will perform the fire ritual at this temple of your family deity Chandi and seek a solution to this dire problem and tell you what the divine instruction is . . .

'Thus, the priest decided to help the king. Meanwhile the king spent sleepless nights and even forsook food. He thought that his existence would become meaningless if he could not help his subjects. He began to feel very guilty and remorseful at the sad plight of his subjects . . .

'After a few days, the priest came and waited on the king . . .

'When the king appeared, the priest saw tears in the eyes of the king and felt pity for him, 'Oh King, you are veritable God on the earth. If you shed tears and become weak in heart like this who would come to the rescue of your subjects? I have performed the fire ritual to propitiate the Goddess Chandi and the Goddess has ordained me to convey her order to you; visit the temple after a day's fast for further instructions directly from the Goddess . . .

'The king felt happy when he received the message and said to the priest, 'Oh Priest Sir, You have served me very nobly in this cause and you will not see me failing to rise to the occasion. I, here, in your presence declare solemnly that I will go on fast and report at the temple, tomorrow itself. I am even prepared to sacrifice myself to the deity for the sake of my people . . .

'The king observed fast the next day itself, for, he wanted to lose no time and he duly went to the temple. Worshipping the family deity, he implored, 'Oh mother, take pity on my people and relieve them from this perpetual misery; I will sacrifice myself at your altar for this favour . . .

The deity appeared before the king and said, 'Dharmapala, I am pleased with your concern for your people and your readiness to sacrifice yourself for them. Go and build a big reservoir of water by linking the two hillocks in the Pandava hill-range in the eastern part of your kingdom. Here is how you do it; on the night of 'amaavaasya'(the moonless night), after having observed fast during the day, go to the Pandava hill, accompanied by your priest. He too must have observed fast on that day . . .

'At the midnight, you start from the terminal point of the hillock on the south; take a big basin and fill it with loose soil, keep the basin on your head. The priest will walk behind you chanting the required hymns I have prescribed; you walk straight southward and while walking go on dropping the loose soil in a straight line. When you have dropped one fistful completely take another fistful of soil from the basin, and go on dropping like that without a break. You must go on doing this continually until you have covered the entire distance between the two hillocks. While you are doing this, you should keep chanting my name all the time; you must not turn or look back—a very important observance, which you shall not violate . . .

'On that moonless night, the king and the priest set out on the sacred mission. The king filled the basin with loose soil and kept it on his head and the priest gave the signal to the king . . .

'It was the darkest of the dark nights; the mountainous area was far from the royal city; it was the prowling time for the poisonous creatures; the wolves and jackals were howling; yet, undaunted by the circumstances, the king and the priest went on with their work, the king chanting the Deity's name and dropping fistful after fistful of soil and the priest walking behind chanting the prescribed hymns . . .

'Now, right from the time he had begun the walk, the king started hearing sounds of anklet bells behind him; he felt curious about the sounds, but remembering the injunction of the deity he curbed his curiosity . . .

'As their walk progressed, the volume of the anklet sounds increased progressively and in place of curiosity a smoldering fear arose in the king's heart and the fear began to increase in proportion with the sounds . . .

'They covered a great part of the distance; only a little stretch remained to be done. Now, fear began to overpower the king; he grew very apprehensive. The darkness of the no-moon night added to the fear; they were in a desolate hilly area. The king remembered that moonless night was the time of the malevolent spirits. As they covered more and more distance, the sounds of the anklet-bells became louder and louder and the king became apprehensive; in that din of the anklet-bell sounds, he could not even hear the hymns the priest was chanting . . .

'The priest did not know the predicament of the king and went on chanting the hymns rhapsodically. Just a small distance remained to be covered; the king was happy that he had almost completed the task . . .

'At that point, the king could not contain his happiness and began to sing in praise of the Deity and as he sang, suddenly and unintentionally he turned back to see the priest. The moment he turned his head, there was sharp slap on his cheek and that was the end of it all! The king's body got petrified into a statue and there appeared in front of the king's statue a breach in the bund! The priest lost his head and ran away wildly, nobody knew where. A little distance away, a small icon of the deity Vindhyadramma appeared. Men going to the forest of the Pandava hills still worship the icon. Around the icon people built a small shrine, in later years . . .

'That was how the king Dharmapala's meritorious attempt ended on a tragic note and despite the benign efforts of his successors the work remained incomplete. All the good that came of it was a small rivulet issuing from the unfinished part of the bund, where a gorge appeared. However, the rivulet turned out to be considerably useful to the people in later times, much later times, since, it boosted the water springs in wells, in the fields downwards . . .'

"What an indiscreet act the king committed and spoiled all the good work he had done! He could have refrained from looking back for just a little more time!" Hussainaiah, who had been listening with interest, remarked.

"No, no, it was not for turning back the king was punished. Some learned people say the Deity was angry with the king, because the king had vowed one thing to the Deity and did not keep his word . . ."

"What was that thing the king had vowed to the deity and ignored?"

"The king had said to the Deity that he was ready to sacrifice his life to the Deity in return for her favour, but forgot that vow and began to think about the steps he would take . . ."

"Oh my God, oh my God . . ."

"That is why, one should be very careful in taking pledges at the temples . . .

"Now, all that remains of the great effort is a vestigial bund. The tank, if filled to its capacity would have nursed thousands of acres of paddy fields; ironically, the Emmellu, who hails from the nearby village has occupied it; he is now cultivating the bed of the tank and is reaping rich harvests of dry-crops, besides deriving profit from the quarry."

Presently, they came into the forest and were surprised to see men engaged in cutting the trees; some of them were loading the logs on bullock carts.

The four pairs of big bullocks, tethered to the tree trunks were masticating the maize grass and appeared to enjoy the state of nature around.

The glen resounded with the sounds of the axe-strokes, and the burly centuries-old trees were tottering and falling to the ground.

They stood wistfully looking at the tall trees, which cast a spell on the onlooker with their majestic beauty.

For the first time in their lives, Kannam and his companions felt a conjoined feeling of thrill and sadness; thrill at the beauty of the nature and sadness at the mindless felling of the old venerable trees.

A little away, in front, the hacked limbs of the trees lay scattered.

All the time, they had been listening to the sounds of concern uttered by the birds.

Sparrows, in particular, sat in a row at a distance, watching the spectacle in disbelief.

"All this is the badmashi of the Malipatel. He bribes the forest guard and loots the forest," Kannam said contemptuously.

They now heard the shouts of the forest guard, "Kaun hai be udhar, kaun hai re chor maa ke . . ."

The local assistant to the forest guard was translating it into the local language, "Who is there, who are these fellows? Who are you, you thieves?"

At that, the workers threw down their axes and stood waiting for the next thing to happen.

Now, Kannam and his companions went and hid themselves behind the bushes, at the suggestion, of Kannam.

"Who is that, Kannam, the saredar?" asked Hussainaiah in whispers.

"No it is the saukidar," Said an unfazed Kannam.

Hussainaiah looked aghast. 'How strange all this is! Why is it that they are not running in panic, until that rotund chowkidar running and panting behind them, stumbled against a stone to fall and lose a tooth or two or all of them? That should be the thing to happen. Isn't it that way it happens normally?'

"Kaun hai tum log (Who are you)?"

"We are the men of the Malipatel of Ramannapet village," One of them answered.

The chowkidar softened up immediately and said with a sardonic smile, "So what? What are you doing here?"

"Kya bol . . . (What are they saying? Who are they and what are they doing here?" Said the saredar (forest officer) and the chowkidar explained to him.

"Malipatel ke hai to . . . (Maybe they are Malipatel's men; but what are they doing here, in the forest? Are they doing 'jamabandi (doing the revenue collections)? Hahaha . . ." Saredar gave a big laugh at his own joke.

The chowkidar dutifully laughed.

Saredar hit a stone, at his feet with his stick and as he paced about, his eyes fell on a trapped rabbit, that lay at the bags of the workers and howled, "Yeh khargoshon . . . (Catching rabbits like this, you people are destroying the forest, what?"

The chowkidar sprang into action; he walked briskly and took possession of the rabbit.

Satisfied with the action he had taken, the saredar ambled away.

"Chalejao . . . (Go away from the forest and soon; otherwise there will be trouble for you. Do you understand what I have said?"

The chowkidar was translating it for them even as the saredar had left the place.

After the duo had left the place, the chief of the workers smiled contemptuously in their direction, "You bloody fellow, at least remember me when eating that dish."

After waiting for some more time, Kannam came out from behind the bushes, "Come out, now; 'the sons of the donkeys' have gone away."

Kannam knew the forest the way he knew the palm of his hand. The places, where one could obtain different kinds of valuable wood like teak, saagwan, nallamaddi, yepe and the like, he knew. He also knew where the water springs lay, and which of the meandering footpaths led to the sources of which kind of wood in the mountain range; like a city-smart that knew the roads, lanes, by-lanes, shops, hotels, and the different landmarks and the sensitive places in different parts of the city, he knew this place. They collected some selectively cut wood and with the loads on their heads, started walking homewards and made it to the tank bund by dusk time.

It was a safe return; they went home and deposited the wood in the backyard; after drinking some water they gathered at the slab.

At the slab, the usual hubbub was not there; but for the subdued voices of one or two, there was silence.

The slab was sparsely occupied. In the poor visibility of the twilight it was difficult to make out who was who; one couldn't even say whether there were a good number of men. Notwithstanding all that, something important appeared to be brewing up.

Nearing the slab, Kannam scented that Nagireddy was there; that perfume always gave him away.

Following the scent, Kannam went to Nagireddy and sat by his side. For one thing, he liked the geniality of this man; he mingled with one and all, but preferred the company of the plebeians more. The other thing that endeared him to the people was that he was one of those unfortunate men who had lost a good chunk of property in the full consciousness of it and yet did not cry over it publicly. That way, he accepted the loss and the consequent slide in the social scale with an even mind; that attitude leant an additional grace to a man of natural charm that he was.

Nagireddy welcomed Kannam and moved a little nearer showing his warmth for the fellow; when both of them were seated side by side, he placed his hand on Kannam's shoulder.

Kannam felt very happy. 'This is a man,' Kannam thought, 'who is true to himself and his word. Born in a family of landed gentry, Nagireddy never betrayed an iota of vanity. To allow someone of a family of his social status to sit by his side is something great,' Kannam thought. 'Then, Nagireddy went to school too. They say he passed the seventh standard. Coming to himself, he passed only fourth class.'

'Then, Nagireddy is a thespian too; has donned, on stage, several roles of epic characters like Rama, Krishna and Arjuna and is noted for his singing of verses sweetly on the stage. When he was on the stage, almost all the verses he sang drew 'en core' shouts from the crowd. At the end of the play, the audience would come to the greenroom and mob him, hungering to hug and even to kiss him! Such a charismatic man is this Nagireddy,' Kannam recalled.

Presently, a debate was on at the slab. Pagadaiah was hammering away, "I am not denying it; Kings, Queens, Ministers and the Court jesters . . . they are all of bygone times. Yes, their time is over; but there is one thing on their side, something of them still remains firm and fresh in the minds of the people! That something the people remembered was that they were righteous in their thought and conduct. They always followed the right path, prescribed by the scriptures, the elders and the traditions whenever they had to take a decision affecting the people and the kingdom . . .

"However, there were some bad kings too, I don't deny that, but even a bad king of those times was far, far better than the present time leaders . . ."

Nagireddy was listening intently.

They were all listening attentively and quite a few of them expressed their approval, on the points, with their nods and gestures.

"Whatever reservoirs of water there are in this country today, a majority of them, at least most of them, are the work of those kings of the bygone era. The Vindhyadramma tank in the hamlet of our small village is one such. King

Dharmapala left his palace in the dead of the night and carried the soil-filled basin on his head to build that reservoir of water. Imagine a king carrying on his head a basin filled with soil! That was the spirit of their commitment to the welfare of the subjects the kings displayed. We have all heard the names of the six great emperors-Harshchandra, Nala, Purukutsu, Pururava, Sagara, and Karthavirya and of course the great Sri Ram . . ."

"Yes, yes, we have all heard about them, indeed. You said many a time that the Vindhyadramma tank came as an achievement of the king and as a boon of the Deity Vindhyadramma; but despite their joint collaboration it had come with a breach in it, like a child with a congenital deformity! What is the use of a reservoir with a breached bund? You praise the king and the deity; the king had not sacrificed his life as pledged at the temple and by not pardoning the king, the deity had shown herself too in poor light. Oh Pagadaiah, it is time you stopped telling these stories . . ."

"Don't misinterpret the things like that, Nagaya; the king forgot his pledge because it was written so on his forehead and the deity ended the king's life because that was the preordained course of events; you may not believe in these things, but everything that happens on the earth is preordained. What is important to note is that the king was so much concerned about the plight of his people and that he prayed and tried to help them and almost succeeded in his mission; some other successor should have closed the breach, but, none did; even the present people's government has not done anything about it and you sing paeans about the People's India! . . .

"When the Deity offered a solution the king received it thankfully and just complied with the command of the

Deity and that too, at the midnight on a no moon night! How many of the present leaders would have done that? They would have peed in their 'undergarments' at the very suggestion of it! Ha ha ha . . ."

There was a roar from the clientele, part of it in approbation and part in relish of the fun.

"Well, well, I appreciate the fact that the king had made at least that much; but he did it because he was duty-bound to do it; wasn't it so? Was he not living on the public money? Therefore, it was his bounden duty to do that. There was no alternative for him. He would have to build tank bunds, excavate tanks or even oceans if the public demanded them. When the public demand a thing, the king has to obey, he cannot wag his tail; there is no escape for him. You must know, Uncle Pagadaiah, that the king is first and foremost the servant of the people."

"It's a blasphemy to say that, Nagaya. You would lose your eyes if you talk such blasphemies. The king is a veritable God on earth, His manifestation; he is like a father to his subjects, people are his children. He is never the servant of the people, never . . ."

"Yes, yes; he is the omnipotent God on earth; that's why he swallows away the public money," Nagireddy mocked.

"No, no; the king never swallowed the money of the people; the king fed the people with his own money, know that."

"His own money . . . ? Where did he get it from, from which grandfather?"

"Oh, 'you've come like that'? Well then, if you say it is people's money, from where did the people get it? From which grandfather . . . ?"

"Well, the people don't get it from their grandfathers and grandmothers; they get it from the sweat of their brow. They work and earn it. They make things; they produce the food and the things the society needs and earn money. State cannot exist even for a day without them; it is their sweat that waters the tree of the State and it is thus the state bears the fruits of wealth; the king and the people owe their daily bread to them—the workers and their toil on the land . . ."

"Oh, is that so? Then, wherefrom did they get the land they work upon?"

"Well, the land they get from the God," Nagireddy deviated just an inch from his theory.

"Ah, that is a good thing I hear from you; so, there is God and you admit that; and tell me this thing Nagaya, do you mean to say that God came down to the earth, gave the land to the workers and went back to his abode; how funny is your talk! No, it is not like that. God placed the king on the earth as His agent to do things at His bidding and as per His plan . . ."

"And the agent began to grab that land, like most of the agents do, isn't it so?" Nagireddy said, "He grabbed the land, grabbed the money, and used them both to build temples, palaces, and tombs for his wives, leaving the people to their fate, to live in poverty in mud walled houses. Instead of wasting away the money like that, he could've built houses and water sources for the people, who, you say, are his children! You say all men are the children of God; then, would a father suffer to see his children live in misery?"

"Well, Uncle Pagadaiah," Mustering up courage Kannam too intervened in the debate, "You say that kings haven't swallowed away the people's money. Then, how did they amass so much of gold, diamonds and jewels with which they made ornaments for their queens and 'keeps'?"

Pagadaiah looked aghast at this daring intervention of Kannam and roared, "Have you seen the kings swallowing away the money of the people? Have you seen?"

Normally Kannam would get devastated by such sallies; but this time he dealt with the situation with some well spun logic, "Well, if you talk like that, haven't you yourself seen it that they had swallowed? You have seen it yourself and have admitted to it . . ."

"Who, 'I have seen it'? What are you talking? Have you lost your head? When did I say that?"

Kannam continued, with Nagireddy laughing and encouraging, "Didn't you say, the other day, how, bedecked in dazzling jewelry, the queens and princesses went to the temple to present precious ornaments to the deities?"

For a moment, Pagadaiah was stunned; he could not recollect the moment and the context in which he had narrated a sequence like that, but felt that it fitted with the way his usual narration went; maybe, he said so his because his scheme of narration demanded it; but the audacious way in which Kannam was quoting and questioning him shook him a little; 'the enemy is rushing straight into my fort,' he thought.

However, at that critical moment, he did not lose his nerve. His hands, of their own volition, untied his slipknot and tied it afresh-his usual reflex in such uncomfortable situations. The shrewdness and boldness of the heroes and valiant warriors of his tales, as sketched by him from time to time, propped up his spirit mysteriously and enabled him to scoop up a stratagem from the 'emergency corner' of his brain; but that exigent action naturally took a little time, driving the slab members to count Kannam a winner; but the assemblage was in for a pleasant twist and a prolonged battle of wits.

"Right Kannam, I admit for the sake of argument, that the kings of old times swallowed the money of the people; what is happening now? Tell me, Kannam. What is happening now in the country? Are the numerous ministers not swallowing the public money? From where are they getting the big loads of money they are amassing? The cars, the big buildings and the big estates and the crores of rupees . . . from where are they getting them all?" Pagadaiah slapped his left palm with the back of his right palm, adding an undeniable force to the challenging questions he posed to his adversaries.

"Have you seen them, the cars, the big buildings and the loads of money . . . Have you seen them all?" A quick reply came from Kannam.

Again it stunned Pagadaiah to have 'the arrow he had released' boomerang on him and he reeled under its effect for an instant.

Nagireddy gave Kannam a pat on the back and when all of them were listening attentively, he floated his pet idea, "That is why my suggestion to all of you is to elect our party of Socialists in the Panchayat elections that are in the offing. What do you say, Kannam?" He pinched on the thigh of Kannam, in a fit of ecstasy.

Kannam felt elated by the sweetness of that pinch and the wonderful time he was having on the slab; this was, to his memory, the first ever instance of Pagadaiah being pushed to his wits' end, on the slab.

"What do you say, all of you, brothers, who have gathered here? What do you say to my proposal? Elect our party in the ensuing election; the tillers would own the land and the toilers would get food. All the idlers would have to starve or else they too must bend their backs and strain their limbs to get some food to eat. How do you like this idea-land only to tillers and food only to workers?"

However, Pagadaiah recovered from the stupor and resumed the fight, "What, what, 'land only to the tillers'?"

Gesturing to his men to wait for his next salvo, he said, "Having squandered your patrimony, how else would one expect you to argue!"

Some laughed at that dig; some thought it was in bad taste.

Pagadaiah continued exultantly, "Well. Keeping aside these things, tell me one thing, Nagireddy; you say all these things to us; but there is your party man, Sundarrao who sits at home lording over the men who toil; he never does even so much as 'scratch his own crotch' and commissions workers to do it for him! How much land he owns, Nagireddy? Just two hundred and fifty acres, you may say, 'small property', nevertheless two hundred and fifty acres still. Then, there is this—what is his name, Um, yes, Narayana; this man, they say, owns 'a paltry three hundred acres.' He is also your party man . . .

"Every peasant in this part of the country knows these facts. Here you are, playing a drama, the actor that you are, parroting the slogan, 'land to the tiller and food for the worker'. Instead, why don't you go there, to them, and ask them to share their land with the landless toilers? What is the use of these sermons to smalltime peasants here, eh?"

Nagireddy remained silent for a while. A hush descended on the slab.

There was no sound of clanging swords; there were no hissing sounds of arrows; but everyone was aware that a fierce battle was raging at the slab; the dramatic tension of it was felt by the members of the assembly.

When the tension began to become oppressive something familiar, happened; Rosaiah announced his arrival by breaking wind. Finish! That was the end of the debate, the end of the tension and the beginning of a hilarious tumult on the slab.

It was familiar to them all; but, today Rosaiah made it a little bit different by mixing it with a chortle that was intended to be a compliment to Pagadaiah on his display of wit and wisdom; however, as was the wont there, it served a greater purpose-the greater delight of the greater number of people.

Some of the victims of the 'broken wind' almost fell from their perches; some acted in time to avert that mishap and some others that were prudent enough sat upright immediately. There were those whose burning tobacco leaf-rolls cast sparks of fire on their bare chests and some were saved from such a mischance by the vests they wore that evening.

Anyway, that was a commotion of a sort, an ever-fresh source of uproarious fun to the slab members.

Despite their minor discomfitures, all of them quickly came into a benign mood and eagerly awaited some more heroics from this 'marvel of nature', the inimitable Rosaiah Sir.

Nagireddy also laughed at that comedy of nature; but he had felt the deep hurt caused by Pagadaiah's remark. His pride spurred him on, to come up with a stronger rejoinder. Concealing his wounded pride, he continued the debate, "Well then, Pagadaiah, it was the fate written on my forehead, as you might say, that I should lose my property; I do not expect anybody to commiserate with me on that; but, Pagadaiah, tell me your say to this, suppose, Sundarrao and Narayana would agree to share their land with the landless, would you also agree to share your land? Tell me, would you also share your land with the landless?"

Pagadaiah was at once confused, as gambled by Nagireddy, "Who . . . ?" He said.

"You, who else . . . ?"

"Me? What . . . ?"

"Share with others . . . ?"

"Share what?"

"Land of course. Share with others . . . ?"

"Who should share with others . . . ?"

"Would you share with others, I am asking?

"Share with others-? Share what?"

Balakoti chipped in, chuckling, to set right this tangled talk, "Cousin Nagaya, the pin has got stuck up; the pin is stuck up!"

Then, Nagireddy tried to straighten up the things and said loudly and clearly, "Would you share your land with others?"

"Why should I share my land with others, Sir? I would not; why should I? I am not a socialist," Pagadaiah summed up his response in the briefest manner.

"Then, why do you want Sundarrao and Narayana to share their land with others?"

"Why do I want them to . . . ?" looking at his men, with a smile, Pagadaiah said, "Well, because they are socialists."

"Socialist or non-socialist, everyone would have to share their land with the landless; there is no alternative and the day for that is not far off," Nagireddy concluded the argument on a warning note; he also waved his index finger at Pagadaiah.

Once again, there was a hush.

It had now become quite dark; still Kannam could spot the launderer Nagaiah passing by and he got down from the bench to meet him.

Presently, Nagireddy began a head-to-head with Hussainaiah, whom he had been befriending for some special reason.

Pagadaiah was satisfied; he thought that he had won the day at the slab; he busied himself in rolling the shreds of tobacco in a green leaf.

There was a lull at the slab.

Rosaiah could not digest this development; he had come to spend a good part of the early night at the slab.

He grunted his disapproval at the abrupt end of the proceedings at the slab, turned and began to walk briskly homeward. When he turned the corner, they all heard him 'do that again'.

They were all disappointed to lose him from the slab so soon—such a natural entertainer and gentleman, Rosaiah Sir . . .

For those that remained at the slab the time had to pass; 'what would they do at home if they went there now?'

Hulakki, the veteran, said addressing the slab in general, "There is no water in our well, barring some ten pans a day, at the most."

"There is no water at all in our well," Said Baswaiah of the northern street, "What would you say to that?"

"But you have that well in your backyard. That never goes dry!"

"Of course, that is saving us; but, for how long?"

"Keeping aside this daily problem of water for domestic use . . ."

"What do you mean by 'keeping aside the problem of water for domestic use'?" Pullamma's man said, in a rasping voice.

An initially surprised Hulakki quickly became thoughtful and nodded his head; he knew this man, Mme Pullamma's husband and his travails. 'It is not easy to live as an adopted son-in-law!' He mused.

"Can a man daily draw up fifty pans of water in the morning and another thirty in the evening, from a well fifty yards from house and yards and yards deep?" Pullamma's husband fumed, "And you sit here at the slab and say 'keep it aside . . . '! Does it make sense to keep aside the problem of 'water for domestic use'? Tell me, you people sitting on this slab, as members of the slab; does it make sense to keep it aside?"

"No, no, it is not right to keep it aside, rest assured," Said Hulakki and renewed his chewing on the gums.

Pullamma's husband was happy at that show of sympathy from Hulakki. 'That man sure knows how difficult the life of 'a son-in-law in adoption' is. A donkey is better off than 'a son-in-law in adoption,' he thought.

To Pullamma's husband this dole of sympathy at the slab was very heartening and he thought of introducing a call attention motion on 'a son-in-law in adoption'; but someone had already taken the floor. Therefore, he turned to the main agenda.

"How are we to proceed with the cultivation work, if this drought situation continues for some more days? How are we to feed the cattle? How are we to keep them alive? Where is the fodder?"

"It would be very difficult to keep the cattle alive; you may forget about agriculture this year, yes we may have to forget agriculture," Hulakki said nodding his head to Pullamma's man.

"We must think of ways to procure fodder for the cattle at least," Said Bushaiah.

Ragavaiah suddenly entered into the debate on remembering something, "There is one very important thing I want to tell you; I don't know how many of you know of it,"

"I for one don't know whatever it is."

"I too don't know."

"How can anybody know without your telling that? First tell us and then ask us whether we know that or not."

"There is no point in asking whether anyone knows it, once I have revealed it," Ragavaiah said smiling.

"We all know that you know many important things; first, tell us what it is, before you yourself forget it," Ramayya said curtly.

"I won't talk if you gibe at me like that. Know that from somebody else, not from me," Ragavaiah pouted.

"Right, then, tell us from whom are we to know the thing. We will ask him rather than falling at your feet. Right . . . ?"

"What is all this perverse talk? Talk meaningfully, if you have to talk . . ." Hulakki's voice sounded like distant thunder; but, surprisingly what he said served the purpose well.

"That is the right kind of talk," came round the man who was the originator of this detour, "As a matter of course, I would've forgotten the thing but for that mention of 'fodder for the cattle' by—by . . . Who was it that talked about the fodder for the cattle?"

Nobody seemed to remember the author of that 'fodder for the cattle'; silence ensued.

"I think it was Mme Pullamma's husband," Carelessly averred Bademaya, who had joined the assembly just then.

"Rre, Bademaya," roared Pullamma's husband, "You are going to die at my hands, one of these days! You attribute to me all the damned things . . ." He was about to lunge at Bademaya; but Kannam skillfully caught him by the waist and prevented a needless scuffle.

Members on the slab were perturbed at the bizarre way things had gone.

Hulakki had to intervene again, "Ssh, stop this insanity and come round to the point. First, what is that important thing? Let us find out. Now tell us that important thing. You—you . . . who was it that said that?"

No one answered.

Anyway, for all their efforts, they would not have found out the man they wanted; for, the maker of the statement had already reached his doorstep, having adroitly escaped from the spot of bother.

The important thing remained a mystery for the night, compelling some of them to brood over it for a part of the remaining night.

It looked like the show was over for the night; one after the other, they began to walk homeward.

Pagadaiah was dismayed at the way the night's proceedings had gone at the slab; nobody had asked for the sequel to the episode in the tale that had abruptly ended a few days ago. He racked his brains to remember at which point he had stopped it; but now, it hardly seemed to matter.

Ruefully Pagadaiah dragged his feet homeward.

The next evening the slab took up the unfinished business. Pagadaiah came, as usual, with his repertoire of stories; but the members sitting on the slab did not show any interest; he sat there biding his time.

The men on the slab broke into groups and busied themselves with a medley of issues.

When the men saw a man with a handbag, walking into the village, they turned their attention to him.

"Why, that is Muneyya!" Naginaboina, who had just come to the slab, recognized the man, "Muneyya, you seem to have gone to the town; do you have any news about the drought relief measures?"

Muneyya changed the bag from one shoulder to the other and wiped the sweat on his brow with his shoulder-cloth, as they all waited for him to reveal the news.

"Muneyya is a diligent man," observed Bushaiah.

"Indeed he is; who else would go to the town in this scorching summer and come back the same evening! Ten miles, by anybody's count . . . Not an easy thing, if you ask me."

"Ten miles . . . ? It could even be more, in my opinion."

"Well, I think it would be in the range of eight to nine miles, if you ask me; but definitely not ten miles, yes, definitely not ten."

"What are you saying? I would put it at eleven to twelve miles; a mile or two more, if anything. Yes."

"Tut, you fellows are at it again! First, know from that man the news about the drought-relief works."

"That is well said! Yes, Muneyya, what is the news about the drought-relief works?

"I would tell you everything; but, right now, my throat has gone dry, would someone fetch me some water to drink?" Muneyya said.

"Yes, yes, let someone go and get some water from someone's house." A couple of men suggested with some concern.

Seeing that none was going to fetch the drinking water, the old man Hulakki got down the 'chimti' bench and started walking.

Kannam quickly went to him, "Uncle Hulakki, what is this you are doing? Don't shame us; you sit there; I will get the water for Muneyya."

"Tut, away from my way, you do whatever pleases you. I am going home; I am tired of these inanities you display at the slab. God knows when you people would come to senses! There appears to be no redemption to this village . . ."

Kannam grasped the truth of Hulakki's remark, paused for a moment, and seeing Hulakki in no mood to relent, proceeded to fetch the water for Muneyya.

When Kannam came back with water Muneyya was not there, "Here is water for you, Muneyya; where are you, Muneyya?"

"Muneyya has just gone home; I saw him going, while I was coming to the slab. I saw him; he was going home, appeared a tired man," Ragavaiah, who had just come back to the slab, replied to Kannam.

"Why did he go away, just like that? He was supposed to drink this water and tell us that news about those drought-relief measures."

"He always does like that, a queer type of fellow he is."

"What a strange fellow, this Muneyya! Such an important news and he slips away without revealing it to the slab!"

"Important thing . . . ? Maybe it is the same thing I was trying to tell you," Ragavaiah said in remembrance.

"So, it was you who gave us the slip last night."

"I didn't give slip to anybody. If you people were not interested in listening to me, what was I to do?"

"That was a great thing you have done. Now, would you tell us that big fat thing without wasting our precious time?"

"I would tell you if your manner of asking is decent."

"What do you mean by 'decent'? Who has ill-behaved with you?"

"Ragavaiah, you are a good man and you care much for the village, we all know that. Now, come, tell us whatever it is."

That worked and Ragavaiah relieved his bosom by telling them that the government was giving subsidy for the purchase of fodder for the cattle, in view of the prevailing drought conditions.

To Pullamma's man and maybe to quite a few others too, the tidings did not appear to contain any good news, "What about men, then? Subsidy for fodder is alright; but what about food for men?"

"You cannot equate men with cattle. Cattle are meek creatures. It is the responsibility of the farmers to feed the cattle."

"Men are also meek creatures, if you talk like that. I tell you; it is the bounden duty of the government to feed them too," Pullamma's husband asserted.

"Are you there? Are you there on the slab, I say? What are you doing there . . . ? Standing here, I am able to hear your blabber . . . Would you like to sleep there, or is there any plan to come home?" The booming voice of Pullamma was quite audible to the men at the slab; half the slab shuddered at that.

In a matter of seconds, Mme Pullamma had her man in front of her and the men at the slab were relieved at 'the loss of the wisdom of Pullamma's hubby'.

Most of the members on the slab thought they too should go home, before a similar embarrassment happened to them; Pagadaiah, however had no such bother; but these recurrent setbacks to his pet avocation of storytelling, were beginning to make him feel disenchanted.

In the prevailing conditions, Pagadaiah did not have any alternative; therefore, he too dragged his feet toward his circular hut to wrestle with and grab the elusive sleep.

Meanwhile, Bademaya, who was dozing, leaning on the plump body of a snoring Siddhappa, woke up with a start, "Yes, Uncle Pagadaiah, tonight you must complete that story of the princess of Malava kingdom," he said as if in a dream, still.

The few men that remained on the slab laughed at that and one of them said, "Pagadaiah has gone home. If you want to know the fate of that princess of the Malava kingdom now itself, well, you have to go to his hut, wake him up and ask for it. If he tells you that, come and tell us too. We will all be waiting for you."

Bademaya sleepily nodded agreement and began to grope drowsily for that rotund body of Siddhappa, who too sleepily adjusted his posture, affording Bademaya the comfort of a cushion.

Kannam smeared cattle dung on the smoked-up pieces of bamboo wood pilfered from the forest and drawing up the coir thread cot, reclined on it for some well-earned sleep.

Hussainaiah for his part could not find dung; he searched in the backyard and foreyard; but little of it was available. He could not ask anybody for it, since they would raise queries.

He wanted to go to bed early.

Meanwhile he heard his wife cursing the buffalo, in the cattle shed; the animal sometimes played tantrums; so he went there and stood in front of the sulking creature, holding up a stick. That usually helped; but, this time, the animal did not budge.

Narayanamma tried in vain to squeeze some milk; but the animal dropped a few clods of dung instead, to the delight of Hussainaiah.

The next morning, Hussainaiah woke up at the first crow of the cock and went to the dwelling of Kannam; Gopaya was already there.

The trio left the village early in the morning, to avoid detection by the nosy creatures of the village. They went past the potters' street stealthily; because nobody could walk past Sonaddiri's house undetected; that man would be always alert. He never slept, he just dozed, especially in the small hours, the time he would be found beating the clay into shape.

They broke the silence only after coming out of the village and Hussainaiah was the first to do so, taking the chance to lament over his woes in collecting a few clods of dung to smear on the wood.

Pilfering pieces of wood from the forest was easy, compared to disposing them of in the town. Townsmen were ever on the lookout for easy ways to acquire money or the things. Three years back, Balakoti paid dearly for his bravado—a week in police station. Still, people took chances, for want of other ways of earning livelihood, especially in times of distress.

By the time the sun was up, they reached the town.

Hussainaiah watched wide-eyed; he saw the townsmen walking to the outskirts, carrying pitchers of water and he wondered aloud, "They have got up now, so late in the morning!"

"They have no worries like the ones we have; they just sit and earn money. Here the lifestyle is different. There is no drawing-up of water, no sweeping the front yard and no sprinkling of dung-water. They don't have to go to the far off fields with ploughshares . . ." Kannam explained.

Presently they reached the east street; government offices lined up on both sides of the street-the Panchayat Samithi office, the Police Station, the Tahsil Office to mention the more important ones.

Hussainaiah gaped, 'People here are different; their habits, their chores, their attitudes and their interests seem to be vastly different from those of the villagers!' He wondered.

"Cousin Kannam, why are we here? Why not go directly to the timber shop?" asked Gopaiah.

"That would be risky," said Kannam, "Unless we have some acquaintance with the timber merchant, we should never go there."

As they reached the end of the street, they saw fodder-loaded trucks in the yard, behind the Samithi Office; men were shifting bundles of hay onto the bullock carts.

An attendant explained to Kannam, "Because of the drought situation, government is subsidizing the purchase of fodder for the animals. In the eastern districts, there are plenty of 'dalva' hay stocks. Government is paying three quarters of the cost of the fodder purchased; so it helps the farmers, doesn't it?"

"Yes, and it helps them-the farmers there much more than the farmers here, obviously," Hussainaiah said promptly, surprising his companions by the spontaneity of his remark.

The attendant too was struck by it and asked, "Whom, whom does it help more?"

Kannam was in for more surprise.

"The farmers of the eastern districts, of course," Hussainaiah added, "Piles and piles of dalva grass is lying in their fields and backyards and they are unable to find a way to get rid of the unwanted stocks. Now, it has become easier for them. For one thing, they are able to rid themselves of the unwanted stock and they are getting paid too."

The attendant looked at Hussainaiah, "Man, enough of it, enough; men do not know the value of a thing when they get it cheap."

At this point, Kannam took over, "We are not getting it cheap; we are paying them more than what it is worth to them . . .

"Any way, fodder for the cattle is alright, what about the men; is there no subsidy for food for the men, in these times of drought?"

"Drought subsidy applies only to cattle, not for men. Man can survive somehow; he would eat roots, fruits, leaves, flowers and when they are exhausted, he would eat birds, goat, sheep and when he has exhausted them, he would turn to his own cattle; every living thing, man would eat; they are all food to him. Only when no other living creature is available, he would . . ."

"He would . . . eat what, then?" Hussainaiah asked in bewilderment.

"Simple, he would eat his own kind."

"Eat men, you mean?"

"Oh yes, what is strange about that? There are many instances of man eating his own children when famines are severe. Man is the only animal that is cruel and unscrupulous among the creatures of God. It is a fact that cannot be disputed," The attendant said in a matter-of—fact tone. Later, he added, "But why go that far, there are plenty of food grains if only you have the money to buy them."

"Would the government give subsidy?"

"Subsidy, subsidy, subsidy, for how many things can the government give subsidy? For the poor, the government has announced the food-for-work program. Shed sweat and earn food . . ."

"Ah, you mean that, a field day for the contractors! In the name of feeding the poor, the government would be fattening the contractors. It is the same familiar story, same old story" Kannam kept waving his head, his lips curved down into an expression of 'Pity, pity'.

The attendant was intrigued by the attitude of Kannam, "Man, you seem to be a communist, judging by the way you talk; I cannot stand the hypocrisy of these Communists; they talk one thing and their eyebrows deny that. There is one man, Sundarrao," a bell cut off his talk and frantically he ran into the office.

"It is quite funny, the way the fellow hurries off . . . as though someone is chasing him," Hussainaiah kept wondering.

Kannam nudged his companion, "Let us get going, Hussainaiah; you have talked enough."

Presently, another man came out of the room, looked them up and down, and asked, "What is that you are carrying on your heads?"

Warding off some embarrassing response from Hussainaiah, Kannam quickly answered, "It is some old wood and some bamboo pieces, that's all."

As Kannam walked ahead, the man came and stood in front stretching his hand across, "Wait, wait man, I know you are here in the town to sell that stuff and you need not go to the timber depot to dispose them off. I am on the lookout for something similar. Now, tell me, how much money you want for them all?"

Hussainaiah looked worried.

Kannam sensed trouble; reluctantly, he waited for the man to make his next move.

The townsman said, "I will give you twenty rupees for each of them; no bargaining, put them down in the yard, take the money and go home."

Kannam waved his head in disagreement and tried to move on; but the townsman was in no mood to lose the deal. "Listen to me, brother. A team of forest officials is in the town right now. I advise you to be cautious. I know the wood is fresh from the forest; you have just smeared cattle dung to make it look old. I know these tricks; I also come from a village. What village you are from, by the way?"

Hussainaiah looked stupidly at his friend Gopaiah, who looked nervous; they awaited the outcome of the haggling, in a resigned manner.

"No sir, each bundle is worth at least forty rupees. We would carry them back rather than sell them so cheap," Kannam tried to wriggle out of the bargain.

"Go then; before you are out of the town they would catch you and straight away you would land in the police station. Do you understand what I am saying? Once you are in the dragnet of the police and forest guards you are a doomed soul; they would dump all unsettled cases on you."

"Oh God, oh God,"

Hussainaia's knees were wobbling visibly.

Kannam sensed that the situation was getting grim, "Give us ten rupees more for each bundle; we have come from a long distance; even then, it is nowhere near their worth."

"Right then, that is some sense you are talking; take what you have said; after all, I too come from a village; I know how hard the things are there."

When the deal was over, Kannam was happy that they had dealt with the situation reasonably well; however, he regretted the loss they had suffered. They could have avoided the loss, he thought, had they not indulged in that foolish talk with that government employee. Next time he would have no truck with someone like Hussainaiah.

Relieved of the load on the heads, they now took the road leading to the timber depot.

At the depot, they saw the gang of the Malipatel of Ramannapet village chatting with the timber yard owner while the men in khaki looked on innocuously.

While they had all heard the fact of this collusion between the forest officials and the Malipatel, the revelation of it dismayed them. What were they to do now onwards? Is the forest no more a source of petty income to the nearby village men in times of distress? Could they too collude with the forest guards, as the Malipatel's gang had done? What would be the terms, then . . . ?

So many questions and doubts arose that their heads started whirling.

"Let us go home, Kannam; I am not comfortable here. At home, I am at ease even on empty stomach. Let us first get away from this place. If one is alive, one can survive even by eating 'balusu' leaves. Let us go home; this has been a foolish venture on our part or rather on my part," Hussainaiah was on a drone.

"Enough of it, Hussainaiah, you stop wailing now. You came on your own; we had not asked you to accompany us and having come, you must take things as they come. Nobody is happy with what has happened; but we must be happy that we haven't been caught and put on remand."

"Whatever it is and whatever you say to me in reproach, let us go home please, just take me home; that's all I want you to do. I don't like the sinister look of this town and the men here."

Without any further ado, Kannam started the return trek to the village.

It was a three-hour walk.

By the time the evening lamps were being lit, they were in the village.

By dusk members gathered at the slab; Hulakki, Mme Pullamma's man, and Pagadaiah were there at the centre.

Kannam was there at a corner; he did not appear to be in his element.

Others were there on the corner points of the slab, Bushaiah, Naginaboina, Balakoti . . .

A few first timers were also there.

Many villagers came to the slab by way of habit; all of them did not partake in the deliberations. However, if decision on any issue required division of the 'house', they counted.

Mme Pullamma's man was a picture of seriousness; two issues were milling in his mind, one—the 'keep-it-aside' point, on the 'water for men' issue, two—precedence to be given to 'food for the people' over 'fodder for the cattle'. He wanted both the issues to be taken up, before the slab turned to other issues.

Knowledgeable members of the slab knew that some very lively debate was in prospect for them. They knew these men for what they were! They could talk on anything for hours and still keep the issue inconclusive at the end of the day. It was not for nothing that they had been doggedly attending the slab meetings, night after night, day after day!

Actually, Mme Pullamma's man had a plan to find out who was going to back who on the issues by just looking at their faces; but it was getting dark and he didn't try that.

Somebody started the proceedings with a call attention motion on 'fodder for the cattle' issue, "The government's idea of giving subsidy for fodder is a good move indeed, otherwise how are the cattle going to last this period of drought. We must all . . ."

Cutting the motion short, Mme Pullamma's man intervened, "First things first; tell me what we are going to do with this problem of water for men? Let us come to a decision on that, first."

"What decision you want?"

"I have told you already. I told even the day before yesterday; can you keep aside the problem of 'water for men' and talk about water for the cattle? Similarly, can you think of fodder for cattle without discussing the issue of 'food for men'?"

Nobody knew what could be said in answer to Mme Pullamma's man; but they wondered at the logic employed by the man, more than about the type of the answer that would be appropriate in the circumstances.

"What is he saying? I don't understand a thing," queried a veteran squint eyed.

Bademaya, who had come unobtrusively, said, "it is the same thing, I have told you," Putting a finger on his temple he turned it round and round signifying a loosened nut, and remarked in a low voice, " . . . same thing; it is worsening . . ."

Surprisingly, Pullamma's man heard the remark in spite of its low decibel level, and though he had not seen the accompanying gesticulation, he guessed what had been said and he pounced in the direction of Bademaya, grinding teeth and swearing at the man, but by the time he reached, Bademaya had fled the place and Ramkishtie, along with his friend had to take the first blows; he managed to escape from the remaining, which fell to the share of those that still remained at the spot—they bewailing and protesting, "What is this, why are you hitting me? Are you mad, stop it man . . ."

"Who are you that I should hit you?" Pullamma's man was in an unabated fury, "Where are you, scoundrel Bademaya, wherever you are, come and dutifully take the blows or you would die at my hands."

"What Bademaya and which Bademaya you are talking about? He has fled the spot long back; calm down and sit there," sitting in a dark corner, Bademaya mimicked, changing his voice and enjoying it all, in the company of his prankster friends.

"They ought to put a lamp here; otherwise, this is what would happen; I knew it would come to this. You want to hit somebody and you end up by hitting somebody else; one can't help it . . ."

"Yes, yes; it always happens like that if there is no lamp; they must put a lamp here," there was somebody to support the motion, after all.

"Why doesn't the 'committee ladia'(community radio) sing today?" a member questioned.

"The 'batri' has exhausted; how can that poor thing sing without a 'batri'? If you want to listen to it you buy it a 'batri'."

"Even if I buy one, can I listen to it in this din?"

"Then, keep quiet."

"Who are you to ask me to keep quiet?" the man shouted angrily.

"Then, keep shouting like that . . ."

"Who are you to order me to keep shouting . . . ?"

"Then, do what you want."

"I don't need your permission to do what I want to do."

"Then, take permission from whoever is competent to give you permission."

This went on for a while and though in the darkness no one distinctly saw who exactly was talking to whom and what exactly was happening, the sound and heat that accompanied the commotion served to highlight the lively piece of exchanges.

Some of the elders openly decried the attitude of the youngsters, "What is happening here? Where do you think you are? This is the slab of the village, not a playground. Don't indulge in these monkey acts and vulgar pranks; do you hear me?"

Despite the darkness, Pullamma's man thought that they were looking at him and those words were addressed to him and shot back, "Why do you say these things to me? You ask that rascal Bademaya what he was saying about me."

Bademaya took a step forward boldly from the corner and objected to the charge, "Whoever said anything about you, man? You are imagining things. We were talking about that Satti, that prophesier. You always think that people have no other business than talking things about you. If you do not change, your imagination would come true, mind it."

"See uncle, he is at it again," complained Pullamma's man.

"See boys, I want each of you to keep in mind the respectability of this place. You must all conduct yourselves with decency and decorum."

Every one of them kept their heads nodding in approval of the elderly man's sermon.

Presently the slab resumed its business.

"So the government is giving subsidy for the purchase of fodder for the cattle. Let somebody contact the VLW (Village Level Worker) and find out the procedure, like, how much money they would pay and how much we have to bear. Find out those details; and then, all of you sitting here must know one thing; slab is a very important place. It is also very powerful place. We do not come here to while away our time; mind it, it is a very important and powerful place. Any decision, taken here, is binding on all of us, yes, binding on all of us."

A first-time visitor to the slab intervened in the debate, "Indeed, the slab of a village is a powerful place. It so happened in a village, once, that a member didn't show respect for the slab; so, the slab imposed a fine on the member for his misdemeanor; the member was asked to pay a fine; he was asked give the elderly members of the slab a grand feast, by way of fine, but the member was adamant and did not pay the fine as ordered by the slab; Then-" the man paused.

"Then . . . ?"

"Then . . . ?" Several members queried anxiously, one after the other.

The first-time visitor had not expected so serious an attention and such and so many prompt enquiries; so, now, he had to conclude the anecdote with a finale of an equally grave nature; so, thoughtfully or thoughtlessly the visitor rounded off the account with, "That member died."

"Oh God, oh God" Members expressed shock.

A few members jumped off the chimti bench and ran into the alley; there they burst into a loud laughter.

The debutant sheepishly looked sideways, in the direction of the alley, head dipped and brow knitted.

Pagadaiah patted on the thigh of the man in sympathy, "Brother Sarvaiah, times have changed. Men of the present generation are not of the same making as we the old timers are."

"Then, of what different make are they?" quipped Kannam.

"Of the same make as that of yours," Pagadaiah said harshly, and added in undertones, "Shut up your bloody mouth."

And Lingaiah now lapped up the chance to educate the members of the slab, "Whether of the old or the present generation, everyone should consider—why a particular man has said a particular thing to a particular group of men at a particular time and then think whether that particular idea of that particular person is good for them in any particular way, and if good, why good and if not good why 'not good', if good, whether that particular idea of that particular person can be of any particular benefit to us, if 'not good', how particularly bad it can be and to how many in particular . . ."

That way, the particular veteran, Lingaiah could have gone on for some more length of time; but Pagadaiah, whose endurance could take it no more, butted in, "That was what I was trying to impress upon them, Lingaiah. Now, with your great wisdom gained from your great age, you have put it very briefly and nicely, uncle Lingaiah. How many are there in this village, with as much wisdom as yours! Barely one more, barely one more . . ."

They nodded their heads in agreement; they knew who the second man was.

"I have been watching uncle Lingaiah right from the time I came to this village, that is, after my marriage. He, uncle Lingaiah comes to the slab regularly; but he talks rarely and when he does, his word is worth bags and bags of rice, if you ask me," Observed Pullamma's man.

"No no, worth pans and pans of water, rather," Bademaya said and fled the next instant.

Pullamma's man was left 'grinding his teeth'.

Grand man Lingaiah's image gained significantly after the session; for a time Pagadaiah had to remain in low profile.

Chewing on his gums, Lingaiah came to a decision; hereafter he would regularly attend the slab meetings.

"My respectful obeisance to Sage Hussainaiah..."
Nagireddy dramatically entered the house, accompanied by
Hussainaiah and mouthing a parody of a dialogue from a
mythological play, his lips taking curvilinear forms, his right
and left palms joined into a theatrical gesture of obeisance.

"Nagaiah, Nagaiah, Come, come" Hussainaiah was
overwhelmed with pleasure at his success in bringing his idol
Nagireddy to his house; hurriedly he fetched a coir-thread
cot, "Be seated Nagaiah, be seated."

To Hussainaiah it was an exciting experience; he might
as well have been witnessing one of those mythological plays
of which he was so fond and that too with Nagireddy in the
lead role-Nagireddy whom he adored so much!

Nagireddy looked charming in a spotless white dress,
clean-shaven, smelling of strong perfume and with lustrous
black curly hair; he looked every inch a thespian.

Kannam, who was passing by got scent of his friend
and benefactor Nagireddy and pushing the front door open,
entered and smiled in greeting.

While going to the grocer, Hussainaiah had seen
Nagiredy on the street and effusively welcomed him to his
house and Nagireddy was so delighted at the invitation that
he readily accompanied Hussainaiah to the latter's house.

Hussainaiah was elated at what he had accomplished and
his face glowed.

Nagireddy took out from his shirt pocket a riffling new currency note and waving it to Kannam, said, "Go to Rosaiah sir's shop and get one cigarette packet and a box of matches," and turning to Hussainaiah asked, "What news, Hussainaiah?"

"What news can there be that you know not, Nagaiah? Things remain the same; the failure of the rains is the only news, these days; all the villagers are despondently praying for rains."

"In spite of the epic-singing . . ."

"Yes, and even after that grand bath to Muthyalamma, things remain the same," Kannam added.

Spurred by the mention of epic-singing, Hussainaiah began to show that he was not lagging behind in the community matters, "Yes, the epic singing was good, though; the harmonium master of Gosseedu and that singer from Ramannapeta-"

"No, no, harmonist from Ramannapet and singer from Gosseedu-that's it," Kannam corrected Hussainaiah.

Annoyed, Hussainaiah pouted, "Yes, that's what I said . . ."

"No, you said 'the harmonist from Gosseedu and the singer from Ramannapeta'.

"Yes, is that not so?"

"No, it is not correct; it can never be so. The harmonist fellow is from Gosseedu and the singer fellow is from Ramannapeta," Saying that, Kannam stopped and bit his tongue for the blunder he too had made; then he carefully put it straight, "The singer from Gosseedu and the harmonist from Ramannapet no, no, the singer from-"

"Tut, both of you had better shut up your mouth," Said Nagireddy, "Do you know why I have asked you both to shut up your mouths? It is because both of you have lost your heads; what do we care who comes from which village? Now, coming back to the main part of the issue, both the strategies have been tried; yet the situation remains the same. You must have scratched the bottoms of the wells,"

"They are all repenting now for having emptied their wells." Kannam said.

"You say 'they', haven't they drawn from your well, for the grand bath?" Nagireddy asked Kannam.

"No sir, I haven't allowed," Kannam said proudly, "And for that act of defiance, he is furious with me—that Pagadaiah."

"What does the great man say now?"

"What else, he has advised them to dig deeper for water springs?" Kannam giggled again.

"Stop that dirty sniggering; as it is you look ugly; you don't have to add to it," chided Hussainaiah and said, "We are all 'dying for want' of rains. If for another week it wouldn't rain . . ." He paused.

"Yes, yes, 'if it wouldn't rain for another week-'? Tell us, what would happen; is there any option left?" Nagireddy asked.

Hussainaiah looked at Nagireddy, expecting from him some solution.

"Why, everybody has to go for 'the stag's food', that is the only option," Said Kannam and ran away laughing, after bringing in that vulgar idiom, "That is what Hussainaiah wants all of us to do," He completed his statement from the other side of the doorsill.

Hussainaiah looked furious; Kannam would have fallen down, if only looks could shove; but all that Hussainaiah said was, "That 'son of a widow' is all set to go mad, there is no escape for him, yes, soon, you will see him, on the streets'."

Nagireddy tried to assuage Hussainaia's feelings, "Calm down, Cousin Hussainaiah. That fellow has a crazy sense of humor; just ignore him, Hussainaiah, ignore him. Let us have some useful talk. Haven't I told you at the slab that these worships and rites will not bring rains?"

Caught in a dilemma, Hussainaiah avoided the issue; instead, he said, "Really, you must do something about this demented fellow Kannam, before others begin going his way. Yes, Nagaiah, that's what I feel."

"Don't worry about him; I will take care of him; but, let's come to what I was saying."

"What were you saying, Nagaiah?"

Nagireddy touched his forehead in anguish and again opened the issue, "If this obsession with rituals and superstitions is not stopped, we will not move forward. We will go backwards, yes, further backwards, "He looked into Hussainaia's face for a trace of impact.

Hussainaiah looked stupefied as he raised his palm and waved it clockwise and anti—clockwise, "Forward where, backward where? I am quite mystified by your talk. I think that fellow Kannam is acting strangely, precisely because of the same predicament."

Nagireddy sighed in despair and said without wasting more time, "Come on, let us go," he put his hand on the shoulder of Kannam, who had presently come back.

"Sit for some more time, Nagaiah. Shall I arrange for some 'kapee' water?" Hussainaiah said.

"Some other time, Hussainaiah . . ." Said Nagireddy amiably and gently nudged Kannam to move out of the house.

All the time, Hussainaiah sat thinking of what had happed, what he had said and what Kannam said and who was right . . . He just did not know why it always happened that way with him and why what he said to the other man and what the other man said in return brought the issue to that state of tangle and things of that kind . . . With quick jerks of head, he too then got up and caught up with them, in the alley.

The elections for the local bodies were due. They had all heard about the impending notification; it might come any time, people were saying. Nagireddy had received an alert from his party's district committee and he was now on the mission.

His was a tough mission. There were hardly two or three men in the village that knew the party lines. Most of the villagers did not know even the broad ideological differences between the Socialist Party and the Praja Party. Regarding the 'who is who' and 'what is what' questions, they were quite accommodative and opined that anybody or anything was as good or as bad as anybody else or anything else. It was against this scenario that Nagireddy had taken upon himself the daunting task of preparing the ground for his party's maiden entry into the village politics.

Hussainaiah ran to keep pace with the duo. Briskly walking he kept looking at the mentor and the protégé, alternately; he guessed that they were on some important work, "Where are we going, Brother Nagaiah-and why so abruptly?"

Nagireddy gave him an indifferent look and a half-smile, "What else can we do, Brother Hussainaiah? Uncle God doesn't seem to like us or our Party."

Just then, he saw Hussainaia's wife.

"Here you are, at last! When did you leave the house and where were you all the time? Where are the tea-powder and sugar you went for? Quite a nice man, you are indeed!" Then Narayanamma bashfully pursed her lips in embarrassment for talking freely in front of others.

Nagireddy stood looking at the woman; he did not hear what she said; presently he asked his protégé, in a subdued voice, "Who is this woman, Kannam?"

Kannam whispered into the ear of Nagireddy, "She is the wife of Hussainaiah."

Nagireddy was intrigued, remembering what he had heard about the lady and what he saw.

He said as if he was questioning himself, "Hussainaia's wife . . . ?"

"That's what they are all saying," said Kannam, suppressing a mischievous smile.

Nagireddy kept looking at the lady with quick darting glances; he was biting his nails all the time; it was obvious to Kannam that his mentor's heart was in a state of pitter-patter.

However, Kannam was not aware that his mentor had already heard about the comeliness of Narayanamma and that he had been eagerly waiting to check up what he had heard with what was real.

"When is this drama to be staged, Nagaiah?" asked Kannam to change his mentor's attention.

"Oh, there is going to be a 'dammra', when Cousin Nagaya?" Cackled Hussainaiah delightedly.

"Not 'dammra', correct yourself. It is 'drr-aa-maa'. Here, say that once; 'drr-aa-m aa'. Now, say that once, yes, say . . ."

Hussainaiah coyly took up the task; in the company of this man he was going to learn quite a few things, he thought. With some difficulty he reproduced the correct phonetic form of the word, "Drr-aa—mma!" and beamed.

"There you are! Really, you are a quick learner, Hussainaiah," Said Nagireddy; then turning to Kannam, he said 'what was actually intended for Hussainaiah', "And Kannam, don't forget to collect the free tickets. Last time, you created a scene, do you remember? Luckily I was there for you; otherwise, they would have thrown you out, remember?"

Kannam nodded his head, half in pretended shame and half in obedience, "This time, I will be careful, you don't worry, Nagaiah."

Like a fish true to its nature, Hussainaiah fell for the bite, "Will you give me too, one 'thickket', Nagaiah?"

Nagireddy feigned inattention and turned to Kannam, "Come on, Kannam; let us go."

"Won't you give me too one 'thickket', Nagaiah?" Hussainaiah dolefully renewed his request.

Nagireddy was delighted, but he didn't show it, "Why one, I will give you two tickets. There will be a separate place for the ladies to sit; no problem; you may come with your woman; Hussainaiah, have you heard me?"

Hussainaiah nodded affirmatively; he was mighty well pleased with himself for what he had achieved, 'Not just one 'thickket, two thickkets!' he thought ecstatically.

Nagireddy left Kannam at the slab and went on his way to Bezwada to finalize the programme of staging a mythological play.

Most of the men in the village came to have only one preoccupation now—a visit to the slab, since their occupation had fallen into doldrums. Once they were there at the slab, things would wind and unwind themselves as though the slab were an automaton. There, they raised issues, discussed problems and aired solutions. Not that their discussions and solutions would resolve the problems; but that was how their wearied minds worked. 'With the rains playing truant, what else was there for us to do?' They asked.

Had a recording of the proceedings been kept, it would have shown that very few men had actually taken part in the deliberations at the slab; the remaining were dumb delegates.

The members who gathered at the slab heard the talk that went on there and appreciated the gumption of the participants, they laughed at their gaucheries too, and remembered them to recollect and laugh on them later. It all served to show that participation in the deliberations at the slab was regarded as a kind of achievement and everybody in their mind nourished an ambition to take part in the discussion at the slab once or twice and win members' approbation.

Bademaya, for one, also wished to take part in the serious deliberations, at the slab and make his mark, at least once, although he was aware of his limitations as a spokesman.

One day he would put forth a proposal at the slab that would earn him the praise of all the members of the slab. Yes, indeed. He had been passing by that stream that issued from that breach of the God-forsaken, age-old and long abandoned water-reservoir, the only remnant of which was the high, long, and breached tank bund. The villagers frequented it whenever they went to the forest. Though the stream had partially dried up now, it flowed full, bank-to-bank in rainy season and part of the winter too. If it could be converted into a live water reservoir, quite a lot of the land downward would be irrigated. At least, three to four villages would be benefitted. It was strange that none of the elders had thought of it!

Bademaya was buoyed up by his thoughts; he bit off a piece of the beedi and took a long puff, kept the smoke suspended in his lungs and slowly let it out, part of it through nostrils; that steadied him up.

He heard someone calling, "Oh Sir, Bademaya sir, I am addressing you, Sir. Where and why are you going at such a pace? You are not even stopping at the slab!"

He stopped and noticed that he had walked well past the slab! Was it not to the slab he was going? How asinine of him to have been caught on the wrong foot, especially by the dim-witted Venkayya, the small! "Oh, I was just going to the north lane; some small business."

"But you are going southwards . . . ?"

'Bungled again!' thought Bademaya, "North lane and south lane, can't a man have some work in both the lanes," He raised his voice a little to silence Venkayya, the small.

"Of course, of course, I was just on my way to the slab; I thought you were also headed there. That's all," Explained Venkayya, the small and turned towards the slab.

"Wait, I am coming there too." Bademaya put his hand on the shoulder of Venkayya, the small and both walked to the slab.

Many of them had already gathered at the slab and still some more were coming; but a debate had already commenced and members were listening with attention.

Reaching the slab, Bademaya caught the thread of the talk.

"By this time, the year before last year, the wet lands had already received the transplantation."

"Now, there appears to be no guarantee of the transplantation; in a few days the rainy season would be over as per the calendar; God knows what is in store for us!"

"The livestock . . . ? How are we going to feed them?"

"There you are at it, again and again! First talk about men; cattle and farm animals come later; they can live by eating grass or foliage. Can men live on them?" Mme Pullamma's man remarked.

To Bademaya the moment appeared to be the right one to intervene in the debate; he said, "We can, if we come to terms with that eventuality, we too can live on grass and foliage; the only thing is we have to practice eating them, right now; let us start tomorrow, shall we?"

There were a few chuckles.

From the direction given to the banter, Pullamma's man briskly concluded that he was the butt of it and gave a war-cry at once; but his voice failed to give it a tune of matching fury; what came out of the effort was a feeble, effeminate shriek.

Some laughed at the miscue, while those who had missed it, frantically queried, "What has happened? What has happened?"

Pullamma's man realized that he had lost in the skirmish and nursing a wounded pride, he muttered abuses and expletives, without taking a name, of course.

Then, the item of the agenda was given up and some of them started discussing private issues.

Bademaya saw that his plan had gone wrong and tried to set it right. He courageously put forth his idea, "If you care for my word, listen; I think, to solve this water problem of our village, there is a plan. We should . . ." Caught in a fit of shaken confidence, he paused.

They waited; that much of patience they always showed to a debutant and an expected silence ensued.

"Yes, we should . . . ? Do what?" A surprised Pagadaiah tauntingly asked; he was a little stunned at the boldness of a non-entity like Bademaya, in putting a proposal before the slab; 'What times have come!' He wondered to himself.

Meanwhile, Bademaya's chums cheered him up, and he tried again, "It is better to . . ." He paused again.

"Yes, 'it is better to' . . ." Pagadaiah was close on Bademaya's heels!

"Across the rivulet . . ."

"Yes, 'across the rivulet' . . . ?" Pagadaiah tightened the grip.

"Build a ddaam!" With a plosive, Bademaya completed.

Pagadaiah was stunned! Of all, Bademaya venturing to make a proposal of such a serious nature at the slab; Bademaya, commoner than the commoners, one of nondescript order and one fated to wait in the wings at the slab, arms bound, making a proposal!

"What! Build a dam across that rivulet-? Have you ever seen that rivulet?" Pagadaiah said jeeringly, "Have you seen it closely, do you have an idea of the steepness of its banks?"

"I have seen it; I go across it and along it, almost daily."

"A man who is drunk can have no idea of the steepness of its banks; to them even a big steepness seems a small elevation," Pagadaiah said in a mocking tone, gesturing one way and looking the other way—a gesture seasoned debaters resorted to.

Members began to pay closer attention; 'now, things would become spicy,' they thought.

"I don't drink, for your information," Bademaya's voice rang loud and new, "Has anyone, sitting here, ever seen me drunk?"

Pagadaiah realized that a point of order had been raised against him and he was not prepared for more of them; therefore he maintained a strategic silence.

As usual, a hush descended on the slab, recreating a familiar scenario.

A few moments passed and then, there came that familiar rib tickling sound, the 'trumpet of Rosaiah sir'. There arose an assortment of sounds, of laughs, sniggers, chortles and what not.

"Oh, Rosaiah sir, please come and grace the slab with your 'sound' butt and wit; you have come at the right time, Sir. In fact, if you had not come, one of us would've come to your shop to bring you to the slab," A slab member greeted the ever-welcome member, a special invitee and a much sought-after artist—all in one!

Men on the slab laughed heartily and welcomed a possible feast of fun.

Rosaiah sir chuckled heartily; he saw that they were all hailing his arrival, for a change; he felt happy, but, he suspected some mischief and started casting side-glances.

A member submitted to Rosaiah sir, the facts of the matter, "Rosaiah Sir, a very important debate is taking place at the slab. We are unable to come to a decision on a point; that is why we were all wishing you were here."

"What is the issue?" asked Rosaiah Sir immediately, assuming an air of authority.

For once, Pagadaiah too was carried away by this ever-pleasant drama, being enacted by the young 'rogues' and with a laugh he too readied himself to give it his full attention.

Rosaiah quickly turned towards Pagadaiah and curtly demanded, "Why are you laughing Pagadaiah? What is the matter? Tell me that first."

"Someone here was telling a joke; that's all," Pagadaiah explained to Rosaiah Sir.

"Then it's alright," Rosaiah turned to the others and asked, "Yes, now tell me; what is the matter?"

"The matter is this, Rosaiah Sir: you know there is a rivulet, in the northern outskirts of our village; we all know that the stream comes from the breach of the Vindhyadramma tank, fed by some underground springs that supply water for six to seven months in a year. Some of us are proposing that a dam be built across that rivulet. It would assure us water, water for men and water for the livestock for most of the year and who knows, it might also help irrigate our paddy fields, they say."

Rosaiah raised his palm, signaling them to stop 'there'; then with his head bent, he began to scratch the ground with his big toe and fondly ran his palm on his rotund tummy; he appeared to be giving the issue some serious thought.

The young 'rogues' pursed their lips; fixing their looks on Rosaiah Sir, they waited, suppressing their laughter.

Even Pagadaiah found it difficult to put his laughter in leash.

A few moments later, Rosaiah raised his head, looked at them and closing the issue, said, "I have no objection; let them proceed."

Finish! That was enough for the pandemonium to break loose; no one knew what had happened to them, as it were. Some nearly fell off the 'bench' but were saved by the quick reflexes of the nearby friends; some ran away from the slab to roar with laughter, at the alley fence; then, there were those that tried to contain themselves but, unable to do so, fell into a mixed paroxysm of cough and laugh.

Hulakki, who was sitting at the centre of the slab, rose and hooted at the young men, "You are all good-for-nothing fellows; to you everything is meant for fun. The situation is very grim and you don't seem to realize the seriousness of it. Useless fellows, rot the way you are fated to . . ." With that he got off the slab and walked homeward.

One scamp watched Hulakki turn round the corner and mimicked, "Hm, now go home, recline on the bed and ponder over the seriousness of the issue. Something good might come out of your dream, who knows!"

The gang was now thinking of the next move and they were murmuring animatedly, when they heard the voices of Nagireddy and his chum Kannam from the street corner; they were delighted to have them in their midst.

Nagireddy came and sat on the slab, with Kannam by his side. He was intrigued by the silence that greeted him; he waited for a while and then broke the silence, "What is this! You are all silent. What for is this silent prayer, if I might know?"

Nobody from the veterans showed any enthusiasm to respond to the query and so it was left to the young brigade to explain and one after the other they related to Nagireddy what had transpired at the slab.

"Cousin Nagireddy, the elderly members of the slab are afraid that the end of the world is round the corner. They won't give the world more than one month, if this dry spell persists."

"To save the world from the calamity, brother Bademaya has suggested the plan of constructing a dam across the rivulet and our Rosaiah Sir has approved it."

"Now, they all want to find out a way to construct that dam, in the nearest possible future . . ."

"If possible, in this week itself . . ." Someone gave the final touch, in a voice choking with a suppressed laugh.

Nagireddy's penchant for fun was as strong as that of anybody there; he took up the cue straight and quick, "Why, it is simple enough; let Uncle Pagadaiah carry on his head a basin full of loose soil, ask Suraiah Sir to walk behind chanting the hymns, and let Uncle Pagadaiah go on dropping the soil straight across the rivulet, without turning or looking back, That's all, it's all a work of—just one moonless night!"

The rogues' gang once again burst into a loud laughter.

The seasoned humorist in Pagadaiah rose to the occasion; he too enjoyed the situation and giving a wry smile, said, "Certainly, certainly. I would love to do as bidden by my young brother Nagaya; but unfortunately for you all, I am not a king, you see!"

"Tut, you smart fellow!" Hulakki who had presently come back, said in appreciation of Pagadaiah's skills at rejoinders and retorts.

Surprisingly, Hussainaiah, of all, found his debating tongue going and said, "That's no big problem; our Patwari Saab would crown you king."

There was a wave of applause for Hussainaiah.

Mme Pullamma's husband butted in; his was a 'fun-or-no-fun, fact is a fact' attitude and he said, "Poor fellow, that Patwari, it is not in his power to crown somebody king. It is the work of the 'kulkatair' (Collector), only a 'kulkatair' can do it. Nobody else can; what can that petty Patwari fellow do . . ."

At that point, Nagireddy got down the slab, "Let's get going, Kannam; folks in your village can do nothing else, than indulge in endless and meaningless talk."

Mme Pullamma's man didn't like the session to end so quickly and abruptly; the beedi was burning right, he had put his right leg on his left knee majestically and was vigorously shaking it; he had made a point in the debate too; was it all to be so short-lived!

Hulakki looked at Mme Pullamma's man with abhorrence, 'How the fellow preens!'

But, in a very short while, the slab began to wear a deserted look; so Mme Pullamma's man too dragged his feet homeward, unwillingly.

Pagadaiah, however, stuck to his perch on the slab. His head was still resonant with those words-'we would crown you', 'kulkatair' would place the crown on your head' . . . He was the last member to leave the slab.

The late night at the slab, however, brought its own rewards; sleeping in his hut, he had an 'undreamt of' dream!

'The erstwhile ruler of a kingdom, in the dream, died issueless and a search party was on to find a successor. A scouting team with a fully caparisoned royal elephant set out, to choose the successor and searched village after village; the elephant was holding the crown in its lolling proboscis . . .

'There was a big crowd, avidly watching the spectacle; the elephant came into their village and there he was, in the back row, innocently watching the pageantry . . .

'Suddenly, the royal elephant caught sight of him and pushing them all aside, adorned his head with the crown and lifting him up with its trunk, placed him on its back; the crowd shouted hysterically, waving hands and hailing the new king, Pagadaiah . . . !

'There was Kannam too; he came to the fore from nowhere and was shouting that the act was foul; he was shouting at a high pitch; but the crowd pushed Kannam away and hailed him as the new king . . .

'The next moment, the royal elephant took him into the queen's wing of the palace; the queen Rattamma, fully adorned with 'the jewelry of the seven weeks' came out of the palace, accompanied by her retinue; she held in her hand, a garland of flowers to put round his neck; but the moment she saw the trunk of the elephant hanging long and loose, she gave a big shriek and swooned; in a flash, that bitch of a woman, the mother-in-law snatched the garland from Rattamma's hand and put it round his neck!'

He was shocked at 'the turn the event had taken' and there the dream ended.

As he got up from the cot, Pagadaiah saw that he was sweating profusely! He walked into the side yard to wash his face and as he walked, he remembered what his mom had always said—the pre-dawn dreams would usually come true.

'Would they . . . ? Would they really come true?'Pagadaiah wondered; his was certainly a pre-dawn dream!

As he lifted his head to look at the noise in front of his hut, he saw the bullock-cart stop and his father-in-law helping the duo of the mother and daughter off the cart.

Two weeks after the arrival of his wife, Pagadaiah still did not see any significant change in his domestic life, barring one thing—now 'she' leant a hand in pounding the millet.

His dwelling was a hut, circular and built around a wooden pillar set up in the center, and strictly speaking meant for one or a couple to live in. With his mother-in-law lumbering in and out, Pagadaiah barely found time to have a clear vision of his wife's face, after that big gap of time. Other times, Rattamma held the fringe of her saree between her teeth to hide her face, the conventional bashful way women did.

Pagadaiah wanted to ask his wife pointblank how long her mother intended to camp in his house. He even framed a few inoffensive phrases and rehearsed them in his mind; but there they remained.

Wherever she was, doing whatever she was, Rattamma was watchful of him, like a lamb wary of the wolf; she would not even bear to have his shadow touch hers, and if that happened she would tiptoe to her mother.

The mother was of a different mold; she was not fussy like her daughter; now she talked freely with her son-in-law and had no 'touch me not' hassles. She did not look her age, though quite old. 'By the way, how old she could be?' Pagadaiah wondered. Not old enough to look old, perhaps, he thought.

Many times the mother told her daughter to mend her ways, come to terms with the reality and live happily with her man. After all, it was not a case of 'poverty'; it was a case of 'plenitude', as she perceived it—and her analysis was right, in her view.

The issue was a delicate one; there could be no open debate on it, the mother thought, nor could she discuss it with her man for fear of hurting the sentiments of the son-in-law; so, there was no other option for her than to wait for the problem to solve itself in the natural course of events.

The daughter continued to be her usual adamant self; 'If you go away, leaving me here, I would hang myself,' she said bluntly.

'If a lone child threatened like that which kind of mother would venture to abandon her to her fate and leave?" the mother reasoned and decided to stay with her daughter, till the God showed a way out.

Pagadaiah's father-in-law, however, had left the same evening of the day; Pagadaiah waited and waited for him to come back with his bullock-cart to take away his 'lady.'

Many a morning passed but the expected bullock-cart never came and the daily dose of disappointment sent him into jitters. 'If she is not interested in conjugal life, why has Rattamma come here at all?' Endlessly the question arose in his mind. 'Why does God create women like Rattamma?'

Pagadaiah suddenly remembered that there was a case like that of Rattamma in the village, though it was a male version!

The saga of 'the Red Lad' was indeed a strange one; like all such cases, the red lad's case too generated a lot of interest among the men at the slab—the slab that was a mill making grist of whatever came to it! That, of course, was the way of the world—one man's worry was another man's fun! Only a few men like him, having known the ways of the world, sympathized with that unfortunate creature—'the Red Lad'.

The story of 'the Red Lad' had started on the same note as that of many a young village lad; like all men in nascent youth, the red fellow dodged the question of marriage. In the beginning, it was dismissed as the usual display of shyness the boys in the incipient youth showed; but as years passed, the Red Lad's parents began to worry about it and decided to summon the help of some experienced family friends. 'Otherwise, the lad's life would be limited to doing community service—driving the village cattle to the foot of the hills in the morning and bringing them back in the evening', the parents thought.

Finally, the job was entrusted to the son-in-law of the family, since he was in good touch with the lad.

One evening, he opened the topic, after a little humoring, "Now, Laddie, I want you come clean on one thing. If you have anything like regard or respect for me—me, your sister's husband, don't hide facts, right?"

Red Lad nodded his head like a good boy and looked into his brother-in-law's face, for a cue.

After a gulp, the brother-in-law asked, "Laddie, Would you like to marry? There is a sweet girl of a family that I know of; what do you say?"

Red Lad gave a quick nod and said, "Oh yes, I will do anything you want me to do."

"You won't back out?"

"No, I won't."

The matter was conveyed to the parents; they were happy that the problem was so quickly solved and the task of finding a suitable match was also entrusted to the son-in-law, who had a girl in his mind. Things moved fast and in a fortnight everything was settled.

The parents and kinfolk were all very happy that the problem was solved at last; but far from being over, the problem took a new twist and became more worrisome.

The news of the new twist was very savory to the members of the slab and they chatted about it no end, enjoying every bit of it and every moment of the chat.

The slab put the tales of Pagadaiah on the back burner and raved about the Red Lad's plight.

A wry smile appeared on his lips as Pagadaiah recalled the public details of a very private problem.

Red Lad had indeed looked a happy youth during the twelve days that preceded the wedding. New clothes were bought in Bezwada and the tailor from the adjacent town was hired to stitch them into fashionable wear.

Red Lad's happy evenings in the company of his friends came to an abrupt end three days before the wedding. Suddenly he stopped going to his friends and began to wear a forlorn look on his face; but he would not reveal anything to anyone.

The evening before the marriage, Red Lad caught his mother alone and with tears in his eyes pleaded that he wouldn't have 'this wedding'.

Had the mother asked her son, the reason would have come out, and maybe, something good would have come out of it; but the mother became touchy and lashed out at the son and at one point swore that she would jump into a well and end her life if the son did anything foolish to ward off the marriage.

That act of his mother threw the Lad into a fit of despair; he loved his mother so much that he would not do anything that annoyed her and so, walked to the wedding place like a lamb to the slaughterhouse.

The wedding over, arrangements for the 'first night' were done on a grand scale; a round hut, at a secluded spot in the backyard of the house was bedecked for the event.

When, the next morning, the old ladies of the family came to test the girl to find out 'whether things had gone right', the bride hissed and chafed and without uttering a word, walked straight into the house where her parents were lodged.

The bride's mother cut a picture of inconsolable grief and on the third day left for home, with tears streaming down her cheeks and mumbling to her grieving child to be patient and wait for an improvement of the situation.

But the situation did not show any improvement and on the fourth day, at dawn, the bride sealed the issue by walking out on them all; the three mile distance to her mother's village she made it on foot and alone!

The slab had non-stop discussion of the issue among small groups of members. Once again family elders held emergency meetings with a bewildered looking Red Lad in the centre. They coaxed him, cajoled him and coerced him into another attempt.

After a week of sustained persuasion, the bride's party agreed, not whole-heartedly though, and arrangements were made afresh.

Red Lad agreed to face the ordeal again.

But, on the eve of the night the girl turned adamant; she would not hear any more of it, "Whatever conjugal life I have had is enough to cry over a life time; I wouldn't take any more of it," she declared, sobbing.

Crying her heart out and cursing the fate, the bride's mother fell into a swoon and at that the defiant girl relented and consented to go into the nuptial chamber, a second time.

Meanwhile, Red Lad and his chums held long sessions of consultation, far and away from his house. Parents appreciated their helpful efforts.

Things seemed to be going in the right direction as the dusk progressed into night.

At the slab, Red Lad's friends waited for the situation to unfold; even the elderly members could not conceal their curiosity and stuck to the slab.

After a long wait, when the members at the slab began to doze off, they were all jolted into awakening by the hubbub coming from the vicinity of the round hut; it was well past midnight then.

Reports poured in to the slab; 'the girl kicked the door open and walked out in a huff; the elders, after a little hesitation, broke into the hut; there was no trace of the Red Lad!

They looked hither and thither and then someone looked up and found a clearing in the thatched roof, wide enough for a man to pass through.

There ended the poignant tale of 'the Red Lad'; where he had run away, no one knew, including his chums.

'It is now close to two years. Red Lad's whereabouts and whatabouts are still a mystery,' Pagadaiah tried to get out of the stupor caused partly by the discomfiture of his plight and partly by the recollection of the tale of the Red Lad.

'What, after all, could lie at the root of it all?' Pagadaiah wondered for the umpteenth time; but the root and whatever lay there eluded him.

'There is a strange similarity between his story and the story of the Red Lad, Pagadaiah thought; perhaps for the same reason he could not help recalling the lad's story.

After Red Lad had fled the place, the lad's mother appeared to have lost her bearings.

When the girl's family came, the lad's mother proposed that the girl should settle down in the in-laws' house and await the arrival of the Red Lad. "I have no doubt, my son would come home; he never stayed away from me this long and I am equally sure that my son suffers from no shortcoming of any kind. Till my son returns home, let her live here with us," she said.

The pendulum swung the other way, when the girl's party, on observing the girl's mindset, wanted to break off the relationship, so that they could have her married off to another boy, at which point lad's mother threatened that she would jump into a well and die, if it came to that.

"First, prove that my son is lacking in manhood and then marry off your daughter to another boy," Red Lad's mother challenged.

'How can a third party prove it?' Slab men wondered.

Lad's father lost temper and demanded the return of the gold bangles, gold chain and the earrings and the nose stud (also of gold) if they wanted to break off.

At that, Red Lad's mother stopped her wailing. Sitting upright and alert, she reminded her man, "What about the silver anklets and the arm-bind? You seem to have forgotten them,"

"Yes, yes, them too. There is no question of forgetting anything, when the issue has come to this state," dutifully he added.

All the time, the arbiters the bride's party had brought, sat silently, trying to understand the thought processes of the parties; they analyzed that both the parties were more impulsive than sensible and realistic. Now, they thought the time had come for them to intervene and set right the things.

"We want both of you to keep in mind one thing. Marriage is a solemn bond ordained by God and it is a sin to annul that bond. You know the story of Sumathi; after her marriage she came to know that her husband was a leper—a leper! Did she break the bond? No. It was the power of her character and her conjugal purity that cured her husband of the abhorrent disease. Take the case of Savitri; when her husband died, as destined by the Fate, she didn't lose her courage and composure. She fought it out with the God of Death, drawing power from her life of chastity and the Lord of Death had to relent and bring back to life Satyavan. That is our tradition; so don't come to hasty conclusions and decide things rashly."

Both the parties gave the arbiters a patient hearing and asked for the next righteous step to be taken.

Pleased at the effect of their sermon, they dragged it a little more . . .

"A fortnight is too small a time to judge such issues; after all, it is a question of two lives, of a young man and a young lady. They are at the threshold of life and cannot judge for themselves. You people have seen life . . ."

The arbiters' preaching worked well on both the parties and the latter asked the former to take a decision and promised to abide by it.

"Are you sure that we should decide? Would you stand by that decision?" the arbiters asked.

"They have to abide by it, if they want the problem to be solved."

When both the families assented, the arbiters took some time and deliberated among themselves.

Then they came and gave their decision.

The families of the girl and the boy were to wait until the boy returned from wherever he had gone. It wouldn't be long, the wait, the arbiters assured. It looked like a case of some false notion or some ill founded belief, as per their perception and it would all end well, they assured.

At the end of the adjudication, there was something for the third party to cheer about; the girl, who was the centre of the storm, came and obediently touched their feet, and that at the bidding of her mother!

Men at the slab were perplexed; what was the factor that induced the two parties to relent? Had they seen any truth in the arbiters' perception? Were they convinced that it would be a sin to precipitate the annulment of the marriage? What was it that weighed, after all . . . ?

Endlessly debate raged at the slab among the members; they sat in select groups of twos and threes and probed the issue. Many inferences were drawn. On one of the conclusions there was near unanimity and that was that they should not have closed the issue in such a hurry.

Nagireddy loved chatting with men who shared interests with him. What attracted the men to him was that he had no status-based vanity and the men, once they gained close acquaintance with him, came to like him for his geniality, helpfulness and above all his sense of humour.

It was an evening in winter. Nagireddy was in the house of Hussainaiah. As usual, Kannam was there by his side; Nagireddy was narrating to Hussainaiah an anecdote from his theatre life.

Kannam was listening to his mentor's experiences dutifully for the umpteenth time.

Reclining on the coir-rope cot, Nagireddy was recalling his essay of the role of 'Krishna of the bedroom scene', in the play—'the Crowning of the Efforts of the Pandavas', a popular mythological play of the times . . .

'The arch rivals Arjuna and Duryodhana go to seek Sri Krishna's help in the coming Mahabharata war. Lord Krishna is in his bedroom in the palace. The shrewd Krishna is aware that the cousins were coming to seek his help; he wants to favor Arjuna . . . Duryodhana has already come and is sitting; so, Krishna feigns sleep as he waits for Arjuna whom he wants to see first so as to give him a preferential deal, on that count.'

Nagireddy was relating the scene and his portrayal of the role of Sri Krishna in the scene . . .

Born in a family of landlords, Nagireddy was barely ten years old when he lost his father. His elder sister took care of him for three years after the death of the father; she sent him to a school that was three miles away; but Nagireddy did not show much interest in the studies, often played truant, fell into bad company and frequently went to Bezwada where he saw four movies in a row and returned the next day with eyes red and swollen. The sister saw that her brother had no love for the studies and tried to push him into farming, with no better result. In a fit of disgust, she gave a big chunk of land to sharecroppers and arranged a steady income and after a few years, she went away to her home, leaving the matters there.

Once, when he was still in his teens, Nagireddy happened to see a mythological play staged by a repertory. Captivated by the glittering costumes of the actors and enchanted by the verses they sang on the stage to the accompaniment of a harmonium, he continued to linger in the vicinity of the venue, long after the play was over.

One lead actor noticed the young fan and took him to where the actors were assembled.

They gave him intimate access, probed his mindset and on finding out his passionate liking for the theatre, offered him the coveted chance of joining the troupe; they promised that he would be trained in accent, modulation needed for the dialogue delivery and singing to the accompaniment of the harmonium and that he would eventually would be put on the stage in a richly costumed role.

The repertory men saw in the handsome young lad, a promising actor and decided to take him in.

Nagireddy, the teenage boy of those years promptly fell for it and left home since he was the master of his own life and decision maker at his home.

The sister was anguished at the wayward nature of her brother and got letters written to the company. They wrote back to her to say that the boy had joined the troupe of his own free will and that he was under no compulsion to stay and could leave if he desired so.

The boy had no desire to leave the repertory; he stayed with it for three years, learned the skills and finally applied cake to his face.

His first appearance on the stage was in the minor role of Vikarna in the court of the blind Kaurava king Dhritarashtra. The young man impressed the repertory with his quick learning; subsequently Nagireddy donned other minor roles; but when he was elevated to the lead roles and did two or three of them, the news came of his sister's demise and he rushed home.

Back home, he was treated as a hero for all the glamorization the stint in the drama company had earned for him.

Sharecroppers sulked when Nagireddy came back and did not show any enthusiasm to pay the arrears; so he dislodged them and gave the land to some other party. When he calculated the loss he had suffered, he was stunned and he decided to give up his theatrical aspirations, at least, for the time being.

However, the itch for the theatre did not ebb in him and he kept up a steady correspondence with the troupe manager and whenever the company performed in a nearby village they offered Nagireddy an important role in the play and he for his part, helped them in whatever ways he could.

Nagireddy's acting talent grew with the experience and with make-up his sweet face showed to good advantage; he became very popular, especially with the womenfolk.

He liked, above all, the role of Krishna and he was aware that girls and women who watched the play liked him in that role.

He was, presently, narrating one of the most eventful episodes of his theatre life to Hussainaiah.

'The Crowning of the Efforts of the Pandavas' was to be staged at Rajupapalem, a village ten miles from his. It was a star-studded programme, with three actors playing Krishna, two playing Duryodhana and two playing Arjuna, in the successive acts. He was to be the first Krishna, 'Krishna of the bedroom scene' so to say; he was to be followed by two celebrities in that role, in the succeeding acts.'

"I was very nervous that night, because famous actors who were part of the troupe would be watching me play Krishna," said Nagireddy as he narrated.

"Why brother Nagaya, you are also famous; why were you so nervous?" Kannam was amused at that statement and asked his mentor.

"I am noted; I know that; but only to people like you. In front of those big actors I was nothing; so, naturally, I was very nervous; when they saw me nervously moving about, they understood my plight. One of the great actors came to me, put his hand on my shoulder and boosted my morale, saying, 'Mr. Reddy, even we too were like you on our debut on the stage. Be relaxed and do it confidently.' That helped me, indeed," Nagireddy gave a little pause, sharpening his auditory powers.

When he heard the sound of the bangles from behind the door, Nagireddy was reassured that all his efforts were going in the right direction and to make it doubly sure, he said to his host, "Hussainaiah, fetch me a glass of water, I don't know why my throat is going dry so much today."

Next moment, the bangles jingled once more and water was handed over to Hussainaiah, who obsequiously gave it to Nagireddy.

Kannam rushed out, feigning a fit of cough, only to have a hearty laugh outside; when he returned, Nagireddy alerted him with his looks and Kannam returned a nod of acknowledgment.

"Are you listening, Hussainaiah? Listen attentively; you will learn how difficult it is to act on the stage."

"Yes, Brother Nagaya, I am listening; it is all very interesting; go on, Brother Nagaya."

"So, as I was telling you, I was very nervous and the great actor reassured me that I would do well. And, who do you think that great actor was? Who? It was the great actor Sheik Meera. Have you heard me, Kannam and Hussainaiah? It was Sheik Meera, world famous actor for the role of Krishna."

Kannam nodded, while Hussainaiah looked on naively.

"Hussainaiah, playing in the bedroom scene is not a joke, do you know that?" Nagireddy said.

Promptly Kannam intervened and suppressing a smile, said, "Why, wouldn't he know that much, even so long after of marriage!"

Nagireddy cast a look of disapproval and chided his protégé, "Stop it, Kannam, shut up your mouth and listen; otherwise go and look after your work, if any, at home."

Observing their demeanor Hussainaiah guessed that Kannam had played some dirty joke; so he wanted to put things in order and said sulkily, "What if married for so long? Is it a rule that one should know that thing you mean, whatever it is?"

Nagireddy thought that Hussainaiah had understood the meaning of the banter and admonished Kannam, "When would you change your ways, Kannam! It's really disgusting to see you behave like this."

Kannam bent his head regretfully, nevertheless enjoying the effect of his joke.

Hussainaiah exultantly remarked, "He would know only after marriage how to behave in a householder's dwelling."

"Have you heard him? Do you want to hear such a thing?" Nagireddy said.

Kannam, now, felt bad; he couldn't take it anymore and head bent, he went out of the house in remorse.

Nagireddy was depressed at what had happened. Obviously, Kannam was hurt; it had never happened like this, between Kannam and himself.

Unable to take it easy, Nagireddy put an end to his narration and like an actor abruptly going into the wings, left the place, leaving Hussainaiah agape in bafflement.

Hussainaiah was shocked by the way things had gone and so quickly; he pined for what had been lost to him. 'When would he get to know what transpired after that point where Nagireddy broke off? Would he get to know the remainder of it, at all?'

'Nagireddy had come to his house for only the second time now; when he came, it was a pleasure to listen to his talk, to both him and his wife; it was as though Lord Krishna himself had come; he had that picture of Nagireddy made up as Krishna, firm in his memory and by God, how resplendent he looked in that gorgeous 'chemky' (glittering) costume! . . .

'That fellow, Kannam was nothing but a spoilsport, as he had proved himself to be time and again, at the slab. Uncle Pagadaiah was never at ease with that fellow among the listeners and 'his tale' never went on smoothly . . .'

Presently Narayanamma came; "Has he gone?" She asked; she had been listening from behind the door and was interrupted by the cackle of the birds in the backyard and when she came back, after putting the birds under the basket, Nagireddy had gone away.

"Yes, he has. What else can happen when that good-for-nothing fellow is around? Next time if he sets foot in my house I will break his legs." Hussainaiah ground his teeth, imagining Kannam's leg between his teeth.

"Why do you talk like that? Nagireddy is a gentleman and he has never done you a bad turn."

"What are you saying? I was talking of that rogue, Kannam," he said.

"Why ask that fellow in, if you don't like him?" Narayanamma said to her husband.

"Who has invited that fellow? He just hangs on to Nagireddy. He is a parasite; always attaches himself to some rich source and for some strange reason, Nagireddy cannot do without him; God knows why!" Hussainaiah lamented.

"Then, the best course of action is to smile it away; otherwise, you would be hurting the sentiments of the man you hold in high esteem. One should always be cautious in such matters. If you allow a prejudice to be formed, it would be difficult to remove it."

Hussainaiah nodded in agreement, "You are right. Hereafter I would be careful. I won't invite Nagireddy if he has Kannam by his side; that would be better; but why would Nagireddy come to my house? What is here for that man, after all?" Hussainaiah heaved a sigh of despair and kept thinking.

They were into the second half of the winter, which was supposed to be the peak period of paddy-field activity; the Rain-God had not shown mercy, the epic singing and the grand bath to the Goddess Muthyalamma notwithstanding. They knew of no other course of action as the next alternative.

The Priest-sir too had wet land, wet in the sense that there was a well in the land and he cultivated paddy with the well water; there were breaches in his seedbeds too. If there was any option mentioned in the scriptures wouldn't he take it up? No, there was no other option; they had to suffer this wrath of God, 'for the acts of sinfulness committed by some men'.

Is God Merciful? Is he the father of all men and the creator of the entire flora and fauna as the pundits say and people believe? Does God take into account the nature of the human acts, in his dispensations? If so, why should God inflict suffering on all, for the sins committed only by a section of the men? Is that the way the divine justice runs? If it is, all nonhuman creatures are put to suffering for no fault of theirs, which is grave injustice. Or, is divine justice different from the justice of human kind? Or is there no such thing as divine justice, as can be understood and interpreted by the humans?

These questions and doubts raged in the minds of the men when they were on the slab, or alone, or in their farms, or wandering about the fields around, looking at the livestock and birds in the backyard and birds perched on the branches of the trees. Finally, when they looked at the sky it appeared to contain the answers to all their questions and doubts, but seemed unwilling to reveal them.

Old men of ripened wisdom often said that incidences such as death, distress and child birth—critical situations in human life pushed men into a mystic mood. The validity of the observation stood proved now, they thought.

When the few men that sat on the slab were in a pensive mood, Big Venkayya came and sat by Pagadaiah; his manner of walking and his demeanor showed that he wanted to break some important news to Pagadaiah.

Pagadaiah guessed it right; he turned to Big Venkayya and gave an enquiring nod.

"Cousin Pagadaiah, Naraiah of the west street had created a flutter, last night, you know?"

Pagadaiah nodded in sympathy, "With the old men, these things happen; is he all right, now?"

"Apparently, but they say his time has come; he is talking strange, it seems."

'So that's it,' Pagadaiah thought; he had seen men heading towards the old man's house, "What do you mean by 'strange'?"

Venkayya appeared caught in a dilemma and moved uneasily for a while and finally let the cat out of the bag, "They say the old man is back from a trip to the other world."

Pagadaiah gaped at the informant, 'A trip to the other world . . . ! God, that sounds terrible,' he got down the slab and said, "Come, let's go and see."

They went to the house of the old man and saw a veritable crowd there.

However, Pagadaiah was received cordially and was soon taken to the side of the old man lying on the bed.

The old man opened his eyes as he heard Pagadaiah's voice and looked disconsolately; it took some time for the old man to come into a talking mood.

Eventually, the old man began to talk feebly, "Brother Pagadaiah, I am in my second life now, so to say."

Pagadaiah nodded understandingly and patted lightly on the old man's shoulder, "I know, I know. Don't worry; now you will live to be a hundred, a hundred."

Naraiah's wife, sons and others looked thankfully at Pagadaiah.

In a while, the old man was chatting.

"To tell you the truth, Brother Pagadaiah, I thought I was more than halfway to the death; the earth under my feet was spinning unsteadily, like a top in its last lap. I felt my eyes sinking into the sockets and my consciousness went into a dimmed state. I just kept meditating upon Lord Narasimha and at that point I lost consciousness altogether, or rather I . . . I went into a different state of awareness . . . !

"Even in that state, I could see that I was a captive; there were two beings, huge in size and black in complexion, one on either side of me; I wondered where they were taking me . . .

"I moved up and up through a white cloud line, feeling very light of my body and eerily happy; I went into a marvelous garden with a wide collection of huge and tall trees with strange formations of foliage; from the high branches of the trees hung clusters of creepers with their own thick foliage and the creeks ran with gurgling sounds; all the time I was flanked by the two wrestler-like, men-like beings of pitch black complexion. It was a place that stunned my sight; I had never seen nor do I hope to see such a place. There, I stood wondering, for, I lost the sense of fear; yes that was it. I didn't feel any fear; I was just in a state of wonder when I was taken to another human-like being, but of immense proportions, dark in complexion and sporting a huge, bushy moustache; there were two big horns on his head."

"Yamadharmaraja . . ." Pagadaiah nodded acquaintance.

"He asked a servant to bring the records; a man came back with a cloth-pack. The big being unfurled the pack and took out a bundle of palm leaves; carefully examining the leaves he picked one leaf and squinted into the matter therein and made some calculations on his fingers, much in the fashion of our Priest-sir; in a while he became furious with those two horned beings that were on either side of me. In a booming voice he said something; it sounded like a mantra and the place reverberated with it for some time and then the big being vanished with an explosive sound.

"The two mountain-like beings trembled at the fury of their master and stood looking dolefully at each other . . .

"Thereafter I was taken out of that place by the two giants and once we were out of the garden, they spoke to me in our language 'Look here, you creature of the earth; there was some confusion in spotting the man whose time had elapsed. By mistake we took you for him; it was a mistake on our part to have brought you here. Our master is very much annoyed with us and has commanded us to rectify this error; we do not know what is in store for us at the end of your case. The system, over which our Lord presides is known to be the most righteous and it has never gone wrong; in our service period of three million years, there has never been such an awful mix up; but what can we do, now? Our service records have been spoiled for once . . .

'Therefore, we are rectifying the thing; we are going to revive your life on the earth. Go back and enjoy your life for the remaining stretch of it.'

"I joined my palms to them in obedience and mumbled, 'your kindness . . .'"

"'However, before we send you back, the Lord has ordained that we do you a favor of his prescription, as a recompense, a favor the like of which you will never have, alive,' and so saying, they took me to a place, the sight of which I can never, never forget."

"Maybe, they took you up to the gates of hell . . ." Pagadaiah ventured a guess.

"No, no, Brother Pagadaiah, it is something I am not supposed to reveal; it's a thing a creature of the earth cannot know," Naraiah gave an unfathomable smile.

Pagadaiah looked, opened-mouthed as he thought, 'How conceited the old fellow looks and talks, for that one experience! Is what he says to be believed? Who can vouch for its truth? If it is his fiction, he will have to pay for it, because, Yamadharmaraja can be ruthless in such matters.'

Then checking himself Pagadaiah said, "So, that is so, that is so? What a wonderful experience you have had Brother Naraiah! You have become a blessed soul indeed; what a blissful experience for a man to have had and come back to life at the end of it! We must go and tell all this to the Priest-sir; he can, perhaps, tell us the significance of it."

"No, no, Brother Pagadaiah, this should be among us only. I don't know what would befall me if I go on making it public, as though it were an incident from my day-to-day occurrences. Let us not make it public," Naraiah showed concern.

"So be it, then, so be it," Pagadaiah said reassuringly, "Well, what was that memorable favor shown to you, in recompense to the embarrassment caused to you by those deputies of the Lord Yamadharmaraja? Do you feel like telling us that; or are you under any divine injunction?"

"No, no, there is no such thing; I will tell you," Naraiah looked a little tired and shut his eyes.

"In that case, Naraiah, I would just like to ask you one thing, only one thing, other things can wait," Said Pagadaiah.

"What is it?" Naraiah said in a weak voice.

"Just this thing, did they take you to one of those two places we all hear about? I mean, those two places called Hell and Heaven—the two places one of which men fear about and the other men yearn for . . ."

"I don't think they make any difference to a man living; they fear the hell and don't want to die and they yearn to go to heaven, yet don't want to die; man is a funny animal, really; but coming to the point, I am not supposed to reveal it."

Naraiah's wife came and covering her man with a sheet of cloth, said, "Let him rest for awhile, Elder Brother Pagadaiah."

Disappointed at that, Pagadaiah reluctantly left the place and walked towards his dwelling, thoughtful.

Pagadaiah stood in front of his house.

In that twilight, he saw the hen moving restlessly in the yard; Rattamma was fixing the evening lamp on the hook; her mother looked very restless as she walked up and down, much like the hen in the yard.

Rattamma saw her man and hurried into the house, as if she had just sighted a ghoul; it hurt Pagadaiah's spousal pride to see his legal wife behave so and morosely he set foot in his house.

"Have a wash and come, Pagadaiah; the meal is ready," said the mother-in-law.

Mechanically he took off his shirt and taking a towel, walked into the back yard; again he saw Rattamma who tried to walk by him quickly.

Pagadaiah took a quick step and caught her by the hand, "Why are you running away like that? I am not a devil; I am your man," he said.

He tried to pull her into his arms.

Rattamma tried to disengage herself from his grip, "Leave me, what are you doing? Mother would watch!"

"Let her watch, after all, I have the right not only to hold your hand . . ." Pagadaiah rejoined, still holding her hand in a tight grip, "Stop these tantrums and arrange our bed inside and put your mother's cot in the backyard, you bitch; otherwise, I will just break your bones in my clasp! Don't act smart with me."

As Pagadaiah loosened his grip, Rattamma wriggled out and ran into the house.

After supper, Pagadaiah went for a stroll and then reached the slab.

There were not many on the slab; but among those present there were a few who bonded with him and they cheerfully welcomed him, dusting the slab for him, as usual.

Sitting on the slab, Pagadaiah lit his leaf-roll cigar; after he had taken a few puffs, the cigar began to burn steadily and he drew on it lustily, enjoying it like never before.

One by one they gathered round him.

"Uncle Pagadaiah, tell us a story, it's a long time since you told us one," entreated one of the cronies.

Pagadaiah gave a happy smile, "Why not, it is story time all right. What type of story you want? Tell me that first," Asked Pagadaiah.

"A story that is interesting, exciting and imaginative, like one that takes us away from this slab, to unseen places, unseen worlds, to big palaces, to kings and queens and their beautiful daughters and to the sorcerers and their magic wands and the fire-breathing gigantic lizards, naughty monkeys that perform the bidding of the hero's sidekick . . . Tell us a tale that mixes all these things."

"Yes, yes, tell us such a tale, for, otherwise, there is no cheer for us, either at home or at the slab; life has become very dull and drab, Uncle Pagadaiah," said another one of the hangers-on.

Pagadaiah was elated, 'It feels good to be sought after so much; after a long time,' he thought.

"And, one more thing Uncle Pagadaiah, the story should be a long, long one; it should run up to midnight."

'A tough demand,' thought Pagadaiah who could not promise any such fare, that night. Already, the picture of Rattamma began to dangle in his thought, clad in that red saree and blue blouse, the pitch-black luxuriant braided hair flowing down to her waist. 'What a picture she cuts!' Pagadaiah wondered.

"Rre, Koti, you give uncle Pagadaiah a pack of beedis and a box of matches."

Pagadaiah began the story of 'The Prince and his Winged Horse.' The skillfully woven tale told about the efforts of a prince to find his dream girl. 'The winged horse is given to the prince by a deity who has been impressed with the penance of the prince; but the horse is of a fierce temper. A hermit reveals a mantra to the prince, with which the prince is able to tame the horse. Then, astride the horse, the prince wanders in the sky, all the time looking out for the girl, through magic glasses, gifted to him by a hermit. Ultimately, the prince finds the girl and with the blessings of the girl's parents weds her and sets out on return journey . . .

'However, the return trip of the prince is fraught with many obstacles and risks. A sorcerer casts covetous eyes on the beautiful girl and wrests her from the prince, using his guiles and sorcery. The prince continues to get timely help from the sorcerer's adversaries and after many adventures regains his sweet heart. During the course of the tale the prince sees lands where animals and birds talk, peacocks dance before the prince and monkeys entertain.'

The story took the listeners to far-off places, showed them bewitching nymphs and mermaids, gave glimpses of seductive dames and showed them a goat's horn that gave an endless supply of food and drinks of choice. It was, indeed, a heavily spiced tale and displayed the charming and captivating power of Pagadaiah, the peerless raconteur and matchless narrator of tales.

The number of listeners swelled as the time went by and the slab wore a rich look after a long time; it pleased Pagadaiah to have a full slab listening to the tale and he forgot himself and the task he had set for himself, that night.

After a satisfying recital of tale Pagadaiah took leave of his clientele and walked homewards. As he walked, Rattamma's figure danced invitingly in his mind, filling him with the thrill of suspense.

Pagadaiah opened the makeshift fence-gate and stood at the door, kept ajar for him.

He hoped to see Rattamma at the door waiting for him, like in stories; but, she wasn't there.

It was very dark and barely a thing was visible; he went inside, groped for the coir-thread cot and found it.

The bangles jingled on the cot, in invitation; he was happy that Rattamma had arranged their bed inside the hut, as bidden by him; he slowly lowered himself onto the bed.

'Silently, silently,' he told himself, 'you should be careful; otherwise, 'the rabbit's ears' would become bitter.'

Again, the bangles jingled and he enveloped her in his bear hug.

The next morning, Pagadaiah got up from the bed promptly before the daybreak and went into the cattle shed to fill the tub and found his mother-in-law and Rattamma huddled together in the cot.

Pagadaiah smiled to himself and went about the daily chores.

Hearing the sound of Pagadaiah's movements and the noise of the pans, the mother-in-law awoke and rose to perform the chores like sweeping and drawing those crisscross lime lines of good luck, in front of the house, while Rattamma covered her face and slept on.

Pagadaiah looked annoyed at his wife's brazen act of sleeping well into daylight; he looked at the mother-in-law questioningly.

The mother-in-law gave a bashful smile.

Pagadaiah couldn't understand the meaning initially, but as he pursued his analysis, it dawned on him that his wife was having some well earned rest; he smiled in understanding.

Hussainaiah was itching to hear the remainder of Nagireddy's first experience on stage—first experience as 'the bedroom Krishna', as Hussainaiah remembered the term; but, he did not get to know the complete version of the anecdote, since Nagireddy was unavailable *for* some days in a row.

However, one day, Hussainaiah luckily saw Nagireddy walking by and grabbing the chance, invited Nagireddy to his house, "I have been waiting for you all these days, Brother Nagaya. Come, come, it's a very chilly day; come in and rest a while, have some tea and give us a full account of your first experience. For men like us, it would be a thing of extreme pleasure."

Nagireddy feigned a feeling of inconvenience, "Actually, Hussainaiah, I am in a hurry; but, since you have invited me, I cannot say 'no'; I am coming, you be on the move; I am just looking for this fellow, Kannam,"

Hussainaia's face lost part of its glow the moment he heard the name of Kannam, but he did not show it and gently pulled Nagireddy by the finger, "Come Nagaya, let us go in; the fellow would anyway get scent and come there."

Presently, they went into the house; Hussainaiah promptly laid the coir-rope cot and put a pillow. Nagireddy smilingly rested on the cot and asked, "Looks like you are alone at home, Hussainaiah?"

Apologetically Hussainaiah said, "Yes Brother Nagaya; but I can make some tea for you, rest comfortably, Brother Nagaya."

"Don't worry, Hussainaiah. I am comfortable and tea can wait; your wife would anyway be coming; she will make the tea, don't worry about the tea now."

"Hussainaiah, do you have Nagaya there?" Kannam's voice sounded at the threshold and as they looked up, a peeping head showed at the door.

Nagireddy cheerfully welcomed the arrival of his minion, Kannam, "Get in, you vagabond, how many places you want me to go, in search of you!"

Kannam gleefully bared his teeth, "I too have gone to many places in search of you Nagaya. That you should be here, of all the places . . . ! How do you think people would expect to find you here, 'Kistaparamatma'?"

Hussainaiah looked glumly as Kannam came in and sat leaning against the wall.

"Nagaya, that day you didn't give us the complete version of your first appearance on the stage as Krishna; you went away, halfway through . . ."

Nagireddy had already assumed the role of Krishna, in his mind, what was left remaining was an exposition of the way he lured the Gopika, his sweetheart.

"See, Hussainaiah, playing the role of Krishna of bedroom scene is not a joke. Listen attentively. As the time for the battle of Kurukshetra is drawing nearer, both the Pandavas and the Kauravas decide to approach Lord Krishna for help; Krishna knows that they would be coming. Just at the time of their coming, he lies on the bed and pretends to be fast asleep . . .

"There are two chairs, one at the foot of the bed and one at the head . . .

"First, Duryodhana comes and vain that he is, sits in the chair at the head of the bed; then Arjuna comes and sits respectfully at the feet of Lord Krishna . . .

"Lord Krishna wakes up; actually he doesn't wake up, just pretends, because he is not sleeping really, it's all pretension; so, he wakes up and sees Arjuna first and sings that verse, 'From where are you coming'; later he sees Duryodhana and sings that verse, 'Cousin, when did you come?'

"So, Hussainaiah, listen carefully. I have told you the scene; now, see how the action goes. After the make-up, I was tensely waiting for the action to start. I went onto the stage and lay on the bed, resting my cheek on my left palm, in style. It took some time to draw the curtain; so I fell into a catnap. They drew the curtain apart; but, there I was, snoozing; funny, isn't it? The contractor, who arranged the play, came into the side curtain and gently poked me, in the ear, with a twig and luckily I woke up and saw. Lo, the two characters, Duryodhana and Arjuna were already there on the stage!" Nagireddy paused.

Hussainaiah urged him to continue, "Don't stop in the midst, Brother Nagaya; I feel as though I am watching the play!"

"Is that so? Nice then; so, waking up, I got up, saw Arjuna and took up the verse, 'From where are you coming?' There were over a thousand, men and women among the audience; ladies were sitting on my right hand side and there were many of them. So, I sang the verse well; it was in the melody, 'kafi'; I like kafi melody and gave it a nice full treatment, bringing out all the nuances.

Nagireddy stopped the narration to see whether Hussainaiah was listening with interest or not.

Hussainaiah came up with a doubt, "Brother Nagaya, you were Krishnaparamatma and you say you took kyapee (coffee); is it alright to take 'kyapee'?"

Nagireddy smiled and explained, "Many people mistake it like this; it is not the coffee we drink, it is a raga, a melody of select notes," After seeing the nod of Hussainaiah, he continued, "So, I sang in kafi and before I took up the dialogue, shouts of 'once more' came from the audience. I was nonplussed and looked at the contractor, who was still in the wings. He gave me a nod to go on; so, cleverly, I went back to the cot and lay on it for a while and then got up, and casting a look at Arjuna, for the second time of course, I took up the verse, 'From where are you coming' and Lo, once again there was 'once more' demand! I looked for the contractor, but he was not there; so, I thought it out quickly and settled the issue by joining my palms to the audience, seeking their pardon. They clapped at my honesty and left it at that . . ."

At that point, they heard the sound of footsteps and next moment, they caught sight of Narayanamma entering the house; as she came, she saw Nagireddy and smiling courteously, went inside.

The moment Nagireddy saw her, a visible change came over him; noticing it, Kannam's lips curled into a smile.

Then onwards, he did not bother much about his ardent fan Hussainaiah and directed it all at his fair lady; but he formally addressed them all to Hussainaiah.

"Hussainaiah, staging a mythological play is a very complex affair; the actors must be good singers, well versed in the art of music; the harmonist must know the pitch and reach of the actors' voices; crowds must be lovers of the mythological plays; of course, they usually are. There are several preconditions that decide the success of a mythological play. Do you understand, Hussainaiah?"

Hussainaiah pouted and turned his palms clockwise and anticlockwise, indicating that he didn't understand a thing.

Undeterred by that gesture, Nagireddy continued, "So. Hussainaiah, going back to the bed, lying on it again, then getting up and singing the verse a second time was a masterstroke on my part; I am not saying this; the famous actors who were part of the troupe had said this and congratulated me. As a matter of fact, Hussainaiah . . ." He stopped abruptly and stared at Hussainaiah.

Leaning against the wall, Hussainaiah was snoring away soundly.

Nagireddy looked at Narayanamma; she too was looking at her husband, amused.

Showing on his face a feeling of mortification, Nagireddy got up and prepared to go.

"Please don't go. I will make some tea for you; it's not every day that you visit our house," said Narayanamma and at that, Nagireddy promptly resumed his seat on the cot.

"Now, would you wake up? You ask the gentleman to your house and when he is here, chatting with you, you drowse; it is time you learnt to be courteous with gentlemen," Narayanamma said and when what she said had no effect on her man, she coyly sprinkled a few drops of water on his face.

With a jolt, Hussainaiah woke up, saw left and right jerkily and then, with the look of a confused man, kept staring at Nagireddy and Kannam alternately, "Hm, what, what is it? What is it?" he said incoherently.

Nagireddy couldn't help laughing at that comedy of the situation and promptly quipped, "It's nothing Hussainaiah; the play is over and the curtains are down. Now go home and have some nice rest."

In the normal course, Kannam would have laughed heartily; but, showing a sense of place and time, he limited it to a chuckle and cryptic remark, "The play is not over,

Hussainaiah; only the first act is over; wait for the second act to begin and then you may go to sleep."

Nagireddy glowered at Kannam.

Hussainaiah, fully awake now, frowned at Kannam and then turning to Nagireddy said, "Would you like some tea, Nagaya?"

In the meanwhile, Narayanamma had already brought the tea and glasses.

Dutifully Hussainaiah got up and taking the kettle from his wife poured the tea into glasses and served it to Nagireddy lovingly and to Kannam grudgingly.

Nagireddy with an apologetic smile said, "We seem to have given you trouble, Narayanamma,"

"No trouble at all, your visit to our house was an act of honor to us, for that matter," said Narayanamma.

Nagireddy felt thrilled; he said effusively, "In fact, whenever I am on my way back from Bezwada late in the night, it always strikes me that I can stay here in your village for the night and go to my village the next morning, rather than walk the two mile-stretch in the dark night, braving the nocturnal creatures; but as it is always the case, I walk home. Luckily, to the date, I haven't been harmed."

"Oh my God, walking like that in the dark night is very risky; it is the time the reptiles are out into the open! Why take so much risk, when you have so many friends in this village?" Narayanamma said with genuine concern.

"Yes, Brother Nagaya, you can camp for the night. Does Kannam know about your risky walks? You can straightaway walk to his house and stay for the night, can't he Kannam?"

Kannam shyly nodded; he knew that was highly unlikely-'Nagireddy staying for the night in my house . . . ! No way, no way.'

"Of course, that is there, he wouldn't say no to me; why, I can even knock on your door, can't I, Hussainaiah?" said Nagireddy.

Before her husband could think of an answer to that, Narayanamma went into the backroom and Hussainaiah gave an evasive smile.

The matter of Nagireddy's overnight stop ended there, for the time being.

Nagireddy felt uneasy at the elusive way the man and his wife responded and he wanted to drive the ploy some more distance and with a smile he said to Hussainaiah, "Hussainaiah, I have told you about my first appearance on the stage; have you listened to it attentively?"

"What happened after 'that', Nagaya? You said that after taking 'kapi' you slept on the cot . . . ; then, what happened?"

Nagireddy patted on his forehead with his palm, in frustration.

After remaining silent for a while, he looked at Kannam and said, "Shall we go?"

Kannam got up in readiness and Nagireddy too got up from the cot, but slowly, expecting a request to extend his stay for some more time.

Hussainaiah got up too, in readiness to see off Nagireddy and his companion.

Nagireddy realized that the curtains had been drawn on the first act. He was not completely disappointed with the day's work; it proceeded in the right direction and was reasonably well done; but 'when could the second act be staged?' he wondered.

With that satisfying feeling of partial success Nagireddy took leave of Hussainaiah and stepped into the street along with his companion, Kannam.

Hulakki had a strange feeling as he walked on the bund of the paddy plot, across field; the paddy grass was unusually tall and each cluster of it, with a cob at the top, moved slowly in the wind. There were angelic faces at the centre of the stalk; with their slow movement in the wind, the plants looked like gravid ladies attending to their chores; their languid smile showed tiredness and yet was sweetly courteous.

Hulakki stood at the centre of the paddy field; the paddy grass was much taller than him; he touched a stalk with warm affection, saying, "I think you are 'rajanalu' (a paddy strain of high quality)."

"We are 'divine rajanalu' a celestial strain; we grow food for the deities."

Hulakki made a reverential gesture, "Ah, how fortunate I am, to have seen you, Mother!"

"How are your paddy fields, on the earth, my son?"

"What can I say 'Mother'! We haven't transplanted yet."

"Sorry to hear that; why, what is the problem, my son," the divine paddy plant asked.

"It's not a plight of this year, 'Mother'; for the last two to three years it has been the case with our fields and agriculture. Some farmers have big wells in their fields and they are managing to keep their seedbeds green; others, they are just looking at the sky, all the time."

"Then, what are you doing about it, son."

"We have done what is prescribed by the tradition, the epic-singing and also a grand bath to the deity, Muthyalamma; still, the Rain-God has not taken pity to on us."

"Pch, my poor children," the celestial paddy sympathized with him, "Go and ask Muthyalamma why she is so unkind; especially when you have complied with the ritualistic prescriptions; don't just leave the matter there and suffer."

Hulakki looked hither and thither and asked, "Is she around, Mother?"

With a nod, the celestial paddy gestured to him to move ahead, "Walk a few paces straight, then turn left and after a few paces turn right; you will find her there. Go and ask her; don't be frightened, my son."

Hulakki nodded and walked ahead, and he heard the celestial paddy cautioning him from behind, saying, "Look here my son, don't take my name there."

"Oh no, Mother, I know that much of the etiquette," Said Hulakki and move on.

After walking as directed, Hulakki found her; Muthyalamma was sitting on the doorsill, combing the nits out; she had a vermillion mark of the size of a rupee-coin on her forehead; she looked questioningly at Hulakki, eyebrows knitted.

Hulakki bowed to her humbly and explained, "Mother Muthyalamma, I am from a village, at the foot of the Pandava Hills and my name is Hulakki; it is my grandfather's name, I mean my paternal grandfather; I have been named after him, Mother,"

The deity nodded a little impatiently, closely examined the comb and then looked at him.

Hulakki understood that she wanted to know the purpose of his visit; summoning up courage he explained, "Pardon me, Mother, there are no rains in the region of our village; for three years in succession it has been the case, Mother. We have bathed your icon with a thousand pans of water; we have also arranged the epic singing of the story of the king Virata. Still, we haven't had any luck, Mother. We are running short of drinking water too. We are all righteous people in our village and we always pay obeisance to the deities; still we are being treated harshly, Mother."

Muthyalamma signaled with her palm asking Hulakki to stop complaining, "Which was your first act, grand bath to my icon or the singing of the story of the king Virata?"

The deity's serious look and the tune in which she questioned, frightened Hulakki; he took a few gulps and apologetically confessed, "Pardon us, Mother, maybe we erred in arranging the epic-singing first; it was only later that we bathed your icon. If it is an impropriety, kindly pardon us for the lapse, Mother. Please shower your mercy on us and save us, our cattle and our paddy fields," he implored Mother Muthyalamma.

"Stop whining here, go to that king Virata and ask him," said Muthyalamma and resumed the combing.

"Where is he, Mother, the king Virata?"

"Who told you about my whereabouts? Go to the same source and find out," said Muthyalamma brusquely.

Hulakki obediently nodded and stepping back he left the place; then he went back to the celestial paddy and narrated to her what had happened.

The celestial paddy gave a thoughtful smile and said, "Right then, go and tell the king Virata your mission; he must be somewhere around, playing dice. What else would he do, the good-for-nothing fellow! Go and ask him; it is he who has to answer."

The celestial paddy gave directions to find the King Virata.

Hulakki saluted and moved on, went this way and that way and finally spotted the king Virata; he was playing the game of 'tiger and the goats'; a flag with a big picture of fish, fluttered in the wind at the place and there were a few earthen vessels with foaming toddy (a lightly intoxicating drink obtained from wine-palm) in them.

Virata took no notice of the arrival of Hulakki and went on with his game of dice. He threw the dice and gleefully shouted, "It's four; it's four . . ."

Hulakki didn't like the looks of Virata, but patiently waited and waited before clearing his throat and when Virata lifted his head, he appealed to the good sense of Virata, "Esteemed sir, I am from a village at the foot of the Pandava Hills; we have been facing drought situation in our region, for the third year in a row. We performed the epic singing of your story, hiring the services of a harmonium player from Gosseedu and a singer from Ramannapet, sorry Sir, the epic-singer from Gosseedu and the harmonium player from

Ramannapet, rather; but we haven't had any rains, so far. Our village is reeling in this dry spell of weather . . ."

King Virata raised his head and said with an insolent look, "I know, I know; I know everything about that epic-singing you arranged. Did anyone listen to it with devotion and attention? Was it performed meticulously well? The singer was going one way and that deaf harmonist was going another way! And those children of your village, Cock or Hen, whatever is the name of the village, they were playing cat and mouse with that slipknot of that poor devoted man, Pathgaiah, no, no, Pagthaiah, no, no, Pagadaiah, a very difficult name to pronounce, indeed! Is that the kind of epic singing you arrange? And here you come and ask for the rains?"

"Oh, no Sir, no; I think you are mistaking me for Pagadaiah; I am Hulakki, Lord-Sir; my name is Hulakki, it's the name of my grandfather, on father's side. Actually, my mother wanted to name me after her father; my father didn't approve of it and he named me after his father. My mother was very angry with my father for that and I have heard it said that my mother didn't talk at all to my father for one full week,"

"Stop all that rubbish and come to the point, straightaway," Virata said peremptorily.

"Forgive me, Lord-Sir, I am telling you the entire truth; how can I hide things to you, Lord-Sir; even if I hide, you would discover the truth the next instant; so, to tell you the truth . . ."

"Oh, you are at it again! Stop that blabber and come to the point or else get lost."

"Pardon me Lord-Sir, I admit that things didn't go right with the epic-singing; your anger is understandable; but, Lord-Sir, it rained heavily in the villages within a radius of ten miles; Molugumadu, Kasaram, and adjacent villages had recorded a rainfall of ten furrows and they haven't arranged any Harikatha. Is that not unfair and unjust, Lord-Sir?"

King Virata frowned at Hulakki and said in a raised voice, "What, what . . . ? You want me to keep listening to your haggling? Do you think you are at the grocery of your Rosaiah Sir to settle the bargain? 'Go the way you have come'; who directed you to me? Now, be off, before I lose my cool," With that, King Virata took a gulp of toddy and took the dice into hands again.

With a forlorn look Hulakki went back to deity Muthyalamma.

Muthyalamma was sitting in a cross-legged posture; she was looking fresh after her bath. She was dressed in a gorgeously brocaded silk saree and looked resplendent in sparkling ornaments; the big vermillion mark on her forehead was awe-inspiring!

A minor deity was there by her side; a few celestial laborers were carrying huge bales of black cotton-like thing; on a closer scrutiny Hulakki discovered that they were rain-bearing clouds.

"How many are you carrying and for which villages?" Muthyalamma asked, "Check them first."

"Mother, they are for the villages of Molgumadu, Marlapadu and Ramannapet, at the foot of the Pandava hills."

Hulakki was astonished at the mention of the names of the villages that were close by to his village and when the deity gave them the nod, he hurriedly appealed to Mother Muthyalamma, "Oh, Mother, they are going to our region; show some consideration for our village too; we have always revered you, Mother . . ."

"Consideration for what?" questioned Muthyalamma, "You say you have given the grand bath; but what came of it?

The water didn't flow into that abandoned well; if it flowed, was the water ankle-deep in the well, after the bath? By what count would you get the rains? It is not that easy, mind it, you won't get them so cheap; understand that."

Prompted by a sudden intuition, Hulakki prostrated at the feet of the deity and wept, "Oh Mother of Mothers, we are your children, and don't forsake us. If you want a sacrifice, take my life, Mother; but don't punish us, the people of Peacock so harshly; oh Mother, oh Mother, there are old men and small kids, ladies and men of all ages in our families and there are dumb live-stock too; there are cows and bulls and oxen besides the buffalos and sheep and goats and of course, the domestic fowl of different varieties and there are also many other creatures like cats, rats and numerous insects, but, I am not pleading for them; of course, all those creatures also need water, all those creatures I have mentioned. Our paddy fields are developing breaches in the plots, Mother, oh Mother, oh Mother, have mercy on us please . . ." he wept inconsolably.

After sometime the deity appeared placated and said, "Oh, you seem to be a stubborn votary. Get up, get up, you have impressed me with your readiness to sacrifice your life for your village. Here, I grant you your wish; but, remember one thing. After I order for the rains, you have to sacrifice yourself at that altar," She showed an altar, a few yards away; on that altar there was big glittering broadsword "Obviously, you cannot return to your village."

Hulakki stared in panic; he had never thought the Deities would take the informal vows of the human beings so seriously, 'Would she really take my life here?' he began to tremble in fear.

Muthyalamma noticed it and laughed hoarsely at him, "What, are you frightened? I can see that; you humans on the earth have got into the habit of taking false pledges even in the presence of the deities, like you do at the time of elections; the elections have taught you that trick, I know; but here, everything you say is recorded and it counts; one can't go back on one's word, hhahha, understand?"

"Oh Mother, I didn't know that, Mother; please pardon me for this once; hereafter, I would never take such pledges, Mother; please grant me pardon, and spare my life Mother."

Muthyalamma said imperiously, "Don't haggle and pester me like that. Once said is said; now, see, I am ordering rain as per your wish and prayer," The deity turned towards the cloud-bearers and ordered them, "Give some good rain to that village, Peacock. Now get up Hulakki, I am pleased with your devotion."

Hulakki saw that things were decided; at least he would become a saint with the sacrifice of his life, he thought and then, with a nagging doubt looked at the load the cloud-bearers were carrying on their heads; later he continued to look at Muthyalamma imploringly.

With widened eyes, Muthyalamma asked, "What now?"

"Mother, they have only those few clouds on their heads and you have ordered them to rain in so many villages; my fear is that our village would only get a pittance of the rain; that will not be sufficient for 'my people's needs, Mother of Mothers."

Muthyalamma gave a big laugh, as she looked benignly at the innocent votary, Hulakki, "How intriguing is your naiveté, my child! You cannot arrive at the true measure of the rain-content of those clouds by what you see; if only a fraction of the full measure of just one of those udders in a cloud comes to rain in your village, the village would be inundated, yes, inundated! Understand?"

Hulakki shuddered at the way the deity explained; at once he slapped himself on the cheeks and asked for forgiveness, "Pardon me, Mother, we are ignorant of the ways of Gods. I would take whatever you give mother; I won't bicker any longer; even if it is a drop of water from you, it would be plenty to my village, yes Mother, it would be plenty for us," He prostrated at the feet of the Mother.

"Get up, my son, I am convinced of your honesty; I am waiving you from the performance of sacrifice; get up," Muthyalamma showed herself in a propitious mood and said smilingly, "You mortals can have no idea of the way the divine scheme is planned and the way the divine machinery works. You wonder how a small-looking cloud can give enough rain needed for the men, their livestock and the fields of crop and the plant life of so many villages. To enlighten you, I will just reveal to you one celestial secret. You have seen the clouds of rain they are carrying and have been wondering whether they would give you sufficient rain; but, you must know that each of the small clouds contains millions of udders, a trickle from one of which is enough for ten villages. Does it give you some idea? To use your own terms of measurement, a trickle from each udder can give you a hundred 'furrows' of rain; but it won't rain fully, since that would be causing huge floods, like the floods of Noah's times and the times of Prithu, understand? Now, go back and don't reveal to anyone this experience of yours. Only one in a billion can have a supernatural experience of this kind; you may go and remember, don't reveal the grant of that waiver of self-sacrifice to anybody, not even to your wife, understand?"

Hulakki nodded with folded hands and took leave of the deity.

"One minute, have a sanctification bath before you go," she turned aside and ordered, "Let somebody pour a pan of water on this devotee's head."

The next moment, Hulakki saw a celestial maid come with a big pan of water; she began to pour on his head, celestial water in jets, steady and sharp. He liked the touch of the celestial water; the spurts of water falling on his head seemed to gain in force; the pouring of water didn't stop.

Hulakki had closed his eyes when the maid came and started pouring water, but now, it began to hurt, the jets of water pricked liked pins.

Writhing in pain under the sharply pricking water, Hulakki pleaded with the lady to stop, "Enough of it, angel sister, enough. Please stop it, Madam."

"What to stop and enough of what . . . ? Wake up and see, Uncle, your son is sleeping like a log, when he should be helping me in drawing up water from the well. Get up, Sir, get up and go to the well; how many pans of water can I manage to get from the well? You must know, it is your work . . ."

Hulakki heard the rumble of his daughter-in-law's voice instead of the thunder of the clouds. He realized that he had just woken up from a remarkable dream.

Then he noticed that his son was sleeping close by and she was awakening him from the deep slumber.

'How nice it would be if the dream came true! He would become a savior to his village!' Hulakki thought.

He recalled the dream and heaved a sigh of disappointment; at the same time, he remembered the vow of self-sacrifice he had made to Deity Muthyalamma and how he managed to get it waived by the Mother; he shuddered. Rain or no rain, he was happy that he was alive.

Then he fully came to senses and got up to find himself at home; he saw his wife cleaning the yard and once again felt happy for being alive.

His wife and daughter-in-law were watching him, amused and surprised.

Hulakki's body ached as though he was just back from a long journey—a long journey to the celestial paddy fields!

Taking two pans and the rope, he trudged his way to the well, looking questioningly at the sky.

He remembered the dream and wondered whether it would come true.

After laboring for half-an-hour Hulakki could fill two pans and with those pans, he walked back.

As he walked back, he saw a group of men coming into the village with pans of water in the slings fixed to the yokes they carried on their shoulders.

"Where are you coming from, carrying water in those yoke—slings?" Hulakki asked.

"We have collected this water from the water holes dug in the sand bed of the rivulet; sweet drinking water and unlike the water from our half-dried up wells, this water is crystal clear; no shade of dirt," said Bushaiah proudly.

Hulakki thoughtfully smiled, "God always keeps some options open for the people in distress."

"Bademaya has been fetching drinking water from the water-holes for the last one week; it is he who told us; though we too know of the source, the idea didn't strike us—funny, isn't it?"

"'A billion kinds of tricks to tide over a million kinds of poverty' they say," Said Hulakki in an aside and moved on his way.

Next morning, the drumbeater went about, announcing the visit of the 'Emmellu' (the MLA) Suryanarayana; there would be a public meeting at the slab and the villagers were to receive important news at the meeting. The meeting would be held at nine in the morning, at the slab.

Villagers began to make guesses on what was in the offing. Some expected the 'Emmellu' to announce a decision of the government on the issue of drought relief, while a few others speculated that the Emmellu would give out the already known 'fodder subsidy' news and there were some who thought that a food for work announcement would be made.

The villagers began to assemble at the slab, much earlier than required; they didn't have any other work at home, barring that of drawing of water, which they had already attended to or assigned to some other member of their family.

At the slab, the men sat in two's and three's, as usual and started a chitchat.

Pagadaiah was the last person to come to the slab and men drew themselves close to him.

"Cousin Pagadaiah, why do you think the Emmellu is coming?" asked a member.

"Uncle Pagadaiah, why have they arranged this meeting?"

"Brother Pagadaiah, do you think some good would come out of this?"

Pagadaiah smiled at these questions and looked at them with his 'big brother' expression, "Time will reveal everything, why this hurry?"

Time passed quickly; but there was no trace of the MLA.

"I have a feeling that something good would come out of this meeting."

"Yes, the drumbeater has announced that there is going to be an important announcement and that thing is bound to be a good one."

There were many in whose opinion something good for the village would issue from the MLA's visit.

"It is not for nothing that the Emmellu comes to our village."

"And it is not often that he comes; after all, he is an Emmellu, and an Emmellu is an Emmellu."

"By the way, Cousin, when was it that he came last, his last visit, I mean?"

"It's difficult to pinpoint the time, but I can say one thing with certainty; it was at the time of my second daughter's second confinement, yes, it was then, I am damn sure about it."

"Oh yes, I get it now; he came three years ago, by your reckoning; yes, exactly three years ago, exactly, not one year less, nor one year more."

"So was it, perhaps, but if you ask me what had brought him to our village, well, I am unable to recollect that."

"Why, he was here seeking our votes, if my memory serves me right, yes, it was for our votes that he came."

"Oh, I get it now, it was at the time of elections; am I right?" The member asked his neighbor.

The neighbor ecstatically laughed and slapped on the back of the member, "Oh my God, you are always right on issues like this, what a memory, what a memory!"

Ignoring the slap, the member affirmed himself, "You may ask me how I have been able to recollect it correctly; here is how I calculated it; at the time of the second confinement of cousin Veerayya's second daughter, my daughter-in-law had a miscarriage for the second time, that's it. That is how I could arrive at the exact time of the visit of the Emmellu."

The neighbor gave the member another good-humored slap and cackled, "Oh God, oh God, the way you remember the things, what a way to remember the events and things by!" The neighbor was ready to give another good-humored slap; but the member had cleverly moved away in time.

Pagadaiah was disgusted at the way the members were talking and when his patience snapped he said to them, "You are very good at recollecting the things, we see that. Now, would you like to come back to the present time or would you like to revel in recollections and corroborations?"

"Why, Cousin Pagadaiah, why are you miffed at it? After all, it was important that we should find out the right time of the last visit of our Emmellu, was it not important?

"Sure, it was important, no doubt about that; go ahead and recollect the times of confinements and miscarriages and the number of times they occurred too; members of the slab would get their memory enriched by your recollections," from a distant corner Kannam said jeeringly.

"Ah, that is Kannam, so you are there, Kannam! Without you there is no spice in any activity at the slab," The neighbor stretched his neck to spot Kannam.

In the mean time somebody saw Nagireddy coming along the northern lane. "Look, Cousin Nagaya is coming; Cousin Nagaya is coming!"

"But, we are waiting for the Emmellu . . ."

Most of the heads turned towards the northern lane.

Pagadaiah fumed at the fellow, "So what? He comes here every alternate day; why are you excited like that?"

Kannam dutifully got up and took a few steps to receive Nagireddy, who amiably placed his hand on his protégé's shoulder.

Kannam dusted the bench for his mentor; after sitting there, Nagireddy surveyed the slab area and said with a smile, "I seem to have come at a very important time; so many villagers have assembled at this odd hour! Is there going to be any public meeting?" he asked Kannam.

Members of the assembly were eager to see some activity and looked from one to the other.

It was Pagadaiah, who started it, "Yes indeed, we are all here for a public meeting; come and deliver a speech."

"My party is not in power; what is there for me to give a speech on? On the contrary it is your party that is in power; so it is appropriate that you give a speech."

Pagadaiah smiled good-humoredly, "Right Sir, then at least, sing a verse from that play 'Kurukshetram'"

Nagireddy too smiled in appreciation and asked Pagadaiah, "Oh yes, I will sing, what is so special about that, but you haven't told me the purpose of this gathering at the slab; pray tell me."

"What is unusual about the gathering at the slab, Nagaya? We assemble here almost every evening and every day, because there is no other work to do."

"Well, there is no secret about it; to tell you the truth the Emmellu Suryanarayana is coming."

The lookout man posted by the Banzardar came running from the west-side alley announcing, "The Emmellu lord-sir is coming, Emmellu lord-sir is coming!"

On hearing that, the Banzardar came out of his bungalow, hurriedly putting on his Nehru shirt and the Gandhi cap.

When they saw the Banzardar coming, all the members stood up and waited.

"Pagadaiah, bring things into order there; ask the people not to sit on the slab; bring some two or three men, let them take the table and the chairs that are there in our verandah and arrange them on the slab; let all the villagers sit in front of the slab; ask someone to sweep it clean, sprinkle water in front of the dais so that dust wouldn't rise. All these things, you have to attend to, Pagadaiah. You are quite experienced in these things, should someone give directions to you? I am really sorry at the way our villagers are conducting themselves!" The Banzardar expressed anguish as a matter of course and asking Pagadaiah to take care of the arrangements on the slab, rushed towards the western alley to receive the VIPs.

And then, Pagadaiah took charge; he asked the men to vacate the slab and the 'chimti' benches and commissioned a man to sweep the place clean; the men from the Banzardar's bungalow came back with the table and chairs, which were duly arranged on the slab. Water was sprinkled on the ground in front of the slab; everything looked trim and neat.

The drone of the vehicle-engine was audible and they waited for the important guests to arrive at the slab.

The sound of the vehicle engine was audible but it remained steady and the same.

Ten minutes . . . twenty minutes . . . half an hour . . . time ticked by; yet the vehicle didn't arrive; the buzz of the engine continued to come from a distance.

Men at the slab did not venture to sit either on the slab or on the side strips; they kept standing in small groups.

Then they heard the sounds of changing gears. In a few moments, the sounds gradually receded and then, they heard them no more.

The lookout man came running from the west lane and broke the news to the waiting men.

"The 'Emmellu' lord-sir and the other lord-sirs went to Kasaram, from where they would go to Molgumadu and the villages in that region. Appaiah Lord-Sir also went away in the jeep."

After giving that message, the lookout kept quiet; there was no further information about the MLA or the meeting or its purpose.

After a spell of dismay the members gradually came back into their familiar mood; they sat on the slab and began to analyze the things in their own way.

Pagadaiah, of course, was a dejected man; all his labor had come to nothing; more than that, he hoped to gain some personal advantage from the programme, though he was not sure about the nature of that advantage.

Kannam was in a hilarious mood; the fiasco of the public meeting cheered him up in an inexplicable way.

"So, the meeting has gone the way the rain had gone! Nothing is lost, because nothing has been gained; when there is no hope, there wouldn't be a disappointment, they say."

"At least, they could've sent a message about the purpose of the Emmellu's visit; they have made us wait this long for nothing. What shall we do now, Pagadaiah?"

Obviously Pagadaiah had no suggestion to offer; so he went ahead with that popular gesture—turning his palm clock-wise and anti-clock-wise.

"Cousin Nagaya, sing for us a verse from that play, Kurukshetram."

"Yes, Brother Nagaya, please sing a verse from the play 'Kurukshetram'; what do you all men say to that?"

"Yes, yes, sing a verse, Cousin Nagaya," There was a chorus of requests.

Other members echoed the same wish and Nagireddy smiled humbly.

They thought it would take some more goading.

Just at that point, Narayanamma came looking for her man; Nagireddy caught sight of her and at once burst into a full-throated rendition of a verse from the mythological play, 'Oh, I haven't ever thought this way, even in a dream!' he also put in a few histrionic gestures into it.

All the members stood spell-bound by Nagireddy's performance and the spontaneity of it.

Narayanamma stood at the corner, staring hypnotized by the sweetness of the voice and the effortless way Nagireddy sang; but, unfortunately for Nagireddy, she was out of sight to him.

Hussainaiah was in a state of rapture; instantly he recalled the offer of two tickets by Nagireddy; he saw himself sitting in front of the stage, then and there itself.

Pagadaiah derived no pleasure from the situation; somehow he felt robbed of the thunder and began to drag his feet in the direction of his hut.

He had not rested for a few moments when the summons came from the Malipatel; so, he had to give up the plan of a snooze.

Going there, he found the Malipatel in a very animated mood, "Come, come, Pagadaiah, the sethsindhi (attendant) was searching for you at the slab. The Banzardar Saab, it seems, asked the lookout to bring you to the end of the west alley; he wanted to take you with him to Kasaram and other villages. When the sethsindi fellow came there he didn't find you."

"Where did I go? I was very much at the slab when the fellow came there. I was there for a pretty long time, listening to that Nagireddy's recital of verses; he has no other work than to keep roaming between his village and ours, idling away the time and spoiling other's time too; 'the braying ass comes to disturb the grazing ass,' they say; it is the same thing with the fellow, and this good-for-nothing Kannam is his sidekick."

The Malipatel was surprised and showed his raised palm, "Stop all that and listen, the MLA Saab would visit our village, maybe, tomorrow. The Panchayat elections are in the offing. The Banzardar Saab wants you to make a survey of the scene and report to him. We must know who are with us in this and who are likely to take a different path. Your job is to find out how many party liners we have and how many there are with the other 'parties'; this is a very delicate job and you must do it unobtrusively, understand?"

Pagadaiah nodded like a disciplined party man.

"This is the message the Banzardar Saab has sent me to be conveyed to you. That's it; now, I am dusting my hands off it; it is you who has to directly deal with the matter, in consultation with 'the lord sir'. Now, you can go and be on the work."

Pagadaiah nodded again and left the Malipatel's house.

'Is there anything for me in this?' he brooded. 'Would the big man ask me to contest in the Panchayat Elections, if so, contest for which post? Is it for the office of Sarpanch or Ward Member? Do I have to spend any money on it; how much could it be? But wherefrom would I get the money . . . ?'

On his way back, he came to the slab again and saw that still some members were there.

Nagireddy was holding the attention of the slab members with 'anecdotes' from his theatre life and the men were listening absorbed.

Pagadaiah went and sat in a corner; one or two among them showed him a place at the centre of the slab but he did not show any enthusiasm to sit there.

'Obviously, he has stopped his narration on seeing me; but what is the thing he has been dealing with', thought Pagadaiah.

Interrupting Pagadaiah's thoughts Nagireddy said, "What is the news, Uncle Pagadaiah?"

"News about what . . . ?"

"About the visit of the MLA; the purpose of the visit, of course,"

"How do I know? I have been here with you all; how do I know?"

Nagireddy smiled to indicate that Pagadaiah was withholding some important news and said, "Considering the access you have to the important men of the village, it doesn't matter where you are. 'If the server is your man it doesn't matter where you sit'." Nagireddy winked to the men close by, spurring them on to note the tricky ways of Pagadaiah.

A few of them nodded and one of them said, "Uncle Pagadaiah is a gentleman and it's quite natural that the village headmen care for his views on important issues."

Nagireddy nodded in agreement and said, "That's how it should be; at the same time they should also care for the opinions of the villagers who hold the same rights as do Pagadaiah and the headmen, what do you say?"

Again a few of them nodded; others were in a fix whether to nod or not.

Nagireddy continued, "When it is an issue affecting the whole village and villagers, it is improper that only a few men take the decision; that is not democracy and we are living in a democratic system. Have I said anything wrong? Tell me, I will correct myself."

"No, no, what you have said is right."

"Yes, yes, Cousin Nagireddy has stated it correctly."

"Cousin Nagireddy always says the right thing."

Pagadaiah felt that Nagireddy was talking in his usual tricky way; 'He is quite tricky, but, let me see through his tricks, for once,' he thought; then, he started a debate, at the same time, taking care to cloak his belligerence, "Nagaya, to tell you the truth, I am not well educated about these things you talk about; what is this 'democracy' you often talk about? Would you please educate me about it?"

Nagireddy chuckled appreciatively at Pagadaiah's foxy stance and kept quiet, mulling over the options—whether to reply or to end the matter with a silent smile.

"Come on, Cousin Nagaya; when he wants to know, tell him what is what; we must give respect to a gentleman and answer his queries, after all," Kannam intervened.

Pagadaiah glowered at Kannam and waited for Nagireddy's response.

'There's no backing out now,' thought Nagireddy and slowly, organizing his ideas, said, "Uncle Pagadaiah, democracy means the way you deal with the problems of a community, in consultation with the public and in accordance with their views. That is the system in practice now, in our country; right, is it clear?"

"Is that possible?"

"Well, that is what our elders thought when they chose that system for our country and prepared a constitution suitable for that ideology."

Pagadaiah nodded like a good boy, "That is very good of course; but tell me one thing Nagaya; do all the members in a community know their problems clearly and supposing that they know, do they all know the solutions to their problems . . . ?

"Second thing; are the interests uniformly the same for the entire community or do different groups have different interests? If interests differ with groups, do they or do they not clash . . . ?

"In the event of a clash, what should be done? If something is done in mitigation of a problem, would all the groups accept the mitigating act . . . ?

"I mean, If there is a solution to the problem of a group, is there any guarantee that that solution would not create a problem to another group or even to a few within the same group? In that case what should be done . . . ?

"Another thing . . ."

"Stop, stop. You say you don't know these things and you come up with so many doubts, Pagadaiah. As regards your first point, I must admit that the answer is 'no'; Leave alone the community; even in a family, all the members do not have a clear idea about the problems of their family; there is no guarantee that the members of the family know the solutions to those problems . . .

"Regarding the second point—the interests are not uniformly the same for the entire community; different groups have different interests and definitely there can be a clash of interests . . .

"In the event of a clash between the interests and the solutions, the government should go by the broader interest of the community and with a foresight. There is no question of a mitigating effort. The best possible solution should be applied firmly and even forcefully, if required . . .

"Finally, care should be taken to see that the solution to a group's problem would not create a problem to another group; if a clash is unavoidable, the government should go by the broader interests of the entire community. However, the members of a community too should show a spirit of understanding, a spirit of accommodation and a spirit of sacrifice; they should always give the interests of the community top priority."

They all heard with rapt attention.

"So, Nagaya, your party seems to share the same views with the Praja party or is it that your party has different views?"

"No, no, no, my party's views are totally different. I have only told about the way the democracy functions in general; my party's ideology is Socialism; it is completely different, completely different . . ."

"In that case, tell us about your party's principles."

Nagireddy said, "It would take an entire day or even more; even then, I might not be able to state all the principles of my party, yes, that is it."

The members saw that the talk fizzled out into an exchange of innocuous generalities from the two peers whose views had always drastically differed, but, today, they didn't appear to be in their elements; it was so uncharacteristic of their dueling nature.

They were disenchanted with the duo and began to fall back into separate small groups to have a more palatable chat.

The next morning, the Banzardar sent for Pagadaiah and Pagadaiah went dutifully and waited in the verandah for the Lord-Sir to come out with some good news.

After Pagadaiah had waited for almost half-an-hour, the Banzardar came out and said, "Pagadaiah, I really don't know when our villagers would change their ways. Yesterday, I went to Kasaram and Molgumadu and saw how prudently the villagers were acting. A spell of drought is sitting heavily on our head and here, all that we do is, assemble on the slab and cry on our plight; even God won't help the inactive wailers. Go and see the men in Kasaram and learn from them how to benefit from the government schemes; almost all the farmers there have availed themselves of the fodder-subsidy scheme. Tell me, has a single farmer drawn the benefit, in our village? Tell me, Pagadaiah, don't just stand there mute; I am asking you a plain yes-or-no question."

"No one has, so far . . ." a dejected Pagadaiah answered, "They cannot be easily goaded into such things; they are like 'mud-eating snakes'. Time and again I told them to shed this attitude and become more purposeful . . ."

"I know, I know, I have heard you telling these things to them on the slab; they are just fated to live like that; I just don't know what we can do about it! . . .

"Anyway, we should not be like that; what do you say?"

After Pagadaiah showed agreement, the Banzardar changed into a pliant mood and said, "I am also feeling the telling effects of the drought like you all; the fodder I have, would last only a few more days and I have decided to apply for the fodder subsidy . . .

"You do one thing for me; go to the Panchayat Samithi Office taking the signed papers from me and apply for the subsidy on my behalf; I will give letters to the officials and the money needed. Get one lorry load of fodder for me. You have to go to Bezwada along with the Samithi officials; there they will help you in the purchase of the fodder and in hiring a lorry; Get a lorry loaded with fodder and come back in the same lorry. It wouldn't take more than three days," and without waiting for any answer from Pagadaiah, he concluded, "Go home, get ready and come here; I will give you the necessary papers and the money."

Pagadaiah waited a while and when the Banzardar did not raise the issue of elections, took the initiative, "Lord-sir, I have made a brief survey at the slab, as bidden by you. The position is not clear; but I have a feeling that a few, only a few of them would follow that Nagireddy,"

"I will listen to all that, later; first, you go home and come prepared to go to the town," said the Banzardar imperatively and went into the house.

Pagadaiah felt a little unhappy and slowly walked back to his hut.

It took Pagadaiah four days to complete the task entrusted to him; two nights he had to spend in that sizzling city, Bezwada; he stayed in a lodge along with three farmers of another village.

It was a crowded city, packed with buildings; roads buzzed with all kinds of vehicles and men; every inch of the city swarmed with people; the roads looked more like canals in flow with men, rickshaws, horse-drawn vehicles and four wheelers—all floating like a tangled mass and then there were the stray animals walking across. On either side of the streets one saw men jostling among themselves to forge ahead of the others-men in hurry, who wouldn't stop to look even if a man had fallen dead!

After midnight, they, his roommates, pushed him into the corridor to recline on a camp cot, while inside the room they spent time playing cards and consuming liquor, supplied by the room boy.

Pagadaiah lay there, cursing his fate and thinking about his hut and his woman.

He wondered whether the place had always been like that and would always be like that!

Two nights and a day later, Pagadaiah went along with the roommates, to the surrounding villages in search of the fodder of their choice.

At all the places he saw a network of canals brimming with water; here and there boats carried men and goods from one bank to the other or along the waterway.

After purchasing the fodder, he sat in the engine cabin of the laden lorry and made good use of a brief stopover at Bezwada, by having a 'darshan' of the deity Kanakadurga in the temple, atop the Indrakeeladri hill; there the Pandava hero, Arjuna had meditated upon Lord Siva and obtained that deadly weapon, the Paasupatha, as per the account of the Mahabharata; a visit to that sacred hill would earn one great merit.

In the temple, Pagadaiah prayed to the Mother to bless and make him the official candidate of the Praja Party for the office of Sarpanch, in the forthcoming elections; he promised to get his head tonsured and worship the deity, in the event of his election as the Sarpanch.

After coming out of the temple, he remembered that he had forgotten to pray for the rains in his region; he pulled his ears in penitence and muttered prayers in atonement.

Pagadaiah was a satisfied man when he started the return journey.

When the lorry arrived in the village, men mobbed Pagadaiah showing their admiration for the venturesome trip he had undertaken; a journey to Bezwada and return to the village with a loaded lorry was no mean achievement!

On the slab, there were Nagireddy, Kannam and Balakoti watching 'the spectacle', bemused.

After giving the papers to the Banzardar and reporting on how he had complied with the instructions given, Pagadaiah went to his hut, took hot water bath and after lunch rested for some time and in the process, caught sleep.

By the time he woke up it was dusk already; so, he prepared to go to the slab; however it took some time to reach the slab.

There the members had already assembled in good number and they were all waiting for 'the most-sought-after' anchorman of the slab.

When he was back on the slab, Pagadaiah expected someone to break news on the local body elections; but, there was no news; they raised a few pertinent queries on his trip.

"Uncle Pagadaiah, you may have seen quite a few places in the eastern country. How is the rainfall there?"

Pagadaiah raised his eyebrows and lifted his hands in expression of wonderment, "Well, well, I must say that, somehow, the God is more merciful to that country and the people there. In fact, people there don't rely on rains as much as we do here. Wherever you go in that country you find water canals, yes, I liked that spectacle, very much indeed; it is really beautiful to see those water canals . . ."

"Even for that, it must rain somewhere in the upper regions," Nagireddy butted in.

"Yes, yes, that is there, the water comes from the reservoir built on the river Krishna . . .

"Yes, that is the thing; there must be some reservoir in the upper regions and it must rain well in the farther regions for the reservoir to collect water; all that is decided by the God, of course. Nothing is in our hands, nothing . . .

"And, there is another interesting thing; at some places there, scarcity of water is not the problem, it is the excess of water that is the problem; they really have a tough time disposing of the unwanted excess of water."

Lingaiah who came to the slab to know the news about the eastern country gave a wry laugh and observed, "Now, what do you say to that! Wonder of the God, that is what I would say. These are the things that are the wonders of the God. Strive for years, labor for years, yet, you wouldn't know the why and how of these things!"

197

Nagireddy grunted his disapproval, "What is so mysterious about it? It depends on the geography of the place, the availability or otherwise of the water; that's all."

Lingaiah cast a look of abhorrence at Nagireddy and conceded the point philosophically, "It's a mystery to ignorant men like me; to the wise like you, everything is clear, everything . . ." saying so, he slowly got down the 'chimti' bench and began to walk away, with a look of hurt writ large on his face.

Nagireddy realized his mistake and hurriedly went to the walking old man, "Uncle, please don't mistake me, I said in a casual way; please don't go away like that, come, come," he tried to lead Lingaiah back to the slab.

The old man gave a pale smile and said, "What is there to mistake you? I am going home; I have to attend to some important work. Leave me and go there to carry on the talk; you are all young and the world is yours!" Lingaiah slowly walked away.

Before anyone could comment, Nagireddy too left the slab, feeling sorry for what had happened.

Most of them at the slab were unhappy at the way things had gone; but, no one looked inclined to make it an issue and so they fell back into their chitchat.

"Uncle Pagadaiah how is the paddy crop there?"

"Paddy, you ask me about the paddy crop there, after all that I have told you? Paddy there is like a healthy, mature, young lady who has just 'missed her month'!" Pagadaiah broke into guffaw, "Maybe, I have put it clumsily, but that is exactly how I felt when I saw the paddy fields there; yes. Please don't be angry with me for that." He joined his palms to them all, seeking their pardon dramatically.

"No, no, you have put it rightly; that sounds nice, in fact; you have said that well."

"Can we and our fields ever attain to that state?" Hulakki wondered aloud, looking up.

"Why not, if you have a river that supplies water like that river Krishna there and if somebody constructs a bund across that river and digs canals as required, then, we can definitely attain to that state."

"Oh God, is that our wise Bademaya talking? I am unable to believe; let somebody pinch me," Gopaya showed his astonishment.

"Come here, come nearer, I will pinch you as much as you want," Retorted Bademaya.

Gopaya laughed and moved away.

"Now, let us stop this chitchat and come to useful talk," Naraiah intervened, "What Bademaya has said merits some serious consideration, really; so, let us think what we can do about it; what do you say, Cousin Pagadaiah?"

Kannam who had come back in the meantime, intervened in the debate, "The first thing that we should do is to get a river to our place, and Bademaya would give us a plan for that," he looked at Bademaya in mock seriousness.

Bademaya got up, whipped his shoulder cloth and, in earnest seriousness, said, "We can do anything that is necessary for the village, but, with a fellow like that in our midst, nothing can be done, I tell you, yes, nothing can be done, with that fellow around."

"That fellow talks like that only; he thinks it is fun to talk like that; but you see, there is an instance of a man bringing a river to his place with the power of penance; we have all heard about the great Bhagiratha who brought the celestial river Ganga to the earth by praying to Lord Siva; Siva was so pleased with the penance of his votary that he agreed to receive the mighty river descending from the Heaven, in his matted hair and then release it to the earth . . ."

Balakoti who was listening keenly, said, "Who can you bring a river for us; there are no Bhagirathas now. If a rivulet will do, we have one already."

At that, all the heads turned towards Balakoti.

A septuagenarian who was there, remarked, "That will do, that will do; all the flowing streams are holy and all heaps of stones are sacred; even a river was a rivulet once and a rivulet can grow into a river, 'what is there'!"

All the heads, then, turned to the old man and nodded in approval.

Promptly, Bademaya came to the centre, "When I said the same thing three days back, all the people laughed at me, this Pagadaiah in particular. Some men think intelligence is their property."

"Agreed, agreed, yours was definitely a clever plan, if you had really announced that three days back."

"'Three days' means—not exactly three days; maybe, it was four or five days back, but I had suggested that."

"Leave aside the silly things; this is a really good idea; let us see how we can proceed with this idea."

"Let us prepare a 'mahjar' (petition), collect the signatures of the villagers and submit it to the government; something good may come out of it, who knows!"

"Oh my God, a mahjar," Balakoti said beating his breast.

"Yes, we can do that; a mahjar to the government requesting for the construction of a bund across the rivulet . . ."

"Good idea, good idea!"

"But, who will prepare the mahjar in the correct way?"

"Pagadaiah can do it; he knows all such things quite well," Kannam suggested mischievously.

Pagadaiah looked keenly at Kannam, "If I can do it, you can also do it, because we both have studied in the same school and under the same teacher and our qualifications are the same; what do you say?"

"Now, you are at it again; keep quiet for some time and let us work upon the idea."

"The grandson of Naraiah is here in the village on vacation; let us go and ask the boy to prepare this mahjar for us; what do you say, Uncle?"

"Yes, that's a good idea, but who'll explain the matter to that boy?"

"Why, Pagadaiah can do that, can't you, Uncle?"

Pagadaiah didn't respond to it; he sat lost in deep thought.

"What, Uncle Pagadaiah, you can tell the boy how to prepare the mahjar, can't you?"

"Yes, yes, he can; there's no need to ask; he can do that."

Finally Pagadaiah answered, "These things can be done well only by educated men; a mahjar is not a child's play; further, the issue has to be debated first and the views of all the villagers should be taken; as Nagireddy has said, we are in a democratic country."

The members thought that Pagadaiah was right and Naraiah voiced the same opinion, "What Cousin Pagadaiah has said is absolutely right; nothing should be done in a hurry in a democratic society."

"They also say 'if we delay, even nectar becomes poison'; when things are clear, there is no point in delaying the issue."

"Now, stop quoting these contradicting adages; we have to consider what is good for us all and go by that."

Most of the heads moved in assent.

At that point, Nagireddy returned to the slab; he went to Kannam and sat by his side; "What is happening here?" He asked.

"The same old thing; they want to build a bund on the rivulet."

"Who is going to build?"

"Who else can do it? The government of course, it is only the government that can do it."

"Then . . . ?"

"They want the government to take up that work of building a bund on the rivulet, so that we can have water for us and our fields."

"That is not a correct idea; instead, it is better to get that breach of the tank filled; that way a bigger source of water, the Vindhyadramma tank can be revived; it would irrigate many more acres, many more acres of land."

"It's impossible to fill that breach," Pagadaiah intervened, "Even if our grandfathers come back to life, that breach cannot be filled."

"That is a perverse talk; science has vastly improved, many machines have been invented, so much so that all kinds of breaches however difficult they might appear to be, can be filled these days," Nagireddy said, "So, it would be a better idea to request the government to fill that breach and restore the tank to its full capacity, rather than working on that petty rivulet, which is nothing but a product of the tank; further, the tank is a very big one and would serve many villages."

Pagadaiah immediately intervened, "The problem is not with the number of villages; the basic problem is that it is an accursed tank and any plan to revive it is fraught with risks; let us not do something that will bring disaster on the village. We have to be very careful."

Nagireddy was astonished, "What do you mean by saying 'it is an accursed tank and reviving it is risky,'? Some party interested in the bed land of the tank has spread that superstitious story; most of us know that, don't we? What I say is that we must go by the consideration of its usefulness to greater number of farmers."

Pagadaiah tensely replied, making that asserting gesture, "Our village would go only for a bund on the rivulet, not for the filling of the breach; so there is no reference to the number of farmers or villages."

Nagireddy's face became red with anger, "That is irresponsible talk; my village is located downwards; wouldn't you take into consideration the adjacent villages."

Pagadaiah looked insolent as he said, "But our village wants to construct a bund across the rivulet only. How can a reservoir, built on a small rivulet, irrigate far off lands; you have to find your own source of irrigation."

Suddenly, the atmosphere became tense; men on the slab were baffled by this sudden and unexpected turn; but no one made an effort to straighten out the thing.

Pagadaiah got down from the slab; addressing none in particular, he said, "Tomorrow we will go to Naraiah's grandson for the drafting of the mahjar; the issue is plain and simple; we will submit a petition to the government for the construction of a bund on the rivulet; that would give us plenty of water, for us, for our livestock and for our fields. That is final."

Kannam did not take kindly to the stand taken by Pagadaiah; he sat watching and listening, with a morose expression on his face.

"Our slab has become a hangout for rootless people; it is time we checked this nuisance," Another blow came from Pagadaiah, stunning them all.

Unable to take it further, Kannam went closer to Pagadaiah and tried to mollify him, "Why Uncle Pagadaiah, why do you utter things like that? Cousin Nagaya hasn't said anything wrong; his village aspiring for the water of Vindhyadramma tank is not unreasonable, after all; it's also in the hamlet of our village, that village of his."

"That is for revenue collection; don't mix up the things and don't try to side 'him' against your own villagers," Pagadaiah cut short the talk.

Kannam was nonplussed and sat pale-faced.

Nagireddy was shocked into silence and so were many on the slab, but none of them opened their mouths to sober up the things.

Nagireddy kept his cool for a while; he observed the silence that prevailed at the slab, looked at the faces of the members and though his face appeared to have 'become smaller', he said in a low, but, firm voice, "The matter is not the exclusive concern of your village; though the Panchayat goes by the name of your village; there are three villages in this 'panchayat' and hamlet and my village is one of the three. If the breach is filled and the tank comes alive, my villagers also would stand to benefit by that; so, it is as much my business as it is yours; we want not a bund across the rivulet but a revival of the tank itself."

The heaviness of Nagireddy's breath was audible to the nearby members.

At that point efforts were made at placation, "Don't take it seriously, Cousin Nagaya; after all, what the government would do to it, no one knows. There's no guarantee that the plan would work; so, don't take it to heart . . ."

"It's not the question of taking it easy or taking it to heart; it is the manner of talking of some people, on a matter which is common and is of such a grave nature," Said Nagireddy.

Meanwhile, Pagadaiah had time to mull over his conduct in the proceedings and began to see things in a clearer perspective; it made him feel mortified and he couldn't raise his head weighed down in that vivid remembrance of what he had said in the heat of argument; it had never happened earlier with him; he smiled nervously and apologized, "I have acted impolitely, Nagaya; I am ashamed of it; please forget it. Think that your elder brother had foolishly talked and annoyed you; pardon your elder brother . . ."

Nagireddy waved his arm brusquely and left the place; Kannam followed him.

Members at the slab sat like dumb witnesses to the proceedings that had gone wrong right from the beginning.

Walking home, Pagadaiah recalled the happenings at the slab. 'It was a bad time; such a rush of blood he had never experienced earlier. It was dusk, the time the malevolent spirits set out on their wanderings, looking to catch unwary men by their tongue to whirl them into such indiscretions. It happened not only with him but Nagireddy too had acted in a bizarre way!'

Pagadaiah remembered that it was a long time since he had offered a bird to the deity Muthyalamma; 'Right tomorrow, I will go and offer a bird to the Mother.'

Next day, Pagadaiah woke up early, took head-bath, wore the 'spun' panche and bade his wife to get ready in the same way; when she complied, he insisted on her walking barefoot to the shrine of Mother Muthyalamma.

Men and women, still busy with chores, looked at this early morning spectacle in wide wonder.

Rattamma, in blood red sari, with her disheveled hair falling all over her breast and a coin-size vermillion mark on her forehead, looked every inch a village deity!

At the bidding of her man, Rattamma washed the stone slabs of the shrine, applied the red vermillion to the deity and to the slabs, after which, Pagadaiah came forth with the cock in one hand and knife in the other.

Then, as Rattamma watched with trepidation, her man severed the head of the bird from its body; the headless body danced in convulsive loops in the air for a few moments in front of the deity and then fell down, still.

Pagadaiah chanted some propitiatory hymns, picked up through rote learning; he looked a man possessed.

The ritual over, the couple went back to their hut and just at that time, a call came from the house of the Banzardar.

Pagadaiah felt exhilarated; this was it, a reward for the devotion he had shown; but could it be something else— some routine message from the Banzardar for some labor that usually went unrequited?

206

Walking to the house of the Banzardar, Pagadaiah thought, 'anything is possible; there is no need to be ecstatic about it.'

The Banzardar was waiting; he looked restless and the moment he saw Pagadaiah he said complainingly, "Come, come, Pagadaiah, you are the only man in this village with any sense of responsibility; now I realize why the Priest-Sir relies so much on you on festival days . . ."

Pagadaiah smiled modestly, "What is the matter, Lord-sir?" He asked.

"Pagadaiah, the matter is quite important; MLA Suryanarayana garu is coming today; he will be here by 10 O'clock and will stay barely for an hour; there would be a public meeting; I have asked the drum beater to announce in the village asking the public to assemble at the slab for the meeting . . .

"Your part of the work is to get the place spruced up for the event; the lord sir is likely to make some important announcement. That is the thing; so go and see to it; there isn't much time."

Pagadaiah nodded and set out on the work, his imagination once again active.

At the slab, he commissioned a boy to call up some men of his choice, to the slab.

He arranged, on the platform of the slab, a table and four chairs as instructed by the Banzardar.

The slab was ready for the event in a short time.

Soon a good number of men gathered.

Pagadaiah also asked the assembled men to sit on the ground, in front of the dais, in readiness for the meeting; but they preferred to stand around the slab, till the 'Emmellu' and party came.

Though he was pleased with the result of his work, the unwanted presence of Kannam and his comrades at a corner point irked Pagadaiah.

Time passed and it was well beyond ten o'clock.

The gathering of men became restive; every five minutes, there was somebody enquiring about the arrival of the Emmellu; it appeared to Pagadaiah that the men were just staying to go rather than going to stay for the meeting.

The lord-sir was inside his bungalow and Pagadaiah could not venture to go and bother him about the inordinate delay and its effect on the men at the slab.

As he stood nonplussed thus, Pagadaiah saw an urchin run in to the slab and tell a member something in the ear; the member in turn confided it to his neighbor and it went on like that for some time.

Then, one after another in quick succession, they began to walk briskly towards the west street; after a while the walk became a run and Pagadaiah stood confounded.

'Oh, this Emmellu!' muttered Pagadaiah in anguish and as he cast his eye over the path leading to the south lane, he found the lookout running fast; 'to convey the news of the arrival of the guests, perhaps' he thought.

By the time the lookout had reached the venue, the slab was empty; Pagadaiah stood there alone, like a palm tree in a desert stretch.

Pagadaiah directed the lookout man to the house of the Banzardar and began to wonder about that mysterious piece of news that had driven the men from the slab to wherever they went; he too felt an itch to go and see what it was; but he could not abandon his post, especially, in his situation.

The Banzardar came out to the gate and watched the slab in wonder, "Pagadaiah, where have they all gone, they were all here a little while back?" he enquired and in added, in haste, "I am going to receive them; meanwhile send somebody to collect men or be on the job, yourself; quick we don't have much time," The Banzardar was almost running, holding his cap in-tact.

In a few minutes the lookout came running to the slab, to announce that the Banzardar and the Emmellu drove away to Kasaram and that they would come back to hold the public meeting in the afternoon.

Pagadaiah was disgusted at the way the Emmellu took the villagers for granted, but, he knew that there was nothing that he could do.

Wearily he too began to walk towards the western lane, wondering what he would see there.

When he reached the place he found a small but closely packed group; men stood behind men and the last man stood on his toes in an effort to catch sight of what was there in front of them.

Pagadaiah went and pulled Balakoti by the shoulder, saying, "Where and what is there, let me see?"

Balakoti pulled away, affording Pagadaiah a comfortable view and with a chuckle said, "It is 'Errodu' there, the runaway 'Errodu' has come back."

For once, Pagadaiah forgot his new responsibility, stretched his neck and widened his eyes to look at the neatly dressed fellow sitting in the midst of the jostling men.

Red Lad looked at the men in rotation and answered a few of their questions in monosyllables and kept smiling all the time; obviously he was enjoying the excitement his return had created.

Pagadaiah went speechless and stood gaping for a few moments—'a long time' for some one of his stature; he couldn't come up with any explanation on the event; he wondered and wondered at what he saw—Red Lad in a resplendent dress and a military cap with a cockade, looking awe-inspiring.

Someone tugged at him; looking back he found the domestic of the Banzardar's house; "Malipatel Lord-Sir wants you to come to the slab immediately," said the man.

Pagadaiah came to senses and addressed the clamoring men, "Come on; let us all go to the slab. The lord-sir is calling us all; maybe, the Emmellu and others have come."

The men in the gathering were in no mood to go back to the slab.

"What would the Emmellu say in the meeting?" Someone asked.

"What for the Emmellu has come?" Another asked.

"The Emmellu can wait; it is we who have made him the Emmellu."

"What is there for us in the meeting?"

Everyone was in a questioning mood.

Meanwhile the sethsindi came, "Patwari saab and Malipatel saab—all are there at the slab. They want every one of you to come to the slab," He said laconically, turned back and went away stiffly.

Pagadaiah looked at the Red Lad closely once more and reluctantly set out for the slab.

On the way he found Rosaiah lumbering to see the Red Lad; he gave Pagadaiah an amiable smile and moved on, breaking wind once or twice as usual, but, nobody taking notice of it for a change.

The message given by the sethsindhi worked and a moderate crowd collected at the slab, to wait for the Emmellu.

Finally, the MLA came.

There were quite a few in the retinue of the Emmellu; a few more chairs were put on the dais and all were seated and the meeting commenced.

After the initial address by the Banzardar, the legislator took over and as he rose to speak the Banzardar promptly garlanded him and the people clapped as guided by Pagadaiah.

"My dear brothers and sisters and mothers and uncles of my assembly constituency,

"I proudly stand before you all, to announce and inaugurate a very important programme being launched by my party in the service of this village and some other villages along the way . . .

"It is the bounden responsibility of a democratic government to take care of its people in times of crisis like this; for the last three years, drought conditions have been prevailing in this region and some other regions also; the nature has not been kind to us; so, we had started this food-for-work scheme three years ago and this is the third year of the scheme; I am proud to say that the programme is successfully running and I hope we will continue this programme in future too. I call upon you to benefit by it and remember that our party always has the interests of the people at the top of its agenda . . .

"I once again request you to keep in mind the fact that it is the Praja Party that takes care of the people and not the other parties. Other parties come to you only for votes and to capture power through your votes; then, they will forget you and would busy themselves with self-enrichment schemes . . .

"The food-for-work scheme is open to the ladies also and they can benefit from it for six days in a week on par with men. However, the wages for the ladies are different from the wages for the men; the supervisors of the work would provide you all those details . . .

"Therefore, my dear brothers and sisters and mothers and uncles, remember that you should all vote for the Praja

Party whenever there are elections and whatever elections they are—be they assembly elections, be they the elections to the Parliament or be they the Panchayat elections. If you want help from the government in difficult times you have to vote for the Praja Party, Jai Praja Party, Jai—Jai Praja Party . . ."

Pagadaiah stood up and guided the people by starting the claps.

After that 'inspired speech' by the legislator, the gathering began to drift; so the scheduled speech by the president of the function, the Banzardar, could not be delivered and he was happy for it and the people seemed happier.

Soon the men were on their trot once again in the direction of the western sector of the village.

Pagadaiah too felt the pull of the west street; but the lord sir wanted him in his train; so, he reluctantly followed the lord-sir.

In the western part of the village, the scene was livelier.

There was a big gathering in front of the thatched house of Errodu and the men in their effort to gain a better view of what lay ahead were getting into a state of skirmish.

At the centre of the encircling group of men, sat the Red Lad; true to his name the lad was strikingly red and in that uniform he wore, he looked quite impressive; the cap and the cockade in it, added to the glitter; his occasional smiling look panned over the assembly of men, lending to the situation an element of drama.

There were many men there and behind them some more; those who could not gain a clear picture were clucking their tongues over their plight; soon there was a recital of clucking.

There were women too, who came to enjoy the event that had suddenly cropped up.

"They might as well have opened it to tickets!" Someone said, but the remark went unappreciated.

Mme Pullamma's man was close by to the gathering and he tried to impose order by poking a stick at the foot of the men and gesturing to them to sit or stand in a line.

The picture of Mme Pullamma's man, with his voluntarily assumed antics, was a source of mirth to the members of the monkey brigade and they grabbed it as a bonus; needless to say, they had been the first to arrive at the show of Errodu.

Then Pagadaiah came to the place and as he saw it, there appeared little chance of his making it to the centre of the scene, but his ardent adherents were able to push him to the centre.

The Red Lad chuckled and greeted Pagadaiah, "Uncle Pagadaiah, how are you?"

Pagadaiah answered with a smile and said, "How are you Laddie? Where did you go from here and where have you been all these days?"

The Red Lad burst into laughter and replied, "I will tell you the entire story, Uncle Pagadaiah; there is plenty of time for that."

The members of the monkey brigade paid no heed to what the elders were saying; the inquiries and the answers meant nothing to them; they just sat there, viewing, in bliss, the spectacle that was right in front of them—the Red Lad in that gorgeous attire and that sparkling red cockade in particular! They sat enjoying the scene.

'Why are these children here? It is an event for 'adults only, after all,' some thought; but who could command them to go away? In fact, they were afraid of them.

Ladies too were there, in the crowd.

Using his baton, Pullamma's man imposed order there and provided separate place for ladies.

Ladies looked closely at the Red Lad, using their full eyesight, so to say. The statue-like figure of Errodu in dark green uniform, with that close-cut crop of hair, feet housed in majestic looking black leather shoes, a baton with a silver knob in hand, a wrist watch and those awe-inspiring goggles sent them into gasps of excitement, so much that they almost wondered aloud saying, 'Oh my . . . It has never struck me that men can be so devastatingly handsome, handsome indeed . . . !'

Bhagyam and her man surveyed the scene and became tense as the crowd kept swelling; no one seemed to be in a mood to quit the scene.

Bhagyam looked anxiously at her man, but he too seemed to have no idea.

Pullamma's man, who had taken on his shoulders the management of the event, was so much overpowered by the 'gate-crashing crowd' that in his jittery imagination he began to 'see himself in the role of the manager of a repertory and was thinking of arranging a second show!'

Who caused the situation to become unwieldy and who could bring things into normal and manageable state, nobody could say.

At that stage, Bhagyam consulted her close relations over the next step and after a few minutes came back to say to the crowd, "Now, that's enough; you have all seen whatever there is to see; we have things to do and plans to make; so, will you all go away please, all of you . . ."

As she repeated the wish a second time, men and women reluctantly began to leave and in half-an-hour, the Red Lad and the members of his family had the entire yard for themselves.

However, members of the monkey brigade settled at the fence, watching from a distance.

Pagadaiah sat for some time, hoping to gather some facts about Errodu's story, but, his effort came to nothing, since Bhagyam cleverly saw him off with, "Uncle Pagadaiah, come after the lamps are lit; we want to sort out a few things on the next course of action."

On his way back, Pagadaiah's eyes widened as he saw the slab full with men; 'Where would they go with that thirst not slaked!' he mused, with a smile.

A few enterprising members of the slab were collecting bits and pieces of information, from the boys, running between the slab and Errodu's place as couriers.

"I went to see the 'food-for-work' road, when I saw a 'biscole' (bicycle) coming towards the alley; there were two men on the 'biscole'."

"Two men . . . ? Then . . . ?"

"When the 'biscole' came closer, I saw that the one who was pedaling was this Errodu; he was attired in a 'direes' (uniform dress). There was another on the backseat; he was in plain clothes. After reaching the alley Errodu got down and gave the 'biscole' and some money to the other man; then that man went away."

"Who was that man?"

"Leave it, that's not important . . .'

"So, Errodu wouldn't walk the distance from the 'tason' (station)! He would rent a 'biscole' to come back to his hut; looks like, he is riding on luck!"

"What, what, you saw Errodu riding the 'biscole' and with two of them on it!"

"Oh yes, and for some time, Errodu was using only one hand! Yes, I saw clearly, because in the other hand he held a 'chiglet' (cigarette); Errodu was smoking a 'chiglet', while riding the biscole!"

That piece of news astonished most of them. 'Errodu riding a 'biscole' that carried two men . . . ', 'Errodu maneuvering the 'biscole' with a single hand . . . ', 'Errodu smoking a 'chiglet',', 'Errodu returning home after a big gap of time . . .' 'Errodu who had been living away from home for such a long time, coming back in style in this manner . . . !' So many heroics accomplished by the same Errodu who had run away 'that night' from the nuptial chamber!

So, many wondrous points of fact and doubt swarmed in the minds of men on the slab and kept whirring about, like wasps.

"No one had recognized him until I pointed out to them; I ran to the slab immediately and broke the news to you when you were busy with that Emmellu's meeting."

The slab members nodded to the boy docilely.

Pagadaiah, who had been listening too, nodded his head and heard someone remark about the boy—informant, "This lad would go far, very far . . . !"

The boy repeated to the latecomers all that he had told the others and then after a pee-break, the slab went into a lengthy discussion on the Errodu-story.

The questions that engaged the minds of the members of the slab, were; 'Why had Errodu run away that night?'., 'Where was Errodu these two years?'., 'Has Errodu become rich and if the answer is yes, how did he become rich, and rich by how much . . . ?'

However, more questions came from Mme Pullamma's man who had presently run back to the slab in a short break—'What would happen now?', 'Will there be a patch-up between that girl and Errodu?', 'Would Errodu come out successful in the forthcoming 'test' that is inevitable?'

The slab held a long session and several compact committees studied in depth, the different aspects of the case of Errodu, before, during and after the discussion

A few hours later,

In the western sector of the village, Errodu, his sister and brother-in-law and the special invitee, Mme. Pullamma's man were deeply engaged in a binge of boozing, chewing pieces of serious debate in between.

By the time Pagadaiah went home, it was very late in the night; the oil lamp was not alight and he groped his way to the cot in the hut, but when he lowered himself on to the bed, he found it empty.

The mother-in-law scented the arrival of Pagadaiah and came asking, "Shall I bring you food?"

"Why not, but, where is 'she'?" Pagadaiah asked.

"Rattamma is asleep in the yard; she is suffering from an acute headache, has just gone to bed," the mother-in-law explained.

"I am not hungry; you may go; send your daughter here," Pagadaiah said dismissively.

The mother-in-law hovered there for some time and went out.

Pagadaiah waited for his wife for some time; the mother was exhorting her daughter to join her man; he was able to hear that and also the whimper of the daughter.

'Why this drama again, especially after she had spent a few nights silently with me?' thought Pagadaiah and couldn't come to any convincing explanation.

He began to compare his plight with that of Errodu; 'Who is the luckier, between the two of us?' he started wondering, as he tossed in bed.

The members of the slab came to know the details of 'the food for work' scheme from those who had joined the line of laborers; it was a 'food for work' programme and the stress was more on 'food' than work and the spot payment of wages made it an interesting proposition.

Therefore, most of the slab members decided to wake up in time next morning to join the line.

As the food-for-work programme progressed many of the villagers, ladies included, joined it.

In the agricultural fields the failure of rains caused wide and deep breaches; they looked like the crying mouths of infants; up above, the sky too looked like a huge mouth of a monster gaping lazily.

King Virata and Muthyalamma were both busy, Virata playing dice and Muthyalamma combing the nits out.

Priest sir Suraiah found no other propitiatory ritual in his stock list.

The townsman, who had taken up the contract of 'the food for work' programme, was himself an enterprising man and the relationship he bore to 'the Emmellu' made him more enterprising.

He scrupulously distributed the wages and on the third day of the work, his own brother-in-law joined in the management of the work and he showed himself to be no less enterprising.

'The brother-in-law' of the 'brother-in-law' opened a liquor store near the entry point of the alley and on the fourth day after the opening of the store, credit facility was extended to all the 'food and drink-for-work' workers and the onlookers of the work too.

The Emmellu paid unobtrusive visits to the work-spot to gain firsthand information on the progress of 'the work' on the road and off-the road.

In the village,

The story of Errodu gradually began to acquire the glamour of a tale of the Knight-errant; boys shared with the others the anecdotes they had collected; some of them had invented a few, too.

According to one, Errodu joined the army; a boy recounted how Errodu had faced a dozen enemy soldiers on the battlefield; another told how Errodu had displayed his gutsiness when his fellow soldiers were in a state of panic; how Errodu raged on the battlefield shooting down an enemy aircraft; then, there was this piece which told how Errodu had saved a lady's honor, risking his life, by taking on a group of the enemy soldiers.

In the eyes of the boys, who circulated the anecdotes, Errodu had become a hero and the listeners on the slab could not conjure up the image of the man without a halo behind the head.

On the slab, members who had been catnapping at the corner points woke up with a start even at the mention of 'Errodu' and huddled round the member that had uttered it.

However, Pagadaiah remained unconvinced about the factuality of the stories and was in no mood to generously accommodate Errodu in the list of the heroes of his tales. 'The credibility of the accounts has to be established first,' his thought reasoned. 'But how long it would take to gain a proof and from what source would the proof come?' was the question that refused to disappear.

'Let it take its own time; after all, the Pandava Brothers did not become heroes overnight!' Pagadaiah reasoned.

Errodu's sister and company finally decided to take the initiative and rearrange the event of 'the first night'; they sent a negotiator to the girl's parents.

At that end, the parents of the girl were just waiting for the call; they had already come to know of the return of the Red Lad; a few of the 'heroics' of the Lad had reached their village too and that boosted the morale of the girl's parents.

'Finally, God has relented and has eased the situation for us', a key-member of the girl's party thought as the party received the emissary.

The negotiations were kept to the minimum and the priest fixed an auspicious time for the function.

There was nothing private or confidential about these proceedings; reports of the things quickly reached the slab and members discussed the matter promptly and thoroughly with alacrity as soon as the reports came.

An interesting aside to the discussion of the issue was that the members polarized in the prediction of the Red Lad's chances of success in the test; some hopefully predicted that the Lad would emerge a winner; some guessed that it would again end up the way the earlier events had ended for the Lad; a third party felt that the element of suspense inherent in the issue was of greater value than the nature of the outcome of it, and that the suspense had to be savored with relish, rather than bother with predictions on the result. 'Ignore the other things; after all, such spicy issues are very few and far between in occurrence; we are lucky to have one such in our lifetime and we will have something of interest to relate to our grandchildren!' the Third Party mused.

Pagadaiah's perspective, as usual, was different. By their very nature, the deliberative bodies or even the issues which called forth deliberation, bred divergence of opinion; one could not expect all the members to think alike. 'That is the beauty or ugliness of the human drama. Divergence is only in respect of thought; when it came to inclination, all of them or most of them sympathized with the Red Lad and wanted him to emerge a winner; as usual there were some who wanted the Lad to fail, thus affording a prolongation of the drama for them?'

The preparations for the trial were made in such a way that the matter no longer appeared to be a family affair; they all leant a hand as if it was a community event. For all the men it was as though the event was a test of their own essence, not just of the Red Lad.

The priest suggested a change of the venue and a few came forward and offered to arrange it in their own dwelling, since the priest had said that the place where the event was held, would be sanctified.

Once again Mme Pullamma's man played a visible role in the decoration of the place; members at the slab wondered whether he had been commissioned for the work or obtained permission to play that role!

The priest asserted that 'this time it would go well', because he had calculated and fixed everything, according to the calendar and 'vaastu'.

Midnight was fixed as the auspicious time for the event.

At the slab, time dragged on for the members.

"Oh, these priests are all alike; the time they fix for these events is always odd!" one member remarked.

"Maybe it looks odd to you, but it serves a purpose," Gopaya explained, "The waiting makes the event more alluring!"

"Oh, is that so? Funny, it didn't strike me!"

"Whether odd or not, whether it serves a purpose or not, it is immaterial; but one thing is there, it sure discomforts us, the timing of the event I mean."

"Yes, yes . . ." many agreed on that point.

They had to pass the time. Pagadaiah was there on the slab, but for a surprising change, nobody asked for a tale. For once, to them, reality seemed to hold greater interest than fiction.

They broke into small teams and started sharing anecdotes.

From the west street, the music played by the hired brass band stopped and at that, the slab became tense.

"Why has the band stopped?"

"Maybe the time has arrived."

There was silence and the silence germinated weird imagination and guess; they saw things happening—men running, Errodu escaping once again through that hole in the roof, the girl coming out of the house, crying; the girl running, her disheveled hair on her face; her mother holding the daughter to her bosom and all of them crying; some men chasing a man, the man turning out to be the priest, the priest running for life . . . Oh God, how funny and interesting could it be if only the imaginations came true . . . !

Presently a member, who had sneaked to the venue of the event, came back and they closed in on him, suffocating him with questions, their eyes bulging, and their ears taut.

The man wriggled out of the huddle, sat on the 'chimti' bench and said with a drawl, "There, all of them are asleep; Mme Pullamma's man is sleeping on the bare ground and his snoring is sounding like the growl of a tiger . . ."

"But, what does all that mean; I don't understand it."

"It means what it means; now, enough of it, I am going home; if you ask me I will advise you all to go home and

222

have a good sleep; tomorrow morning we will all come to know about the happenings, anyway."

They were not impressed with the advice and stuck to the slab.

Pagadaiah sat alone in a corner and brooded-'There is something in this series of events that holds a key to the matter,' he mused, 'what could that be?"

From a corner of the slab, Hulakki slowly walked up to Pagadaiah and said in a hushed up tone, "Pagudaya, what do you think of the matter?"

Pagadaiah was astonished to find the man, "Uncle Hulakki, you here still? Have you been here, all the time? But, why are you still here, Uncle Hulakki? You should have gone home long back; you have seen plenty of these things in your life. No, you go home, Uncle Hulakki; come, I will take you home," Pagadaiah gripped the old man's arm.

Hulakki loosened the grip on his arm and said in a firm voice, "Of course, I will go home, I will go home; but I want to tell you one thing," he looked right and left to check whether the place was safe.

Pagadaiah was astonished further, 'Maybe, the old man knows a thing or two!' he thought.

Hulakki set out from the chimti bench and lightly tugged at the arm of Pagadaiah, 'Come, Pagudaya, I have something to tell you," he led the way in the direction of the alley.

Pagadaiah followed the man, 'the old fellow is acting strange,' he thought, even as he walked with the man towards the thicket in the alley.

Hulakki saw two men coming to join and stopped till they met him, "Where do you think we are going? Pagudaya is taking me home; it's nothing more than that; now, you go back to the slab," he waved his hand.

They stood there for some time and walked back, 'Strange fellow, this old man!' the two men thought.

Relieved at that, Hulakki firmly held the arm of 'Pagudaya' and led him away from the alley, into the lane that led to his house.

Once they were at a safe distance from the members, Hulakki opened up, "Pagudaya, there is something the matter with this affair; you cannot find fault with Red Lad for running away, the first time. He had done the right thing then; even now, he should do the same thing. Any other fellow in his right senses would've done the same thing."

"What are you saying, Uncle Hulakki?" Pagadaiah asked in wonder, "What do you mean by this thing you are saying?"

The old man gave an enigmatic smile, "Come, I will tell you everything, but not here; at my home" and he led 'Pagudaya' almost to his house.

But, Hulakki couldn't wait; stopping short of his house, Hulakki began to talk in a hushed up voice, revealing to Pagadaiah some new facts on the case.

Pagadaiah stood aghast when the old man opened up and laid the things bare.

At the slab, the departure of Pagadaiah along with Hulakki had intrigued the members; their faces began to wear a quizzical look; in a while they began to leave the slab, one by one and in a short while, the slab became empty barring two or three youngsters who were soundly asleep.

The next morning, the slab members were surprised by the latest news from the hut in the west street, where they had gone.

A few men from the town had come in a jeep and asked for Errodu. First, they went to the house of the Police Patel, were closeted with him for a few minutes and then drove to the dwelling of Errodu.

The parents of Errodu were told tersely that the lad had secured a job as a domestic in the house of a retired army officer, two years ago, and then, about a fortnight back, had run away from his post, without obtaining the master's permission.

When asked about the fate of the lad, they told the parents that it would be decided by the military officer in a way that fitted with the military officer's establishment; they could not say how long the completion of the formalities would take or whether the parents would be kept informed, and finally, whether the lad would be free to return to his village.

The men went to the house of 'the event', in the west street.

They saw the wailing parents of the lad and the girl; the girl looked a little unnerved, but showed a brave face; 'maybe, the Lad had told her the facts and reassured her that things would end well,' they thought.

After the jeep had left the village, the men flocked at the slab and began a postmortem of the events; it went on for a long time; one or two of them queried about Pagadaiah whose presence, they thought, would throw more light on the things, but most of them did not seem to bother very much about the presence or otherwise of the raconteur. If anybody felt strongly about anybody's absence, it was Gopaya who wished Kannam were there with him.

"Narayana, I wish Kannam were here with us now. He has been away for just a few days, but you see how it feels like a long time!"

Just at that moment, Kannam showed up, turning the corner; behind him came Nagireddy.

"There comes the devil!" Gopaya gleefully shouted at the sight of his friend.

Narayana too was delighted, "Indeed, there he is!"

Kannam came smiling in response and Nagireddy too accompanied him; they sat by the side of Gopaya.

"You look very happy, Gopaya; what is the matter, here?" asked Nagireddy.

"Matter . . . ! You say 'matter'! Oh, Nagaya, there is so much of it, Nagaya; there is so much of it, indeed!"

Meanwhile, others joined them.

Balakoti said, with a mix of laughter in his voice "What else, Errodu has come and is gone, like our monsoon!"

"What, Errodu has come and gone, just like that?"

It was a cool evening at the slab; darkness was gathering. A sizeable number of members assembled, all of them thirsting for fresh tidings on Errodu's case.

Pagadaiah and Hulakki were sitting together and waiting for someone to open up 'the discussion'.

Kannam was at his usual perch flanked by Gopaya and Narayana.

For a long time no one spoke, expecting somebody else to come up with the latest.

At last it was left to Mme Pullamma's man to break the silence with a succinct remark that highlighted his role in that event of importance, "All the effort and labor have gone waste!"

They pounced on him with questions, "Why, what do you mean by that?", "What happened there last night?", "Did the event go well?", "How did 'the Red Lad' fare in the test of his essence?" . . .

"First let him break the news; you can come up with questions later," said the veteran Hulakki and Pagadaiah nodded agreement.

"Yes, yes, tell us all that has happened there; don't leave out anything, tell us everything, yes, everything."

Mme Pullamma's man appeared confused as he looked into their faces.

After giving him some time, the members once again closed in on him with queries.

Guardedly looking at those inquirers once again, Mme Pullamma's man retraced his steps to a safe distance and from there said in a low voice, "After festooning the hut with colour papers, I lay down and in no time fell into sleep. By the time I woke up, the place had become very calm and there was no one around; so I went home and slept. In the morning I woke up late and when I went to draw water from the well, I heard their voices from sister Bhagyamma's hut and leaving the pans there I rushed to the place; there I saw the jeep with men and Errodu in their midst."

They heaved sighs which were sounds of disgust and disappointment, "Well, there you have it, his account of it, for what it is worth; now, tell me, can you make out anything from it?"

"What else can you expect from that man; poor Pullamma; she must be having a horrid time with the fellow!"

"But, the man has told you all that he can; why should you pick on him like that! If you are so much itching to know what exactly happened there, you should have posted there your own man."

"But, he has given us some information, after all. There is no point in blaming him; he is a man of helping nature, poor chap, don't blame him."

"Why, he had a good sleep last night, that is evident, isn't that clear enough, Cousin Gopaya?"

Hulakki clucked his tongue and said, "There, there, they are at it again, Pagudaya! Would you see to what we can do with these wayward fellows?"

Pagadaiah intervened, in deference to the wish of the Uncle Hulakki and amiably said, "'It's not like that', Mme

Pullamma's man; we just want to know from you whether the last night's event was successful or not."

With a sudden loud laugh the man said, "Oh Lord Pagadaiah Sir, what a wonderful man you are—the questions you pose! Do you think I can divine on that? How can anybody answer that query of yours, except Errodu?" the Man continued to recall the question and enjoy it as a joke.

Pagadaiah realized that, for once, he had been caught on the wrong foot and looked downwards sheepishly.

"It's better to ask a log at sister Bhagyamma's house; you might get some intelligible answer," said Hulakki.

"Go and ask a log then, there are many of them, at that house; you know where the house is or shall I show it to you?" pouted Mme Pullamma's man.

"Enough of it, now, you have shown us how clever you are, enough of it," Pagadaiah showed his palm to Pullamma's man, in a mild reprimand.

Hulakki heaved a long sigh of helplessness and left the issue to untangle itself.

Pagadaiah, however, carried the issue forward, "Marriage is a serious ritual; you have to be very careful in fixing a marriage; the stars have to match and one has to check out on the lines on the palms of the boy and the girl and more important than that, you have to ascertain whether any important birthmarks are there on any part of their bodies and if there are any, get them read by some person knowledgeable in that science; otherwise, things will not go smooth."

"What, look for the birthmarks before you fix a marriage?" wondered aloud Hussainaiah, "and wherever they are?"

"First learn to listen to the elders, Hussainaiah; that is the correct way of gaining common sense and a knowledge of the etiquette and the facts of life," said Hulakki, "don't talk like that, like an imbecile; where would the birthmarks be, they would be on the body of the person; it is as simple as that!"

Hussainaiah looked angrily at the veteran, but kept quiet for the time being.

Pagadaiah continued, "Leave it, but the point is . . ." At that he lost the link and tried to recollect, "Now, what was I saying, what was I saying . . . ?"

"You were saying 'what was I saying; what was I saying?'" Kannam provided the link from a remote corner.

There were chuckles.

Pagadaiah glowered at Kannam; 'if only looks can . . .' thought the nearby members.

Hulakki gave Pagadaiah a gentle slap on the back and said, "Ignore their remarks, Pagudaiah; we cannot conduct any business if we keep heeding these foolish remarks; come to the point or you want me to take over?"

At that, Pagadaiah discovered the lost link and at once went ahead with the issue, "Yes, these are all sciences, members should note. When you are building a house you must know what features and forms of the house are benign and what of them are blemishes. It's important, because you build a house once in a lifetime and you want to live in it happily with your family. If you ignore a point you may have to pay the price and who likes that!" Pagadaiah was regaining his eloquence.

Now, the slab was back into its customary state of silence and deference, with members paying attention to what the honorable veteran was positing.

Pagadaiah skillfully presented the points on the topic he took up, " . . . so, don't jeer at these things; instead try to understand what our ancestors have bequeathed to us in the form of these sciences, the science of Vaastu (building a house), the science of the Nevi and the science of the tumbling House-lizards-"

"What did you say, Uncle Pagadaiah, the science of the tumbling House-lizards? Is there a science of that too?" Asked Muneyya; he had just come to the slab.

"Yes, yes, there are sciences of everything, if only you wanted to learn; but, to come back to the point, this science of the Nevi-the birthmarks, is very important for the smooth running of a man's life; it can make or mar a life, yes that's what it can do; keep it in your minds, all of you, if you want to do well in your life."

Many heads in the gathering nodded docilely, yielding a point to Pagadaiah.

Hussainaiah queried, "Wherever the birthmarks are . . . ?"

"Again, the same query . . . ? Yes, wherever they are, I say," Pagadaiah thumped his right fist into his left palm, "One has to know whether any important birthmarks are there on the body of the prospective spouse."

Catching Pagadaiah in the midst of his say, Hussainaiah wondered aloud, "Wherever the marks are, even on the body of a nubile girl?"

Pagadaiah caught the point and tackled it with the shrewdness he is known for, "Yes, yes, Hussainaiah, I get your point. Now, that is not a big issue, Hussainaiah, because the parents and the close relations would anyway have been watching the child right from its birth; so, there is nothing secretive about it and you can say the entire community is in the know of these things, isn't that so?"

"Maybe so, but suppose the birthmarks appear at a later stage?"

"How naïve you people are, birthmarks are congenital marks, if they appear at a later stage, they are not birthmarks;

they are just body-marks! We have nothing to do with them; they have no effect, whatsoever," Ruled Pagadaiah.

"What kind of effect can a birthmark have? If a girl has a certain birthmark, would that affect her life only or would that affect her husband's life also?"

"Why are you asking all these questions now, Hussainaiah, you are married for some years now?" Kannam asked innocently.

Members relished the element of fun in that observation and even Pagadaiah smiled at that.

"The birthmarks of the man and wife affect each other; that is why each party should check on the other's birthmarks."

"Why are we discussing the birthmarks now?"

"In order to know the fate of Errodu, of course; what else can it be for," Hulakki intervened.

"But, Errodu knows it all," Ramkishty, a close associate of the Red Lad, averred.

The slab was aghast at that revelation, "Errodu knows it all?"

Pagadaiah and Hulakki wondered, "You say so, how do you know?"

Koti, another close companion of the Red Lad said, "Why, we all know that."

"You all know? How many of you know?"

"There are many of us," another young lad shot in, "We all know that and Errodu knows that we know; he also knows that we know that he knows it."

Pagadaiah wondered, 'How smart these gabby bastards are, and they rarely open their mouths at the slab!'

The point, now, was revealed to be an open secret; Hulakki's naïve assumption—that he was the exclusive privy to the knowledge of the secret—lay shattered. With a groan he got down the slab and firm-fixed the plait of his garment.

Pagadaiah stuck to his place; he wanted to know from the young lads more on the issue and befriending Ramkishty asked, "Rre, Ramkishty you are aware of the plight of your friend and yet didn't try to be of help, is that the way a friend should behave?"

That mild rebuke was enough for Ramkishty to come out with more; with an endearing address he laid bare the facts of the case, "Uncle Pagadaiah, as a matter of fact, many of us know the thing; we also know that the girl is of a very comely appearance and that many suitors coveted her for wife; all of them changed their minds when they came to know of it . . ."

"Came to know of what?" Hussainaiah asked, confusion writ all over his face.

Hulakki's face lost the initial proud look; he sat glumly, 'holding his pride with the remaining teeth of his'.

Pagadaiah, however, presented a bold front; but, he gave the young fellow a respectful hearing and this change in Pagadaiah's attitude didn't go unnoticed by the members of the slab.

Now, it was left to Ramkishty to round up the debate with some telling revelations, such as the one on, how the lone son of a landlord fell for the girl and strongly wanted to marry her, the birthmark notwithstanding, and how the despondent parents of the lad frantically searched for a strong ruse to dissuade their son from that fatal decision; then, how a government teacher wooed the girl to the point of persuading the girl to an elopement with him and how the plan was scented by his students and was divulged to the girl's parents and how as a result of the disclosure of his plan, the teacher had to run for his life leaving the job he had secured after several attempts and . . .

The slab listened to Ramkishty's testimony with unwavering attention, a fact meticulously observed and noted by Pagadaiah, of course.

"Where was that birthmark on the girl's body, I say?" Hussainaiah said in anguish; 'nobody cares to find out that important point . . .'

The query was greeted with chuckles, which went on for some time and at the end of it, Kannam quipped with, "That is a secret, Hussainaiah, to be revealed only to the suitors."

Pagadaiah saw the loss of seriousness among the slab members and sensing it, Hulakki nudged Pagadaiah suggesting an exit from the slab.

However, Pagadaiah was in no mood to leave the field; 'it would amount to surrender,' he thought; so, gamely he stuck to his place and waited for a favorable turn, which by his count 'wouldn't be long in coming'.

It was Gopaya who unwittingly steered the issue Pagadaiah's way, as he said, "Now, all of you go home and start a search for the birthmarks!"

"Especially, the married ones," said Kannam.

"No, no, Kannam, it is now the head-ache of only the unmarried lads, more than being that of the married ones, I mean the lads like you," Pagadaiah said, his panning finger covering Kannam and Ramkishty and his gang.

The slab relished the humour and a member took it even further, "I would suggest that the lately married men check on the birthmarks of their spouses in case things haven't been going well for them."

Hussainaiah looked this side and that side in a self-conscious way.

"Uncle Pagadaiah, keeping aside all this, please explain this science of the birthmarks; that way, you would be doing a favour to the young men, I mean the unmarried young men."

"Yes, yes, the married are married already, I pity them if the Nevi are working against them; at least the young men's lives can be saved from the troubles if they are instructed, in advance, on what can bring them good luck and what could cause them trouble; please reveal these things, Uncle."

Pagadaiah was pleased at the propitious turn and gave an endearing smile to the members, "Oh yes, 'what is there in it', I have always tried to help the young fellows; it is only they that have spurned me."

Pagadaiah took a deep breath in preparation and the next instant he found the sethsindhi in front of him, "Lord Sir is calling you, Pagudaya."

That was a big disappointment to the young men.

With a sigh Pagadaiah rose to go to the Banzardar's house, saying "Some other day I will tell you."

"Uncle Pagadaiah, first tell us about the birthmarks; the visit to the Lord-Sir's house can wait," The young ones pleaded.

Pagadaiah held his protruding tongue between his teeth and waved his index finger to show the boys the impropriety of it and walked towards the Banzardar's house.

Young men were dismayed at the abrupt end to what promised to be a useful instruction on the benefic and malefic effects of the birthmarks on the human lives.

"Pagadaiah, come, come you lucky man, you are indeed a lucky man, Man," The Banzardar greeted effusively, "The Praja Party has chosen you as its candidate for the office of Sarpanch in the ensuing elections. Go at once to the temple and break a coconut; ask the priest-sir to prepare tamarind rice and give people a bowl of it to each; that is the way to celebrate, Pagadaiah. Of course, you know all these things better than anybody . . ."

Pagadaiah showed his respect for the Banzardar with the usual gesture—palms joined web-to-web, head bent and nodding reverentially; he felt in his body the thrill of the sweet news! To him the experience was the first of its kind; he did not have any formula-type response to offer; but from his wide repertoire of creative skills he dug out an apt gesture of thankfulness and chose a fresh collection of words that sounded new even to himself; he bent some more and said, "It's all the result of your kindness, Lord-Sir; where would I be without your blessings, my Lord!"

The Banzardar was pleased with Pagadaiah's genuflections and went out of the way in offering a stool to him, "Sit on that stool, Pagadaiah; don't hesitate; it is time we started recognizing your worth. Anyway the Praja Party has seen your worth. I am happy they have chosen you; any other man wouldn't have been as acceptable as you. God sees to the fitness of the things he orders, you see."

Pagadaiah didn't relent on the display of loyalty and obedience; he instinctively knew that more was in the offing on the issue and waited patiently.

"So, Pagadaiah, that's it; I have done whatever is there in my hands. My part of it is over; I have conveyed to you the decision of the Party. There are other things you have to consider for yourself, like working your way into the goodwill of the voters, winning over people from the rival's camp; of course, we know that already you are popular with the men of our village; but, as of now, we do not know who the other candidate is."

"Lord-Sir, the other candidate means the Socialist Party candidate, isn't that so, Lord-Sir?"

The Banzardar waved his arm in a vague gesture, "Maybe, you are right, maybe, you are wrong; you see, we don't know what lies on the other side of the fence, Socialists or 'Vocialists', whoever it is, the Party has chosen you as its candidate and you have to fight against the other Party's candidate, that is the important thing . . .

"Now, Pagadaiah, there are other things you have to take care of and I think you know what they are," The Banzardar looked Pagadaiah in the face, with a meaningful big smile.

For a time, he continued the look and the smile.

Pagadaiah could not decipher the meaning of the smile and the gesture; so, he met the looks of the Lord-Sir with his innocent looks.

The Banzardar felt that he had come to the end of the tether and said in a matter of fact way, "You would need to spend some money, yes, that's it, Pagadaiah; you have to arrange for yourself some money; I don't know how much, but it definitely cannot be less than ten thousand rupees."

"Ten thousand rupees . . . ?" Pagadaiah's eyes bulged; his heart missed a beat!

The Banzardar stared at Pagadaiah in surprise, "Yes, ten thousand and what is so startling about it? After all, you cannot go into an enterprise without an investment, can you? Tell me; Pagadaiah, tell me . . .

"And out of that ten thousand, five thousand would go to the MLA Sir; what remains is for your campaign expenses; it is simple, Pagadaiah . . .

"And, one thing I must tell you, Pagadaiah; the Party has chosen you on the basis of the information gathered by it. They have chosen you because they have seen a winning candidate in you, yes, that's it.'

There was no positive response from Pagadaiah for a long time.

The Banzardar for his part kept looking at Pagadaiah as if he was looking at a stranger.

Pagadaiah walked away, head bent, after making an indistinct gesture of respect to the Lord-Sir; the initial thrill he had felt when the news was broken, was now gone and in its place a sense of social loneliness and economic despondency made their distracting presence felt.

Till he reached the turnstile he neither looked back nor did he lift his head.

The lord looked on, baffled; did he go wrong in the choice of the man, on behalf of the Party?

As he stepped into the street, Pagadaiah looked at the slab; there were still some members there; 'were they waiting for him, waiting for an exposition on the Science of the Nevi or on the Science of the Dreams? Should he go there and explain to them the effects of the fall of the House-lizards?

For a time he stood listless and undecided where to go; a good part of the night had passed; there was no point in going to the slab now, especially after what the Lord-sir had told him.

One or two of them from the slab appeared to look at him in expectancy; but Pagadaiah could not see things clearly in the faint moonlight and he was in no mood to go to the slab.

Avoiding the slab, he turned to the left and walked to his hut.

The first quarter of the night was ending; it was the ninth or tenth night of the waning moon. He unhooked the door and walked into the hut; it was pitch-dark inside the hut; Rattamma hadn't lighted the bed-lamp.

Pagadaiah took off his banian hung it on the clothesline and went into the yard to have a wash.

He heard the snore from the cot; 'it's that devil of a woman, the mother-in-law' he muttered under the teeth.

Back in the hut, after the customary short prayer, Pagadaiah groped for the cot and heard the jingling sounds of the bangles. Trying to shake off the feeling of depression, he lowered himself onto the bed.

He gave a jerk in disbelief as the surprisingly eager hands of his bedmate dragged him closer.

'What a pleasant change in Rattamma's attitude!' he thought and began probing her body, working up himself into a romantic mood.

Then, he stopped for an instant wondering at the coarseness of the skin his hands had felt; he came to himself and resumed the amorous activity; but the next moment, he suddenly wondered at the identity of the partner and sat bolt upright at the edge of the cot, suspecting a foul play.

"What has happened, Pagadaiah?" huskily the partner asked.

At that Pagadaiah jumped up in horror, as if waking from a nightmare.

The mother-in-law!!!

Pagadaiah trembled at the horrible mix up; he began to sweat and his pulse started to throb at a frightening rate.

'What would happen now? Would he be counted for a sinner and would he be dragged into the hell to be fried in an oil pan or to be trodden under the pillar-like feet of the elephants or to be put under the cutting saw?'

It was a horrible sin; had he committed it? A mother-in-law is one of 'the five mothers', the tradition says; what a horrible thing he had he done?

Pagadaiah recollected the happenings of the recent nights with a feeling of guilt and fright; 'what had I been doing, committing a sin of the worst nature? Did Rattamma know of it? How mean she would brand me to be? Would she ever touch my hand again, my sinful hand, my sinful body? Would she ever forgive me?'

"Don't take it to heart so much; after all, everybody is asleep in the lane, Ratti is sleeping like a log; even otherwise, I can manage her."

Pagadaiah's mental state was such that he could neither see in her direction nor could he talk back to her, "I am damned, I have become an accursed," he hid his face in his hands and let out a long wail.

The lady tried a bold approach, "There is no point in crying and cursing yourself like that . . . I am not going to blame you publicly for what you have done; after all, I am the one sinned against; so, pull yourself together; these things happen by the evil designs of the malevolent spirits reveling in the night; so, calm down; lie down and have some, some . . . sleep," coming into a sitting posture, she tugged at his hand.

Pagadaiah pulled his hand away and rushed out of the hut even as the lady tried to dissuade him in a hushed up voice; soon, she heard the sound of the man's steps recede into the street.

However the lady kept her nerve and tried to find a way out.

In the backyard, the daughter was sublimely asleep.

Presently, Pagadaiah came back and taking a shirt and a 'panche' he walked out of the hut.

As he stepped out of his yard, Pagadaiah noticed that the time was nearing midnight; the lanes were frighteningly empty. He was unable to decide where to go and what to do; in anguish he meditated on his favorite deity, Mother Durgamma.

He walked along the way his feet dragged.

Reaching the slab, he found it empty; going to the base of the giant Bo tree he reclined there, on sidewise, his feet curled up, and head resting on the forearm.

Thoughts raged in his mind. 'Would this act of his be recorded as a deadly sin, in the account book of Chitragupta, the assistant of the Lord of Death, Yama? If yes, what punishment would be meted out to him?' He recalled the long list of punishments, read out once by the Priest-sir from the Garudapuranam and began to shudder. The next thing, he chanted the Mother's name and implored her to intercede in his behalf and mitigate the case.

Slowly he slipped into sleep.

After a long time, Pagadaiah woke up; already the lanes were abuzz with men and women, busying themselves with the morning chores. Luckily for him, no one appeared to have noticed him and his feet started the return-drag to the hut.

At the hut, the same silence still prevailed; neither the mother nor the daughter had woken up.

He went to the niche in the wall wherein he kept the small idol of the Mother and groping behind the idol, he took money; putting on a washed shirt he went out.

He hesitated for a few moments, weighing the options; should he go and explain his predicament to his sister? He debated the issue and chose not to do that; 'the element of mystery might help me in some way with the blessings of the Mother!' he thought and walked on with determination.

Luckily for him not a soul saw him leaving the village.

In the morning when the sethsindhi came on the Banzardar's errand, Pagadaiah was not there in his house and the inmates were climbing into the bullock-cart brought for them, by Rattamma's father.

For a few days, the slab missed the enterprising presence of its chief anchor.

Hussainaiah, Mme Pullamma's man and a few other members of the slab went to Pagadaiah's house, which was closed; then they went to his sister, but, there they only encountered the forlorn looks of the lady.

Even the veteran Hulakki was unable to give any lead.

'What could be the reason for this mysterious and abrupt disappearance of the man; normally he wouldn't do anything without informing his sister, why this . . .' Balakoti mused.

At that juncture, Nagireddy and Kannam arrived on the scene; Nagireddy noticed that, despite a low-key chat by some, there was an unusual silence at the slab.

The attendance at the slab had been somewhat thin since the start of 'the Food-for-work' programme; only those that shunned the 'liquor on credit' chose to come to the slab.

"What is happening here, you folks look glum?" Nagireddy said, asking none in particular.

"It is three days since one has seen Pagadaiah; even his sister has no clue on where he has gone."

Nagireddy smiled, "Maybe, he has gone to meet the Praja Party leaders."

That was an interesting piece of news to the slab and was soon taken up for discussion.

"What has he got to do with the Praja Party?"

At that, Nagireddy smiled again, "You people don't seem to notice what is happening around you; the election notification is set to come 'this evening or tomorrow', as they say; has any one of you heard that, at least?"

They showed gestures of negation, "We haven't heard any such thing, Nagaya; even then, what has he got to do with that?"

"Why not; maybe, he has been picked by the party to be its candidate . . ."

"Candidate, for what . . ."

"For the office of Sarpanch, what else it can be?"

"But, we have a Sarpanch already . . ."

"His term is over; moreover he has not submitted the accounts so far; he cannot contest."

"So what, the accounts would not disappear? He would show the accounts someday, if necessary."

"Not 'if necessary', submission of accounts is necessary if he wants a second term."

"Maybe, he doesn't want a second term."

"Second term . . . ? Why, is one term not enough for one man . . . ?"

"You people do not know a single thing right about the power of the Panchayat," Nagireddy touched his forehead with his palm, in an expression of disgust and commiseration for them.

"Leave away all that talk; help us find out where Pagadaiah has gone."

"Brother Nagaya says he might have gone to Ellavupalem, that is, to the Praja Party office; maybe, that is true."

"We haven't heard any such thing from Pagadaiah."

Nagireddy looked at their faces one after the other, and said in an undertone, audible only to Kannam, "It is well-known to all that you don't hear anything, you don't say anything, you don't see anything," then turning to the members, he opened up, "You are all good followers of Mahatma Gandhi, indeed . . .

"Well, whatever is the case with Pagadaiah, I am here, presenting my case to you all." Finding that he had gained the attention of the slab, he stood up and said firmly, "I am 'standing' for the office of Sarpanch and I request all of you to support me and elect me Sarpanch," Mr. Nagireddy joined his palms displaying a newly found respect for the slab.

All the members opened their mouths in wonder; one queried, "But, have you met the Emmellu?"

"Why should I? I am contesting from my Party, the Socialist Party of India."

"Would you win, Nagaya?" Hussainaiah asked, wondering.

Many on the slab shared the benign concern.

"Why not, he would win, he would win," a few of them said.

"Yes, yes, why not, he would certainly win," Others joined.

"If not he, who else would win?"

Once again, Nagireddy joined his palms to them in a 'Namaste', "If you all show the same spirit of support, I will definitely win and let everyone of you in this gathering hear from me and in their turn tell the others; I will serve you all without fear or favour and true to the spirit of democracy and upholding the constitution of India . . ."

They looked at one another again, mouths still open.

"What is the meaning of the thing you have said, Nagaya?" another member asked ingenuously.

"I will explain that," Said Nagireddy enthusiastically, "What I mean by that is, that I swear that I will work to fulfill your demands, whatever you want, I mean, for the people, of the people and by the people."

"Would you get us water, Nagaya, water for us and our fields?"

"Yes, yes, that is the first thing I will take up. If you all support me, I will fight for the repair of the Vindhyadramma tank breach and the sluice."

"If you fight, will they take up the repair of the breach, Nagaya?"

Kannam watched as his mentor skillfully presented his case to the members of the slab; he noticed that they were listening to him in pin-drop silence.

Then suddenly all of them broke into guffaws.

Nagireddy was bewildered, but, the next moment he too heard that familiar trumpet-like sound and fell into laughter, helplessly.

"Rosaiah Sir is coming, Rosaiah Sir is coming!" Somebody announced.

They all saw Rosaiah hurling himself towards the slab at a fierce pace.

Rosaiah gasped as he reached the slab and said, "Oh my God, so many people have assembled on the slab, this evening! Something important is happening! What is 'the story' of the day?"

"The story of the day, Rosaiah Sir, is that, Nagaya is saying that he would have the Vindhyadramma tank breach repaired if we elect him Sarpanch."

Rosaiah chuckled, "As simple as that? Then, let us lose no time; we will all elect him Sarpanch today itself."

Nagireddy smiled in good humour.

They all liked the man's cheerfulness, "Rosaiah Sir, there is nobody like you, Sir; you are the only person who wishes the village well. Oh, how I wish I could put a lump of sugar in your mouth, Oh Rosaiah Sir,"

"Oh, Rosaiah Sir, God bless you, Sir."

"Not simply bless, bless you with a long life, Rosaiah Sir."

Rosaiah cackled ecstatically, "Why, why, why all this sudden effusiveness; even God can't say when you people would rumble and when you would rain."

"Today we are doing both, Rosaiah Sir; what can we do, Sir; the Rain-God is not doing either of them; so, we are doing both the things, Rosaiah Sir."

Rosaiah gave a hearty laugh, running his palm fondly on his potbelly.

One of the men made place for him; he even dusted it for him.

"Don't worry, don't worry, I am not going to sit; I've just come to see what is happening at the slab; maybe the customers are waiting for me at the shop; I have got to go," Said Rosaiah and the next moment he deftly turned round and breezed past the slab.

Soon, the slab heard 'it' again.

After that short interlude, all the men on the slab felt refreshed and picked up the thread of the discussion.

"But, one thing I don't understand, Nagaya, our Pagadaiah says it is better to go for a bund across the rivulet rather than take up that long-abandoned bund, what do you say to that?" Balakoti asked.

Kannam felt intrigued; 'how would Nagireddy tackle this query?'

Nagireddy dealt with the issue easily and plausibly, "If you ask me why Pagadaiah is saying like that, my answer is simple and straight; Pagadaiah believes in that story—the story of the King, the Priest and the Deity Vindhyadramma; he thinks that tank is accursed and that anyone who tries to tamper with its state of ruin would stand to be ruined; that is that, short and simple."

Hussainaiah fell into a fit of imagination and began to see Nagireddy glittering as Krishna, in a dazzling costume, even as his ears heard the latter's analysis of the issue in question.

"There is a point in what Pagadaiah feels about 'the bund'," Hulakki took up the brief for his friend, "That the ruined tank is an accursed thing is an undeniable truth; you want proof? Well, there the bund is, there the breach is and there the idol of Vindhyadramma, the deity and the king turned into stone, are. Anybody who sees it would tell you that it was meant to be a water-reservoir but that was not to be because of the curse; how long it had been like that, nobody knows. Anyone can see that the entire thing is old, very old, rather of ancient times and it had been like that from times immemorial; it is clearly discernible to anybody who sees it; so, it is not only me, anyone in the right state of mind would agree with Pagadaiah on that."

"Uncle Hulakki, I am not denying what you have said; it would definitely have been a big reservoir, a very big one; it was a well intended act on the part of the king," Nagireddy said diplomatically, "but, the work was far beyond their skills and strength, the skills of those old, very old times; they didn't have the big machines and things we have today. Regarding that idol of Vindhyadramma it is clear to all of us; they placed it there for whatever benefic influence it can cast; we all place such idols in our houses, even in our fields; don't you think so, Uncle?"

"Even at the centre of the village," said Hussainaiah, in a veiled reference to the unrelenting deity, Muthyalamma.

Hulakki frowned at Hussainaiah; however, he realized that he had no further points to advance the argument; still, he stuck to his stand, "Whatever you say, Nagaya, I am of firm opinion on that; it is an act of risk to think of reviving that cursed tank; let Pagadaiah come, I am sure he knows more on that; he is a wise man."

Nagireddy could not venture to say more on the issue, especially in consideration of his election prospects; so, he maintained a tactical silence; it was not clear to him which line of thinking appealed to the slab-members.

Kannam intervened, "Whatever it is, I think, Pagadaiah was wrong in his contention."

"What is it?" Hulakki enquired; taking a look at Kannam, he wondered if the fellow was drunk, but, he remembered that villagers had long been abiding by the convention of attending the slab, only when sober.

"That day Pagadaiah said the issue of the 'tank' belonged exclusively to our village; how can he talk like that when our Panchayat has three constituent villages? 'Even if the litigant is one's own brother, one must give justice on the basis of the merits of the case' as they say," Kannam observed.

Hulakki didn't like this gibe of Kannam at Pagadaiah, particularly when the latter was not there to defend himself; he thought he must curb the crass attitude of fellows like Kannam; so, he went into an appraisal of values, a process he had found to be suitable for all times and climes, "Ragavaiah, it is really funny the way the world is changing; back in my childhood days, it required guts to come and sit on this slab. Even if one came, rarely one opened one's mouth in front of the elders. They learnt the etiquette step by step, observing the people and listening to the elders for a number of years; then they learnt how to talk, how to talk in different sets of gatherings, on different issues, on different . . ."

Kannam cut into Hulakki's talk, "So, you mean to say that only old men should talk and the younger ones should always listen, isn't that it? 'An old woman is the only chaste woman', you seem to say."

After glaring at Kannam for a long time, Hulakki got off the slab and walked homeward, lips pursed.

Nagireddy saw that Kannam's belligerent attitude was going to harm his case; so, he pulled Kannam by the hand and muttered, under his grinding his teeth, "You idiot, you still have not learnt any lesson; I told you several times to avoid talking in such serious situations. If you don't change your ways, stay away from me, I tell you."

Kannam's smile faded; he bent his head as the colour of his face lost its sheen.

While every member at the slab saw, heard and noted the men and their talk, none appeared to have noticed the sethsindhi who lurked a little away, well behind the men, making a mental dossier on who had said what.

The Banzardar, sitting in the easy chair in the front verandah of his bungalow, was also able to hear the talk; later he would corroborate his version with that of the sethsindhi.

The food-for-work grind was crawling on, at the site, which was now at a distance of three kilometers from the village.

With the passage of time, the relations between the two kinds of beneficiaries smoothened to exude a look of camaraderie; part of the credit for such transformation went to the works-manager and the other part went partly to the women-workers' perceptive abilities and inventive skills and partly to the conniving shrewdness and studied tolerance of the men-laborers. If, still any rough edges cropped up, the liquor store took care of them.

The Praja Party dignitaries were happy with the tidings they got from the lower rungs of the party, that 'the food-for-work' was progressing nicely and could prove to be a nice build-up for their party, in the local body elections.

The MLA daily met the visitors from the different segments of his assembly constituency and one or two from the press. He was a happy man; this venture would certainly catapult him into the ministry.

The only thing that pinched him occasionally was the ignorance of the right forms of democratic terminology the people displayed in their conversation. 'Democratic culture has not yet taken firm roots in the constituency,' he regretted; 'the country must undergo a 'cultural revolution,'

Whenever someone uttered that distorted word 'Emmellu', he would knit his eyebrows in anguish; the word

251

'Emmellu' rhymed with Mallu, Chillu and that sounded very distasteful to him.

"Even simple things, they cannot master; M L A is a simple word but, they always say Emmellu, and that sounds very nasty, you see." The MLA said to the Minister.

"I think even the educational functionaries aren't well-versed in this respect; I have my own experiences, Sure-naraina."

The MLA blinked at the distortion of his name by the Minister.

'This man never ceases to be strange,' thought Suryanarayana. 'Ganjibabu, by name, the man comes from an aristocratic family; educated in England, he registered as an advocate but had never taken the profession seriously. He inherited, along with a large property and a few industries, the legislature membership too from his father; he has been a member of one cabinet after another cabinet, because no Chief Minister liked to leave him out of his cabinet; in fact, he remained the star attraction of the State Cabinet; despite all that Ganjibabu's interest in active politics was dilettantish. He would start with the address 'Mr. Chief Minister' and would go on to criticize the actions and decisions of the Government as though he were an opposition leader; still, the Chief Minister would take it with a humble smile and even take back or change a decision or two and ask for his wise counsel every now and then! No wonder that every legislator liked to be in the train of that man for the coattail benefits.'

"Mr. Sure—Naraina, if you care for my opinion, our concern for democracy should not end with the elections; besides taking interest in the policies of the Party the political functionaries should also strengthen their minds with an account of the evolution of democracy and its philosophy . . ."

"You must read the constitutional history of Britain to know how the political wisdom of the people got fine tuned over a period of time; to know about the growth of republicanism and modern nationalism; you must study the histories of Italy, Germany and East Europe and to know how they all impacted the Eastern Countries you must read the story of the Sick man of Europe," Minister averred.

'Quite a tall order for me, now,' thought the MLA, whose education had ended with the Bachelor Degree.

'In the present scenario, a politician does not require any educational background, much less a thorough reading of the Principles of Politics and Political thought; Plato to Marx and Mao all theoreticians look irrelevant now, especially in the Indian context.' the Legislator mused.

However, Ganji Babu appeared to him as the Christian trekking towards the Delectable Mountains, undeterred by hurdles and hindrances.

The dialogue between the two representatives would have gone on for some more time and maybe, would have fruitfully ended in the finalization of some remedial programme for the democracy at the grass-root level, but presently an office-boy came with a letter for the MLA, sent by the Banzardar Appaiah Dora.

MLA Suryanarayana took it; it was a long envelope and on the top of it there were underlined words, 'Personal and Important'; so, he excused himself and went into the antechamber.

When he had read the letter the MLA became a disconcerted man; something 'sinister' appeared to be brewing up, a move by some men of his own constituency that had the potential to upset his applecart in every way!

He had never imagined that things could happen the way outlined by the Banzardar in his letter.

'How fickle they all can be—the People, the Destiny and the Lady called, the Fortune!' the MLA wondered.

The MLA felt restless as his mind conjured up the unsavory possibilities and thought that he should go to the constituency at once; he would meet the Banzardar and have firsthand information on the issue. Still, his mind not at rest, he returned to the room where the Minister sat playfully imagining the possible distortions of the democratic terminology and 'the modicum of truth' each one of them seemed to contain.

The Minister was happy with the activity his mind had avidly taken up; 'surely, digressions like these would add taste and flavor to the work of a minister which, otherwise, is dull and drab,' he thought, 'the only silver lining is that it is, of course, a very respectable position,' he consoled himself.

"So, Mr. Sure-naraina, as I was telling you . . ."

Three days later, the MLA felt relieved when he sat face to face with Appaiah Dora, the Banzardar.

"Don't you worry unduly about it, Suryanarayana garu; I was only hinting at distant possibilities, in that letter; there is no certainty of the things happening; but, you see, one has to wield 'big stick to kill even a small snake', as they say."

The MLA nodded pensively; the big expanse of fertile land and the recently planted orchard of lemon trees, dangled in his mind; his family had been cultivating that land and quarrying the stones thereabouts for generations. For some time he had been thinking of getting it recorded as their family property in the 'qasra forms' or whatever it was; but that was a clandestine act. If the public clamored for the revival of that long-dead huge tank of water-'the Vindhyadramma tank', and the government relented to it, what right his family would have to prevent the land from going under water again? By no stretch of logic or maneuvering of law, it could be shown to be their ancestral private property; people would call it unauthorized occupation of public property. Of course, there would be some loopholes in the law that could be taken advantage of, as was being done by most of them, these days, in a similar predicament; but, that would be the last resort and one uncertain to succeed; even if it succeeded, it would be a short-lived success and it would cost 'all the goodwill' acquired over the years.

Presently, the sethsindhi came, along with Pagadaiah; both of them stood at the door.

The MLA greeted Pagadaiah amiably, "Come, Pagadaiah, come," He had not seen the man; he had only been informed about his suitability for the office of Sarpanch.

Pagadaiah waited with his arms folded across the chest; his head was shaven.

'Obviously, he had gone for a tonsure, at some shrine,' the Banzardar thought, "Have you gone on a pilgrimage, Pagadaiah?"

"Lord-Sir, I went to the temple of Mother Durgamma"

"Oh, Mother Durgamma, the Mother of the three Mothers, so you went to offer thanks to the Deity for this luck of yours, then," Said the Banzardar, looking at the tonsured head of the man.

Pagadaiah smiled humbly.

The Banzardar returned the smile and turned to the MLA, "This is the person I have told you about, Suryanarayana garu. His name is Pagadaiah; he is a nice person and he has a good image in the village. He is the only person who helps the priest and the village officials in the smooth celebration of festivals and the public meetings in the village."

"Yes, yes, I have seen him helping us with the last meeting we had here; looks a nice person; his face and his manners show him to be a nice common man, indeed," observed the MLA.

Pagadaiah joined his palms to the MLA and waited.

"Pagadaiah garu, our party has chosen you as its candidate for the office of the Sarpanch, as has already been informed to you by my friend, Appaiah Dora garu. Now, we want, rather, the Praja Party wants you to stand by the party, on all issues; yes, on all issues. You have to stand by 'me' firmly, even against the villagers if required, because I represent the Party and the villagers do not know what is good for them, as much as the Party knows; yes, the Party is above the villagers and the village; in short, the Party is above everything, so to say. Do you understand what I am saying, Pagadaiah garu."

The Banzardar nodded his head to show Pagadaiah how to respond.

Pagadaiah nodded hesitantly and after satisfying the MLA with his docility came to the point, "But, Lord-Sir, I cannot stand as Sarpanch, as commanded by the Praja Party; I do not have the big money, required by the Party."

"What big money, required by the Party . . . ?" the MLA expressed surprise.

The Banzardar quickly intervened, "I told Pagadaiah that he would need to invest to the tune of ten thousand rupees—the party fee and the campaign expenses, I mean," he concluded with a wink.

The MLA understood quickly and solved the problem, "Money is not a big question, Pagadaiah garu; money is fickle, as they say; it comes today and vanishes tomorrow. It is the Man and his true measure that are important. I have never given importance to money in my life; ask anybody who knows me; I cherish our traditional values . . ."

"Who can say you are money-minded? The entire constituency knows you, Sir" the Banzardar intervened.

Pagadaiah indicated with gestures that he had no such thought about the character of the MLA.

The MLA was satisfied and said to Pagadaiah reassuringly, "You trust me, Pagadaiah garu; I will take care of the money aspect. Don't worry about that; all I want is that you should be the Party candidate; I have full confidence in you and your abilities and I trust you; that's all; so, it's all settled now, isn't it?"

Pagadaiah nodded his consent and with a parting obeisance went out of the Banzardar's house, into the street.

He took a look at the slab; there was a small gathering; they were all looking in his direction. Should he go there? Should he announce to them his candidature, right now?

Pagadaiah took his first step and first decision as a politician and moved towards the slab.

It was all the merciful work of the Goddess Durgamma, he thought as he took measured steps; he was a shaken man, especially, after what had happened to him in his hut, in that fateful frightful night.

Bademaya dusted a spot on the cement bench for Pagadaiah and looked with reverence at the latter's tonsured head; the others too showed their veneration for the raconteur's tonsured head.

Pagadaiah sat on the dusted place of the bench and ran his fingers lightly on his pate, now, a little rough with the incipient hair; he reverentially recollected the image of the Mother Durgamma.

A member, sitting at the far end of the cement bench, got up on a sudden impulse and walking up to Pagadaiah, touched his feet, in a gesture of reverence to Mother Durgamma.

On observing it, the remaining men on the slab too lined up to Pagadaiah to touch his feet, one after the other, so as not to fall behind in earning some easily available merit.

Pagadaiah showed them each, his raised palm in a gesture of acknowledgment of their devoutness.

"What made you dash to Bezwada so suddenly, Uncle Pagadaiah?" Venkaiah, the senior asked.

Pagadaiah gave a blissful smile and nodded his head in a partial explanation and followed it up with, "One day, you too would do the same thing, on an appointed day of yours."

Narayana looked at Venkaiah, the senior with a wry smile and took up the explanation for Pagadaiah, "It is the Mother's Call, know that, you naïve fellow; sometimes, a call comes like that, to the chosen few; you and I are far, far from that stage."

Pagadaiah sat, his palm still held high and eyes half-closed, like the male version of the Mother.

Members on the slab looked at Pagadaiah and his sacred pate, part in respect, part in curiosity.

"I too have been contemplating a visit to the temple of Mother Durgamma, for some days; don't know when my day would come!" Mme Pullamma's man who had just come to the slab, said with a drawl.

Pagadaiah lifted his head and gave him a consoling smile, "Don't worry Mme Pullamma's man; in the divine plan of the Mother, there is a set day for everything and on that day the call would definitely come, smashing all obstacles; that is the power of the Mother Durgamma."

Mme Pullamma's man bobbed his head, half in belief and half in doubt and went and sat in a corner like an obedient boy.

"By the way, Cousin Pagadaiah, I too have been longing to know the thing; why did you so suddenly take up that trip to Bezwada?"

Pagadaiah did not answer; his mind was repeatedly recalling that late night's incident; he wondered how many of them knew how much of what had transpired in his hut. He was here on the slab, a fortnight after that incident.

A gnawing presentiment sat heavily on his mind; 'a few of them may have come to know,' he thought as he looked at them with a persistent suspicion. 'But how,' his mind reasoned, 'how could anyone have come to know about the incident that had transpired in his hut, in the later part of the night, not a soul was awake, then?'

"Yes, Cousin Pagadaiah, why did you so suddenly go? You had, not even once, hinted about the trip to Bezwada or that you had a vow to Mother Durgamma to discharge. We too would have come with you."

Pagadaiah didn't respond to the doubts and questions the members raised; he gave a vacant smile and kept nodding occasionally and that pushed them into respectful silence.

Presently, Kannam and Nagireddy arrived at the slab; the atmosphere turned mundane.

Members of the slab came closer to the duo; one of them asked Nagireddy, in a matter of fact way, "Are we set to have the Panchayat elections soon, Nagaya?"

Nagireddy beamed, "Yes, why doubt that! The notification would come, anytime, now."

"Are you 'standing', Nagaya?"

"If you want me to contest I will; otherwise I will not. As a matter of fact, today, I have come to finalize that, because, my party has asked me to be ready for the elections. If I say no, they will select someone else."

"Who is that someone else, Nagaiah?"

"Anybody, it could be you, it could be he or it could be another; but the man should be a member of the Party. My party believes in the principle of equality and fraternity of the men" Nagireddy said.

To Pagadaiah the time looked appropriate and he dived into a debate with Nagireddy. Clearing his throat, he asked, "Does that mean that even you and the Banzardar Lord-Sir are equals, as per the principles of your party?"

"Why not, not only we two, even you can call yourself our equal, I mean, so far as our public life is concerned; of course, in a personal and private way our situation in life would make it different, that's it; otherwise, we are all equals in a democratic society; liberty, equality and fraternity . . ."

"Don't drag me into it, Nagaya; I don't see myself as equal to the Lord-Sir," he turned to the other members and asked, "Do you all think that you are the equals of Lord-Sir?"

"We and the Lord-Sir . . . equal! My . . . we would go blind, if we think so!" they averred, beating their breasts.

Nagireddy knit his eyebrows in disgust.

Pagadaiah smiled in triumph as he looked, nodding questioningly at Nagireddy.

Nagireddy shrugged his shoulders in concession, "It's a matter of one's line of thinking."

"So, you see, Nagaya, things do not always conform to the Party lines; society has a way of organizing itself, and I, rather, we believe in that."

Nagireddy countered, "Maybe; but it's difficult to say who thinks what, unless they all register their thoughts and beliefs; can you say with certainty that Venkaiah believes in this, Narayana believes in that and Balakoti believes in another thing?"

Venkaiah, Narayana and Balakoti smiled happily at the mention of their names.

"Everyone has to fall in line with what the society demands; otherwise, the society would be pulled apart," Pagadaiah exultantly ruled, "Different parties say different things for their existence; but, it is the society that takes care of its members."

Nagireddy nodded, but, with an expression of a doubt on that statement of Pagadaiah; after a while, he pointedly asked, "Uncle Pagadaiah, tell me without dodging; are you contesting?"

Pagadaiah gave an enigmatic smile, "What is your view? Do you want that I should . . . ?"

Nagireddy felt irked by the question and gave a late reply, "Do I have a say on that? It is up to you to decide."

"Then, why were you asking others whether they thought that you should contest?" Pagadaiah laughed and said in conclusion, "Nagaya, it is a game which all can play equally well; don't you think so?"

"Agreed, all can play equally well; but, in the final analysis only one of them can win; I think you know that," Kannam said.

"Yes, yes, now I come to know that, because you have told me; yes, I know it now."

Kannam saw that for once, his mentor was on the defensive and showed some grudging admiration for his bugbear. He was about to say 'it's time we moved.'

A stranger came to the slab and asked, "Who is Nagireddy garu? I have a message for him."

Nagireddy welcomed the reprieve; he got off the slab answering, "It's I; I am Nagireddy."

Clasping the hand of the man, Nagireddy took him away toward the alley to know the purpose of his visit; Kannam limped behind.

The attention of the slab was now focused on the twosome at the alley, 'Who is this stranger? On whose work has he come? What is the message . . . ?'

Hussainaiah, in particular, was inquisitive about the stranger and his message.

As the members on the slab looked in curiosity, Nagireddy and the messenger walked farther and farther away from the slab, talking; in a while, they were gone.

Pagadaiah was unhappy at the way the discussion got aborted, especially when his eloquence was working.

In a couple of days, Hussainaiah came to know that the repertory would be staging a play in the school ground and it was none other than Kannam, who revealed it, coming to his house.

Hussainaiah was excited, as Kannam went on with the details, "You remember, Hussainaiah, the other night at the slab, Nagaya and Pagadaiah were talking about the Panchayat elections and at that time a stranger came to the slab asking for Nagireddy, and he brought a message . . . ? That man was a messenger from the Drama Company Nagaya worked in."

Hussainaia's eyes bulged at that and for once all his animosity for Kannam vanished, "Come, come, Kannam, sit down and tell me everything about it," He showed Kannam the palm-leaf mat to rest and sat near him.

Having settled himself on the mat Kannam broke the news, "Exactly fifteen days from today, you will be seeing Nagaya as Krishna; the play is 'Udyoga vijayam'; so, remember that and don't fail to witness the play; Nagaya has asked me to remind you that his promise on the tickets stands; yes, you will have two tickets."

Hussainaiah was very happy at that and asked Kannam, "Which Krishna Nagaya is playing-is it bedroom Krishna, or Royal Court Krishna?"

"Why, it is Krishna of bedroom, of course; Nagaya acts only as Bedroom Krishna; in subsequent scenes other actors would be playing that role."

"That means, he would put on that chemky (glittering) dress, wouldn't he, Kannam?"

"That thing I don't know," Kannam scratched his head. And, after a time he added in a low volume, "Hussainaiah, I will tell you something Nagaya is thinking; but don't ask Nagaya about this, because I am not supposed to reveal it to you."

"No no, I wouldn't tell anyone, but what is it, tell me?" Hussainaiah asked eagerly.

"I will tell you; but I am not very sure whether Nagaya was being serious about it . . ." Kannam showed hesitation.

"Don't worry about all that; first, tell me what the matter is," Hussainaiah said impatiently.

Kannam pouted to hide his smile and said, "Nagaya wants to give you a role in the play; he says he wants to see how you would look in a chemky dress."

Hussainaiah opened his mouth cavernously and struggled to breath and with difficulty asked, "Me . . . ? Me putting on a chemky dress! Nagaya wants to see me in chemky dress-? Are you telling me the truth, Kannam?"

"Of course, how can I utter a lie in these matters?"

"Me, me in chemky dress?" Hussainaiah choked in ecstasy, "Oh, my . . . what are you saying, Kannam? Me acting in chemky dress . . . not just witnessing the play, but straightaway acting, and in chemky dress . . . ! Oh, this Nagaya, the way he thinks and acts, he is really a Kista Paramatma, indeed!"

"Yes, but, first tell me, just tell me, are you willing? Tell me; wouldn't you like to put on the chemky dress?"

Hussainaiah was still unable to talk freely and was gasping.

Kannam was wondering how his mentor hoped to achieve the fulfillment of his wish, with these strange ideas.

Hussainaiah said in a voice that still trembled, his mind hovering between awareness and trance, "Oh, what are you saying, Kannam? I don't understand what is happening to me! Oh, Kista Paramatma, what are you doing to me?"

Narayanamma who had been seeing and listening to all this, intervened and said with concern, "Oh, he is losing his mind, Kannam; ask Nagireddy garu to leave him out of this plan; such things are beyond this man . . ."

Hussainaiah swirled round and hissed like a cobra, robbed of its prey and gave a full-throated shout, "You keep out of all this, I tell you; what do you know of these things that you should intervene and talk, foolish woman! Go back into the other room, that's where you belong."

Narayanamma's face showed hurt as she walked away quickly on him; they could hear her muffled crying.

"No, no, you shouldn't have talked that way; after all, she was being careful that you shouldn't lose your face on the stage; she was right in her apprehension. Is it not a fact that you had not gone on the stage even once? And then, Hussainaiah, acting on the stage is not easy," Kannam mildly rebuked Hussainaiah.

Hussainaiah was already regretting his foolish outburst at his wife; he quickly turned round to face Kannam and said angrily, "You have been the cause of all this; who asked you to come to me with that news from Nagaya? You are a nuisance man; all that you do is this; go from house to house and disturb 'the placid waters'."

Staggered, Kannam looked intently at Hussainaiah for a while and said, "You have taught me a good lesson, Hussainaiah; I will not come to your house a second time."

Hussainaiah watched helplessly as Kannam walked out into the street and then, after some quick rethinking, ran hurriedly to catch and pacify him in an effort to prevent damage to his budding theatre career.

Managing to catch Kannam, Hussainaiah offered a few explanations, walked along with him to the kirana shop of Rosaiah, bought him a bundle of beedis and a box of matches and succeeded in extracting a promise that Kannam would not reveal to Nagireddy what had happened.

After cajoling and coaxing he took leave of Kannam and walked back to face turbulent weather at home.

The water holes in the sand bed of the rivulet were not collecting water as fast as they did earlier and had to be dug deeper and deeper. Around each water hole men and women gathered expectantly with pans, pots and other containers; yoke-slings lay piled up, by the side of each water hole. Men squatted on the sand dunes as the women folk struggled with water-collection.

"I think we are destined to witness the end of the world, judging by the way seasons are failing."

Pagadaiah was also there among the men with the yoke slings; he heard the comment and gave a wry smile.

Balakoti who was going round, deepening each water hole, came to the place wielding a crow-bar; "Step aside, Bathukamma, this one needs deepening; just wait for a little time, I will make it easier for you."

"Oh my, God give you a hundred years of life, Balakotaya!" Bathukamma then turned to the other men, "a man should be like him, helping the womenfolk. You are all standing and watching as though it is a game. This task of collecting and carrying water is weighing down our waists. Why is the God troubling us like this; if His intention is to punish, why doesn't He straightaway end our lives."

Pagadaiah said, "If at each difficulty people ask God to end their lives to end their misery, the entire world would be emptied in no time."

"Let it happen so; the animals would thank God for it and would live happily."

"Facing difficulties is a part of life and you have to try and find out a solution," Pagadaiah sermonized.

"Then, find a solution to this water problem; it is the work of men—this finding of solutions for the problems. You men sit there on the slab every night and chat for hours and hours; what you all do there, we, the women do not know."

At that, the men chafed and the women laughed exultantly.

Water welled up slowly in the deepened holes.

They began to fill their containers, one after another.

Balakoti moved from one water-hole to another in supervision; sometimes he helped a woman in lifting a pan and fixing it sideways on her waistline; womenfolk were impressed with his helping nature.

Then, Pullamma's man came with his yoke-sling and pans.

Pagadaiah looked on thoughtfully at the spectacle before his eyes; the spectacle of so many of them gathering on the sand sides of the rivulet, for water; the remark made by the lady, though casual, definitely carried some truth—it definitely was the duty of the men-folk to find out a solution.

By the time they all collected water and carried it home it was well past noon.

Lazily moving clouds got hitched on, one to one, and by the afternoon the sky became cloud-cast, cooling the day.

Back in the village, men assembled at the slab, in good number.

Pagadaiah and Hulakki joined late.

The cool wind and the cloud-cast sky cheered up the members and one of them said, "Yes, Uncle Pagadaiah has come; it is a long time since we heard a tale."

Before Pagadaiah could react, Hulakki took up the issue, "It's time we opened our eyes; forget the tales and chit-chat and do something practical; you discussed the issue of water a hundred times at least, on this slab. Has anything, useful, come out of it? Somebody proposed reconstruction of the Vindhyadramma tank; another proposed a dam across the breach-rivulet; you talked of mahjars and representations to the 'kolkoter'—so many things you have said. The moment you are away from the slab you forget all the things, like those 'beggars of Budipadu' . . .

"But for that timely 'food-for-work' programme many would've starved," Hulakki paused and nodded his head questioningly at the members and said in conclusion, "So, be serious and do something that would help the community in these tight times."

"Whatever you have said is true, Uncle Hulakki; the other day, Uncle Pagadaiah talked of mahjar and nothing has come out of it."

"Yes, yes, and somebody has also suggested that we should approach Naraiah's son for the drafting of the mahjar."

"Yes, yes, yes" Hulakki mimicked, "Somebody said something and somebody said some other thing; what were you doing and what did you think?"

"We must get the mahjar prepared today; would someone go and call that boy, Naraiah's grandson to the slab?" Pagadaiah suggested.

Balakoti promptly got down the chimti bench and ran to the house of Naraiah.

"That's how it should be," Somebody said appreciatively.

"You are right; that should be the spirit of a slab member," Another member seconded the compliment.

"I think, by tomorrow, the dam across the rivulet would be constructed; so, let the slab fix the water-rate," Kannam remarked.

The remark caused ripples of chuckles.

The veterans knitted their brows in distaste.

Mme Pullamma's man arrived on the scene; after observing the slab for a while, he floated an enquiry, "I see a very serious atmosphere at the slab; what is happening here?"

"Come; we are all waiting for you."

"'Waiting for me', what do you mean, Bademaya? Is your head spinning? Do you want some treatment?"

"Shh, don't start that again, for once," Hulakki chided.

Mme Pullamma's man continued to caste menacing looks at Bademaya, who continued with his mischievous smile and mumbling remarks.

Meanwhile, Balakoti came back limply and the members looked at him questioningly.

"Naraiah's grandson left the village two days ago."

Kannam suppressed his chuckles. As others waited for the things to unfurl, the slab became silent.

"Now, what shall we do?"

"What can we do? So many are there at the slab and not even one can write a mahjar, that is the plight of this slab!"

"Let us all go to the Lord-Sir; maybe he will show us a way out."

"Not all; only one or two."

"In that case, let Uncle Pagadaiah and Uncle Hulakki go to the Lord-Sir; only the two of them,"

The delegates went to the house of the Banzardar.

The Banzardar smiled at them, "What brings you two veterans here?"

Their explanation over, the Banzardar asked them, "What do you want, you tell me that first? Do you want that old Vindhyadramma tank to be revived or you want a fresh dam built across the rivulet? The other day that man Nagireddy was proposing the revival of the Vindhyadramma tank, whereas, you seem to prefer a dam across the breach-stream; that shows there is a clash of ideas among you. What would you write in the mahjar?"

"But, Lord-Sir, Nagireddy is not from our village; who is he to decide what should be done? We want a bund across the rivulet; we would not revive that accursed tank; yes, that is it, Lord-Sir," Pagadaiah said conclusively.

The Banzardar silently nodded and gave an intriguing smile, "Pagadaiah, you know what is what, and you are talking like this! There are three villages in our Panchayat and any decision taken should protect the interests of the three villages. Further, that Vindhyadramma tank is not in the revenue limits of our village . . ."

"But, Lord-Sir, we don't want that, we want only a bund across the rivulet,"

"I know, I know; you have said that, but, the rivulet also issues from the breach of that tank-bund; you have to remember that," the Banzardar explained.

Pagadaiah stood gaping.

The Banzardar smiled at them, amiably, "Don't worry; I will tell you what to do; but, remember that you have called on me for help and I am showing you a way; I am not forcing you into anything; is that clear? . . .

"Take two white papers and collect the signatures of the villagers on them and give me those papers; let me see what can be done with them. Right . . . ? Now, go and be on that work," The Banzardar said dismissively.

"Lord-Sir, the signatures . . . ?"

The Banzardar gave an indulgent smile, again, and twisted his lips, "If not signatures thumb-impressions; it's all the same. Do whatever you can; the minimum that you have to do is collect the thumb-impressions of all that have gathered at the slab."

They were satisfied with that and with a nod of obeisance took leave of the Lord-Sir.

They came back to the slab; the members looked at them for the next move.

"Pagadaiah, no time to be lost now," Hulakki turned to the slab members and said, "We have done part of the work; now, let someone go to Rosaiah-Sir's shop and fetch two or three white papers, and . . . and . . . and . . . a fountain pen.

"Of what use is a pen for us; how many of us can sign?"

Each of them looked at the others.

Only one of them held his hand high, and that was a smiling Kannam, "But you haven't told us what for we want a pen and papers."

"Lord-Sir has said he will get the mahjar written and all that we need to do is collect the signatures of the villagers," Hulakki explained.

"Not signatures, say thumb-impressions, thumb-impressions and you don't require a pen for that,"

"Yes, yes, thumb-impressions; it's all the same, Lord-Sir has said; what difference is there?"

"How are we to know what would be written on that paper?" Another member queried.

"Lord-Sir has asked us about what should the mahjar contain and we have explained; the same would be written, of course," Pagadaiah said after a pause, "Now, has anyone gone for the papers?"

Balakoti came running with the papers; "Rosaiah Sir wants to know what for we want white papers; he is coming here," Balakoti gasped.

Members looked towards the alley and saw Rosaiah-Sir hurrying to the slab and they smiled in appreciation, "Oh, come Rosaiah Sir, come; there is no better omen than your arrival."

And Rosaiah came in his usual style and straightaway came to the point, "Pagadaiah, what is the matter; why have you sent the man for white papers?"

Pagadaiah explained and Rosaiah nodded with satisfaction, "Then, it is all right; but what are we going to have, a bund across the rivulet or filling of the breach to revive the Vindhyadramma tank? Tell me that first."

"That, of course, is to be decided by the Lord-Sir; we will have one or the other."

"But, Pagadaiah, you were saying the old tank is an accursed one and would bring bad luck to the village . . . ?"

Pagadaiah noncommittally nodded his head and said, "Let us see what it would all come to. Nothing is in our hands; it is the One above that decides all things," he pointed his index finger at the sky.

"Of course, of course, 'that is always there'," Members endorsed it

"So, that's it, then; but, don't delay the things, Pagadaiah; good things must be done at the earliest," Rosaiah turned to the slab, "Right then, I must be going now; maybe, customers are waiting for me."

"Rosaiah Sir, keep coming to the slab; your wise counsel is very much needed."

"Certainly," Said Rosaiah, looking back over his shoulders.

"Rosaiah Sir is a nice man, I say; he never refuses a beedi, you see."

Quite a few of them nodded in approval.

"Uncle Pagadaiah, the slab has done its duty; now, let us have a tale."

"Yes Uncle, you must tell us a good tale today."

Pagadaiah felt happy.

However, Hulakki was not for the tale; he said, "No, no, we haven't even started the work and you are saying 'the slab

273

has done its duty,' No tale, no 'vale'; now, first let us collect the signatures, I mean, the thumb impressions of the slab members. Now, Balakoti, have you brought the inkpot?"

Balakoti bit his tongue and looked stupidly.

"The fellow is always like that; does only half the work assigned."

Balakoti resented the remark and looked angrily at the member; then he turned to Hulakki, "That sounds wonderful, did you ask for an inkpot? You said, 'white papers', and I have brought them; if you mentioned an inkpot I would've brought that also, hmm," Balakoti expressed his displeasure.

Hulakki twisted his lips at the perversity of the man and then added, "Okay, now I am telling you, go and bring the inkpot, quickly."

Balakoti stood sulking.

"Come on, be quick, go and get the inkpot."

"You are ordering me as though I am your servant; I wouldn't bring any inkpot or 'winkpot'; let somebody else do that. Am I the only one to do everything here?" Balakoti pouted.

Hulakki touched his forehead in disgust and looked at Pagadaiah.

Pagadaiah twisted his lips philosophically.

"Okay, Uncle Hulakki, I will get the inkpot," Kannam said.

Members were astonished at that gesture from an unexpected quarter and looked at the sprinting Kannam; they came to appreciate the man, "The fellow isn't that bad, after all; when the slab needs a thing he would always oblige."

"Yes, yes, actually, the problem is with some of the slab members; the thing is that they always try to make him look a black sheep."

"You are right, Venkaiah the little, I too feel the same way."

There were more 'I too's,' on that and it was now the turn of Hulakki to pout.

Presently, Kannam came back empty-handed, "Rosaiah Sir has refused to give inkpot; 'already I have given three white papers; how much more you want freely from me?' he said."

Members gaped.

At that point, Rosaiah came, carefully holding the inkpot, with both hands; coming to Pagadaiah he said, "'It's not like that', Pagadaiah; if it's a thing of small price, I wouldn't hesitate to give; haven't I given three white papers? Now, ink bottle is a costly thing and there is only one in my shop; suppose, I give you that and you open it and use it and then send it back to me, who would buy that? It is very rare that a man comes for an inkpot and when that man comes and asks for it, can I give an opened inkpot? You have to understand my problem too. I am not tight-fisted as some of you, perhaps, are thinking. Ask the men here; every now and then a buyer comes and asks for a free beedi and I never say 'no'; sometimes, a buyer also asks for a free 'cigret' too, though it happens rarely; I give away 'cigret' also; but, you have asked for an inkpot and what can I do; here, I have brought it; take it and if you think that it is in the fitness of things to pay, you pay for it; let anyone pay, not necessarily now; a few days later, at least. Here, take it and do whatever you want to do with it. I am going," Keeping the inkpot in the stretched hands of Hulakki, Rosaiah went away.

They were all stunned again and silence ensued.

"What a big sermon he has given over a small inkpot!"

"'Sometimes' he is 'always' like that; quite a strange fellow, this Rosaiah,"

"You are right; you know what happened one day? I bought four 'tolas' of cooking oil; he weighed it and gave it and then, when I asked for a 'cigret' he threw a beedi at me and said, 'it's beedi you should smoke'. After that, I never asked for a cigret; I asked only for a beedi. Very queer fellow, this Rosaiah . . ."

"Let it be so, one day what happened you know . . ."

"Stop it, all of you; now let this business of taking the thumb impressions start," Shouted Hulakki, stretching his hand for someone to take the inkpot.

Pagadaiah gave a start at that shout, but, checked himself and took the inkpot; he realized that Hulakki was upstaging him and intervened to say, "let us attend to the first things, first."

They started the process of taking the thumb impressions of the members present at the slab; members vied with one another to lend a hand.

On one paper, they took the thumb-impressions, one below another.

The work went on at a good pace; all the three papers were filled with thumb-impressions. Pagadaiah and Hulakki looked satisfied with what they had achieved.

As usual, the sethsindi lurked at the Bo tree's base.

"Now, I will show these papers to the Lord-Sir," Pagadaiah said and picked up the inkpot to fix the screw-lid, only to lose his grip on it; the pot fell from his hands straight on the papers, spreading ink on them, all over.

Pagadaiah's heart skipped a beat and he stared in horror at what happened.

For a time, nobody spoke.

Pagadaiah and Hulakki stood like statues, their eyes fixed on the mess-up.

The other members were all looking in wonder at what Pagadaiah and Hulakki, of all, had done or failed to do

Then, that boy, who had impressed the slab members with his news coverage on the return of 'Errodu', came sprinting to the slab and broke some sensational news, "Errodu has come; he came on a biscole, on 'double—sawari' (two men on a bicycle), a chiglet in one hand and riding the biscole with the other hand . . ."

All the heads turned towards the reporter-boy.

Pagadaiah and Hulakki stood like statues, staring at the botch-up for a long time.

When they looked back they saw the last man leaving the slab.

Both the veterans watched the exodus, too perplexed and too late to ward off.

Pagadaiah asked in a weak voice, "What shall we do now Uncle Hulakki?"

Hulakki said "Don't be unduly perturbed over what has happened; such things happen, because of the bad spirits hovering above our heads, at dusk time . . .

"But, Pagadaiah, I am sure, you have handled inkpots earlier; how did it go wrong, this time?"

Pagadaiah answered with a pale smile, "I might have touched an ink-pot once or twice when I was in school; in those days, we used to practice writing only on sand with the index finger, and occasionally a slate, and may be once or twice I touched an inkpot; but that was a long, long time back; now, after such a long gap, who remembers these things?"

Hulakki gave an understanding smile, "It is no big thing, Pagadaiah; you have to hold the ink-pot in your left palm, like this, and then, with the thumb and index finger of your right hand turn the screw tight, like this, slowly . . . Slo . . wly . . . like t-h-i-s," Hulakki gave a nice demonstration on fixing the screw-lid of an inkpot.

"Enough, Uncle Hulakki, enough," Said Pagadaiah showing the hurt of humiliation on his face, "don't teach me these things now, at this age; the question is, 'what should we do now?'"

"Why, why are you so much upset, Cousin Pagadaiah, "Nothing has happened; it is straight and simple; go to Rosaiah's store and get three more papers and start the process again, that's all."

"But, do you think, Rosaiah would give papers again?" Pagadaiah expressed a doubt.

"Leave it to me, if not from Rosaiah's store, from some other place," After giving it some thought, Hulakki slowly said, "if my memory serves me right, there are some papers, at my home; yes, I think so . . ."

Pagadaiah heaved a big sigh of relief, "Oh, Mother Durgamma, you have saved me from an embarrassment; I will break a coconut, the next thing! Oh, Mother Durgamma . . ." then he suddenly turned to Hulakki and asked, "But, Uncle Hulakki, it is really very surprising to hear that you have some white papers with you; How did they come to your house?"

Hulakki laughed it off, "Oh that happened long time back and there is a lengthy story behind it; some other time I will tell you," He wondered at the uneasiness of his ally; putting his friend's agitating mind at ease, he said, "Stay here, at the slab; I will go and get the papers."; he rushed away.

Pagadaiah sat on the slab; he recalled the news of Errodu's return, but resisted the idea of going to the western lane.

In a while, Hulakki came back with a roll of white papers; Pagadaiah was pleased at the sight of the roll of papers.

"Now, Pagadaiah, is your mind at rest now?" Hulakki asked his friend, fondly.

Pagadaiah was about to smile; but, the bigger problem of inkpot loomed in his mind and he said, "And, Uncle Hulakki, wherefrom shall we get the inkpot?"

"Eh, why didn't you remind me of the inkpot?"

"What if I did?" asked Pagadaiah.

"I have an inkpot too, at home."

Pagadaiah was astonished, 'he has an inkpot too!' he wondered.

"But, what is the use of getting the papers and ink; they have all gone to the west lane; it will take a while for them to come here; and then, there is no guarantee that they would come to the slab; they might go home. What shall we do?" Hulakki asked.

Pagadaiah had no ready answer to that question.

"Or shall we do one thing; let us also go to the west lane and see what is happening there; then we will herd the men back to the slab; what do you say?"

Reluctantly, Pagadaiah agreed.

"In that case, I will keep these papers at home and come back; stay here itself, I wouldn't be long," Hulakki walked briskly to his house.

Pagadaiah sat on the slab pensively, still unable to take off his mind from that bungling act of his.

At the house of the Red Lad there was a crowd, as expected; men were jostling their way to get a better view.

Pagadaiah and Hulakki didn't like to push their way to the forefront; after all, the mess up at the slab had diminished the aura around their heads.

Resignedly they kept back.

However, Red Lad's sister caught sight of the two veterans and warmly called out, "Come, come, Uncle Pagadaiah and Uncle Hulakki; now, give way to the elders, you men; why are you all surging like that; is a puppet show on, here? Go home, go away," She pushed the huddle apart to make way for the duo.

The crowd tottered on their feet, but, after the duo advanced to the front line, their feet regained the balance and they tried to forge ahead.

Then, the veterans saw Errodu sitting on the coir-cot, in the open courtyard and his lady lying on the floor, in front, sobbing inconsolably as she clutched and hugged her man's feet to her bosom.

Women in the crowd, wept unashamedly at that poignant sight, "Oh my child, oh my child, you have come out unscathed in this ordeal; oh my child, oh, my sweet child . . ."

Tears welled up in the eyes of Pagadaiah too; furtively he wiped them, 'This, indeed, is the kind of wife a man dreams of; blessed is the man who gets such a spouse!'

Hulakki, for his part, was unmoved by the sentimental touch of the scene in front.

Pagadaiah appeared to be in no mood to leave the spot; he was aware that he was in a vicarious surge of emotion and he made no effort to come out of it.

"Let us go to the slab, Cousin Pagadaiah; let us ask them all to come to the slab; we must complete the work this evening."

Pagadaiah calmly showed his raised palm, "Don't worry, Uncle Hulakki, we can do it tomorrow; why hurry up the things!"

Hulakki fidgeted, but didn't talk back.

Errodu consoled his wife, fondled her, and now and then, wiped away the tears, hers and his too.

Bhagyam, crying now, talking now, came and sat near Pagadaiah and narrated the unrevealed part of the tale, "God give that big 'military lord a long life; he has kindly released my brother; Uncle Pagadaiah, tell me, what ceremony I should perform at the shrine of Muthyalamma to pacify the angry deities . . ."

Pagadaiah nodded with empathy, "I will tell you, I will tell you."

Errodu intermittently looked at the veterans and the crowd with a pale smile.

Meanwhile, Pullamma's man arrived at the scene and straightaway assumed charge and began to put the jostling crowd in order, "Get back a little, move back a little; don't cross this line, I tell you"; he drew a line with the small stick he wielded.

Presently, Bhagyam noticed that the eyes of the men were riveted on the wailing lady; quickly, she went to the lady and tugging at her wrist, prompted her to get up and follow her into the house.

281

After a while, Errodu too took leave of Pagadaiah and went into the house.

With both the central characters gone, the crowd reluctantly began to drift away.

"Oye ye men, don't go home; all of you, go first to the slab; we have to complete that work of collecting the thumb-impressions," Hulakki called out to the men.

Sensing that they were in no mood to comply with, Hulakki said again, "Oye men, this is important for us all; gather at the slab, all of you."

"Don't worry Uncle Hulakki, we would anyway come there tomorrow; where else would we go to pass the time and what else is there than to pass the time?"

"Uncle Hulakki, go home and have some sleep; you have been fretting all the day, with that thumb-impressions business,"

"And, Uncle Hulakki, do you honestly think these mahjars would help? The Emmellu, the kulkatair—all of them know about the Vindhyadramma tank; who doesn't know? If they really want to help us, these mahjars are not required."

Their remarks unnerved the veteran Hulakki and he looked at his ally and at the drifting men, alternately.

However, a few men stood a little away, and were waiting; Hulakki saw them and joined them, "I am going to the slab, Pagudaiah; come there; we all will be waiting for you, come soon."

Pagadaiah, then, stood up and called out to the drifting crowd, "Oye, ye men, gather at the slab; don't go home; we have to give those papers to the Lord-Sir, tomorrow."

They listened and didn't reply; however, they changed the course of their walk and proceeded in the direction of the slab.

Pagadaiah noticed it; he was satisfied that his stock was still intact.

He too reached the slab and for some unknown reason looked keenly at the sky; the tenth day waxing moon was bright in the sky; but a few clouds were lurking by, waiting to ambush Him.

The members were there in good number; they were all waiting for Pagadaiah; he noticed that Uncle Hulakki had brought a hurricane lamp.

"Shall we begin, Uncle Hulakki?"

Hulakki nodded and unfurled the roll of papers. He spread them out and kept a few pebbles on them as paperweights; then, he carefully unscrewed the lid, asking Pagadaiah to watch closely.

The work commenced and the gathering on the slab watched curiously.

The sethsindhi watched the activity unobtrusively.

Hulakki went on with the job like a professional; he called up the members, one after the other, smeared the ink on their thumbs and took the impressions on the papers.

Pagadaiah sat close by and supervised the work with his looks.

The work did not take a long time and at the end of it, Hulakki gave a long sigh, "So, our part of the work is over,"

"With the grace of Mother Durgamma," Pagadaiah added.

"But how is one to know which thumb-impression is whose? That has to be written; now, we can't even get it written because there is no way we can identify the impressions!"

Hulakki was aghast and looked open-mouthed.

However, the members did not disperse and appeared to be waiting for some clarification on something.

"Don't bother; it doesn't matter whose name is written for whose thumb-impression," Pagadaiah said in disgust.

"What are we waiting for?"

Hulakki trying to please Pagadaiah, said smilingly, "Perhaps they are waiting for you to recite a tale."

Naginaboina hastened to say, "No, no, it's not for a tale or vale; some of us want to know why Errodu ran away from his wife then and what is it that has now brought him back, yes, that's it."

"How can anyone explain that? Only Errodu can tell you the reasons for it," Hulakki laughed, but seeing that no other member shared the joke, quickly gave up his laughter and waited for some other member to take up the issue.

This time, it was Balakoti; he said emphatically, "We are all waiting not for a tale; we want to know about the effect of moles on the lives of men."

It hurt Pagadaiah's ego to listen as the slab members spurned the tale for once, the tale for which they had bothered him a hundred times, at times; in fact, he was longing and ready to recite a story.

He had many stories in his repertoire; there was this story of the celestial beauty, Urvasi and the great emperor Pururava; 'the emperor who is head over heels in love with the beauty, wins her with his valor but eventually loses her by unwittingly committing a breach on the stipulated conditions and wanders like a mad man, in search of her; then, there was that saga of Yayati, a great ancient emperor; the emperor craves for carnal pleasures, even in ripe old age and makes demands on his son, whose youth he wants to be transferred to him. The tale of the Sage Viswamitra and Menaka never lost its appeal with the members; Menaka, a danseuse in the heaven, is sent by the Indra, the lord of the Heaven to distract the Sage from his severe penance; she beguiles the Sage with her beauty and tempting dance and the Sage falls for her and loses all the spiritual power acquired over years of severe penance. They listened to these tales again and again; but, he knew that a raconteur should never lose patience; like a good shepherd, he should tend to the 'straying creatures' . . .

Pagadaiah chose to 'get the sheep inside the fenced up square' and said, "So, you want to know why Errodu had run away and why he chose to return, isn't it that? Well, it shouldn't take a long time for the story to come out; sooner or later we will come to know that," Pagadaiah assured the members.

At that, the members fell into an animated talk, and Hulakki and Pagadaiah heard them with attention.

Then came a surprising disclosure, "Uncle Pagadaiah, it is no more a secret; almost all of Errodu's friends know that; if you permit me to talk, I will reveal that to you all," Ramkishtie said, suppressing his smile.

Pagadaiah was intrigued, "Yes, yes, go ahead; tell us whatever that is."

"If you knew that, it is time you told the slab."

"You are supposed to inform all such important things to the slab, first thing; no permission or girmission."

Even before Pagadaiah opened his mouth, several members demanded Ramkishtie to divulge 'the secret'.

Ramkishtie, however, addressed his explanation to Pagadaiah, "Actually, Uncle Pagadaiah, the thing is known to everyone in the village of that girl, and that is the thing all the suitors have been afraid of and have given up the idea of marrying her; but, after Errodu's marriage with her, they are all ruing their rejection of the girl, now."

"Stop that husk and come to the point; whhaatt was ththat reason? Tell us that first, yes, tell us, without wasting time, if you want to save your skin, yes," Someone said in a good-humored way.

"What are you talking? Why would I need to save my skin, what crime have I committed?" Ramkishtie shouted.

"There, there, back to the same old ways again; what can you do now, Cousin Pagadaiah; 'crooked is dog's tail and crooked it would remain'!" An exhausted Hulakki turned to Pagadaiah.

Pagadaiah was also itching to know the sneaky reason, "Alright, alright, Ramkishtie, now tell us whatever it is,"

Pagadaiah's word didn't work

Even while sulking, Ramkishtie pointed to the young men, sitting at a corner of the slab, "They are also Errodu's friends and all of them know it; ask them to tell," with that, Ramkishtie left the slab in a huff.

The slab observed the customary silence and at the end of it came back to the point, as Pagadaiah said in exasperation, "This is not the way things should go on at the slab; members getting angry even over words said in good humour is not right; anyway, let someone spill the truth, whatever it is."

Finally, a young man made a quick, loud and brief revelation of it, "That girl has a snake-like birthmark on her right thigh; people say, whoever courts a lady with such birthmark would die the very first night."

They listened with open mouths, Pagadaiah and Hulakki included

Pagadaiah thought, 'So, this is the reason why they were all clamoring to know the facts on the Science of the Nevi!'

In time, all of them pursed their lips and started thinking, witnessing some visuals in their minds and debating the issue.

Pagadaiah wondered what they would do after they were home; he smiled wryly, as he thought, 'What would I do, if Rattamma were here, in my hut?'

Balakoti came to Pagadaiah from a far off corner of the slab and said, "Uncle Pagadaiah, now, you must tell us about the effects of these birthmarks on the lives of men."

"Yes, Uncle Pagadaiah, that day you promised to tell us," Bushaiah endorsed.

"Uncle Pagadaiah, it is very important that we should know these things."

"Yes, Uncle Pagadaiah, today, we wouldn't go home without learning about the significance of the birthmarks."

'This is all very nice,' thought Pagadaiah; he showed his palm and nodded his head, "Okay, don't worry, I will tell you whatever I know of it; but, first, let someone give me a beedi and matches."

"It is getting very dark; looks like it would rain; is it not better that we go home," Hulakki cautioned the members.

"We wouldn't mind getting drenched, let it rain as much as it would."

"Yes, yes, Uncle Pagadaiah, we must know this mystery of the Nevi, tonight."

"But, where is my beedi?" Pagadaiah stretched his hand in the thickening darkness.

They came forward with beedis and matches groping for Pagadaiah's palm, 'Take as many beedis as you want, but you must tell us this thing.'

Hulakki saw that they were in no mood to heed the rain; he got off the slab, "Pagudaiah, I am leaving."

Pagadaiah watched as Hulakki walked towards his home.

Then he lit a beedi, lustily drew in the smoke, and began, "The most important thing about the birthmark is that, it wouldn't fail to affect the lives of men. Like Palmistry and Astrology, the Science of the Nevi is absolute in its effect. One important thing to be kept in mind is that, the birthmarks differ in their effect on people's lives, gender wise; for example, if a man has a birthmark on his right side of some organ, it has a benefic effect, but, in case of women, the mark must be on the left side for a benefic effect . . . Of course, there are some exceptions to this rule . . .

"Birthmarks appear in different colors; birthmarks in green, red and honey colors are auspicious; the black ones are harmful; they affect men's lives adversely; usually, the birthmarks form congenitally on different parts of the body, but in some cases, they can be inside the body too and they are more harmful, because they are not visible to the eye of a novice and so no neutralizing measure can be taken . . ."

"Yes, yes, I heard my great grandfather say this; if a person has a black mole on his tongue, his word on critical issues would come true; is that reading correct, Uncle Pagadaiah?" Venkaiah, the middle asked.

"Yes, yes, there you are. It is correct . . ." Pagadaiah endorsed.

"So, as you have said, the bad effect can be neutralized . . . ?"

"Yes, yes, but one has to be very careful."

"Careful . . . ? How . . . ?"

"Yes, yes, one has to be very careful about it. One must take the help of a person who is well-versed in the Science of the Nevi and act as per the prescriptions."

"But, Uncle Pagadaiah, priests see only the palms and decide whether the girl and the boy are well-matched; they don't check these nevi . . ."

"That is also there; but a priest's theory usually goes by the birth stars, not by the birthmarks; if the stars are mutually compatible, other things wouldn't count, in that line of thinking, of course."

"Uph, uph, raindrops are falling; yes, looks like, it would rain . . ." Bushaiah fussed.

"Oh, stop it man; if you are so much worried, beat a hasty retreat to your hut; don't disturb us."

The slab ignored the threat of the rain by a good majority; however, one or two members left the place in dissent.

"And then, Uncle Pagadaiah, suppose, the stars of the boy and girl match as per the reading of the priest, would their lives be happy even if some bad birthmarks are there on their bodies?"

Pagadaiah scratched his pate, "That is something only an expert can say."

"What factor must have helped Errodu, then?"

Pagadaiah looked pointedly at Bushaiah, "So you haven't gone home," He gave a hearty laugh and after an instant said, "If you so badly want to know that, Bushaiah, you must go, check and find out the birthmarks on the body of Errodu; find out and report to me; I will then tell you what has worked against what and what has neutralized what; okay?" Pagadaiah nodded questioningly at Bushaiah.

They relished the joke, but did not ease up on the topic; "Uncle Pagadaiah, let us come back to the birthmarks," Naginaboina pleaded.

Pagadaiah realized that he must be careful; so, he proceeded cautiously, "I too don't remember all of them, but I can tell you of some; first one of them is that a man would be blessed with wealth, if there is a mole on the right side of his forehead, or on the right temple or on the right side of the pupil of the eye, or on the right side of the nose; even if there is a mole on either side of the neck that will do; the man would be blessed with wealth . . .

"Suppose, a man has a mole on the right thigh, he would beget wealth through his wife . . ."

They chuckled; a member enquired, "Is Pullamma's man around? If he is, let somebody search for the birthmark on his thigh."

"On the right thigh, right thigh, don't forget that; is the fellow around, anyway?"

"You are lucky, he is not here."

"Oh my, the raindrops are falling, indeed . . ." Again some members expressed concern.

"Shh, let them fall, what will happen, haven't you ever been in rain, before?"

Venkaiah, the little came up with another doubt, "And then, Uncle Pagadaiah, I remember my grandfather saying that a man would become hugely wealthy if there is a mole on the right side—the right side . . ."

"Right side of . . . what—?" Bademaya asked impatiently, "Come out with that quickly-"

"I will, but please don't laugh, all of you, okay?" Venkaiah the little said shyly.

"Right, agreed, we wouldn't laugh," Three or four voices said in a chorus, "Now, you don't take too much time; on the right side of, what . . . ?"

"I wouldn't take much time, but, actually, the thing brings laughter to me too; but, don't laugh; please don't laugh if I say that."

"Oh my God, it looks like it would be morning by the time you cough it up; say that quickly or shut up your mouth."

"I will say Sir, don't be so rude, for that matter you are not my . . ."

Pagadaiah quickly intervened, "Alright, alright; now, what was it your grandfather said, 'on the right side of—of'—what?"

Finally, Venkaiah, the little was about to 'vomit' the word, stuck up in his throat, " . . . on the right side of the," again he checked himself and finally came out with a euphemism, "'the Pouch', yes, that's it, on the right side of 'the pouch'."

Instantly, they all grasped it and broke into a wild laughter; the slab echoed and re-echoed with the word 'Pouch'.

Pagadaiah too couldn't suppress his laughter, "'Pouch', Oh, Venkaiah, the little, you have almost swamped me with that word of yours, 'Pouch', yes, your grandfather is right, a mole on the right side of 'that' would make a man very rich."

"Have you checked it up; do you have it there, do you have it on your 'pouch'?"

Venkaiah, the little pouted in resentment at the jibe.

"Just for fun; don't take it seriously, Little Venkaiah, am I not you friend? Take it lightly, take it lightly."

Little Venkaiah relented and came back to the point, "But Uncle Pagadaiah, for a woman, the mole should be on the left side, am I right?" Venkaiah the little asked innocently.

The slab burst into laughter again, "On the right side of her 'pouch'! Hahhahha . . ."

"Oh, my poor grandson, my innocent darling, you are not getting the 'Pouch' factor right, dear," They mimicked.

Once again the slab resounded with that word and laughter. It took some time for the slab to come back to the Science of the Nevi, only on Naginaboina's request.

And Pagadaiah continued with his exposition on the Science of the Nevi, "One more fact, if there is a mole on the left side of the right palm, there would be a windfall for that man, yes . . ."

"Yes, that's it; check your right palm." A member said to his neighbor."

"But, how can I? It is quite dark . . ."

"Alright, then, search for it tomorrow, the first thing,"
They laughed.

"We will anyway do that, but everyone must check for 'that mole on the pouch', before the other things, I tell you."

"Sure, I will, I will search for all the birthmarks; there is no question of leaving out anything on any part . . ."

"Oh my, they are really big, these raindrops; they are big indeed; I am leaving."

"Yes, go, go; I will tell you where to search for, tomorrow"

"Uncle Pagadaiah, please postpone it to tomorrow."

"Then, it is alright with me," Pagadaiah got off the slab.

"No, no, Uncle Pagadaiah, please continue; it's not raining, it's only the pitter-patter of raindrops, just 'cat's piss', that's all."

"At least, tell us about the more important ones of the Nevi; we can listen to the remaining, tomorrow."

"Yes, do that, Uncle Pagadaiah."

"Alright then, I will give a quick check list and postpone it to tomorrow," Said Pagadaiah; then, he began, "Here is a brief list; a mole in the right eye, above the eye or on any one of the temples, on the tip of the nose, on the right side of the chin or cheek, on the front tip of the tongue or on the downside of it, on the right side of it, on right and left sides of the neck, downside of the right wrist . . ."

"Oh, you are going through it too fast for us . . ."

The raindrops began a fast beat, thud thud thud . . .

"Enough for tonight, the rest of the birthmarks, we will hear tomorrow . . ."

They lumped and jumped off the slab and began to sprint in different directions to reach their dwellings.

The Rain started slowly as if to alert the slab members, gained in momentum as if to warn them and then became fast and furious as if to teach them the lesson that they could never take things lightly, with Him, the Rain God.

Soon, it turned into a downpour; the lanes became slushy and in no time turned into canals, flowing from the brim of one side to the brim of the other.

The thatch of the roofs that had become dry and brittle in the unduly long summer broke into bits and fell into the lane-turned canals and the mice living in the cushy thatch scampered out only to tumble into the swirling water.

Slab members went home, all of them soaked to the bone.

On the slab, the jets of the rainwater beat on the forgotten thumb-impressed papers and pounded them into pulp, some of which dispersed on the slab and some fell off the slab to lose identity in the flowing waters that hurried towards the abandoned well at the end of the alley. The inkpot jerkily moved in the spasmodic wind, fell on a stone at the basement and broke, the ink lending a fleeting streak of colour to the rushing waters.

It rained continually through the night dampening the wind and chilling the weather.

The gusts of the dank wind whistled into the dwellings, through the openings in the twig screen-doors and windows.

None of them, locked up in their homes, slept; to them, things appeared to be heading for a cataclysm and they helplessly mumbled prayers to their Gods.

In between, a dazzling lightening nearly blinded them and they heard a deafening thunder, which almost fell on them or their huts; they shrieked in terror and quickly chanted the several names of the middle member of the Pandava brothers, "Arjuna, Phalguna, Pardha, Kiriti, Swethavahana, Bheebhatsu, Vijaya, Krishna, Savyasachi, Dhananjaya . . ."

The collective effect of the rain, gale and darkness was so devastating that they heard a rumble when there was none and had hallucinations of a deluge that was swamping their village.

The night seemed interminable and it rained all through the night. Where, in a house there were young and old, they all nestled together like sheep and lamb as if their proximity would save them like a shield; hours passed by like that.

At long last, on the heights of the Pandava hills there appeared an amber patch of brightness that heralded the morning, bringing with it some cheer and courage.

As if summoned by a call, they all came out of their dwellings and converged on the village outskirts to see to believe what had happened during the night.

The River of Sticks was in spate; the distance from the village to the river shortened by half, the river now so close as if the Gods had relented to provide a water-source to the village.

'But, where is the breach-rivulet? Where is the rivulet? We see only a wide, very wide stream, of the River of Sticks or have the two met; in that case, how big the rivulet has become?'

'Yes, yes, I see that; we are unable to spot the rivulet in this colossal stream. My God, has it rained so much, so much . . . ?'

"Maybe, we are seeing an abated flood; it was bigger a little while back, just see the silt here."

They could now see logs, tree-branches and some indeterminate clumps of mass floating on the swirling waters.

Some of them remembered the times their grandfathers had recounted about—times when the flood of the River of Sticks carried bodies of men, women and livestock in big mixed-up lumps.

'It matters only when they are alive; in the end, they all come to mean the same indistinguishable mass, afloat in the flood.'

It was an awesome sight to those viewing it from the outskirts of the village.

On one side there was a huge deluge terrifying and mystifying; on the other, there were dogs, swine and birds and fowl, straying and sniffing at the things on the ground, in the water and in the mire, foraging for food, oblivious of their mutual antagonism and the raging fury of the nature by their side, highlighting the power of the survival wish.

To those who looked up, the rain-bearing clouds still hovered in sky, 'it's not over, not yet . . .'

Soon, it started again, starting with slow paced showers and quickly gaining in momentum; soon the rain dismissed all of them from the spot, the men folk, the quadrupeds and the arboreal.

Burrows were engulfed in the waters, occupants were washed away in the rushing waters; the chance survivors lurked in bush and bramble—'now, they have to raise a family, afresh . . .'

'All seasons work the same way; they create, support and destroy the life; what happens when to who is what is called the destiny!'

Pagadaiah was busy at home; there were several leaks in the thatched roof. Installing a ladder, he climbed onto the roof and began to mend the thatch in the way he could.

The weather was chilly; but, the thing had to be attended to; he had no sleep all through the night, shifting his bedstead one place to another to escape the icy water drops from the leaks.

"Uncle Pagadaiah, I think the world is nearing its end; I have just seen the River of Sticks in its colossal spate; where did the river flow yesterday and where is the river now? A distance of two, no, three miles! My God, has anyone seen a thing like this . . . ?"

"Don't worry, Narayana, you will live to see worse things," Pagadaiah said as he climbed down, "So you have seen the deluge . . ."

"Yes, yes, it is really awesome, Uncle Pagadaiah; you must see the spectacle; shall we go?"

Pagadaiah nodded and putting on his banian, he pulled the twig-door shut and walked out.

'Really it is an awe-inspiring sight,' thought Pagadaiah as he surveyed the panoramic view of the intermixed floodwaters of the river and the rivulet; then, his eye got fixed on a spot; turning to Narayana he said, "But, Narayana, where is the hut of the snake-charmer Neeladri? This is where it was until yesterday and now the ground here looks eroded."

"Do you think Neeladri and his hut have been washed away," A frightened Narayana asked.

"What is surprising if they have been? He is also a mortal like them who have been washed away; by the way, have you seen any human bodies in the flood, has any one reported so?"

"Human bodies in the flood waters . . . ?"

"No, we have seen only the bodies of some animals, both white and black and of course, chunks of mass that looked like birds," Said Balakoti, who had joined them.

Pagadaiah pursed his lips for a brief while and then laconically said, "Soon you will see; the flood has not abated; it is rising; the culprits can't escape."

Narayana looked bewildered, "Who are the culprits?"

"Those that are yet to be washed away . . ."

"Who are yet to be washed away . . . ?"

"The culprits, of course . . ."

Then they heard the wailing of a man; "Oh my lords, my benefactors, my hut has been washed away and my three snakes too!"

They turned back and saw the snake charmer; "Oh Neeladri, here you are, safe; thank your Gods."

"But, my snakes, my lord . . . ? And, how sweet those three snakes were! Can I ever get the likes of them! Oh my God, how can I live now? Those beauties, Rambha, Urvasi, Menaka . . ."

Pagadaiah couldn't help laughing, 'Rambha, Urvasi, Menaka . . .'

The unmarried snake charmer had been eking out livelihood with the snakes he caught, displaying their dance; once in a while he helped villagers by catching snakes moving around their homes.

"Don't worry Neela; now you will have plenty of snakes to catch; all the holes have been invaded by the flood waters; at least, until it becomes dry again, they will be living outside for you."

Neeladri still cried disconsolately, "Oh my darling ones, why did you leave me alive; why didn't you take me too with you . . ."

It took three days for the floodwaters to recede completely and a fortnight for life in the village to fall back into a groove. Relieved from the survival fears, they now began to wonder what they should do with their fields, ploughshares and farm tools.

They discussed it once. The black cotton soil would take some time to dry enough for plowing; after plowing, what would they sow? Should they go for a dry crop or opt for paddy? One must ask a veteran like Hulakki or Naraiah and others of that age; their hair had grayed and in some cases had fallen off in this uncertain activity called 'farming'.

When would they all go to the slab again like they had done before the havoc of rain and river? When would they be rid of the worry? Would they ever win in this gamble with the monsoon? Questions, questions, questions all the way . . .

The slab lay in a low profile for a month. If it were endowed with life, it would have vanished from the village; 'the members cannot solve the problems of the community; they don't know how to tackle a problem and those that are intervening to help are further complicating the issues. What is the point of my existence in their midst!'

Pagadaiah recalled his spouse more frequently now. It was many months since she had gone away with her mother; he had not heard anything from them or about them since then.

His sister suggested that he should take another spouse; but he didn't agree to that idea. Whatever had happened, Rattamma had given him a son; maybe she would change her ways with the passage of time. Further, where was the guarantee that a fresh one would be different; after all, the problem centered on his anatomy?

One day, surprisingly he ran into an itinerant tenant farmer from his in-laws' village. In that chance meeting he gathered the news that they were all doing well and that-that-that—his 'mother-in-law was in the family way again, after a long, long time!!!

Pagadaiah was stumped by the news and his mind lost its composure; 'so, a record of his guilt was in the making.'

For quite a few days after he had received the news, he looked a shattered man; the onlookers were baffled at the sight of a forlorn-looking Pagadaiah; they enquired after his health and tried to know the cause of his plight; but he managed to avoid an embarrassment.

As predicted by Pagadaiah, there were reports of the presence of reptiles; Neeladri was able to catch two cobras and a rat snake; it made them all happy that the flood had spared Neeladri when it carried away his hut and they agreed among themselves that they should help him build another hut.

They approached Hulakki and Naraiah for their wise counsel and as usual they gave different advices on the farming activity to be pursued; with that, the farmers vacillated between the alternatives.

Finally, things improved and slowly men began to gather at the slab. Shrugging of the effects of the storm, the slab went into its business.

The issues that came up for a serious discussion were, the uncertain rains and the reasons for them, the progress the parents of the nubile daughters had made in finding suitable boys for their girls, the status of the human kind vis-a-vis the value system, the lives of Errodu, Pullamma's man, the status of the deity Muthyalamma . . . Among the subjects that were casually considered were the questions of water for cultivation, water for men and cattle, and the question of Vindhyadramma water tank read with the issue of a bund across the breach rivulet. There were also other minor issues, touched during the guillotine time, such as the Panchayat elections.

The staging of the mythological play 'Crowning of the Pandavas' efforts' hanged in suspense, rain and floods playing spoilsport; the proposed venue for the erection of the stage and auditorium was flooded and slushy even fifteen days after the cyclonic rain.

Hussainaiah who was to apply paint to his face and don a 'glittering costume' was terribly disappointed and was waiting to ask Nagireddy about the new date fixed for the play.

For some reason, Nagireddy had never showed up for more than a fortnight. His minion Kannam appeared listless and was querying all and sundry about the whereabouts of his patron.

It was in these circumstances that, one late morning, the Banzardar looked out from the verandah of his bungalow and found no one on the slab.

None of his servants was readily available to carry an important message and there was not even a boy in the vicinity; so, an upset Banzardar came out half-clad and shouted, "Who is there? Is anybody there on the slab? Would somebody go and ask Pagadaiah to see me, at once?"

After that shout, he went back into his bungalow thinking that someone would carry the message and that Pagadaiah would respond.

There was nobody near the slab; so, the message remained undelivered.

The Banzardar waited and waited, but the man didn't arrive and he had to go a second time and make the same announcement.

Disgusted, he went into the backyard and found two of his domestics chatting ecstatically.

He cursed them and sent one of them to Pagadaiah.

The summons was duly conveyed, but Pagadaiah, distraught with the news from his in-laws' village, failed to respond in time and the Banzardar fumed at the misdemeanor of the man.

Putting on his khadi dress, the Banzardar went and sat on the slab, like a plebeian.

Rosaiah came there looking for Pullamma's man who had bought some provisions at his grocery, but had slipped away without paying the bill. Seeing the unusual presence of the Banzardar at the slab, he stopped, paid obeisance and enquired with an obedient smile, "What is this I see, Lord-Sir sitting on the slab?"

The Lord-Sir smiled back, nodded and replied, "Times Rosaiah, it is the power of the times; who knows what would happen when? Hadn't Vasudeva clasped the feet of the donkey?"

Rosaiah grasped the meaning of the allusion and folding his arms across the chest, politely asked, "Is there anything this humble servant of yours can do for you, Lord-Sir?"

The Banzardar smiled again as he looked the man up and down, "Yes, Rosaiah, why don't you dress up fully before you come to a public place; see, sometimes, there would be young men at the public places; why do you frighten them in this half-naked condition, Don't force them to become recluses; instead, dress up nicely; you are not an old man and you have a happy family; are you getting what I mean?"

Rosaiah smiled and nodded in appreciation of the jest and head bent, scratched on the ground with his toe; then clucking his tongue, he said philosophically, "What is left for me in this world now, Lord-Sir, 'both the beans and farts have exhausted'!"

The Banzardar raised his eyebrows in mock surprise; he laughed and remarked, "Ah no, they say the latter have not exhausted; I hear them extolling your prowess at that, after all."

Rosaiah chuckled with pleasure, "Oh, Lord Sir, it's all God's grace, not at all my prowess, I am a pretty common creature and it's all in their love and affection they say these things about me; otherwise, I am a pretty ordinary man, Lord-Sir, pretty ordinary . . ."

The Lord-Sir controlled his laughter, "Anyway, Rosaiah, what brings you here?"

"My work can wait, Lord-Sir; but is there anything I can do for you?"

"In fact, I am waiting for Pagadaiah; I have sent the message; I don't know why he has not come so far. There is an important matter . . ."

Before the Banzardar had finished, Rosaiah walked away in high speed to Pagadaiah's hut, conveyed the message and in a short while, was back to the slab, bringing the man with him.

The landlord pursed his lips and knit his brows, "What is this Pagadaiah? I have sent a man to you, not for any personal work of mine. Men who want to attain a goal in life must qualify themselves with their promptness and punctuality."

"Forgive my lapse, Lord-Sir, actually I am not feeling well; so, I have taken a little time; Forgive me Lord-Sir, I am your servant, at all times."

"No, no, Pagadaiah, there is no need to be so humble, take it easy. The matter is, M.L.A. Suryanarayana garu is coming here tomorrow; so, the news has to reach the people; he might want to give a public speech. If you can take care of the matter, it is alright; otherwise, I have to search for someone who can attend to it."

Before Pagadaiah could respond, Rosaiah bravely said, "That is not a big thing Lord-Sir, I can go and contact the trumpeter Kasee and deliver your message."

And again, before the Banzardar could say a thing, Rosaiah walked away at the known pace of his, in the direction of the colony where the trumpeter lived.

Both the Lord-Sir and Pagadaiah were amused at that sudden spurt of obedience on the part of the grocer.

The Banzardar sat silently and Pagadaiah stood in front of him, but, lost in thoughts of his own; after some time, the Banzardar got off the slab and walked away to his bungalow; Pagadaiah looked at the lord-sir but failed to get into his looks; in a state of uncertainty he lingered there for a while and then trudged home.

The Banzardar looked back and saw that Pagadaiah had not followed him to the bungalow; the 'protocol' had been violated.

'Whatever the reasons, the fact of violation can't be ignored,' thought the Banzardar as he ruminated on the incident.

The trumpeter had made the announcement, covering all the village lanes and as expected a sizeable number of villagers gathered at the slab in that late morning and a long wait for the Emmellu ensued.

They waited and waited at the slab; but the visit got more and more delayed.

Someone expressed the inevitable disgust, "The Emmellu never comes in time; how long should we to wait?"

Rosaiah who desired to be in the thick of the things, intervened, "No, no, don't talk like that; in this business with the big people we have to be patient. After all, visit to our village is not the only work they have; they are big people and their programme is also big."

Many heads turned toward Rosaiah in surprise.

Normally, Pagadaiah took care of these things; but he stood in a corner, sidelined as it were.

"What has happened to Uncle Pagadaiah; today he looks dejected?"

Of all the men it was Kannam who showed concern for Pagadaiah; the man who had been his critic and adversary so long, now went to the man and amiably asked, "Why do you look so much out of spirits, Uncle Pagadaiah; do you have a problem?"

Pagadaiah gave a pale smile, "I am all right."

Kannam became friendlier, "No, there is some problem; I can see that. Tell me, Uncle Pagadaiah; is there anything I can do for you, tell me?"

Pagadaiah felt touched and he reassured Kannam, "There is no problem, Kannam; I am all right, but feeling a little dull; that's all. It happens once in a while to everybody."

Kannam was not convinced, but didn't press it further.

Meanwhile, there was a flutter and the next moment they all heard the sound; a jeep was coming down the alley.

"Rosaiah, ask the people to get down the slab. Ask them to sit in an orderly manner; I hear the jeep coming. The MLA is coming, I think."

All of them raised their eyebrows in surprise and looked at Rosaiah, Banzardar's new agent.

"Don't stand helter-skelter like that and don't stand at a distance like that; don't stand apart, like that; come together," Rosaiah tried to bring the things into order at the slab.

"Right, right, Rosaiah Sir, we know how to stand; this is nothing new for us; but, what are you doing here half-naked in that loin-cloth and leaving your kirana shop business? Maybe customers are waiting there; this new business wouldn't bring you any profit, after all!"

"Shh, here comes the jeep . . ."

The jeep stopped with a roar and the MLA stepped down from the vehicle; clad in khadi of Ponnuru, he joined his palms to the people of his constituency; there was another important looking guest who got down the jeep and offered namasthe to the crowd.

Meanwhile, the Banzardar came running to receive the VIPs; after the greetings and exchange of courtesies, the guests were taken to the bungalow.

The men placed a table and three chairs on the slab; back of the table, they fixed a spread out flag of the Party.

The crowd watched the proceedings bemused.

The landlord, the legislator and the other guest came out; the Emmellu got his obese body hauled onto the slab with a stool and Rosaiah's shoulder as spring-board; the landlord and the unknown guest also climbed onto the stage; the three were duly seated.

After they were seated on the dais, the landlord gesticulated to Rosaiah to be seated on the slab.

With lips curving into a smile Rosaiah paid obeisance to the trio on the dais and joining his palms to the crowd, sat on the edge of the slab, looking austere in his loin-cloth.

The landlord gestured to Rosaiah to garland the guests, at which the new agent of the lord got up in alacrity, but, seeing the half-naked man, the legislator asked the Banzardar to do that and asked Rosaiah to move away from the slab.

Playing host, as it were, to the meeting, the legislator introduced the other guest to the crowd, "I am very happy to introduce to my people, the esteemed Minister for Rural Development, Sri Ganji Babugaru. He has studied in England and is highly educated. Born in a family of Zamindars, Sri Ganji Babugaru had given up his thriving practice as an advocate and chose to serve the people of the state. He is an intellectual and a comparative study of the societies of different countries of the East, is his favorite avocation . . ."

Men looked at each other mystified.

"Sri Ganjibabu garu has chosen the Ministry of Rural Development when asked by the Chief Minister to join the Cabinet and this is his first visit to our constituency; please give a big clap in welcome of the Esteemed Minister . . ."

The crowd duly clapped.

The Minister confided something in the ear of the legislator and the legislator communicated the same to the gathering, "The esteemed Minister would be meeting a delegation of the people, after the conclusion of this meeting.

With these remarks I request the Banzardar saab to conduct the proceedings of the meeting, Jai Praja Party."

Rosaiah gave a signal for claps and the gathering ungrudgingly obliged.

The Emmellu then gave a brief speech, much of which was unintelligible to the crowd; in conclusion he said more clearly and buoyantly, "Soon, the elections to the Panchayat are going to be held; this village has always been a strong citadel of the Praja Party and I am sure that you would elect, this time too, the nominees of the Praja Party with a resounding majority; I request 'my people' to bear this in mind. Please repeat, 'Jai Praja Party', 'Jai Praja Party', and 'Jai Praja Party.' Namasthe,"

Later, the Minister spoke about the importance of the villages, 'unless the villages develop, the country cannot be called a developed country.' He quoted Mahatma Gandhi, 'Gandhiji said, 'India lives in villages and that the gramaswaraj should be at the top of the agenda for the Governments . . .'

At the end of his speech, the Minister said he would like to meet a small group of the delegates of the people to know their problems, "I have come to get a firsthand account of your problems; you can write to me, you can meet me and you can talk to me about your problems; I am always available to you . . ."

After a sumptuous lunch the Emmellu settled down for a siesta; while the Minister went out to the slab to meet a group of delegates who were waiting.

They stood up when the Minister came to meet them; the Minister gestured to them to sit at ease on the slab and he sat amidst them, "We are all one, one for all and all for one; there is no need to observe any disparity . . . First, I would like to know what your problems are . . ."

The delegates nodded enthusiastically.

"Our biggest problem is lack of water source; we need water to irrigate our fields, we need water . . ."

"We need water for men and cattle," Madam Pullamma's man who had joined the delegation unobtrusively, chimed in.

The delegates looked at him in surprise.

"It is not easy to draw from the backyard well fifty pans of water in the morning and in the evening, Lord-Sir . . ." Pullamma's man continued.

"So, you have a well in the backyard," Minister turned to the others and asked, "Do you all have wells in your yards?"

"Yes, Lord . . ."

"Please don't call me 'lord'" Minister intervened, "you may call me 'brother', and, yes, proceed . . ."

"Most of us have our own wells; but the problem is, if the rains fail they go dry and rains often fail in this region . . ."

"We have wells in the fields too, but, even there we face the same problem . . ."

"Do you have a school in the village?"

"Yes, Lord-Sir; there is a singer-teaser school (Single Teacher School) . . ."

The Minister nodded, "Yes, a Single Teacher School, I understand; but, do you all send your children to the school?"

"A few of us do, Sir, but, that is not a problem; our main worry is that of water . . ."

"Our Emmellu lord-sir knows everything."

"I think, recently they have laid a road up to the nearest railway station; are you satisfied with it?"

"That is no problem; actually we do not move out much; the main problem is 'water' . . ."

The Minister gave them a patient hearing, "Tell me, I am hearing you . . .

"Do the Extension Officers of the Samithi often come here to advise you, on matters of agriculture, compost preparation and such things . . . ?"

The delegates looked at each other and nodded their ignorance of it.

"What do you sow mainly; are you getting the seed in time, for the sowing?"

Again they exchanged glances, "We always preserve the best seed from our produce; that is our age old practice; we sow mainly millet, both bajra and jowar; we like to cultivate paddy; but, what can we do, there is this problem of water . . ."

"What type is your soil?"

"Mostly it is black cotton soil; soil-soaking requires good rains and it takes a good time to dry up; but, what can we do about it; soil is a God-given thing, of course, water is also a God-given thing . . ."

"Has it ever occurred to you that you can get the soil tested and take the counsel of soil scientists?"

Their looks pleaded they have no knowledge of those things.

"What do you do when the rains are delayed, I mean, how do you prepare yourselves, to face a delayed monsoon?"

"What can a man do in such a situation, Brother-Sir? We bathe our village deity Muthyalamma or go for a singing of the epic-song of the Virataraja . . . and of course, keep praying . . . In fact, for a solution of most of our problems, we pray, pray and pray; but water is our main problem," Said a delegate with moist eyes.

Ganjibabu was touched; he talked about their leisure time pursuits.

The delegates mentioned the puppet-show and the street-plays.

It was evident that the villagers were not interested in anything except water.

"I can see water is your main problem; what do you want the government to do to help you."

There was no response.

"Tell me; how does the government know unless you represent your problems . . .

"Do you have a source of water anywhere near, a river, a big rivulet, something like that?" the Minister tried another approach.

"The River of Sticks is there; but, it is at a lower altitude that our region; but . . ."

Presently, Pagadaiah came to the slab and stood at a little distance; noticing him, one of them said enthusiastically, "Here is our big brother, Pagadaiah; he is a man who knows many things from MaaBharatham and Bagotham; also, he knows many stories; he tells us a tale a night, very interesting stories . . ."

The Minister wondered, 'What useful things can I get from this man?'

The members called the man into their midst, "He is our big brother; he will tell you . . ."

"Nice meeting you, Pagadaiah. Tell me, do you have a good source of water, around?"

"Yes, Lord-Sir, there is one and that is a rivulet; it is not very big; it issues from the breach of the Vindhyadramma tank," Pagadaiah said.

Surprised, the Minister said, "So, you have a 'tank' here; none of you has told me about it; then, what is the problem in getting water from that?"

Then, Pagadaiah warmed up to the occasion and related the facts; 'the tank has always been there, Lord-Sir, though none of us has ever seen it with water; even our ancestors said

311

that they had never seen it with water; our fields haven't ever been irrigated by the waters of that tank in our lifetime.

"For us it has always been a tank with a breach. As a matter of fact, no one knows when the tank was built and for how long it had been useful . . ."

The Minister heard with interest and showed enthusiasm "What you say sounds very strange; are there any inscriptions, I mean stones with writing on it?"

"Some of our ancestors said there were some, but we haven't seen any?"

"If it is a big reservoir of water that is good thing; it can be revived? Anyway, first, I would like to see the tank; how far is it from the village, is it very far . . . ?"

"It is not very far; but, what is the use of seeing it when there is no water in it? The entire bed of the tank is under cultivation and different kinds of cash—crops are grown; they have planted an orchard of lemon trees. There is no trace of the tank except the bund," Kannam who had joined the delegation, curtly put it.

The Minister turned his head and asked promptly, "Who is cultivating the bed of the tank?"

They didn't reply and sat with heads bent.

"Who is cultivating the land? Don't you know or don't want to reveal . . . ?"

Pagadaiah explained, "That, you can get to know anytime, Lord-Sir; but, if you want to see the Vindhyadramma tank I, rather, we would take you there; but, the jeep would not go there. I am afraid we have to walk, Lord-Sir."

The Minister said with alacrity, "I can walk the distance, I can walk; I walked great distances in my childhood, across the fields around my village. Shall we go?" He rose prepared to walk.

The villagers wondered at the Minister's prompt response, but didn't know what to say.

Kannam quickly rose and said, "Uncle Pagadaiah, come on, let us go and show the Vindhyadramma Tank to Lord-Sir, yes let us go, Uncle Pagadaiah . . ."

Pagadaiah was caught in a dilemma, 'Is it proper to take this Lord-Sir to the tank, without telling the Village Lord-Sir?'

Along with the Minister, the delegates, including Mme Pullamma's man got ready to go.

The Minister was ready to walk.

"Keep walking, I will just go and inform our Lord-Sir and will catch up with you," Pagadaiah said and walked to the bungalow of the Lord Appaiah.

The Banzardar and the M.L.A were in the midst of an after-lunch siesta and couldn't be disturbed.

Pagadaiah mulled over for some time and decided to show the bund and the breach to the Minister, come whatever.

The Minister and the delegates walked together cheerfully; apart from the chosen delegates, a few others also volunteered to accompany the team.

The Minister seemed to enjoy the walk; he looked at the wild plants and trees on the way and identified them as if he was remembering old friends.

The accompanying villagers were pleasantly surprised at the amiable way the minister conducted himself in course of the walk.

The distance was considerable and the terrain not very friendly; but, it looked short, the way the walk went.

In half hour they were on the bund of the Vindhyadramma tank.

The minister felt exhilarated when he looked downwards from the steep bund and surveyed the environs of the place.

"Undoubtedly the tank is a work of the Kakatiyas," He observed, "Kakatiyas constructed hundreds and hundreds of tanks in the country and contributed to the economic welfare of the people; the more one sees these stupendous works the more one gets convinced that monarchy was not so bad a system of government as decried by the protagonists of the modern systems of government."

The villagers looked on innocently and the Minister realized that they were not in a position to appreciate his observation; he felt a rush of enthusiasm to teach them the salient features of monarchy, republicanism and socialism. Checking himself he rued for the umpteenth time how the political leaders of the country rushed into a new system of government without initiating a suitable Cultural Revolution in the country first; then, he minded the place and time he was in and looked at the men.

"Anyone knows any story about this tank of water?" The Minister queried.

At the suggestion of the men, Pagadaiah narrated the prevalent popular story and then showed the Minister the icons—of the deity Vindhyadramma and the King, as per the account of the story.

"There must be some stone inscription somewhere here; the kings always placed them at such public works; has anyone seen any such thing?"

"We haven't heard about anyone seeing such a thing, but, there are pieces of stones at the temple in the village, with strange figures on them; I have seen them," Pagadaiah said.

"We will see them; they can throw some light on the matter," the Minister said, as he walked towards the breach.

'The breach bears traces of human authorship,' thought the Minister; there were dumps of dug-out earth that aged with the times and looked like a secondary bund; the breach showed the springs that fed the rivulet.

They climbed down the bund and spent some time examining the rivulet.

"Something good certainly would come out of this visit, I feel," said one of the men to the others who nodded heads showing agreement.

"Usually, at such places inscriptions show the name of the king or some high official who got this work done; unfortunately, here, we see none; let us hope the stones at the temple would reveal something."

The villagers looked anxiously at the Minister.

Turning to them, the Minister said reassuringly, "I will do my best to help you to revive this grand reservoir; trust me."

They looked at him thankfully and joined their palms.

"Do one thing; as soon as you reach your slab, collect the signatures of the villagers on white papers and give it to me; that is the first thing I advise you to do."

They nodded.

They started their trek back and made it to the village in quicker time.

The Minister saw the legislator and the Banzardar and a few men waiting for them at the slab.

The Minister himself greeted them and said, "Have we kept you waiting for long?"

"It's nothing like that Babugaru, but, had you informed me I too would've accompanied you. Anyway . . . have you gained any useful information on that abandoned place," the legislator asked.

"Not much, I'm afraid, Surenaraingaru."

The Minister took leave of the villagers with a 'Namaste' and the visiting guests were taken into the bungalow of the Banzardar.

Night was about to set in and the legislator proposed camping in the village for the night; "Tomorrow we would take out a procession as a buildup to the coming Panchayat elections; this village is very important, particularly, for me."

The Minister nodded casting a probing look on the legislator.

"In that case, I would send for that man, Pagadaiah, to mobilize the men," Banzardar said.

"Not necessarily that man; you were telling about a grocer who wishes to be the Sarpanch-candidate, better send for him," Suryanarayana said.

The Banzardar quickly camouflaged his surprise with feigned enthusiasm, "I will attend to it immediately; we shouldn't lose time."

Rosaiah came as soon as he got the call—this time fully dressed and took instructions from the Emmellu Lord-Sir.

Pagadaiah too was sent for and was ordered to mobilize the men for a public procession.

Next morning a banner and a flag were brought from the baggage of the MLA and were fixed on poles. The important persons got ready and went to the slab where a sizeable number of men were waiting.

Rosaiah was kept at the head of the procession and a man from the legislator's entourage was ready with a list of slogans.

The men were instructed on the slogans and the procession started.

Women stood at their doors and watched curiously as the men in the procession raised the slogans. The men gave wrong responses; where they were to say 'Zindabad' (long live) they said 'Murdabad (Down with) and vice versa.

"Things can't be done better than this, especially when the procession is taken out at such a short notice," the Legislator said to the Minister who showed a wry face.

"In that case, we shouldn't have taken out the procession at all."

The procession went on with some of the men dropping out at each corner; half the men in the line were unable to master the refrain and gave only lip-movement.

Luckily, by the time the procession went round the village and came back to the slab, a few remained in the line.

"Whatever it is, it is a good beginning," Suryanarayana said and the Minister looked wondering at that observation.

On the slab, tables and chairs were arranged but the Minister appeared so much disenchanted with the 'tamasha' (a funny show) that he asked it to be called off.

Rosaiah who was readying himself to give a fitting speech was disappointed.

A little later the dignitaries left the village; a good number of men came to see them off.

After the departure of the legislator and the Minister, Kannam and Pagadaiah lost no time and in a short while they brought white papers from the grocery of Rosaiah and collected the thumb-impressions of as many villagers as they could muster.

As the jeep drove on the return trip, the legislator asked the Minister, "What did you see and hear at that ruined tank-bund, Babugaru?"

"I have seen a very old historical site; it is a marvel of work, keeping in view the times in which it was built; Kakatiyas were really great rulers; the hundreds of water-reservoirs they built across the country are a testimony to their love for their country and people . . ."

"It's not that I am referring to, Babugaru; have they made any representation for its revival; perhaps they had expressed that wish . . ."

"Naturally, there is nothing strange or wrong if they wish a revival of the tank; the vagaries of the monsoon and its effect in this region make such an effort imperative on the part of the government. I think the government should take the initiative and revive that great reservoir . . ."

"All that is ok; but, you see Babugaru, the people here firmly believe that it is an accursed reservoir, revival of which would surely bring disaster to the village and the region; that is the perception of the people and the government cannot ignore the traditional beliefs of the people . . .

"That, Rationality and Scientific temper should be the guidelines of policy for the government is alright; as a party man I accept that; but, the government should also give due weight to native wisdom and traditional beliefs of the people; otherwise their sentiments would be hurt and the Party would lose its image."

"Yes, yes, Surenaraingaru, I agree with you; please don't mistake me in this. What I mean to say is that in line with the times, our policies also should be amended; take the events like the American war of independence; they also suffered the effects of Colonialism like our country; they announced at the close of the War of Independence the Declaration of Human Rights; take the case of France, people there suffered the evil effects of the 'ancien régime' and released their version of the Human Rights, after the revolution. Even among the Asian countries, take the case of Japan and China; in Japan the Emperor Mutsuhito proclaimed the Five guiding Principles to steer the country into the modern age; interestingly, in Japan the abolition of feudalism did not evince any bloodshed as was the case in France; in China Mao Ze-dong ushered in a cultural revolution to acclimatize the people to a new socio-economic climate in the country. That step, unfortunately, was not taken in our country; after so many years of freedom, people still can't distinguish between Gandhi and Nehru and they don't seem to distinguish between feudalism and democracy; haven't you heard their 'lord-sir', 'lord-sir' addressing. It's rather ironical to see this state of affairs after decades of freedom and republicanism!"

The legislator put an end to the dialogue; silently they moved ahead, each lost in his thoughts.

'It looks like I have to make another visit to the village alone and do some spade-work,' thought the legislator.

'This village presents state of nature of a kind; I must help these innocent villagers to find a solution to their problems; otherwise, my being a Minister for Rural development would become meaningless,' The Minister reflected.

The dry spell of the weather continued. Most of the families resorted to rationing, and soon a meal a day became the order of the times.

In the cattle-shed, the inmates rummaged the feed-bunk to catch a good stack of fodder worth a bite and when they found none, angrily stampeded and demanded the day's ration; the owners got up and fetched whatever they could and put it in the trough. The cattle moved cheerfully, shaking their dewlaps and bending their heads into the trough.

One evening . . .

The village was still, and in that stillness, the intermingled sounds of a harmonium and men's voices reached the ears of the men, resting at home.

Pagadaiah lay on his bedstead, tossing from side to side, as his mind played back precisely those incidents he so much wanted to forget—the night, the dark hut, the jingling sounds of the bangles, and the husky voice of the 'demon-in-law' . . .

Unable to bear the burden of the recollections, he got up from the bed and went out; then, he heard the sounds of verses sung to the accompaniment of a harmonium, coming from the adjacent lane.

He lighted his leaf-cigar and drew on it in quick succession; the cigar began to burn steadily and, leisurely inhaling the smoke, he came into the foreyard.

Now, he began to hear the sounds clearly; the melodious voice of Nagireddy was audible singing that verse, 'How they (the Pandavas) are in those forestlands and what did Partha say?'

'Nagireddy has a sweet flexible voice; when he sings those verses, touching the different levels of the notes, he must be feeling serenely happy and relaxed! If I too could sing like that, how nice it would have been, especially when the mind is distraught with unpleasant things!'

He had heard someone say that Hussainaiah, that bumpkin, was now all set to get onto the stage as a character in the mythological play, Nagireddy doing him that great favour!

For once, Pagadaiah blamed himself for the ruffled relations with Nagireddy; if he had maintained friendly ties, Nagireddy would have given him too, a chance like that! Who could say 'no' on that? Now, how mortifying it would be to watch that imbecile fellow donning a role in a play of the Mahabharata and would the fellow sing too, to the accompaniment of a harmonium? What a disconcerting experience that would be!

For once, freed from the thoughts that had been driving him to distraction, Pagadaiah came into a somewhat cheerful mood and took a walk in the direction of those musical sounds.

He discovered that the sounds were coming from the dwelling of Hussainaiah.

Walking up to the house of Hussainaiah, Pagadaiah stopped at the doorsill; the door was shut and hesitantly he stood outside; he 'had never entered this house' and now, should he knock on the door, seeking entry?

As he stood undecided, the door opened and Kannam came out; seeing Pagadaiah, he greeted warmly, "Uncle

Pagadaiah, how long have you been standing here? Would you like to come in?" He took Pagadaiah's hand and ushered him in.

Nagireddy was surprised, "What is this, Uncle Pagadaiah, you here?"

Pagadaiah gave a friendly smile, "Yes Nagaya, actually I was looking for you; I heard you singing the verse and came."

Nagireddy came up to him and still in a surprised state, asked, "Is something the matter? You want me to come out?"

"No no, I have come to be in your company for a while; can I sit and watch?"

"Why not, come, sit here and watch, if you like to,"

Pagadaiah sat on the coir-cot smiling at the men; he took a look at the gathering.

'Quite a few strangers are there,' He thought, 'maybe, they are from the repertory.'

The rehearsal recommenced.

The harmonium player looked an accomplished artist; playing on the instrument with nimble fingers he was guiding the actors in catching the correct pitch in the rendering of a verse.

The melodic scale the harmonist played was very sweet and Pagadaiah felt fascinated by it.

Then, the actor sporting a grey beard picked up the pitch and began the rendition of a verse.

Pagadaiah was thrilled as the actor's voice and the notes from the instrument fused nicely into a harmonious sequence, the notes ascending and coming down to the base in a manner very soothing to the ears; 'who could this artist be?' wondered Pagadaiah.

Nagireddy observed Pagadaiah listening in an absorbed manner; delighted, he asked, "Uncle Pagadaiah, you liked it?"

Pagadaiah said in appreciation, "It is very nice, Nagaya, very nice, indeed; he is singing very sweetly, really!"

"And, Uncle Pagadaiah, do you know who the actor is—the one that has sung that verse?"

Pagadaiah curled out his lips expressing ignorance.

"It is our Hussainaiah, Uncle, it is our Hussainaiah," Kannam smilingly apprized.

Pagadaiah opened his mouth and looked at Kannam; "Are you kidding me?" he looked at Nagaya for help.

Nagireddy nodded affirmatively and endorsed, "It is Hussainaiah, very much; see through that grey beard, Uncle, you will see it is Hussainaiah."

Pagadaiah looked closely; it took him some effort to see that 'the fellow' was laughing under the thick beard. Amused with the trickery the make-up had done, Hussainaiah said "Why, it is I, Uncle, Hussainaiah."

Pagadaiah gaped in surprise, "Hussainaiah, you . . . ?"

All of them laughed.

Pagadaiah continued to wonder, "Hussainaiah singing so nicely . . ."

Nagireddy added to the surprise, "Actually, it was not he that was singing; it was this man, sitting hidden behind, who sang the verse for Hussainaiah," he pointed out the man who was the play-back singer.

Hussainaiah didn't like Nagireddy giving away the secret.

Pagadaiah was baffled by the experience and sat stupefied.

Then the rehearsal restarted and the verses and dialogues of the mythological play came in waves, unabated, for more than an hour.

Pagadaiah couldn't help glancing time and again at Hussainaiah who too, now, began to look an accomplished thespian.

Hussainaiah for his part continued to smile; clearly he relished the experience.

At the end of the rehearsal, Narayanamma served tea and some 'khara' to them all.

Pagadaiah now felt happy and relaxed.

The incident, in a way, changed Pagadaiah's attitude towards Nagireddy, Kannam and others. A feeling of bonhomie and concord replaced the old contentiousness and discord.

Nagireddy and Kannam also felt the purging effect of that meeting with Pagadaiah, in a new setting.

As the curtains were drawn on the rehearsal, the artists from the repertory and the support technicians dispersed from Hussainaia's house; most of them went to Nagireddy's place in the neighboring village and Nagireddy stayed back to coordinate the work of construction of the stage and an enclosure for the audience, made up of big twig-screens.

Now, Nagireddy looked at Pagadaiah, inquiringly.

"Nagaya, shall we go out?"

The trio went out and walked towards the usually vacant area at the alley.

It was quite intriguing to Nagireddy and his protégé; neither of them could guess what was in Pagadaiah's mind.

Once they were at the alley, Pagadaiah opened up, "Actually, Nagaya, I had tiffs with you many times over squabbles; I want you to forget all that and listen with an open mind; let us open a new chapter in our relations and work together for the benefit of our community.?"

Nagireddy nodded with a wry smile, still, evincing interest.

Pagadaiah explained, looking amiably now and then at Kannam, "The other day, the Minister and the Emmellu came; Kannam must have told you. That day, the Minister came and sat with us on the slab and talked freely with us. He asked us to tell him the problems we the villagers were facing. We all liked it very much; the Emmellu had never done that to us, you know . . ."

Kannam kept his head bowed and nodded approvingly to what the veteran was saying,

"It is the first time, Nagaya that an important visitor to our village showed a genuine interest about our problems; are you getting the point, Nagaya . . . ?

"Yes, yes, I understand, proceed."

Pagadaiah continued, "Kannam was there and Mme Pullamma's man and others were also there. We told that lord-sir about our water-problem; the gentleman wanted to see the Vindhyadramma tank and he walked with us to the place. Such a thing has never happened with our Emmellu, you know . . .

"Why would our Emmellu go to see the tank; what he is interested in is the dry bed of the tank; it's nothing new," Nagireddy gesticulated.

"What do you think we should do at this seemingly favourable juncture? Don't you think we should do something?"

Nagireddy asked, "What is the best course of action in your opinion, Pagadaiah?"

"I don't know; but, I feel that we must think seriously and come up with a clever plan. To me, it is a God-given chance; if we lose it now there is not going to be a second chance for us; yes, I think so."

They stood lost in thought.

Nagireddy sighed and said, "I agree with you; but, on what should be done, let me think it over. Let me be done with this drama affair first; only then, I will be able to think on it and tell you my opinion."

Pagadaiah nodded understandingly; they parted at that.

Taking leave of Nagireddy and Kannam, Pagadaiah walked straight to the temple of Lord Narasimha.

He was surprised to see the Banzardar there; the Priest-Sir Surayya and the lord-sir were debating some important issue; normally, the Banzardar summoned the priest to his house, but, today, it was different.

The Banzardar went away and Pagadaiah was surprised when the priest-sir came straight to him, "Who is that, there, sitting?"

Hurriedly Pagadaiah presented himself, with an obeisance.

The Priest-Sir smiled in surprise, "Pagadaiah, how long have you been waiting here and at this hour?"

"Lord-Sir, I just came to bow to the lord; I saw that you sirs were talking about something important and so I waited outside."

"This is an odd hour, even for a bow to the Lord; is anything bothering you, Pagadaiah?"

Pagadaiah stood head bent.

The Priest understood that the man was in a disturbed state of mind and said to Pagadaiah, "You may come in if you like; come and rest for some time in the temple pavilion; that might ease your troubled mind."

Obediently Pagadaiah followed the Priest.

When he sat for some time in the pavilion facing the icon of the Lord Narasimha, Pagadaiah felt relieved and began framing in his mind the questions he would ask the Priest.

After pouring some oil into the lamp-bowl, the Priest came back and sat by the man he had always trusted and leaned on, in times of need on festival days.

The Priest knew that the man's domestic life was in shambles; he also knew that, being one committed to old-time values, the man always took the 'right path' when he faced a dilemma; but, for all that, the man's outspokenness earned him more critics than friends,

The Priest heard Pagadaiah clearing his throat and sat waiting for the man to come out with the matter that appeared to sit heavily on his mind.

Pagadaiah again joined his palms and said, "Esteemed sir, what is the extent of truth in this story we hear about the Vindhyadramma tank? Who built it; when was it built? For how long had it been in its present breached state?

With a broad smile the Priest patted on the back of his 'crucial-time assistant', "Why, what do you want to do with that? It is also a story like many other such stories . . . You yourself are a good story teller and should be able to find out for yourself how much of truth it contains . . ."

"But, Lord-Sir, telling stories is one thing and true story is another thing. Going by the version of the story we hear, the tank must have come to life by the magnanimous act of a king, but we do not know who the king was or when the tank was built; the question is, 'what caused the breach and why wasn't it repaired?' We do not know the lengths of the times involved—for how long it was a tank and for how long it had been in breached condition in which we see it today . . ."

The Priest brooded over it for some time; then he coolly said, "I have seen it in breached condition all my life. Even my father said it had always been like that in his lifetime and I cannot go farther back in time than that . . ."

Pagadaiah took a deep breath; he chose his words carefully and uttered them clearly, all the time moving back and forth as if in a trance, "Lord-Sir, can a person ever own the land which forms the bed of the tank? While it is a fact that the tank-bund has breached and it is no more a live-tank, can anybody cultivate the bed land of the tank, and if one can, by whose authority and sanction can one do so?"

The Priest pursed his lips and nodded his head across helplessly; he knew the purport of the questions Pagadaiah posed; but, what could he say in answer? 'It was not that none in the village knew the answers to the questions in question; it was that none in the village new a solution to the questions?'

"Lord-Sir, there must be some proof, somewhere, of the truth or otherwise of the things we hear; the proof has not come out, because no one has made any effort to find it out . . ."

The Priest looked at Pagadaiah wondering what lay at the bottom of the man's move.

"And Lord-Sir, I have heard you say often that according to the scriptures, works useful to the public, like wells with steps to climb down, water reservoirs, temples and books written etc., are like one's own children; they earn merit to the makers . . ."

"Yes, the Sapthasanthana (the seven kinds of offspring) 'vaapi koopa thadaka . . .'" The Priest quoted.

Pagadaiah sat in the same posture and persisted with the same back and forth movements like one possessed.

The Priest wondered and kept staring at the man, 'something is going on inside this man . . .'

Suddenly, the Priest remembered something and touching the shoulder of Pagadaiah, he disclosed it, "I don't know how far it would be interesting and useful to you, but there is something I want you to see; however, you can see it only tomorrow, in daylight; you see, it is quite dark now; there are a few stones with strange figures on them."

Pagadaiah queried, "I have heard that, but, what do they say, Lord-Sir? If it interests you it must be relevant; Lord-Sir, what is it they say?"

"Yes, I think those stones can reveal a fact or two on the issue, if carefully examined; they are stones, of course, dumb witness, but a witness all the same."

"Stones can tell us several things, Lord-Sir; where they are relevant they testify more truthfully and flawlessly than a man does. Further, the stone always gives you the truth and doesn't lie; yes, it does not lie."

The Priest smiled and said, "Yes, you are right, indeed; lying is a patent human trait; no other creature of God can do that."

Pagadaiah appeared a little relieved.

"So, we will see those stones tomorrow; now, go home, and have some sleep, forgetting these things."

Pagadaiah gave cryptic smile and said, "Lord-Sir, permit me to spend the rest of the night here; I will pray a little and maybe, I will have some sleep too,"

The Priest could not reject the request and said, "Alright, then; I will fetch a mat for you."

Pagadaiah tried to dissuade the Priest, but the Priest had already gone into the residential part of the temple; in a few moments, he was back with a mat and pillow, and then placed a bowl of food in front of Pagadaiah, "Now, have some food; one should not sleep on empty stomach."

Pagadaiah was taken aback; he could not look into the eyes of the Priest; his eyelids batted like the wings of an insect and he pursed his lips tightly to choke away a surging spurt of emotion, the cause and meaning of which were unfathomable to him.

Pagadaiah bowed to the Priest and moving to a corner ate the food reverentially.

The stage and the auditorium had been neatly arranged for the play.

On the day of the play, right from the daybreak villagers kept coming and going round the place; they were delighted to see that a theatre, though a makeshift one, had come to their village after a long time.

Children climbed on to the stage and mimicked the actors they had seen some time back; some even crooned the verses they had heard many times, played on the microphone in the village, on days of all kinds of celebration; even a cowherd of the village could render that verse 'Lo, there is the city Dwaraka and there the kine . . .'

Nagireddy and some men of the repertory assembled at the house of Hussainaiah. Moving in and out like ducks they caused much embarrassment to Narayanamma; however, she put her temper on leash, knowing how her man craved for this theatre activity.

For Nagireddy this was the prelude to the play he had authored and was about to stage at the thought of which his heart felt sweet tremors; for him it would be the play of a lifetime; a lady had never won his heart as much as did this dame.

At every half-chance he found occasion to talk to the lady, who politely spoke back, nicely and cleverly cutting short the talk.

Nagireddy wondered whether the lady, who looked so charmingly artless, had read his mind, but, was reciprocating timorously, only because, it was a new experience to her.

At times, Hussainaiah appeared to be playing a watchdog, but that did not bother Nagireddy much. Whenever he had such doubt, he quickly referred to a point of detail in Hussainaia's role in the play and that served to keep the imbecile man happy and oblivious of 'the other things'."

Nagireddy even prided himself for masterminding the play, but cautiously put on a plain face.

Pagadaiah had visited the venue of the rehearsal two more times; after that, his interest in the play and rehearsal waned. Nagireddy ignored it. Kannam, however, showed some concern.

Hussainaiah who was one of the centerpieces in both the plays (one that was about to be staged and the other one being engineered) was blissfully preoccupied with the stage role; he even fantasized himself as Krishna in a sparkling costume, sometimes going to the extent of crooning that familiar verse, 'Cousin, where are you coming from . . . ?'

Narayanamma once caught her man doing that verse, and was all smiles as she quipped, 'that's not your verse, not your verse!'

Hussainaiah for his part smiled back and said with a wink, "You just watch; one day I would sing that verse on the stage!"

And Narayanamma burst into a hearty laugh as she imagined 'her man miming as Krishna, while a hidden playback singer sang the verse; the verse was nice but her man's lip-movement was going awry!'

Hussainaiah continued the joke, "Alright, alright, laugh as much as you can; but, my day would come one day."

Once Nagireddy had caught the couple in this act of playful talk and wondered whether his plan was going right.

As he looked at the sky, Nagireddy saw clouds gathering; knitting his eyebrows, he worried aloud, "What is this I see, an untimely collection of the clouds! Would they spoil the programme?"

"Don't worry Nagireddy Sir, the Rain-God is just playing a joke," A repertory man said, "Rain-God wouldn't do anything amiss; he knows that we are staging the play involving Krishna and Arjuna and he wouldn't dare earn their displeasure. I think the Rain-God still remembers how guided by Krishna, Arjuna had kept him at bay, while the Fire-God devoured the Khandava forest! Now, can he take chances again with the same duo?"

Nagireddy gave an appreciative smile at that clever allusion, but kept looking at the clouds.

Meanwhile a bullock cart rolled to a halt in front of Hussainaia's house; Narayanamma's parents got down the cart . . .

As the party went into the house, Nagireddy forgot about the gathering clouds and began to imagine things unpalatable; soon he heard the guests and the inmates of the house chatting joyously.

With a pale face Nagireddy drove his men to the theatre; it was already 'looking houseful' and he took steps to vacate the place, so that a checkup of the arrangements could be made.

Fortunately for them, Pullamma's man had already arrived on the scene; sensing Nagireddy's mood he took things into his hands; he had, in fact, come in readiness for the role, carrying a cane.

The boys started leaving the place as soon as they saw Pullamma's man, but not without paying their 'compliments'.

Undeterred by their heckling faces the man went ahead with 'his work', which he knew would earn him a free pass; Nagireddy allowed the man to do the odd job.

The harmonium with the foot-operated bellows was set in the pit in front of the stage and the public address system running on generator was fixed.

The generator was started and the technicians began to test the working of the system.

The musician sat behind the harmonium and said to Nagireddy, "Nagireddy Sir, sing a verse," Then he asked the PA technician, "Now, here we go with the verse; ready?"

With a smile, Nagireddy climbed onto the stage and stood before one of the hanging mikes; clearing his throat he took up the verse, "Ah, Son of Nanda, take into your hands the reins of my chariot; with you there resplendent like the noon time Sun, may my chariot glitter . . ."

"Once more . . ." Shouted Pullamma's man and laughed.

The musician gave finishing touches to the melody and took up another melodic scale, "Nagireddy Sir, sing that verse, 'When the picture of the king of monkeys, Lord Hanuman is shining on the flag, a row of white chargers is arrayed in front, and I am handling the reins of the chariot and Arjuna is pounding your forces with his weapon Gaandiva, none would listen to your entreaties for peace, oh, King of the Kurus . . ." Nagireddy gave the raga a long treatment and Pullamma's man shouted 'encore' once more.

Nagireddy gave the fellow a stare and said, "Would you do the same thing when the play is in progress? In that case I wouldn't give you a pass."

Pullamma's man wailed mockingly and touching the ears promised he wouldn't do that.

The repertory men had a hearty laugh.

They went on merrily for some more time, testing their preparedness and indulging in some warm-up exercises.

The curious men that gathered outside peeped through the gaps in the twig-screens and were happy with a free preview of the stage they had.

Nagireddy remembered that he had forgotten to take care of a point; he caught the hand of Kannam and took him onto the stage and from different angles showed a spot in the quarter allotted for ladies, "That is the place where Narayanamma should sit, understand?" He pointed a finger at it.

Kannam suppressed his smile and nodded, wondering at the intensity of his mentor's infatuation.

The contractor of the play looked at the sky, but, in the darkness he could see nothing; he prayed for a rainless night.

Soon the make-up men called up the actors and the process started.

Nagireddy noticed that Hussainaiah had not yet come and hurriedly dispatched his protégé to bring him; then, he had to sit for the make-up; he knew that the makeup of Krishna would take time.

He sat for the makeup, praying to God to take care of everything and promised two coconuts in return.

In a while, Kannam came with a nervous looking Hussainaiah who saw Nagireddy sitting bare-chested before the make-up man, but could not recognize him.

Seeing that Hussainaiah was in jitters, Nagireddy tried to put him at ease with reassuring words and asked the technician to give the man the minimum of make-up and a 'chemky dress'.

The opening scene was that of Krishna's bedroom; they had laid a cot there with a light mattress and a pillow on it and the stage was ready for the scene.

They sang the Prayer, 'Parabrahma . . .'

Arjuna and Duryodhana were ready to go on the stage.

Nagireddy waited for Kannam to come and break the news of the arrival of Narayanamma; but the fellow was nowhere to be seen and Nagireddy didn't know what to do.

Everything was ready and they were just waiting to draw the curtains open.

Tensely, Nagireddy—now fully made up as Krishna, went onto the stage and peered through the curtains; he saw Kannam who had just arrived and was showing Narayanamma the place reserved for her; she wore that parrot-green saree and blood-red blouse and looked ravishing!

Nagireddy stood looking at the lady and would have stood there for an eternity, had not the programme manager come and smilingly poked him in the ribs, "What Bedroom Krishna Sir, are you looking for your Gopika?"

Nagireddy chuckled and came back into the greenroom. 'You cannot hide these things from the repertory men; they can 'count the bones inside you when you yawn,' he thought.

The manager queried with a gesture whether everything was ready and when his men nodded in the affirmative the curtains were duly drawn apart and the stage with Krishna reclining on the bed opened up for the audience.

There was a big roar of applause, the improvised auditorium resounding with it.

'Bedroom Krishna' Nagireddy had already fixed the place and angle of the bed on the stage so that he could see not only Arjuna but more importantly, he could see the lady in parrot-green saree clearly.

The play began.

Krishna saw Arjuna first and broke into that familiar verse . . .

His eyes fixed on the lady, Nagireddy took up an elaborate treatment of the melodic scale in the rendition of the verse; he saw the stamp of ecstasy on Narayanamma's face as she looked at him with wide eyes.

As expected, an ardent fan of the mythological plays, stood up and shouted, "Once more,"

Drawing from experience, Nagireddy went back to the bed, lay on it for a while, got up and sang the verse a second time, his looks all the time fixed on the lady. At the end of it, emboldened by 'her' looks, he stole a quick moment and gave a good clean wink to the lady.

The act was aimed at the lady only, but as it happened, quite a few of the women thought it was made at them and were shocked at the brazen act of the man; it seemed to matter little whether it was Krishna or Nagireddy.

In a fit of resentment a small group of ladies got up from the auditorium and walked away cursing with gestures.

Krishna and company were stunned, but with the manager gesturing feverishly, they continued as if nothing had happened; most of the men from the audience, after a few queries among themselves, fell in line with the play and the repertory men drew a sigh of relief.

Nagireddy, however, could discover that some men from the adjacent village were preparing for a showdown; he felt thoroughly shaken; for a moment he wondered what would happen; he could clearly see a change in the mood of the spectators in the front row.

Somehow, he managed to do his bit of the role and was a relieved man when his part of the role was finally over; in the auditorium, still, a part of the crowd was restive; he could sense that.

He went into the greenroom and there he saw Hussainaiah, made up as Dhritarashtra; sitting alone he was trembling and the minute he saw Nagireddy he sprang up and fell on the mentor's feet, "Nagaya, now, this is beyond me, yes, I tell you, Cousin Nagaya, it is beyond me; I cannot go onto the stage; if you send me forcibly onto the stage I will fall dead there. Please leave me out of this and save my life, Nagaya, you will earn merit for that; I will go home . . ."

Nagireddy lifted the kneeling man, "Hussainaiah, there is no reason to fear; you have a man behind you to sing the verses and if you so wish, I will also see that the man even speaks for you; after all, with your thick beard nobody can discern whether you are talking and singing or not. Be bold; it was you who longed for it and asked for it. I have arranged this for you, taking risks, even against the wishes of the Company and now, you want to give it up and go away. No, no, you cannot go away like that; I will lose my face with the Company . . ."

Hussainaiah now began to cry, "Nagaya, please save me; I will never ask you again for a chance; leave me; here, I am going away . . ."

As Nagireddy stood bewildered, Hussainaiah took to heels, with the mustache and beard set and the glittering costume on, and in a trice was gone.

"Hussainaiah, listen to me; I will be with you in this . . ." Nagireddy ran after the man, but Hussainaiah was able to beat him in the run.

Nagireddy had done some quick thinking even as he ran after the man.

The repertory men stood gaping at the spectacle of the two actors sprinting away, with make-up and costume on, 'just like that!'

Hussainaiah ran like a deer being chased by a cheetah and reached home.

Just as Hussainaiah was about to close the door, Nagireddy caught up with him and pushed the door open.

Then he saw the lady of the house enter the scene.

In a flash she rushed to the door and hissing like a cobra, pulled her man in and banged the door shut on 'the Bedroom Krishna's' face.

Nagireddy trembled at the expression on the lady's face; turning back he ran towards the auditorium, covering his cake-applied face and costume wearing body with his shoulder cloth.

Halfway to the venue of the play, he heard a big commotion; he could hear whistles and shouts and noise of things being messed up; he came to an abrupt stop; he knew from experience what those sounds meant and began to panic; 'should he go there now and force an 'encore' from the wild crowd?'

Even as he trembled, Nagireddy's mind recalled a similar incident, involving a theatre celebrity . . .

'Nagireddy Sir, I am running to Gosseedu; please take care of my box; it contains the most valuable collection of my theatre life, the epaulets, the wrist-bands, the 'golden crown', the velvet apparel and some costume knickknacks. If I am alive I will come back someday and take them back, otherwise, give them to my family . . .'

'That was 'the world-famous actor' Patimpadu Pitchiraju, noted for his role of Krishna', recollected Nagireddy, 'that night, the great actor had run a distance of three miles to Gosseedu, in complete make-up and costume as 'Krishna' of the bedroom scene; no other actor can boast of such a brave run, indeed!'

He heard the shouts and noises coming in his direction and without losing much time ran fast towards his village, in an unpremeditated emulation of the great 'world-famous actor'.

Back in his house, the bedroom Hussainaiah groaned in a state of fever and growled at his foolish craze for the cake and costume, "Why didn't you warn and tell me it would be such a difficult thing to do?" He reproached his wife.

"Enough of it; now, shut up your mouth and stay calm," Narayanamma shouted.

With a whimper Hussainaiah turned to the other side.

The next day's evening saw the members gather early in good number at the slab.

Naraiah was unable to understand the reason for the silence that prevailed at the slab; "are we waiting for someone?" he queried but, getting no answer, he sat back and started chewing on his gums leisurely.

The next moment they saw Kannam at a little distance, walking heavy footed; the slab became attentive.

"He definitely knows the details," Said somebody in an undertone.

Kannam sat at a distance from the centre of the slab; his movements didn't show his normal élan.

"Come here, Kannam; why are you sitting far away; members want to know many things from you," Balakoti said warmly to Kannam.

Kannam obliged but not with his usual warmth; he went and sat by Balakoti.

Members sitting at a distance craned their necks eagerly.

Only a few of the slab members had gone to witness the play, not all of them; it was an expensive thing in their plight then, but prying on the things didn't cost anything and interested everyone; so, they would not lose that treat.

"Where is Pagadaiah, we don't see him much these days?"

"These days he is more at the temple than at home."

"A temple is always a safer place than the dwelling, they say."

"Pagadaiah didn't show any enthusiasm even to witness the play, though Nagaya offered him a free ticket," Said Kannam, finally intervening.

At the mention of the play those sitting at a distance stretched their necks again; they had all come to know that the programme had ended in a fiasco; they relished the news, but wanted to know the details.

"It was good that I hadn't bought a ticket; is it true that the play ended after the second act itself, Kannam? I have also heard that the crowd went after some of the actors and that some actors had run away from the spot to save their skin; was anybody hurt?"

"Is that true, Kannam?"

Kannam reluctantly affirmed it with a nod and gave no further particulars.

"Why don't you open your mouth and tell what happened there?"

"I can tell you everything only if I know everything, and I tell you I don't know what happened there; that's all I can tell you," Kannam said and avoided eye-contact with them.

"The fellow is not revealing the truth, it's obvious," A member remarked.

Then they saw Mme Pullamma's man arguing with a member over a beedi.

"Oye you men stop that fuss over beedis; you become cantankerous the minute you come to the slab. This is not the place for . . ."

Someone gave a beedi to Pullamma's man and another lit it, "Come now and sit here, the slab wants to know from you what happened last night."

Immediately Pullamma's man turned towards Kannam for guidance.

Kannam avoided his looks rose and walked to a corner of the slab; that was clue enough for Pullamma's man.

Pullamma's man came up with his version of the incident, "Actually I too don't know what happened, because just at that time I went out to 'fold my legs' and by the time I came back it was all over; if only I had known that things would go bad like that, I wouldn't have gone to 'fold my legs'. They were all shouting; I heard that one of the actors didn't oblige when they said 'once more'; yes, that's it; the company men tried to pacify the shouting men but the men were adamant; they broke the furniture, tore the curtains to pieces and stampeded on the stage." He turned to Kannam with 'have I done a good job of it?' look.

"But, what was Nagaya doing all the time? He is a local man; he should have controlled the situation . . ."

"Nagaya tried his best to bring things under control; but what can one man do in such a melee? At that point I came away; I don't know what happened later."

Members of the slab knew that they had not received a faithful account of the fracas; but there was nothing else they could do; 'truth would come out one day, anyway,' they comforted themselves.

At that point they saw Pagadaiah walking wearily to the slab.

When they looked at him they felt a surge of sympathy for him; the raconteur looked thinner and weaker; nevertheless the sight of the man cheered them, one and all.

Kannam in particular took a few steps and stretching his arms, held the raconteur in a warm hug as he guided him to the slab.

Many of them raised their eyebrows at that, 'what a turnaround!'

The slab left off the issue of the aborted play and took up the other issues.

Next morning when Kannam and a few others were there at the slab, a jeep came and stopped at the slab.

A government official got down the jeep and asked, "We have come from the Minister Ganjibabu garu; can we see the gentleman named Pagadaiah?"

Kannam got down the slab at once and took him to the hut of the Raconteur.

After a brief talk, Pagadaiah gave the thumb-impressed papers to the messenger.

In a few minutes the jeep drove off.

The Banzardar who had come into the verandah at the sound of the vehicle stood staring at that quick development; he recollected the report the sethsindhi had given about what had transpired at the slab, on the day of the Minister's visit.

Promptly, the Lord-Sir sent for Pagadaiah.

The Banzardar listened to what Pagadaiah said; then, pursing his lips he went into the house without any further talk about it, dismaying the man.

Kannam and the others were waiting outside for Pagadaiah.

He told them what had happened and all of them walked to the slab, together.

The Banzardar busied himself drafting a letter to the legislator.

Two days later, shortly before the dusk, the legislator's jeep arrived in the village and stopped in front of the Village Lord's house.

The Banzardar, who had been waiting for the sound of the jeep, came out and the Banjardar and the Legislator went into the house.

Soon, many villagers assembled at the slab.

They sat in grave silence; all of them had a presentiment that something very important had been set in motion, 'Was it going to affect them in a good way or was there something serious in store for them', each of them asked themselves.

The Banzardar stood on his verandah and said to them in a raised voice, "Oye men, sitting on the slab, all of you come here, all of you; Emmellu Lord-Sir wants to speak to you; come quick."

The men hurriedly obeyed the Lord-Sir; they sat in the open ground in front of the verandah.

"Lord-Sir, they are all here . . ." Banzardar informed the legislator who was sitting inside.

The MLA came out and stood on the verandah facing the men, "I am your representative in the legislative assembly, I hope you remember?" he said with a Namasthe.

They all stood up dramatically and joined palms to him apprehensively.

The MLA gestured to them to sit at ease and addressed them, "You have elected me to represent you in the assembly and to help you in solving your problems; even otherwise, I come from the same region; my village is just fifteen miles from yours; I have so much of love for this region; I think you all know that I belong to this area . . ."

They nodded obediently.

"If you have a grave problem you should tell me, either by coming to me or when I am here, but, choosing to seek the intervention of 'a third man' is wrong . . . Ganjibabu may be a Minister; but he is not your representative; anything concerning this area should come to me and the thing would go to him only through me. He cannot do anything here without consulting me; without my consent not a bird can ly in this constituency, understand that . . .

"The other day we both were here; yes, we both were here and you chose to take him to that place, without informing me; maybe you requested him to get that tank revived; he sent an officer to receive some papers from you, I am told; have you written anything on them; who wrote it for you?"

"No, Lord-Sir, none of us can write; we just affixed our thumb-impressions; they are blank papers."

"How foolish of you to have done that; now, anything can be written on the papers and it would be binding on you . . .

"Now, listen, all of you, I am revealing a very important fact to you. Listen carefully, all of you, particularly 'that great man, Pa-ga-da-iah'; listen, my family has a strong link with that Vindhyadramma tank; yes, it was built by my ancestor Pagadanayudo, hundreds of years ago," the Minister now raised his voice, "Have you heard me, the builder of that tank was my ancestor, Pagadanayudo . . .

The men were stunned at the revelation; they began to talk to each other animatedly in hush.

After giving them some time, the Minister continued, "The tank was an ill-fated one and my ancestor paid for it with his life; it was the short-sighted advice of the priest that cost my ancestor his life. Now, only the self-sacrifice of a descendant of Pagadanayudo can revive that tank; do you all know that?"

The men nodded.

"Yes, as descendant of my illustrious ancestor, I am prepared to sacrifice my life, if only that would help in reviving the tank for you, my people. Yes, I am ready to sacrifice my life; I will go there, slit my throat and consecrate the breach with my warm blood; you can all see my body lying at the breach, bleeding to death . . ." The legislator thundered, his voice choking with emotion.

The men clapped.

"But we are living in modern times and we have to be modern in thought and action. Don't think that I have slept over the matter for so long; no, I haven't slept over it; I got the place examined by the Geologists, men who know all about the strata of the earth, the tectonics etc., they were with me for two days and tested everything at the place; they have said the breach cannot be filled; the effort would be futile, they said. Even if we fill the breach, the breach can reoccur anytime and that would be a disaster, a big disaster! Even if we build it completely 'with lead', it would not last, they say. Now, what can you do? I ask you to tell me what is to be done. Should we go ahead foolishly and bring a disaster not only to your village, but to many villages in this region as well? Tell me . . ."

The men were silent.

"Therefore, give up the idea of reviving the Vindhyadramma tank; forget about it; I am trying to forget it, though my family is sentimentally connected with the place; let us think of an alternative; for every problem there are alternatives . . .

"Don't act hastily and foolishly. Now, go home, all of you . . ." The legislator concluded.

Men slowly left the place and came into the street.

"What shall we do now?" Balakoti asked.

"Sh, don't talk here; let us go and assemble at some other place."

"But, where . . . ?

"Let us gather at a far off place," Kannam said and walked; the men followed him.

They went and sat on those two small cemented bench-like structures on either side of the door of Mme Durgamba's house.

" . . . It is now or never; that gentleman came as though God had sent him on the mission; let us draw benefit from it . . ."

"But, why has the Emmellu come now, all of a sudden? Normally, he keeps us waiting . . ."

"What the Emmellu says about the tank is astonishing; do you think really his ancestor built the Vindhyadramma tank?"

"I will never accept that; he is bluffing; what proof is there that his ancestor had built it; there is no stone proclaiming it to be so."

"And, he says he would slit his throat, sanctify the breach with his blood and revive the tank . . ."

"Aahaha, a great man and a great descendant of a king he is indeed!"

The remarks continued like that for some time.

Then Kannam intervened, "All that is alright, but, what is the course of action open to us now? If we have to do something, it can only be with the help of the Minister lord-sir; how to send him the news about the situation here?

"The only way is to go to 'Patnam' (City); who would go and where is the money for that?"

Kannam asked, "How much do we require?" and when no one responded, said, "I will find out all those details and arrange the money too; leave it to me. Now, who will undertake the journey?"

"Pagadaiah is the right man for that."

They endorsed it and persuaded Pagadaiah to go on the mission; who would be the second man was to be decided by Kannam.

Next week, on the same day Nagireddy and Pagadaiah met the Minister in his Chamber and gave the details.

It was obvious to the Minister that the legislator would resort to every conceivable trick; he was intrigued about the claim made by the man, that the Vindhyadramma tank was the work of his ancestor.

Pagadaiah and Nagireddy maintained that they had never heard that version and that even the legislator had never made such a claim earlier.

"I think it is a false claim; since there is no historical evidence he has made that spunky claim; if it can be disproved, he can be effectively silenced . . . . You were telling me about some stones in the temple premises?" the Minister turned to Pagadaiah; what is the information they contain?"

"What can a man like me gather from those stones, Sir? Maybe they are a proof of something, but only to one who can read them."

"Don't worry, I will find a way-out and maybe I will come there at an opportune time to study the things there," the Minister said, "I advise you to be united; united you stand, divided you fall, know that."

The Minister patiently talked with them and arranged food for them; later he sent a man to escort them to the railway station, buy tickets and see off.

They came back to their village.

The Banzardar got the news of the absence of the two men in the village, but, beyond that he could get to know nothing.

They were back into summer. The water, the storms had given them the previous year, stood them in good stead in the initial part of the year.

On the traditional New Year Day (Ugadi) the priest read out to them the calendar; it was forecast that there would be copious rainfall and the crops would give good yield.

Pagadaiah as well as his clientele had now lost their appetite for the tales; the Vindhyadramma tank never disappeared from their minds and they saw visions of a full tank almost every waking hour and in sleep saw dreams of thriving paddy fields.

One day, in the early hours of the morning, his sister came to Pagadaiah's hut and said to him, "How long would you live like this, Pagada; it's time you brought your wife back. You should go to bring her back; that is the right way; it is not good for you or for the boy to live away from her for so long; I have told you what I feel; 'later it is your wish'."

Pagadaiah remained silent.

"Think it over," She said and went away.

Pagadaiah put on his banian and went out. As he went past the Banzardar's house, he heard the grocer Rosaiah in conversation with the Lord-Sir. For a fleeting moment he reflected on his forfeited candidature.

With head bent he went past the bungalow.

At the slab Hulakki was alone; so, he went and sat by him

353

"Pagudaiah, I don't like the way you look; listen to me; go and bring home your wife; don't drag the issue till it snaps; every man has to bend and bow before his wife; otherwise, the home becomes a hell; it is uniformly the same for every man, king or common man," Hulakki advised, "If you want somebody to talk on your behalf, I am prepared to come; I tell you because, I have been seeing you become thinner and thinner; I want to see 'the old Pagadaiah' in you again."

Pagadaiah smiled modestly. His in-laws' village was ten miles away and the way passed by the Vindhyadramma tank. He didn't have a bullock-cart, but, if he went there, maybe, they would send Rattamma in their cart, he thought.

Slowly the desire to bring back his wife became stronger, but, he shuddered at the thought of facing his mother-in-law and then, 'would Rattamma agree to come with me forgetting and forgiving all that had happened? What is in her mind, now?' He wondered.

That evening Pagadaiah told his sister he was going to in-laws' village the next day; she felt happy at that.

Two days later, the Minister's jeep came and stopped in front of the Banzardar's house. There were a few officials in the Minister's retinue.

The Minister smiled at the surprised village—lord, "Appaiah Doravaru (Lord-Sir), maybe, I have surprised you; the point is I am trying to help your villagers in the revival of the Vindhyadramma tank. The problem is—there are a few issues; they have to be resolved before the Government takes up the work; a few technologists have come with me," He showed them and they paid obeisance.

The Banzardar took the Minister into the guest room; the technologists sat comfortably in the drawing room and signals were given for the follow-up courtesies.

The Banzardar feigned interest and smiled to the Minister as the latter took his seat on the sofa; 'So, the thing has gone very far; now, can I still be of help to the legislator?' he thought.

The Minister asked, "Where is that gentleman, Pagadaiah? Lord-Sir, would you please send for him?"

"Lord-Sir, he is not in the village, has gone to his in-laws' place, I am told."

The Minister seemed a little disappointed.

He went to the temple, accompanied by the epigraphist and other technicians, greeting the men who had gathered at the slab, on hearing the news of the Minister's arrival.

They saw the stones in the temple premises.

The epigraphist didn't take much time to identify the figures and explained, "Sir, these are the broken pieces of a Kakatiya inscription, rather; a figure and isolated words are there on them; otherwise they mean nothing; the figure on that stone is of 'a boar', it appears on the royal seal of the Kakatiyas; rest of them are function words; we can't make out anything from them; we have to see whether any inscription is still there, though I am not sure of them being there, especially after seeing these pieces here. What shall we do, Sir?"

"Thank you, Mr.Shastri, what is the use of looking at them? The point in question eludes us; shall we go to the Vindhyadramma tank," The Minister said.

The epigraphist obediently said, "Yes Sir, maybe, if we are fortunate, we will see something that throws light on the point."

They took up the walk to the tank bund; the Banzardar too accompanied them.

Kannam and company were dismayed that the Village lord was also coming with them.

Presently they reached the tank and climbed onto the bund

The epigraphist openly remarked, "Ah, this is a marvel of construction; all the Kakatiya constructions are awe-inspiring, whether they are temples or tanks! I don't know whether you have seen the Ramappa tank, Sir; it was built about seven centuries ago, it is still strong and is irrigating thousands of acres of paddy fields. When I sat at the waterside there, the first time, I felt as though I was sitting on seashore . . .

"When we look at the terrain of this place and consider the times it was built in, this work is really a marvelous feat of engineering."

Then, they went to the breach. They felt sad at the grievous state of the tank; they got down to the spot of the breach and saw; the engineer examined it closely.

"What do you see there, Mr. Das?"

"Sir, this appears to be a man-made breach; if it was natural the debris of the breach would have been washed away in the flow of water; this secondary bund, here, is made up of the dug-out soil and the soil-dump has become compact; I think it is man-made," the Engineer asserted.

"That is quite surprising, indeed," the Minister explained the matter to the villagers.

Kannam muttered gravely in hushed tones, "We are not surprised; on the contrary, we are happy that things are clearing up!"

"How old is this secondary bund; can you just give a time scale, like, when it was built when the breach occurred and how long it remained like that," the Minister queried.

"It is difficult, Sir; but, it appears to be fairly old."

Then they moved into the tank-bed and for a considerable time searched for a stone-inscription or a piece of it; they could find no such thing; but, they found a recently planted orchard and a stone quarry at which they raised eyebrows.

On their return trip, the epigraphist enumerated a few prevalent methods of investigation in epigraphy, "Sometimes, in addition to a stone inscription, the kings issued a copy of the inscription on copper plates also; they were usually given to the concerned beneficiaries where land-grant was involved; sometimes the non-royal authors of public works kept with themselves copper plate version, as a copy of the stone-inscription; now, it's very difficult to trace them; because in most cases, the copper plates would've been melted and used to make vessels; our sense of history is not very strong, unfortunately."

"You are right; even I cannot excuse myself in that respect; in my childhood I destroyed many palm-leaf bundles using them to make toy-windmills. Men must value historical data, preserve and transmit them to the succeeding generation."

Presently, they returned to the village and were surprised to find the legislator waiting for them, at the slab.

"I am sorry Ganjibabu garu, I should've accompanied you as per the protocol; but, there was an important public work I had to attend to; so, I have come today to catch up with your program," the legislator said with an obeisance.

The Minister smiled, "Don't worry Mr. Sure naraina; we have to go by the spirit of the rule rather than by the word. It's good you have come; we are pursuing the matter . . ."

The Banzardar intervened to say, "But, Lord-Sir, our MLA Lord-Sir says that he has a record showing the name of his ancestor as the author of this work; we have to consider that also."

"No no, I have never said so," the Legislator hurriedly contradicted, "What I have always said is that there is a strong belief in my village that one of my ancestor created this tank; there is no written proof of it; people say that on inscription was there; but some vandals broke that hexagonal pillar and men took away the stone pieces as curios; two such stone blocks are there in our yard and some are there in the temple yard in this village, I have heard . . ."

The Banzardar stood aghast at the way the legislator gave a twisted version of his earlier statement.

Kannam, Balakoti and others too were astonished at that volte face by the Emmellu.

The Banzardar nodded, ostensibly in agreement; but, thought it was clearly a case of equivocation by the legislator.

The Minister wanted to know whether Pagadaiah had returned.

The sethsindhi went and finding the door closed, went to the Raconteur's sister.

Aademma was worried why people were enquiring so much about her brother and showing concern, she herself went to the slab where the Minister and his retinue sat in an informal setting, at the slab.

"If only we can get hold of a copper plate copy of the destroyed stone-inscription, the mystery would be solved," the Minister was saying, "but, where can we find those copper-plates?"

Precisely at that moment Aademma came there.

Kannam thought of the attics of the houses.

Aademma who had 'now' arrived at the slab and heard what the Minister was saying, analyzed the point in her own way and after some hesitation made a submission to the Minister, "They are at my house, Lord-Sir; we didn't steal them from anybody or anywhere; they have been in the attic of our house, since the times of our forefathers. Last year I thought of using them to make a cauldron; but, my man asked me to preserve them carefully for what they were worth and I kept them like that . . ."

The Minister was astonished and exclaimed, "That is some wonderful news! Madam, would you kindly bring them and show them to us?"

Aademma fell into a dilemma and said in a weak voice, "But, Lord-Sir, they have been in our house for generations; we haven't stolen them from anybody; they are ours; I would swear on any deity!"

The Minister smiled at the innocence of the woman and looked at the epigraphist.

The epigraphist intervened and clarified the matter, "'It's not like that', Madam; the Minister Sir would like to see them only for some information; they would be given back to you, you need not worry."

The Banzardar intervened, "Aademma, have no doubt on that; bring them and show them to the Lord-Sir; it's important, yes."

Her face still showing confusion and doubt, Aademma went home; the cloth bundle with the plates was taken down from the attic; she took it as it was to the slab and gave it to the Minister; she noticed how their faces beamed when they saw the bundle; tensely she stood there wondering whether it concerned some treasure.

The Minister gave the bundle carefully to the epigraphist.

All of them stood watching curiously.

Even the Banzardar looked mystified by the series of events that had climaxed in the discovery of the copper plates.

Presently, the epigraphist meticulously unpacked the bundle and took out the metal sheets containing the historical data.

"This is really fortuitous and wonderful, Sir. A remote village at the foot of this Pandava hill range here becomes the provenance of crucial historical data!"

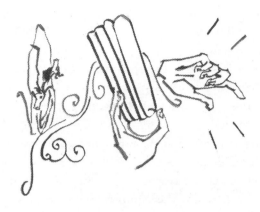

The Minister looked with curiosity at the epigraphist who was looking into the metal sheets.

"We are used to these wonders, Sir; but, let us see whether these plates contain any information on the issue in question," Epigraphist dusted the sheets, gently wiped them with his palm and began to study the content.

It took some time; they all waited with bated breath for an affirmation or negation on the issue.

"The inscription is in Devnaagari script, Sir, and the language is Sanskrit," the epigraphist slowly read out the inscription to the Minister.

Kannam and his men looked happy that something had been found which would help their cause, though they did not know the 'what and how' of it.

The Epigraphist then read out the relevant part of the Sanskrit inscription, a second time.

"Swasthi sree Jaya sake, Varshe Aseethyuttara ekaadasa satha samyuthe, Roudreenaama samvathsare, Vaisakhamaase, Suddha Paadyamyam, Brihaspathi vaasare . . .

"Sree Ganapathi Deva Mahaaraajasya Raajyakale . . .

"Mayura Mandalaadheesa Mayura gothrodbhavah Pagadanaayakaha, thasya Jyeshtaputhrah Surana lenka naamno, Puthrapremnaa . . .

"Mayuragraamaath Prachyatho dise, Vindhyadevi thadaakam srijyatha . . ."

Then, the Epigraphist paraphrased it in Telugu, "May it be good to all; in the year One thousand one hundred eighty of Saka Era, the regnal year of Sri Ganapathideva Mahaaraaja, corresponding to the year 1258 A.D., in the Telugu Year Roudree, on the first day of Vaisakha month, on Thursday, the first day of the Waxing phase of the moon . . .

"The Chief of Mayuramandala, Pagadanaayaka of Mayura gothra, got excavated the Vindhyadevee thadaakam, to the east of the village Mayura, in loving memory of his eldest son, Suranalenka . . .

"That is the main content of the inscription, Sir," Concluded the Epigraphist.

Unable to contain his delight, the Minister went to the epigraphist and hugged him; at that, the men clapped.

Pensively, Banzardar too clapped.

"So, this village, Peacock was once the headquarters of an administrative division called Mayura mandala of the Kakatiya Empire and Pagadanayaka of Mayura gothra, which means 'Nemali', was its chief . . . isn't it so, Sastry?" the Minister exulted, "Does anyone, here, know who Pagadanaayaka of Nemali gothra could be?" the Min asked in wonder.

Veteran Hulakki, who had been listening to the paraph content of the inscription, nodded in confirmation, "It mu Pagadaiah's ancestor, Lord-Sir; Pagadaiah's lineage is 'Ne (Mayura)."

The legislator's face went white, then turned blacl remained so.

361

"That is really wonderful; it's great news! This is how you come to know the meaning of the adage: 'Carts become Ships and Ships become Carts.'"

Slowly it dawned on the Village Lord-Sir that Pagadaiah's ancestor, Pagadanaayaka was the lord of this region at one time, which meant that he held a position immensely greater and higher than his 'at present'; the same thing dawned on the legislator too. They felt humbled though they did not show it on their faces.

"Could you get any other interesting data from those plates, Mr. Sastry?" the Minister eagerly asked the Epigraphist.

"Yes Sir, the elder son of Pagadanaayaka was Surana; this Surana was a 'lenka'; Kakatiyas maintained bodyguards called 'lenkas'; the lenkas dedicated their lives to the king; they not only risked their lives in the service of their patron, but, when the king died, they even immolated themselves on funeral pyre."

"My God!" exclaimed the Minister.

The Minister heard hiccups-like sounds and turned to see.

Kannam covered his face with his shoulder cloth and was crying as his troubled mind recollected the comments made by the raconteur in different contexts, at the slab, about kingship and the greatness of the kings, their concern and love for their subjects, their charitable nature and the spirit of sacrifice that permeated their acts and thoughts; he tried to stop crying, but, unable to do so, ran away shaking his head, perhaps, in remorseful scorn of himself for having hated and harmed the raconteur at the slab, at every step.

The other men—Pullamma's man, Balakoti, Gopaya, Naginaboina among them, were stunned and looked dumbstruck, at the grieving Kannam whom they had always seen as an arch-critic of the Raconteur.

Soon more and more men came and the slab and its environs were filled with the villagers; they had come to know of the tidings, the copper plates revealed and stood wondering about the power of 'the Time'.

They all visualized Pagadaiah and recalled his remarks, his firm convictions and his comments on kings and kingship.

'Where is our Pagadaiah now? When is he going to be amidst us?' Most of them wondered.

Aademma who didn't understand it, wondered why they were making so much fuss about those metal plates; 'were there any cryptic clues in them about some big treasure?' She wished they were there and then with her, her man and her brother, 'One can never trust these lettered men; they would do anything for money.'

The Minister gave back the plates to Aademma, after the epigraphist had taken the photos and noted down the Sanskrit text of the inscription; he asked her to preserve them carefully till some govt. official came to purchase them.

Kannam was surprised to see that Nagireddy too was delighted at the news.

"It is more than a week since my brother has left home at my suggestion, to bring back his wife. I don't know what has happened at that end and where my brother is!" Aademma cried disconsolately as she walked back to her house.

The news of Pagadaiah's illustrious pedigree spread pervasively in Peacock and the nearby villages.

The villagers expressed sympathy and made enquiries, especially after coming to know about the facts revealed by 'the copper sheets'.

As Aadamma and her man sat grieving in front of their house, Kannam came and stood before them; it was obvious from his manner that he came to break some news.

"Come Kannam, 'my brother', have you gained any news about your friend? Tell us he is safe; just tell us he will be coming today or tomorrow, wouldn't you? If my father comes in dream and asks me what I had done with my brother, what answer can I give!" Aademma said as she sobbed.

Kannam went close to her and reassuringly said, "Sister Aademma, tomorrow morning Gopaya and I are going there to find out the thing; rest assured that we would come back with Pagadaiah; be courageous."

Aademma nodded controlling her grief, "Oh Lord Narasimha, show mercy on us."

The Minister and his men bade the villagers well and taking leave of the Village-Lord went back to the city; the legislator violated the protocol a second time and stayed back in the village, on the plea that he had to make a trip to his village.

Later, accompanied by his burly attendant, the legislator set out for his village in a bullock-cart; en route, he wanted to see the tank's bed which had been his family property de facto, for generations, always giving a good yield, unaffected by the vagaries of the monsoon.

'Now, if the newly set course of events is not checked, the land would soon pass under the waters of the revived reservoir . . .' The legislator sat thinking as the bullock-cart went on a bumpy run.

Kannam, Gopaya and Balakoti who went on the search mission, reached the village of Pagadaiah's in-laws, but, they didn't have to go to the house of Pagadaiah's in-laws for news.

When they were at the head of the wooded passage leading to the village they ran into a longtime acquaintance.

Kannam told him the purpose of their visit; he also told the man the developments that had taken place, "It has been discovered that Pagadaiah is the descendant of a former ruler of this region; more importantly it was his ancestor who had built the great Vindhyadramma tank. This revelation has come to light because of the interest taken by that noble Minister lord-sir . . ."

The local man listened with interest and nodded in wonderment.

"Pagadaiah's sister is concerned about her brother; we have come in search of the man; we understand that Pagadaiah came here a few days back to take back his wife," Kannam said.

The local man clucked his tongue and knitted his brows, "I am afraid I don't have good news for you, Cousin. Now, I don't advise you to go into the village; I strongly advise you to beat a retreat from the alley itself."

"But, why, what has happened, Cousin?" Kannam asked perplexed.

"Cousin, there is nothing cheerful about what has happened here. Unpleasant things have happened; Rattamma's mother—your friend's mother-in-law, has given birth to a still-born boy. A day after that, Bakkayya, your friend's father-in-law, hanged himself to death; the village is agog with weird rumors about it all. Listen to my word and go back to your village; don't enter this village, because the man you are searching for is not there; they had literally hounded out the man. What is destined to happen would happen; why do you go into the village and invite trouble . . . ?"

Kannam wanted to go into the details, but, the local man was not inclined to talk anymore on the issue.

Kannam and his friends wondered 'what Pagadaiah had done to get such a raw deal from his in-laws; after all he had come to take back his wife!'

When they were back in Peacock, they didn't dare to go to Aademma with the news they had gathered; so, they went directly to the slab.

At the slab they all gathered and were waiting for news on Pagadaiah—youngsters, adults and old men like Hulakki, Naraiah and Lingaiah-all of them appeared very much concerned.

Kannam told them the news he had gathered.

Pagadaiah now became the focal point of an animated talk at the slab.

Some of them made guesses and analyses; but, nobody talked derogatively about the raconteur.

A sense of loss, a sense of despondency and a wish for divine intervention were written on the faces of the men; at the same time, a fear of the unwanted thing happening and an apprehension of the logical end of the sequence, loomed large in their minds.

"It is unbelievable that Pagadaiah is not here on the slab today; we have always sought that man's views on issues for what they are worth and he has always given us a point which is uniquely his!" Naraiah was saying.

"Why do you talk like that Uncle Naraiah? You are talking as though we have seen the last of Pagadaiah; please don't talk like that; it hurts us to hear one say that," Kannam said.

Naraiah broke down at that, "I am not forecasting anything bad. It is my fear and concern that are compulsively coming on to my tongue like that! What can I do, tell me!" He covered his face with the shoulder cloth.

Men on the slab were sad and kept hoping that their fears would be proved wrong and that Pagadaiah would soon be seen coming to the slab, dressed in his 'neerkavi' colour dress and turban, walking languidly along the western alley, smiling and longing for a chat with them on the slab.

To the Banzardar things still appeared to be in a fluid state; he thought the revival of the Vindhyadramma tank could not be taken for granted 'even at this stage', especially when the stubborn and unyielding Suryanarayana was there in the picture.

The local body elections were postponed; grocer Rosaiah felt cheated at the news of the postponement; daily he was doling out something or other to the customers who were craftily taking advantage of his candidature. Not only free beedis, even cigarettes were becoming freebies.

One day, the villagers heard the trumpeter announce that there would be a public meeting the next day in the morning and that the Emmellu and Minister would be addressing the people.

"What now? They are arranging meeting after meeting . . ."

"Since the Minister Ganjibabu lord-sir is coming, we can say that they are going to lay the foundation stone for the breach-repair work on the Vindhyadramma tank," Someone made a guess.

"Is it so? How nice it will be if it really comes true!"

In a surprising departure from the usual way, the dignitaries came early for the public meeting; however, the curious villagers didn't find their benefactor Minister in the party; instead, there was a stranger.

The Banzardar and Rosaiah welcomed the Guests.

In a short while, the meeting commenced and it was the legislator who took the mike first.

" . . . the Praja Party knows the pulse of the people; it knows what is good for the people and how to do a thing that is good for the people . . .

" . . . we understand your apprehensions and your beliefs; true, they are valid; but, sometimes it is easy to get carried away by a fanciful idea; but, wise men are in no hurry; whatever they do, they do with forethought and circumspection . . .

"Take the case of the water problem you have been facing; it is an old problem-as old as your village. There are two solutions; one to build a medium irrigation project on the rivulet; it would cost less and would benefit you very much in the long run and more importantly it is free from risks . . .

"On the contrary, you have that God-forsaken reservoir called Vindhyadramma tank; some of you might be longing for its revival; but, remember, it is a tank that has taken the life of its builder. Our elder citizens say it is an accursed reservoir and would bring disaster to anyone who tries to revive it . . .

"We respect your beliefs and we value your wisdom. We don't want to initiate something that might bring disaster to your village and the villages nearby; so, there is no question of reviving that old tank. We would consider building a dam across the rivulet and go for lift irrigation technology even, if the situation so requires . . ."

They exchanged looks in disbelief, "Why didn't the Minister Ganjibabu lord-sir come?" One of them said aloud in dismay.

"Ganjibabu would not come here anymore," Said the legislator curtly; he had heard the villager's query, "Praja Party wouldn't allow the politicization of the public issues and that is precisely what he has done; he has been removed from the cabinet; he will not come here anymore . . .

"At this juncture I would like to introduce to you our new Rural Development Minister, Rambabugaru who has been a legislator for thirty years; give him a big clap"

Kannam nodded his head across, "Lord-Sir, why did you remove Ganjibabu garu from Government?"

Banzardar wrinkled his forehead in disapproval at the open way Kannam interrupted and questioned the Minister;

he brusquely waved his hand commanding Kannam to sit down.

Kannam refused to be cowed down, "Ganjibabu lord-sir promised us that the tank would be revived and that too well in advance of the 'first rains'; now, you are telling us a different thing . . ."

"I have told you that Ganjibabu is not in the government anymore; why are you talking about him and his promises, again and again; I am your legislator, and being a local man, I know the problems of this village and the villages nearby . . ."

Kannam got up and walked away, showing resentment.

Even as the dignitaries watched aghast, a few others too walked away.

The face of the Banzardar became pale-'bloodless even to a cut with knife!'

The Dignitaries had a hush-hush confabulation and the legislator was about to resume his speech; but, the men continued to file past the venue.

As the Village lord-sir stood 'small faced', Rosaiah tried to stop the men; but they didn't look back.

"This signals a new era in the village, certainly. I just don't know what more is in store for us!" Banzardar was heard saying.

The next day the Village woke up to shocking news.

The community cowherd hurried back to the village from the Pandava hills with the news that he had seen the spread-eagled body of Pagadaiah in the breach of the Vindhyadramma tank, with its throat slit, the body already getting infested with insects.

As the news spread like wild fire, villagers started running towards the tank and the women rushed to the house of Aademma who was wailing for her brother.

The women sat round the bereaved woman and cried their hearts out, a woman caressing her disheveled hair, another clasping her in anguish and sympathy, and another whimpering and wondering on ways to console the woman.

They brought the body and kept it at the slab.

The Banzardar came and saw the body; the throat was slit deep and long; it couldn't have been self-inflicted cut nor could it have been done in any combative fight.

"It clearly appears that someone-" the Banzardar stopped abruptly and left the remark incomplete.

"It clearly appears, Lord-Sir, that someone has slit his throat," Kannam completed what was left vague by the Banzardar.

Instantly, the Banzardar looked at Kannam and came to wear a look of bewilderment; he desisted from making any further comment.

Kannam was astonished at the way the lord-sir had fumbled into an inadvertent remark and began to analyze the developments in his own way.

As the time ticked by, they kept looking at the body, unable to come to terms with the reality.

A debate ensued on the reasons for the tragic event.

"Lord-Sir, you are our father and mother; call the police and find out who killed my brother; have you ever heard of my brother harming anybody, Lord-Sir; has anyone heard my brother injuring anybody, brothers? Then why did they do this treacherous thing to my brother? Who is that 'son of a widow', that bastard, that son of . . ." Aademma went into invectives even as she cried her voice hoarse.

They stood pale faced and listened to her in silence, nodding to whatever she said.

Nagireddy who had heard the news, rushed to Peacock.

The moment he saw the dead body of Pagadaiah, tears rolled down his cheeks; he went close to the body and touched its hands, shoulders and face, nostalgically remembering a host of things and reliving 'the moments'.

Bademaya cried openly and unashamedly.

Nagireddy and Kannam embraced each other and grieved, watching 'Pagadaiah' who wouldn't argue or dispute or contradict any point anymore.

The Policepatel came along with the Malipatel and they drafted a report to be sent to the Sub-Inspector of Police.

The matter was reported to the Police through a courier; they waited for 'the Panchnama'; the funeral rites could be performed only after that.

Next day Rattamma came wailing for her man; she came alone in the bullock-cart and seeing her man's body at the slab, she got down wailing.

Aademma was furious at the sight of the woman who had never conducted herself as a dutiful wife to Pagadaiah.

"Why did you come here, you devil? You are responsible for all this; now what is there for you here? You never wanted that man. You made life horrible for him; you would go to hell after your death; but, oh God, women like you would not die soon; 'the sinners live long,' they say. Go away this minute and don't desecrate the place with your presence . . ."

Rattamma didn't talk back; she cried and slapped herself on the cheeks and plucked at her disheveled hair, "Oh my God, take me with you; I know I wronged you, but, I didn't know what I was doing; I have sinned; I am a sinner; let somebody end my life in the same way; I will take it; I can no longer live this unworthy life. Oh God, take me to wherever my blessed man is. I would atone for all my sins, fall at his feet and break my head . . ." She touched the feet of Pagadaiah with her head and then hit her head repeatedly on the slab floor.

Women joined in her wail, in empathy and the place resounded with their shrieks.

Pagadaiah's body was to be cremated at the Vindhyadramma tank, as decided by the members of the slab.

Kannam, Nagireddy, Bademaya and Mme Pullamma's man bore the garlanded body to the Vindhyadramma tank; Balakoti and Naginboina partook by 'changing shoulders'.

The Banzardar, Policepatel and Malipatel and Priest Suraiah walked in the funeral procession.

Pagadaiah's son, Balaraju lit the pyre; Pagadaiah's friends stood respectfully as the pyre went aflame; in a while the body turned to ashes.

Many of them went into a mystic mood and wondered about the transience of life, as men always did on such occasions-'graveyard mysticism', as they called it.

They came back to the village and sat on the slab for a long time.

For once, the village lord-sir and other headmen of the village too sat on the slab, at a little distance from the plebeians.

Nagireddy suggested that they should arrange a condolence meeting on the slab, and the men agreed with him. He also proposed that they should install a bust of Pagadaiah at the slab and another on the Tank-bund, by the side of the statue of the King; he would bear the cost of it, he said; they nodded appreciatively.

"Kannam, go to sister Aademma and find a photo of Pagadaiah; there must be a photo taken at the Veerlapadu fair . . ."

Kannam went to the house of Aademma.

"I am still unable to understand how this has happened; it comes as a stunning revelation that Pagadaiah has sacrificed his life for the revival of the Vindhyadramma tank; it is as though he has upheld the truth of the story and the validity of the stipulated condition; it was he who had popularized that story and now it is he who has proved it right, as it were . . ." Nagireddy said.

"You are right there, Nagaya,"

"But, he had no inkling of his pedigree; he died completely unaware of it; how could he have sacrificed his life when he didn't know that he was a descendant of that family?"

"I have never heard a story which is stranger than this horrible sequence of events!"

"If anybody has killed Pagadaiah what could have been the motive?"

There was a hush at that.

"If you examine the relevant factors deeply, you wouldn't fail to identify the man . . ."

"Ssh, keep quiet, the village headmen are there."

One, two, three . . . heads nodded in agreement, though none of them took any name.

The Village headmen who sat at a distance on the slab turned their heads.

"But, now, do you think the story would come true with the revival of the Tank?"

"It should; the Government cannot ignore the issue anymore, now."

"Even when there are men opposed to it-?"

The next day the MLA and his brother-in-law came to Peacock; for the last one week the Banzardar had been sending a courier to the town regularly so that important news could be conveyed to the legislator over phone.

As usual, a table and chairs from the bungalow of the village lord-sir were about to be arranged on the slab.

The legislator dismissed the formalities and chose to sit on the bare slab; he even asked the village elite to sit on the slab; they obliged.

It was Nagireddy who spoke first; he fondly recalled his association with Pagadaiah, "He always gave high priority to the Village and Community in his scheme of things. He was blunt in his arguments but he was soft as a man . . ."

Next the Village elite spoke and at the end the legislator gave a long account of his brief acquaintance with the man; "Pagadaiah always impressed me with his spirit of service and social awareness; whether in arranging meetings or maintaining order in the conduct of the festival events, he showed a rare maturity and vision . . .

"Our Banzardar always spoke about Pagadaiah's respect for the traditions and customs. Though not educated he had a good knowledge of the Epics, I am told. The way he sacrificed his life for the welfare of the village makes him an exemplary man; it is very appropriate that Nagireddygaru and his friends have decided to install his statue at the slab . . ."

"Even on the tank-bund," Kannam harshly broke in, waving a small photo of Pagadaiah.

"Yes, yes, even on the tank-bund," the Legislator hastened to add.

There ended the condolence meeting.

In a few days the busts of Pagadaiah were brought from Bezwada and one was set up at the base of the Bo-tree.

The second bust was taken to the Vindhyadramma tank-bund in a procession, Kannam carrying the bust on his shoulders; the legislator along with his brother-in-law walked in the procession.

The arrangements for the installation of the bust had been already done; the bust was set up near the Statue of the King.

While returning to Peacock the men broke into groups and talked.

Kannam walked along with Nagireddy and Bademaya, heeding to the Emmellu's talk with his brother-in-law.

"It's a picturesque site really,"

"And, imagine how wonderful it would look, if a pleasure boat or two are added to the revived tank!"

"Add to the picture, a nice Restaurant and a Bar . . ."

Kannam and his friends exchanged meaningful looks.

One or two men felt the touch of raindrops on their heads and looked up.

The sky became cloud cast and the atmosphere became cool.

"See, how the clouds are collecting on the sky; it looks as though the Deities are pleased with what we have done!"

"Will we reach the village before it starts raining," Naraiah said.

"I think we cannot, but what difference would it make? Once in a while we must get drenched in the rain; it is good for us."

"Not at our age . . ." Hulakki said looking at Naraiah.

They looked up and saw the movement of clouds in the sky and the changing colour of the clouds.

It was the month of Sravana, the starting point of the two-month peak period of rainy season.

"We thought the tank-bund would be repaired in time for 'the first rains'; but, now, it looks like we have to wait until the next 'first rains' . . ."

"Even then, it is not bad. Let the government do it."

Hulakki nodded his head, "We cannot hurry up the things with our thoughts; everything takes place at the time fixed by the Destiny."

Hulakki was breathing with difficulty; Kannam noticed it and went to him, "Uncle, would you like to rest for a while?"

Hulakki philosophically waved his hand, "No no, I will walk, don't worry about me; you proceed; maybe, you have things to take care of; I have learnt to live with this . . ."

They looked at the sky; now it had become completely black; they had done only half the distance.

They quickened the pace of their walk.

It was becoming difficult for the veterans and Nagireddy and Kannam walked by their side.

"Nagaya, have you heard that talk between the Emmellu and his brother-in-law? That fellow who laid the 'famine-road' and ran a liquor store at the 'famine-road' now wants a hotel and liquor shop at the tank-bund too; maybe, he would open both of them, with the help of his brother-in-law . . ."

"Maybe, he would open a cinema hall too."

"No, no, who would allow all that? Hereafter, we will thwart such smart ideas." Nagireddy asserted, Kannam nodding.

Now it began to rain steadily and young men started to run, but, within a short time the black cotton soil became slippery, making it a hazardous option.

They all came back to Peacock fully drenched.

Adding to their discomfort the wind became cold; the veterans shivered.

The legislator and his 'crony-in-law' were taken to the bungalow of the Banzardar.

The men sat on the slab, though it was raining; some of them stood close to the trunk of the Bo-tree; none of them was in a mood to go home.

They wrung their shoulder-clothes and wiped their wet bodies with the wet cloth.

It continued to rain and never looked like abating; they looked at the sky for the umpteenth time and found it dark and unwilling to tell what time it was.

Now, in the verandah of the Banzardar's bungalow the domestic hung a hurricane lamp and that proclaimed it to be nighttime.

The rumble became thunder now and after a time they discovered that they had to leave the slab and go home.

However, Kannam sat on the slab, unmindful of the rain, and kept a wary eye on the verandah of the bungalow, his ears taut; he could not see, but, when he heard the clinking sound of glasses he understood what was happening-'a celebration'?

He went home very late, fully drenched.

It was a cyclonic storm, quite familiar to them and one that helped them often when regular rains failed; but, a cyclonic storm always tested their level of endurance.

None of the villagers slept that night; whenever they heeded they found it raining and raining.

'Where would we find the River of Sticks tomorrow morning? Would we see it in more awesome state? Would the waters of the rivulet and the river flow together as a colossal flow of water? Would we live to see the morning or would the village be washed away in the flood!'

The Villagers spent the night asking themselves questions and woke up the next morning to find answers.

In the morning some of them woke up early and went to the village outskirts and saw that things were more ominous than they had imagined.

Kannam and his friends were there watching the broad expanse of water.

"Wait, Kannam, let me join you."

Kannam looked back and was astonished to find the legislator wading in the water, 'did he call my name?' he wondered.

In the couple of days he stayed in Peacock, Suryanarayana had been trying to befriend the young villagers-the spirited ones in particular.

Kannam, Balakoti and others looked at each other.

The Emmellu looked uneasy and was tottering on his feet; the effect of the last night's binge was evident in the legisltor's movements and talk.

"Be careful, Sir, there are ditches under the water," Kannam said anxiously.

"Don't worry, Kannam; these things are not new to me; they can't even move my little finger, I tell you; I can take care of myself; after all I am also from-" the high profile man stumbled and fell into that abandoned well now treacherously filled with the flood water.

"Oh my God, the Emmellu has fallen into the abandoned well!" Kannam shouted, frightened, "Come from that side, Bademaya, quick," Spontaneously he yelled to his friend.

With that Kannam leaped at once into the water-trap and begant to wrestle with the flood water and its waves.

From the other side Bademaya too dived into the waters.

The legislator dipped and rose twice, as he gulped water; before he took the third fatal gulp, Kannam came under the body and lifted it up; from the other side Balakori reached the body to catch the Emmellu by the shoulder; together they pulled the body out of the waters.

Once the body was taken out of the waters it took four men to carry the body to a house; when they laid the body in the yard there, they saw no movement in the body and were perplexed.

Now, Kannam got down to the body and began to press it from the sides onto the stomach; the body started spewing ruddy water; he did that a few times and the body threw up a large amount of water.

The stench of undigested food and alcohol was unbearable to the men; they held their noses tight with fingers.

"That will do; wait a little while; he would regain consciousness now."

They waited but the body showed no sign of movement.

"Someone should go and bring the Priest-Sir."

The Priest, the Banzardar and other Village Headmen came anxiously enquiring.

After a considerable time the body showed symptoms of life and they were relieved at that.

The news of the series of events that had happened at Peacock reached the Capital and the higher echelons of Power rather late, because of the inaccessibility factor.

In a belated reaction, the Home Minister, the Minister for Rural Development and other dignitaries descended upon the village; the former Minister Ganjibabu was also there in the team.

Led by Kannam and Nagireddy, the villagers—slab members in particular, raised slogans demanding justice and action against the perpetrators of 'the crime' on Pagadaiah.

A team of Police Officials had made an inquest of the event, but, they had been unable to solve the mystery of the suspicious death of Pagadaiah; they had asked the Villagers to give their views; as decided among themselves, the villagers gave no names, but, stuck to the theory of conspiracy.

The investigating team had showed reluctance to go by the obvious leads holding that the leads were highly hypothetical and motivated.

Ganjibabu was very much saddened by the tragic death of the man who appeared to personify the benign character of the Village and the Villagers; it touched his heart with its poignancy.

The former Minister knew the entire background to the gory incident; but, there was no way he could consolidate it into a valid thesis.

The Home Minister who had given a patient hearing to the appeals of the villagers promised that the Government would redress their grievances by doing the needful.

It took the legislator a fortnight to become his normal self. He heard from the Banzardar how the two young men from the village had saved his life, by risking their lives and what had happened in the fortnight. 'What would have happeded to him and who could have prevented it, if the two men had played 'swing baskets' with his body? He shuddered at the thought and was doubly happy that he was alive

"This short period of time has taught me what I had failed to learn in my life-time. I will plead with the Government and to lose no time in reviving the Vindhyadramma tank; maybe, that way I would atone for all that I and my family had done and caused misery to the villagers of Peacock and the villages nearby . . .

"Even then I don't think that would be enough to expiate me completely . . ."

'What a transformation, what a transformation!' The Banzardar wondered looking at him, but, is it real!'

Three months passed; the villagers waited anxiously and hopefully for the revival of the Vindhyadramma tank.

"The Lord-Sirs have promised us publicly; they cannot go back on it; so, it is just a matter of time," they thought.

In the meantime, the MLA came to Peacock a few times and hobnobbed with the young and old members on the slab; twice he also brought for them the finest variety of sweets from a city confectionary. He also asked Kannam if he would like some wine from the city and was disappointed when the latter replied, "I don't drink, Lord-Sir."

One evening, camping in Peacock the legislator tuned on the pocket radio and enabled the members of the slab to listen to the news: "the Government has decided to revive the historic Vindhyadramma tank, built during the times of the Kakatiyas; the tank, built in a sylvan setting amidst the Pandava hills, near the village Peacock, is a big one and can irrigate more than three thousand acres. When the tank is revived many villages at the foot of the Pandava hills would come to wear a rich look of opulence; the decision of the Government came as a result of the unrelenting efforts of Sri Suryanarayana, who represents the Backward Peacock Constituency in the Legislative Assembly . . ."

The men on the slab clapped their hands in alacrity and appreciation.

The next week,

The Rural Development Minister came to ceremonially start the work of the repair of the breach of the tank.

The legislator and the Village lord-sirs were there at the function.

The Legislator whose mind was richer with new ideas after his traumatic experience in flood waters, called on Nagireddygaru and Kannamgaru to adorn the dais and when they were surprised and shyly declined, the legislator personally went to them and ushered them onto the dais, amidst thunderous applauses from the gathering.

After the speeches from the Dignitaries were over the vote of thanks was to be offered by the gentleman-contractor who was to take up the work of repair of the breach and revival of the Tank.

The Villagers' faces began to wear a look of bewilderment and anxiety when they saw 'the famine-road' brother-in-law of the legislator, who came to propose a vote of thanks.

—THE END—